THE TOILERS
OF THE
SEA

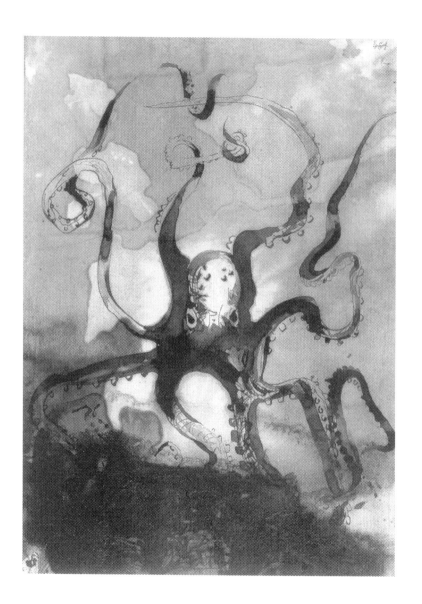

VICTOR HUGO

THE TOILERS

OF THE

SEA

A new translation by James Hogarth

Introduction by Graham Robb

Notes by James Hogarth

THE MODERN LIBRARY

NEW YORK

LIBRARY OF CONGRESS CATALOGING-IN-PUBLICATION DATA
Hugo, Victor, 1802–1885.
[Travailleurs de la mer. English]
The toilers of the sea / Victor Hugo; introduction by Graham Robb;
translated, with notes, by James Hogarth.—Modern Library paperback ed.
p.   cm.
ISBN 978-0-375-76132-4
I. Hogarth, James.   II. Title.
PQ2289.T7 E5513 2002
843'.7—dc21   2002022342

Modern Library website address:
www.modernlibrary.com

Frontispiece: Octopus with the initials VH (ca. 1866).

146122990

VICTOR HUGO

Victor-Marie Hugo was born in 1802 at Besançon, where his father, an officer (eventually a general) under Napoleon, was stationed. In his first decade the family moved from post to post: Corsica, Elba, Paris, Naples, Madrid. After his parents separated in 1812, Hugo lived in Paris with his mother and brothers. His literary ambition—"to be Chateaubriand or nothing"—was evident from an early age, and by seventeen he had founded a literary magazine with his brother. At twenty he married Adèle Foucher and published his first poetry collection, which earned him a small stipend from Louis XVIII. A first novel, *Han of Iceland* (1823), won another stipend.

Hugo became friends with Charles Nodier, a leader of the Romantics, and with the critic Sainte-Beuve, and rapidly put himself at the forefront of literary trends. His innovative early poetry helped open up the relatively constricted traditions of French versification, and his plays—especially *Cromwell*, whose preface served as a manifesto of Romanticism, and *Hernani*, whose premiere was as stormy as that of Stravinsky's *Rite of Spring*—stirred up much protest for their break with dramatic convention. His literary outpouring between 1826 and 1843 encompassed eight volumes of poetry; four novels, including *The Last Day of a Condemned Man* (1829) and *Notre-Dame de Paris* (1831); ten plays (among them *Le Roi s'amuse*, the source for Verdi's *Rigoletto*); and a variety of critical writings.

Hugo was elected to the Académie Française in 1841. The acciden-
tal death two years later of his eldest daughter and her husband devastated him and marked the end of his first literary period. By then
politics had become central to his life. Though he was a Royalist in his
youth, his views became increasingly liberal after the July revolution
of 1830: "Freedom in art, freedom in society, there is the double goal."
Following the revolution of 1848, he was elected as a Republican to
the National Assembly, where he campaigned for universal suffrage
and free education and against the death penalty. He initially supported the political ascent of Louis-Napoleon, but turned against him
when Louis-Napoleon established a right-wing dictatorship.

After opposing the coup d'état of 1851, Hugo went into exile in
Brussels and Jersey, launching fierce literary attacks on the Second
Empire in *Napoleon the Little, Chastisements,* and *The Story of a Crime.* Between 1855 and 1870 he lived in Guernsey in the Channel Islands.
There he was joined by his family, some friends, and his mistress, Juli-
ette Drouet, whom he had known since 1833, when as a young actress
she had starred in his *Lucrezia Borgia.* His political interests were supplemented by other concerns. From around 1853 he became absorbed
in experiments with spiritualism and table tapping. In his later years
he wrote the *Contemplations* (1856), considered the peak of his lyric ac-
complishment, and a number of more elaborate poetic cycles derived
from his theories about spirituality and history: the immense *The Legend of the Centuries* (1859–83) and its posthumously published succes-
sors *The End of Satan* (1886) and *God* (1891). In these same years he
produced the novels *Les Misérables* (1862), *The Toilers of the Sea* (1866),
The Laughing Man (1869), and *Ninety-Three* (1873).

After the fall of the Second Empire in 1870, Hugo returned to
France and was reelected to the National Assembly, and then to the
Senate. He had become a legendary figure and national icon, a presence so dominating that upon his death in 1885 Émile Zola is said to
have remarked with some relief: "I thought he was going to bury us
all!" Hugo's funeral provided the occasion for a grandiose ceremony.
His body, after lying in state under the Arc de Triomphe, was carried
by torchlight—according to his own request, on a pauper's hearse—to
be buried in the Pantheon.

CONTENTS

THE TOILERS OF THE SEA
THE ARCHIPELAGO OF THE CHANNEL

PART I: SIEUR CLUBIN

BOOK I: THE MAKING OF A BAD REPUTATION

BOOK II: MESS LETHIERRY

BOOK III: DURANDE AND DÉRUCHETTE

BOOK II: THE LABOR

BOOK III: THE STRUGGLE

BOOK IV: OBSTACLES IN THE PATH

PART III: DÉRUCHETTE

BOOK I: NIGHT AND MOONLIGHT

BOOK II: GRATITUDE IN A DESPOTISM

BOOK III: THE SAILING OF THE *CASHMERE*

List of Illustrations

Drawings by Victor Hugo

INTRODUCTION

Graham Robb

Most eminent writers learn to protect their reputations. They capitalize on success at the risk of being accused of self-parody, avoid ridicule at the risk of becoming tedious, and appear humble in the face of public acclaim. Victor Hugo (1802–85) destroyed his own reputation so many times and with such spectacular disregard for the consequences that he seemed to have several lives to spare.

After the fall of Napoleon I in 1815, the boy poet had been the angelic voice of the restored monarchy, "the hope of the muses of the fatherland." Ten years later, Victor Hugo was the *enfant terrible* of French Romanticism, the author of a play, *Hernani,* which filled the Comédie Française with long-haired hooligans, and a novel, *Notre-Dame de Paris,* which appeared to celebrate the victory of the 1830 Revolution. In the 1840s, he was elected to the conservative Académie Française and made a peer of the realm. The idol of the young Romantics had become respectable. As one of his former disciples put it, "What was the point of going to all the trouble of becoming Victor Hugo?"

The collapse of the monarchy in 1848 heralded a new succession of Hugos. There was the Hugo who fought on the barricades in Paris, the political exile who broadcast to his international audience from an island in the English Channel, the visionary poet, the defender of the *misérables,* the national hero who helped to found the Third Republic. The 2 million people who attended his funeral in 1885 were a fair reflection of his encyclopedic career: anarchists, feminists, war veterans, civil servants, politicians, and prostitutes. Every layer of society was represented.

This mass outbreak of Hugophilia was seen by some as evidence of the poet's hypocrisy: his continual changes of tack were attributed to cynical opportunism. Hugo's refusal to separate morality from politics had always had an inflammatory effect on his contemporaries. Before and after his death, he was insulted and admired more than any other writer: "sublime cretin" (Dumas fils); "as stupid as the Himalayas" (Leconte de Lisle); "Victor Hugo was a madman who thought he was Victor Hugo" (Jean Cocteau). Hugo might have retorted with the words he quoted in *William Shakespeare* (1864): "Remember the advice that, in Aeschylus, the Ocean gives to Prometheus: 'To appear mad is the secret of the sage.' "

Now, in 2002, the bicentenary of Hugo's birth is being celebrated in France. The face that appears on television and on newsstands is the white-bearded sage of the Third Republic, the politically correct Father Christmas figure who used to stare down from classroom walls at children who were forced to memorize his poems. At Hugo's funeral, armed policemen confiscated the banners of socialist clubs. At his bicentenary, the boisterous rabble of his writing is being drowned out by official platitudes.

This neutralization of France's greatest writer is significant. Hugo was always the voice of his nation's bad conscience. His parents had stood on opposite sides of the great chasm in French history: the monarchy and the republic. His father was an important general in Napoleon's army in Spain. His mother, meanwhile, joined a conspiracy to depose Napoleon. For Hugo, to take one side or the other was to betray a part of his own past.

Hugo may have practiced autobiography as a form of fiction, but he grew up in a country that obsessively rewrote its own history. He saw Napoleon twice defeated and the monarchy twice restored in less than two years. In 1848 and 1871, he saw the government of which he was a member massacre hundreds of its own citizens. These traumatic events were also personal catastrophes. They showed that it was possible to follow the dictates of one's conscience and yet not be on the side of Good. Above all, they revealed the terrible truth that human battles are acted out on a background of unfathomable darkness: "The solitudes of the ocean are melancholy: tumult and silence combined. What happens there no longer concerns the human race."

The powerful, strangely insecure language of Hugo's magnificent novel *The Toilers of the Sea,* with its sporadic omniscience, its startling images slowly hammered into unexpected truths, its relentless questions and baffling answers, is the sound of a forensic hand forcing doors, lifting lids, unearthing ghastly secrets. Baudelaire claimed that "nations have great men only in spite of themselves," but they also have the great men they deserve. Victor Hugo, the secular god of official celebrations and poet laureate of the tourist industry, is also the Victor Hugo who wrote *The Toilers of the Sea* and other half-forgotten works of genius—the nervous voice of a nation whose modern history is crowded with ghosts: the Dreyfus Affair, the Vichy government and the deportation of Jews, the Algerian war, and, more recently, the rise of the National Front. As Hugo wrote, "Some crayfish souls are forever scuttling backward into the darkness."

———

When Hugo wrote *The Toilers of the Sea,* a chasm lay between him and his home country. In December 1851, Louis-Napoleon (later, Napoleon III) dissolved Parliament, bribed the army, and conducted a coup d'état. Hugo hid in Paris for several days, trying to stir up a revolt. Eventually, he fled from Paris on the night train to Brussels disguised as a worker. He spent the next nineteen years in exile, most of them in the Channel Islands, first on Jersey and then on Guernsey. His polemical works—*Napoléon le Petit* and *Châtiments*—were smuggled off the island and inspired revolutionary movements throughout the world.

Even in exile, the supposedly monolithic Hugo changed as often as the weather in the English Channel. He was a lyric poet in *Les Contemplations* (1856), an epic poet in *La Légende des Siècles* (1859), a social reformer in *Les Misérables* (1862). All these works were rooted in his earlier life, but *Les Travailleurs de la Mer* (1866) was conceived and written entirely in the Channel Islands. It showed, triumphantly, that Hugo's imagination had thrived on banishment and defeat.

A key to the workings of this imagination can be found in the extraordinary séances conducted in the first years of Hugo's exile on Jersey. The practice of enlisting the spirits of the dead in after-dinner conversation had been introduced to the exiles as a parlor game, but the mind of Victor Hugo turned it into a terrifying series of metaphysical visions.

The Hugos and some of their fellow exiles sat in a darkened drawing room, with the sea wind rattling the windows, and were astonished to find themselves talking to Hugo's first daughter, Léopoldine, who had drowned on her honeymoon nine years before. For the next eighteen months, until one of the participants went mad, the table tapped out its mystic words: one tap for an *a*, two for a *b*, and so on. Once transcribed, these messages—from Homer, Socrates, Jesus, Joan of Arc, and many others—all sounded remarkably like Victor Hugo.

One of the stars of these séances was a moody, irascible Ocean, which appeared in the spring of 1854, twelve years before it reappeared in *The Toilers of the Sea*. The Ocean wanted to dictate a piece of music and listed its musical needs:

> Give me the falling of rivers into seas, cataracts, waterspouts, the vomitings of the world's enormous breast, that which lions roar, that which elephants trumpet in their trunks [...] what mastodons snort in the entrails of the Earth, and then say to me, "Here is your orchestra."

Hugo politely offered a piano. But, as the Ocean pointed out, a piano could never express the synaesthetic dialogue of sounds, sights, and scents. "The piano I need would not fit into your house. It has only two keys, one white and one black, day and night; the day full of birds, the night full of souls." Hugo then suggested using Mozart as a go-between: "Mozart would be better," agreed the Ocean. "I myself am unintelligible."

> HUGO: "Could you ask Mozart to come this evening at nine o'clock?"
> THE OCEAN: "I shall have the message conveyed to him by the Twilight."

These ghostly conversations are often used to show that Hugo was insanely gullible. He seemed to believe that this flotsam of his unconscious mind had come from beyond the grave. He showed no surprise when the spirit of Shakespeare told him, "The English language is inferior to French," nor when he heard himself described by "Civilization" as "the great bird that sings of great dawns."

Hugo himself knew that, if published, these séance texts would be greeted with "an immense guffaw." His credulity was a deliberate ploy. By suspending his disbelief, he was summoning up the wild-eyed, holy sense of horror that kept the channels open between the writing hand and the deep unconscious.

The séance texts were a kind of rehearsal for his novel. Hugo was talking to his characters, conducting interviews with his own imagination. In *The Toilers of the Sea,* the tidal-wave syntax that sweeps up small details until the horizons of the page are filled with a single mighty metaphor, the thudding epigrams and crashing contrasts, the sudden silences and bathetic plunges were an attempt to provide the Ocean with its orchestra.

———

Hugo wrote his novel—originally titled *L'Abîme* ("The Abyss" or "The Deep")—between June 1864 and April 1865. The harrowing process of revision took almost as long. The novel was eventually published in March 1866. The introduction, "L'Archipel de la Manche," which is still the best general guide to the Channel Islands, was omitted. It did not appear until the 1883 edition.

Visitors to Guernsey today can not only talk to Hugo's ocean, they can also explore the house where the novel was written. From the street, Hauteville House, on the hill above St. Peter Port, appears to be a normal Georgian town house. Inside, it looks like a homemade Gothic cathedral. Hugo filled it with his own carvings and paintings and objects picked up on the beach or discovered in old barns. From the primeval gloom of the entrance hall to the blinding light of the "lookout" on the roof, Hauteville House is a model of Hugo's cosmogony, a seven-story poem in bricks and mortar.

It was in the "lookout" that he wrote his novel, standing up, battered by the wind, with a view of the harbor below and the thin gray line of the French coast. A glass panel in the floor allowed him to peer down through the layers of his domestic universe like a medieval god.

The intimate and grandiose architecture of the house is perceptible in *The Toilers of the Sea.* Huge blocks of text are coordinated as if they were parts of a giant sentence. The structure is littered with bizarre linguistic artifacts, picked up on beachcombing expeditions through manuals and dictionaries. And, like the house itself, the novel can be explored on several levels.

The ship that runs aground is the ship of State, piloted by a greedy hypocrite (Clubin or Napoleon III), and redeemed by a lone hero (Gilliatt or Victor Hugo). The title of the novel—literally, "*Workers* of the Sea"—has a socialist nuance. Technical progress and honest toil will triumph over the old feudal systems. But this was also part of a greater struggle. Gilliatt's task, like that of any engineer, is to conquer gravity and thus, in Hugo's symbolic view, the dumb weight of original sin.

At the center of the novel, the two towers of the Douvres, with the ship lodged between them, are one of Hugo's giant monograms, like the *H* of the guillotine in *Ninety-Three* or the *H* of the twin towers of Notre-Dame. This vertiginous structure is the concrete form of Hugo's mental discipline, around which the other allegories are entwined: the self-destructive nature of love, the civilizing mission of the lone hero, and his metaphysical fear of the void, embodied in that half-imagined, ungraspable creature, the *pieuvre*, "one of those embryos of terrible things that the dreamer glimpses confusedly through the window of night."

———

The Toilers of the Sea was a huge popular success, which says much about changes in reading habits. "Nineteenth-century novel" was not yet synonymous with dainty drawing-rooms and etiquette, although, even in 1866, a novel about an illiterate sailor and "the silent inclemency of phenomena going about their own business" was considered somewhat eccentric.

Five editions hurtled off the presses in the first three months. French critics were predictably frosty. In France, to insult the exiled Victor Hugo was to show allegiance to the régime of Napoleon III. One pedant published a brochure titled *A Badly Mistreated Mollusc, or M. Victor Hugo's Notion of Octopus Physiology*. Critics, said Hugo, are people who look at the sun and complain about its spots. A noble exception was Alexandre Dumas, who threw a *pieuvre*-tasting party in honor of the novel. Most writers remained silent. Like the Dreyfus Affair, the exile of Victor Hugo is one of the great moral touchstones in French history.

An English translation appeared almost immediately. Unfortunately, it sanitized the text. Gone were the underwater pebbles resembling the heads of green-haired babies, the evocation of springtime as the wet dream of the universe, and, of course, the nightmarish anatomy of the *pieuvre* with its single orifice.

British critics chortled at Hugo's extraordinary attempts at English. Captain Clubin was greeted with a hearty "Good-bye, Captain." A "cliff" in Scotland was called "*la Première des Quatre*" (the Firth of Forth), and the bagpipes turned into a "bug-pipe." Hugo was sensitive to reviews and found these comments strangely discourteous. He had dedicated his novel to the people of Guernsey and even gave the first word to England: "*La Christmas de 182 . . . fut remarquable à Guernesey.*" As Robert Louis Stevenson pointed out, these blunders were part of Hugo's weird charm. In fact, his fondness for the craggy consonants of Anglo-Saxon, the mad desolation of Celtic myth, and the swirling hallucinations of fog and forest give his Channel Island novels—*The Toilers of the Sea, The Laughing Man,* and *Ninety-Three*—a curious Britishness reminiscent of J.R.R. Tolkien and Mervyn Peake.

Hugo's so-called faults did nothing to harm the book's success. Eight English editions were published in the first six years. Later, a sixpenny edition brought the novel to a vast audience. *The Toilers of the Sea* remained a bestseller until long after Hugo's death. In 1900, some 3,250 copies were being sold every year in Britain.

Since then, Hugo's vast oeuvre has effectively been whittled down to a few hundred pages. *The Hunchback of Notre-Dame* and *Les Misérables* are now the only visible peaks of a literary continent that comprises seven novels, eighteen volumes of poetry, twenty-one plays, a small museum of paintings and drawings, and approximately 3 million words of history, criticism, travel writing, philosophy, and coded diaries.

Hugo would not have been surprised by this submersion of his work. All his novels end with images of erasure and decay. He knew that even masterpieces fall into disrepair and are eventually engulfed by incomprehensibility.

But in *The Toilers of the Sea*, it is still possible to experience the great outdoors of an inexhaustible imagination. This is not a novel for tidy minds who like to read classic fiction in their Sunday best. As the genteel reviewer of *Fraser's Magazine* remarked in 1866, after reading "A Word on the Secret Cooperation of the Elements," Hugo seems intent on "troubling us, offending us, buffeting us in the face; we come out of this chapter in a dishevelled unseemly condition."

———

GRAHAM ROBB's many books include *Victor Hugo: A Biography,* which won the 1997 Whitbread Biography Award. He has also written major biographies of Balzac and, most recently, Rimbaud.

I dedicate this book to the rock of hospitality and liberty,
that corner of old Norman soil where dwells
that noble little people of the sea;
to the island of Guernsey, austere and yet gentle,
my present asylum, my future tomb.

V.H.

PREFACE

Religion, society, nature: such are the three struggles in which man is engaged. These three struggles are, at the same time, his three needs. He must believe: hence the temple. He must create: hence the city. He must live: hence the plow and the ship. But these three solutions contain within them three wars. The mysterious difficulty of life springs from all three. Man is confronted with obstacles in the form of superstition, in the form of prejudice, and in the form of the elements. A triple *ananke*[1] weighs upon us: the *ananke* of dogmas, the *ananke* of laws, the *ananke* of things. In *Notre-Dame de Paris* the author denounced the first of these; in *Les Misérables* he drew attention to the second; in this book he points to the third.

With these three fatalities that envelop man is mingled the fatality within him, the supreme *ananke*, the human heart.

Hauteville House, March 1866.

THE TOILERS
OF THE
SEA

THE ARCHIPELAGO
OF THE
CHANNEL

I

ANCIENT CATACLYSMS

The Atlantic wears away our coasts. The pressure of the current from the Pole deforms our western cliffs. This wall that shields us from the sea is being undermined from Saint-Valery-sur-Somme to Ingouville; huge blocks of rock tumble down, the sea churns clouds of boulders, our harbors are silted up with sand and shingle, the mouths of our rivers are barred. Every day a stretch of Norman soil is torn away and disappears under the waves.

This tremendous activity, which has now slowed down, has had terrible consequences. It has been contained only by that immense spur of land we know as Finistère. The power of the flow of water from the Pole and the violence of the erosion it causes can be judged from the hollow it has carved out between Cherbourg and Brest. The formation of this gulf in the Channel at the expense of French soil goes back before historical times; but the last decisive act of aggression by the ocean against our coasts can be exactly dated. In 709, sixty years before Charlemagne came to the throne, a storm detached Jersey from France. The highest points of other territories submerged in earlier times are still, like Jersey, visible. These points emerging from the water are islands. They form what is called the Norman archipelago. This is now occupied by a laborious human anthill. The industry of the sea, which created ruin, has been succeeded by the industry of man, which has made a people.

II

GUERNSEY

Granite to the south, sand to the north; here sheer rock faces, there dunes. An inclined plane of meadowland with rolling hills and ridges of rock; as a fringe to this green carpet, wrinkled into folds, the foam of the ocean; along the coast, low-built fortifications; at intervals, towers pierced by loopholes; lining the low beaches, a massive breastwork intersected by battlements and staircases, invaded by sand and attacked by the waves, the only besiegers to be feared; windmills dismasted by storms, some of them—at the Vale, Ville-au-Roi, St. Peter Port, Torteval—still turning; in the cliffs, anchorages; in the dunes, sheep and cattle; the shepherds' and cattle herds' dogs questing and working; the little carts of the tradesmen of the town galloping along the hollow ways; often black houses, tarred on the west side for protection from the rain; cocks and hens, dung heaps; everywhere cyclopean walls; the walls of the old harbor, now unfortunately destroyed, were a fine sight, with their shapeless blocks of stone, their massive posts, and their heavy chains; farmhouses set amid trees; fields enclosed by waist-high drystone walls, forming a bizarre checkerboard pattern on the low-lying land; here and there a rampart built around a thistle, granite cottages, huts looking like casemates, little houses capable of withstanding a cannonball; occasionally, in the wildest parts of the country, a small new building topped by a bell—a school; two or three streams flowing through the meadows; elms and oaks; a lily found only here, the Guernsey lily; in the main plowing season, plows drawn by eight horses; in front of the houses, large haystacks on circular stone bases; expanses of prickly furze; here and there gardens in the old French style with clipped yew trees, carefully shaped box hedges and stone vases, mingled with orchards and kitchen gardens; carefully cultivated flowers in countryfolk's gardens; rhododendrons among potatoes; everywhere seaweed laid out on the grass, primrose-colored; in the church yards no crosses, but slabs of stone standing erect, seeming in the moonlight like white ladies; ten Gothic bell towers on the horizon; old churches, new dogmas; Protestant worship housed in Catholic architecture; scattered about in the sand and on the promontories, the somber Celtic enigma in its various forms—menhirs, peulvens, long stones, fairy stones, rocking stones, sounding stones, galleries, cromlechs, dolmens, fairies' houses; remains of the past of all kinds; after the druids the priests; after the priests the rectors; memories of falls from heaven; on one point Lucifer, at the castle of the Archangel Michael; on another, Icart Point, Icarus; almost as many flowers in winter as in summer. This is Guernsey.

III

GUERNSEY (CONTINUED)

Fertile land, rich, strong. No better pasturage. The wheat is celebrated; the cows are illustrious. The heifers grazing the pastures of St. Peter-in-the-Wood are the equals of the famed sheep of the Confolens plateau. The masterpieces produced by the plow and pastureland of Guernsey win medals at agricultural shows in France and England.

Agriculture benefits from well-organized public services, and an excellent network of communications gives life to the whole island. The roads are very good. Lying on the ground at the junction of two roads is a slab of stone bearing a cross. The earliest known bailiff of Guernsey, recorded in 1284, the first on the list, Gaultier de la Salle, was hanged for various acts of iniquity, and this cross, known as the Bailiff's Cross, marks the spot where he knelt and prayed for the last time. In the island's bays and creeks the sea is enlivened by the multicolored, sugarloaf-shaped mooring buoys, checked red and white, half black and half yellow, variegated in green, blue, and orange in lozenge, mottled and marble patterns, which float just under the water. Here and there can be heard the monotonous chant of a team hauling some vessel, heaving on the towrope. Like the fishermen, the farmworkers look content with their lot; so, too, do the gardeners. The soil, saturated with rock dust, is powerful; the fertilizer, which consists of sand and wrack, adds salt to the granite. Hence the extraordinary vitality and richness of the vegetation—magnolias, myrtles, daphnes, rose laurels, blue hydrangeas; the fuchsias are overabundant; there are arcades of three-leaved verbenas; there are walls of geraniums; oranges and lemons flourish in the open; there are no grapes, which ripen only under glass but when grown in greenhouses are excellent; camellias grow into trees; aloe flowers can be seen in gardens, growing taller than a house. Nothing can be more opulent and prodigal than this vegetation that masks and ornaments the trim fronts of villas and cottages.

Attractive on one side, Guernsey is terrible on the other. The west coast of the island, exposed to winds from the open sea, has been devastated. This is a region of coastal reefs, squalls, careening coves, patched-up boats, fallow land, heath, poor hovels, a few low, shivering hamlets, lean sheep and cattle, short salty grass, and a general air of harsh poverty. Lihou is a small barren island just off the coast that is accessible at low tide. It is covered with scrub and rabbit burrows. The rabbits of Lihou know the time of day, emerging from their holes only at high tide and setting man at defiance. Their friend the ocean isolates them. Fraternal relations of this kind are found throughout nature.

If you dig down into the alluvial soil of Vazon Bay you come upon trees. Here, under a mysterious layer of sand, there was once a forest.

The fishermen so harshly treated by this wind-beaten west coast make skillful pilots. The sea around the Channel Islands is peculiar. Cancale Bay, not far away, is the spot in the world where the tides rise highest.

IV

THE GRASS

The grass of Guernsey is the same grass as anywhere else, though a little richer: a meadow on Guernsey is almost like a lawn in Cuges or Gémenos.[2] You find fescues and tufted hair-grasses, as in any other grass, together with common star-grass and floating manna grass; mountain brome, with spindle-shaped spikelets; the phalaris of the Canaries; agrostis, which yields a green dye; rye grass; yellow lupin; Yorkshire fog, which has a woolly stem; fragrant vernal grass; quaking grass; the rain daisy; wild garlic, which has such a sweet flower but such an acrid smell; timothy grass; foxtail, with an ear in the shape of a club; needle grass, which is used for making baskets; and lyme grass, which is useful for stabilizing shifting sands. Is this all? By no means: there are also cocksfoot, whose flowers grow in clusters; panic millet;

and even, according to local agricultural experts, bluestem grass. There are the bastard hawkweed, with leaves like the dandelion, which marks the time of day, and the sow thistle of Siberia, which foretells the weather. All these are grasses, but this mixture of grasses is not to be found everywhere: it is peculiar to the archipelago. It requires granite for its subsoil and the ocean to water it.

Now imagine a thousand insects crawling through the grass and flying above it, some hideous, others charming; under the grass longicorns, longinases, weevils, ants engaged in milking aphids, their milch cows, dribbling grasshoppers, ladybirds, click beetles; on the grass and in the air dragonflies, ichneumons, wasps, golden rose-beetles, bumblebees, lace-winged flies, red-bellied gold wasps, the noisy hoverflies—and you will have some idea of the reverie-inducing spectacle that the Jerbourg ridge or Fermain Bay, around midday in June, offers an entomologist who is something of a dreamer or a poet who is something of a naturalist.

Suddenly, under this sweet green grass, you will notice a small square slab of stone inscribed with the letters *WD*, which stand for War Department. This is fair and proper. It is right that civilization should show itself here: otherwise the place would be wild. Go to the banks of the Rhine and seek out the most isolated corners of the landscape. At some points it is so majestic that it seems pontifical: God, surely, must be more present here than elsewhere.

Penetrate into the remote fastnesses where the mountains offer the greatest solitude and the forests the greatest silence; choose, let us say, Andernach and its surroundings; visit the obscure and impassive Laacher See, so unknown that it is almost mysterious. No tranquillity can be found more august than this; universal life is here in all its religious serenity; no disturbances; everywhere the profound order of nature's great disorder; walk with a softened heart in this wilderness; it is as voluptuous as spring and as melancholy as autumn; wander about at random; leave behind you the ruined abbey, lose yourself in the moving peace of the ravines, amid the song of birds and the rustle of leaves; drink fresh spring water in your cupped hand; walk, meditate, forget. You come upon a cottage at the corner of a hamlet buried under the trees; it is green, fragrant, and charming, clad in ivy and flowers, full of children and laughter. You draw nearer, and on the corner of the cottage, which is bathed in a brilliant alternation of shadow and sunlight, on an old stone in the old wall, below the name of the hamlet, Niederbreisig, you read 22. LANDW. BATAILLON 2. COMP.

You thought you were in a village: you find that you are in a regiment. Such is the nature of man.

V

THE PERILS OF THE SEA

An overfall[3] extends along the whole of the west coast of Guernsey, which has been skillfully dissected by the waves. At night, on rocky points with a sinister reputation, strange lights—seen, it is said, by prowlers along the shore—warn or deceive. These same prowlers, bold and credulous characters, distinguish under the water the legendary sea cucumber, that infernal marine nettle that will set a man's hand on fire if he touches it. Some local names, for example, Tinttajeu (from Welsh Tin-Tagel), point to the presence of the Devil. As Eustace (the name of Wace) says in the old lines—

> Then surged the sea,
> The waves 'gan swell and stir,
> The skies grew black, and black the clouds.
> And soon the sea was all aroused.

The Channel is as unsubdued today as it was in the time of Tewdrig, Umbrafel, Amon Dhû, the Black, and the knight Emyr Lhydau,[4] who sought refuge on the island of Groix, near Quimperlé. In these parts the ocean puts on *coups de théâtre* of which man must beware. This, for example, which is one of the commonest caprices of the winds in the Channel Islands: a storm blows in from the southeast; then there is a period of dead calm; you breathe again; this sometimes lasts for an hour; suddenly the hurricane, which had died down in the southeast, returns from the northwest; whereas previously it took you in the rear, it now reverses direction and takes you head on. If you are not a former pilot and an old sailor, and if you have not been careful to change your tack when the wind changed direction, it is all over with you: the vessel goes to pieces and sinks. Ribeyrolles,[5] who died in Brazil, jotted down from time to time during his stay on Guernsey a personal diary of the events of the day, a page from which we have in front of us:

1st January: New Year gifts. Storm. A ship coming from Portrieux was lost yesterday on the Esplanade.

2nd: Three-master lost in Rocquaine Bay. It hailed from America. Seven men dead. Twenty-one saved.

3rd: The packet did not arrive.

4th: The storm continues.

14th: Rain. Landslide, which killed one man.

15th: Stormy weather. The *Fawn* could not sail.

22nd: Sudden squall. Five wrecks on the west coast.

24th: The storm persists. Shipwrecks on all sides.

There is hardly ever any respite in this corner of the ocean. Hence the seagull shrieks, echoing down the centuries in this never-ending squall, uttered by the uneasy old poet Lhy-ouar'h-henn, that Jeremiah of the sea. But bad weather is not the greatest peril for navigation in the archipelago: the squall is violent, but violence is a warning sign. You return to harbor, or you head into the wind, taking care to set the center of effort of the sails as low as possible. If the wind blows strong you brail up everything, and you may still come through. The greatest perils in these waters are the invisible perils, which are always present; and the finer the weather the more they are to be dreaded.

In such situations special methods of working the ship are necessary. The seamen of western Guernsey excel in such maneuvers, which can be called preventive. No one has studied so carefully as they the three dangers of a calm sea, the *singe,* the *anuble,* and the *derruble.* The *singe* or *swinge* is the current; the *anuble* ("dark place") is the shoals; the *derruble* (pronounced *terrible*) is the whirlpool, the navel, the funnel formed by underwater rocks, the well beneath the sea.

V I

THE ROCKS

In the archipelago of the Channel the coasts are almost everywhere wild. These islands have charming interiors but a stern and uninviting approach. Since the Channel is a kind of Mediterranean, the waves are short and violent and the tide has a lapping movement. Hence the bizarre battering to which the cliffs are subjected and the deep erosion of the coasts. Skirting these coasts, you pass through a series of mirages. At every turn the rocks try to deceive you. Where do these illusions come from? From the granite. It is very strange. You see huge stone toads, which have no doubt come out of the water to breathe. Giant nuns hasten on their way, heading for the horizon; the petrified folds of their veils have the form of the fleeing wind. Kings with Plutonian crowns meditate on massive thrones, ever under attack by the breakers. Nameless creatures buried in the rock stretch out their arms, showing the fingers of their open hands. All this is the formless coast. Draw nearer, and there is nothing there. Stone can sometimes disappear like this. Here there is a fortress, there a crudely shaped temple, elsewhere a chaos of dilapidated houses and dismantled walls: all the ruins of a deserted city. But there is no city there, no temple, no fortress—only the cliffs. As you draw closer or move farther away, as you drift off or turn back, the coast falls to pieces. No kaleidoscope is quicker to disintegrate. The view breaks apart and re-forms; perspective plays its tricks. This block of rock is a tripod; then it is a lion; then it is an angel and unfolds its wings; then it is a seated figure reading a book. Nothing changes form so quickly as clouds, except perhaps rocks.

These forms call up the idea of grandeur, not of beauty. Far from it: they are sometimes unhealthy and hideous. The rocks have swellings and tumors and cysts and bruises and growths and warts. Mountains are the humps on the earth's surface. Madame de Staël, hearing Chateaubriand,[6] who had rather high shoulders, speaking slightingly of the Alps, called it the "jealousy of the hunchback." The grand lines and great majesties of nature, the level of the seas, the silhouette of the mountains, the somber shades of the forests, the blue of the sky are affected by some huge and mysterious dislocation mingled with their harmony. Beauty has its lines; deformity has, too. There is a smile; there is also a distorted grin. Disintegration has the same effects on rocks as on clouds. *This* one floats and decomposes; *that* one is stable and incoherent. The creation retains something of the anguish of chaos. Splendors bear scars. An element of ugliness, which may sometimes be dazzling, mingles with the most magnificent things, seeming to protest against order. There is something of a grimace in the cloud. There is a celestial grotesquerie. All lines are broken in waves, in foliage and in rocks, in which strange parodies can be glimpsed. In them shapelessness predominates. No single outline is correct. Grand? Yes. Pure? No. Examine the clouds: all kinds of faces can be seen in them, all kinds of resemblances, all kinds of figures; but you will look in vain for a Greek profile. You will find Caliban, not Venus; you will never see the Parthenon. But sometimes, at nightfall, a great table of shadow, resting on jambs of cloud and surrounded by blocks of mist, will figure forth in the livid crepuscular sky an immense and monstrous cromlech.

VII

LAND AND SEA MINGLED

The farmhouses of Guernsey are monumental. Some of them have, lining the road, a length of wall like a stage set with a carriage gate and a pedestrians' gate side by side. In the jambs and arches time has carved out deep crevices in which tortula moss nestles, ripening its spores, and where it is not unusual to find bats sleeping. The hamlets under the trees are decrepit but full of life. The cottages seem as old as cathedrals. In the wall of a stone hovel on the Les Hubies road is a recess containing the stump of a small column and the date 1405. Another, near Balmoral, displays on its façade, like the peasant houses of Ernani and Astigarraga,[7] a coat of arms carved in the stone. At every step you will come across farmhouses displaying windows with lozenged panes, staircase turrets, and archivolts in the style of the Renaissance. Not a doorway but has its granite mounting-block. Other little houses have once been boats; the hull of a boat, turned upside down and perched on posts and cross-beams, forms a roof. A vessel with its keel uppermost is a church; with the vaulting downward it is a ship; the recipient of prayer, reversed, tames the sea. In the arid parishes of western Guernsey the communal well with its little dome of white stonework set amid the untilled land has almost the appearance of an Arab marabout.[8] A perforated beam, with a stone for pivot, closes the entrance to a field enclosed by hedges; there are certain marks by which you can distinguish the hurdles on which hobgoblins and auxcriniers[9] ride at night.

All over the slopes of the ravines are ferns, bindweed, wild roses, red-berried holly, hawthorn, pink thorn, danewort, privet, and the long pleated thongs known as Henry IV's collarettes. Amid all this vegetation there multiplies and prospers a species of willow herb that produces nuts much favored by donkeys—a preference expressed by the botanists, with great elegance and decency, in the term Onagriaceae. Everywhere there are thickets, arbors, all kinds of wild plants, expanses of green in which a winged world twitters and warbles, closely watched by a creeping world; blackbirds, linnets, robins, jays; the goldfinch of the Ardennes hurries on its way at full speed; flocks of starlings maneuver in spirals; elsewhere are greenfinches, goldfinches, the Picardy jackdaw, the red-footed crow. Here and there a grass snake.

Little waterfalls, their water carried in channels of worm-eaten wood from which water escapes in drops, drive mills that can be heard turning under the boughs. In some farmyards there can still be seen a cider press and the old circle hollowed out of stone in which the apples were crushed. The cattle drink from troughs like sarcophagi: some Celtic king may have rotted in this granite casket in which the Juno-eyed cow is now drinking. Tree-creepers and wagtails, with friendly familiarity, come down and steal the hens' grain. Along the shore everything is tawny. The wind wears down the grass that is burned up by the sun. Some of the churches are caparisoned in ivy, which reaches up to the belfry. Here and there in the empty heathland an outcrop of rock is crowned by a cottage. Boats, laid up on the beach for lack of a harbor, are buttressed by large boulders. The sails seen on the horizon are ocher or salmon yellow rather than white. On the side exposed to rain and wind the trees have a fur of lichen; and the very stones seem to take their precautions, covering themselves with a skin of dense and solid moss. There are murmurings, whisperings, the rustling of branches; seabirds fly swiftly past, some of them with a silver fish in their beak; there are an abundance of butterflies, varying in color according to season, and all kinds of tumults deep in the sounding rocks. Grazing horses gallop across the untilled land; they roll on the ground, leap about, stop short, offer their manes to be tossed by the wind and watch the waves as they roll in, one after the other, perpetually.

In May the old buildings in the countryside and on the coast are covered in wallflowers, and in June in lilacs. In the dunes the old batteries are crumbling. The countryfolk benefit from the disuse of the cannon, and the fishermen's nets are hung out to dry on the embrasures. Within the four walls of the dismantled blockhouse a wandering donkey or a tethered goat browses on thrift and blue thistles. Half-naked children play, laughing; on the roadways can be seen the patterns they have drawn for their games of hopscotch. In the evening the setting sun, radiantly horizontal, lights up the return of the heifers in the hollow ways as they linger to crop the hedges on either side, causing the dog to bark. The wild capes on the west coast sink down into the sea in an undulating line; on them are a few shivering tamarinds. As twilight falls the cyclopean walls, with the last daylight passing between their stones, form long crests of black lacework along the summit of the hills. The sound of the wind, heard in these solitudes, gives a feeling of extraordinary remoteness.

VIII

ST. PETER PORT

St. Peter Port, capital of Guernsey, was originally built of houses of carved wood brought from Saint-Malo. A handsome stone house of the sixteenth century still stands in the Grand'Rue. St. Peter Port is a free port. The town is built on the slopes of a charming huddle of valleys and hills clustered around the Old Harbor as if they had been thrust there by the hand of a giant. The ravines form the streets, with flights of steps providing shortcuts. The excellent Anglo-Norman carriages gallop up and down the steep streets. In the main square the market women, sitting out in the open, are exposed to the winter showers, while a few paces away is a bronze statue of a prince.[10] A foot of water falls on Jersey every year, ten and a half inches on Guernsey.

The fish merchants are better off than the sellers of farm produce: the fish market, a large covered hall, has marble tables with magnificent displays of fish, for the fishermen of Guernsey frequently bring in miraculous drafts. There is no public library, but there is a Mechanics' Institution and Literary Society. There is a college.

The town builds as many churches as it can, and when they are built they must be approved by the Lords of the Council. It is not unusual to see carts passing through the streets of the town carrying arched wooden windows presented by some carpenter to some church. There is a courthouse. The judges, in purple robes, give their judgments in open court. Last century butchers could not sell a pound of beef or mutton until the magistrates had chosen their meat.

There are many private chapels in protest against the official churches. Go into one of these chapels, and you will hear a country-man expounding to others the doctrines of Nestorianism (that is, the difference between the Mother of Christ and the Mother of God) or teaching that the Father is power, while the Son is only a limited power—which is very much like the heresy of Abelard. There are large numbers of Irish Catholics, who are not noted for their patience, so that theological discussions are sometimes punctuated by orthodox fisticuffs.

Sunday is, by law, a day of stagnation. Everything is permitted, except drinking a glass of beer, on Sunday. If you felt thirsty on the "blessed Sabbath day" you would scandalize worthy Amos Chick, who is licensed to sell ale and cider in the High Street. The law on Sunday observance permits singing, but without drinking. Except when praying people do not say "My God": they say instead "My Good"—the word *good* replacing God. A young French assistant teacher in a boarding school who picked up her scissors with the exclamation "Ah mon Dieu!" was dismissed for "swearing." People here are more biblical than evangelical.

There is a theater. The entrance is a doorway in a deserted street giving access to a corridor. The interior is rather in the style of architecture adopted for haylofts. Satan lives here in very modest style and is poorly lodged. Opposite the theater is the prison, another lodging of the same individual. On the hill to the north, in Castle Carey (a sole-cism: the right form is Carey Castle), there is a valuable collection of pictures, mainly Spanish. If it were publicly owned it would be a museum. In some aristocratic houses there are curious specimens of the Dutch painted tiles with which Tsar Peter's chimneypiece at Saardam is faced and of those magnificent tile paintings known in Portugal as *azulejos,* products of the high art of tin-glazed earthenware that has recently been revived, finer than before, thanks to initiators like Dr. Lasalle, manufactories like the one at Premières,[11] and pottery painters like Deck and Devers.

The Chaussée d'Antin of Jersey is Rouge-Bouillon; the Faubourg Saint-Germain[12] of Guernsey is Les Rohais. Here there are many handsome streets, finely laid out and intersected by gardens. St. Peter Port has as many trees as roofs, more nests than houses, and more sounds of birds than of carriages. Les Rohais has the grand patrician aspect of the fashionable quarters of London and is white and clean. But cross a ravine, pass over Mill Street, continue through a narrow gap between two tall buildings, and climb a narrow and interminable flight of steps with tortuous bends and loose paving, and you find yourself in a bedouin town: hovels, potholes, streets with broken paving, burned-out gable ends, ruined houses, empty rooms without doors or windows in which grass grows, beams traversing the street, piles of rubble blocking the way, here and there a shack that is still inhabited, naked small boys, pale-faced women: you might think yourself in Zaatcha.[13] In St. Peter Port a watchmaker is a *montrier;* an auctioneer is an *encanteur;* a housepainter is a *picturier;* a building worker is a *plâtrier;* a foot doctor is a *chiropodiste;* a cook is a *couque;* to knock at the door is to *taper à l'hû.* Mrs. Pescott is *agente de douanes et fournisseure de navires* (customs agent and ship's chandler). A barber told his customers of the death of Wellington in these words: *Le commandant des soudards*[14] *est mort.* Women go from door to door selling trifling wares bought in bazaars and markets: this is called *chiner.* The *chineuses,* who are very poor, are lucky if they earn a few doubles[15] in a day. A remark by one *chineuse* is significant: "You know, I've done well: I've set aside seven sous this week." A friend of mine, encountering another *chineuse,* gave her five francs, whereupon she said: "Thank you, sir: now I'll be able to buy wholesale."

In June the yachts begin to arrive, and the bay is filled with pleasure craft, most of them schooner-rigged, with some steam yachts. Some yachts may well cost their owner a hundred thousand francs a month. Cricket prospers, while boxing declines. Temperance societies are active; and, it must be said, they perform a useful function. They hold processions, carrying banners in an almost masonic display that softens the hearts even of the innkeepers. Barmaids can be heard saying, as they serve customers overfond of drink: "Have a glass, not a bottle."

The population is healthy, handsome, and well-behaved. The town prison is very often empty. At Christmas the jailer, if he has prisoners, gives them a small family banquet. The local architecture has its peculiarities, of which it is tenacious. The town of St. Peter Port is faithful to the queen, to the Bible, and to sash windows. In summer the men bathe naked. Swimming trunks are an indecency: they attract attention. Mothers excel in dressing their children: it is pretty to see the variety of toilettes they so skillfully devise for the little ones. Children go about alone in the streets, showing a sweet and touching confidence. Small children take the babies. In the matter of fashion Guernsey copies Paris, though not always: sometimes vivid reds or harsh blues reveal the English alliance. Nevertheless we have heard a local dressmaker, advising a fashionable Guernsey lady, say: "I think a ladylike and genteel color is best."

Guernsey is renowned for the work of its ship's carpenters: the Careening Hard is lined with ships under repair. Vessels are hauled ashore to the sound of a flute. The flute player, say the master carpenters, is a better worker than the workmen. St. Peter Port has a Pollet[16] like Dieppe and a Strand like London. A respectable gentleman would not be seen in the street with a book or a portfolio under his arm, but he will go to the market on Saturday carrying a basket. A visit by a royal personage provided a pretext for erecting a tower.[17] The dead are buried within the town. College Street runs past two cemeteries, one on either side. Built into a wall is a tomb of 1610. L'Hyvreuse is a little square planted with grass and trees that can stand comparison with the most beautiful gardens in Paris's Champs-Élysées, with the additional bonus of the sea. In the windows of the elegant shopping mall known as the Arcades can be seen advertisements such as this: "On sale here, the perfume recommended by the 6th Artillery Regiment."

The town is traversed in every direction by drays laden with barrels of beer and sacks of coal. A stroller about town can read a variety of other notices: "A fine bull to be hired out here, as in the past."—"Highest prices given for rags, lead, glass and bones."—"For sale, new kidney potatoes of the finest quality."—"For sale, pea stakes, some tons of oats for chaff, a complete set of English-style doors for a drawing room and a fat pig. Mon Plaisir farm, St. James's."—"For sale, good hay, recently threshed, yellow carrots by the hundred, and a good French syringe. Apply to the Moulin de l'Échelle, St. Andrew's."—"It is forbidden to dress fish or deposit refuse."—"For sale, a she-ass in milk." And so on, and so on.

IX

JERSEY, ALDERNEY, SARK

The Channel Islands are fragments of France that have fallen into the sea and been picked up by England. Hence their complex nationality. The people of Jersey and Guernsey are certainly not English against their will, but they are also French without knowing it. If they do know it, they make a point of forgetting it. Some indication of this is given by the French they speak. The archipelago consists of four islands—two large ones, Jersey and Guernsey, and two small ones, Alderney and Sark—together with various islets: Ortach, the Casquets, Herm, Jethou, and so on. The names of the islets and reefs in this old Gaul frequently contain the term *hou.* Alderney has Burhou, Sark has Brecqhou, Guernsey has Lihou and Jethou, Jersey has Les Écrehou, Granville has Le Pirhou. There are La Hougue Point, La Hougue Bie, La Hougue des Pommiers, the Houmets, etc. There are the island of Chousey, the Chouas reef, etc. This remarkable radical of the primitive language of the region, *hou,* is found everywhere: in the words *houle* (entrance to a rabbit's burrow), *huée* (booing), *hure* (promontory), *hourque* (a Dutch cargo vessel), *houre* (an old word for scaffold), *houx* (holly), *houperon* (shark), *hurlement* (howling), *hulotte* (brown owl), and *chouette* (screech owl), from which is derived Chouan,[18] etc.; and it can be detected in two words that express the indefinite, *unda* and *unde.* It is also found in two words expressing doubt, *ou* and *où.*[19]

Sark is half the size of Alderney, Alderney is a quarter the size of Guernsey, and Guernsey is two-thirds the size of Jersey. The whole of the island of Jersey is exactly the same size as the city of London. It would take twenty-seven hundred Jerseys to make up the area of France. According to the calculations of Charassin, an excellent practical agronomist, France, if it were as well cultivated as Jersey, could feed a population of 270 million—the whole of Europe. Of the four islands Sark, the smallest, is the most beautiful; Jersey, the largest, is the prettiest; and Guernsey, both wild and smiling, has the qualities of both. Sark has a silver mine that is not worked because it yields so little. Jersey has fifty-six thousand inhabitants, Guernsey thirty thousand, Alderney forty-five hundred, Sark six hundred, Lihou one. The distance between these islands, between Alderney and Guernsey and between Guernsey and Jersey, is the stride of a seven-league boot. The arm of the sea between Guernsey and Herm is called the Little Russel, that between Herm and Sark the Great Russel. The nearest point in France is Cape Flamanville. On Guernsey you can hear the cannon of Cherbourg; in Cherbourg you can hear the thunder of Guernsey. The storms in the archipelago of the Channel, as we have said, are terrible. Archipelagos are abodes of the winds. Between the various islands there is a corridor that acts as a bellows—a law that is bad for the sea and good for the land. The wind carries away miasmas and brings about shipwrecks. This law applies to the Channel Islands as it does to other archipelagos. Cholera has spared Jersey and Guernsey; but there was such a violent epidemic on Guernsey in the Middle Ages that the bailiff burned the archives to destroy the plague. In France these islands are generally known as the English islands, in England as the Norman islands. The Channel Islands coin their own money, though only coppers. A Roman road, which can still be seen, ran between Coutances in Normandy and Jersey. As we have seen, Jersey was detached from France by the ocean in 709, when twelve parishes were engulfed. There are families living today in Normandy that still have the lordship of these parishes. Their divine right is now under water: such is sometimes the fate of divine rights.

X

History, Legend, Religion

The original six parishes of Guernsey belonged to a single seigneur, Néel, viscount of Cotentin, who was defeated in the Battle of the Dunes in 1047. At that time, according to Dumaresq, there was a volcano in the Channel Islands. The date of the twelve parishes of Jersey is inscribed in the Black Book of Coutances Cathedral. The seigneur of Briquebec had the style of baron of Guernsey. Alderney was a fief held by Henri l'Artisan. Jersey was ruled by two thieves, Caesar and Rollo.[20] *Haro*[21] is an appeal to the duke ("Ha! Rollo!"); or perhaps it comes from the Saxon *haran,* to cry. The cry *haro* was repeated three times, kneeling on the highway, and all work ceased in the area until justice had been done. Before Rollo, duke of the Normans, the archipelago had been ruled by Solomon, king of the Bretons. As a result there is much of Normandy in Jersey and much of Brittany in Guernsey. On these islands nature reflects history: Jersey has more meadowland, Guernsey more rocks; Jersey is greener, Guernsey harsher. The islands were covered with noble mansions. The earl of Essex left a ruin on Alderney, Essex Castle. Jersey has Mont Orgueil; Guernsey has Castle Cornet. Castle Cornet stands on a rock that was once a holm, that is, a helmet. The same metaphor is found in the Casquets (*casques* = helmets). Castle Cornet was besieged by the Picard pirate Eustache, Mont Orgueil by Du Guesclin[22]; fortresses, like women, boast of their besiegers when they are illustrious. In the fifteenth century a pope declared Jersey and Guernsey neutral. He was thinking of war, not of schism. Calvinism, preached on Jersey by Pierre Morice and on Guernsey by Nicolas Baudouin, arrived in the Norman archipelago in 1563. Calvin's doctrines have prospered there, as have Luther's, though nowadays much troubled by Wesleyanism, an offshoot of Protestantism that now contains the future of England. Churches abound in the archipelago. It is worth considering them in detail. Everywhere there are Protestant churches; Catholicism has been left behind. Any given area on Jersey or Guernsey has more chapels than any area of the same size in Spain or Italy. Methodists proper, Primitive Methodists, other Methodist sects, Independent Methodists, Baptists, Presbyterians, Millenarians, Quakers, Bible Christians, Plymouth Brethren, Non-Sectarians, etc.; add also the episcopal Anglican church and the papist Roman church. On Jersey there is a Mormon chapel.

In St. George's Fountain, at Le Câtel, girls see the image of their future husband. Another spring, in St. Andrew's, I think, compels liars who have been unfortunate enough to drink from it to tell the truth. If a woman scrapes a stone in a dolmen, mixes the resultant powder, known as *pérelle,* into water, and drinks it, she is sure to have sturdy children. The wall of a church can be scraped with similar success. In every bay there lives an elf who, if a child gives him a cake, will in due course, according to sex, give the little girl a dowry when she reaches marriageable age and the boy, when he becomes a man, a fully rigged boat. There are two giants: the giant Longis, father of Gayoffe, father of Bolivorax, father of Pantagruel,[23] and the giant Bodu, who has now been transformed into a black dog, having been punished by the fairies for his dalliance with a princess. This black dog, Bodu, competes in old wives' tales with a white dog, who is Gaultier de la Salle, the bailiff who was hanged. Connoisseurs of phantoms have all sorts of varieties to study in the Channel Islands: *drées* are not the same as *alleurs; alleurs* are not the same as *auxcriniers; auxcriniers* are not the same as *cucuches.* In these parts anyone encountering a black hen at nightfall feels some apprehension.

In certain parishes there has been something of a return to Catholicism. At present crosses are beginning to grow on the tips of church spires. It is a sign of Puseyism.[24] The organ is now heard in churches, and even in chapels, which would have aroused John Knox's indignation. Saintly persons now abound; some of them possess to a very remarkable degree a horror of "miscreants." In many people this horror seems innate. Protestantism excels, no less than Catholicism, in promoting it. A woman of the highest society in London is famous for her ability to faint in houses where there is a copy of Dr. Colenso's book.[25] She enters a house and cries: "The book is here!" and then swoons. A search is carried out and the book is found. This is a very valuable kind of faculty.

Orthodox Bibles are distinguished by their spelling of Satan without a capital, "satan." They are quite right.

Speaking of Satan, they hate Voltaire. The word *Voltaire,* it seems, is one of the pronunciations of the name of Satan. When it is a question of Voltaire all dissidences are forgotten; Mormon and Anglican views coincide; there is general agreement in anger; and all sects are united in hatred. The anathema directed against Voltaire is the point of intersection of all varieties of Protestantism. It is a remarkable fact that Catholicism detests Voltaire and Protestantism execrates him. Geneva outbids Rome. There is a crescendo in malediction. Calas, Sirven, and so many eloquent pages against the dragonnades count for nothing.[26]

Voltaire denied a dogma: that is enough. He defended Protestants but he wounded Protestantism; and the Protestants pursue him with a very orthodox ingratitude. A man who had occasion to speak in public in St. Helier to gain support for a good cause was warned that if he mentioned Voltaire in his speech[27] the collection would be a failure. So long as the past has breath enough to make itself heard, Voltaire will be rejected. Listen to all these voices: he has neither genius nor talent nor wit. In his old age he was insulted; after his death he is proscribed. He is eternally "discussed": in this his glory consists. Is it possible to speak of Voltaire calmly and with justice? When a man dominates an age and incarnates progress, he cannot expect criticism: only hatred.

XI

OLD HAUNTS AND OLD SAINTS

The Cyclades form a circle; the archipelago of the Channel forms a triangle. When you look at a map, which is a bird's-eye view for man, the Channel Islands, a triangular segment of sea, are bounded by three culminating points: Alderney to the north, Guernsey to the west, and Jersey to the south. Each of these three mother islands has around it what might be called its chickens, a series of islets. Alderney has Burhou, Ortach, and the Casquets; Guernsey has Herm, Jethou, and Lihou; Jersey has on the side facing France the semicircle of St. Aubin's Bay, toward which the two groups, scattered but distinct, of the Grelets and the Minquiers seem to be hastening, like two swarms of bees heading for the doorway of the hive, in the blue of the water, which, like the sky, is azure. In the center of the archipelago is Sark, with its associated Brecqhou and Goat Island, which provides a link between Guernsey and Jersey. The comparison between the Cyclades and the Channel Islands would certainly have struck the mystical and mythical school that, under the Restoration, was centered on de Maistre by way of d'Eckstein[28] and would have served it as a symbol: the rounded archipelago of Hellas (*ore rotundo,* harmonious in style), the archipelago of the Channel sharp, bristling, aggressive, angular; the one in the image of harmony, the other of dispute. It is not for nothing that one is Greek and the other Norman.

Once, in prehistoric times, these islands in the Channel were wild. The first islanders were probably some of those primitive men of whom specimens were found at Moulin-Quignon,[29] who belonged to the race with receding jaws. For half the year they lived on fish and shellfish, for the other half on what they could pick up from wrecks. Pillaging their coasts was their main resource. They recognized only two seasons in the year, the fishing season and the shipwreck season, just as the Greenlanders call summer the "reindeer hunt" and winter the "seal hunt." All these islands, which later became Norman, were expanses of thistles and brambles, wild beasts' dens and pirates' lairs. An old local chronicler refers, energetically, to "rat traps" and "pirate traps." The Romans came, and probably brought about only a moderate advance toward probity: they crucified the pirates and celebrated the Furrinalia, the rogues' festival. This festival is still celebrated in some of our villages on July 25 and in our towns throughout the year.

Jersey, Sark, and Guernsey were formerly called Ange, Sarge, and Bissarge; Alderney is Redana, or perhaps Thanet. There is a legend that on Rat Island, *insula rattorum*, the promiscuity of male rabbits and female rats gave rise to the guinea pig.

According to Furetière,[30] abbot of Chalivoy, who reproached La Fontaine with being ignorant of the difference between *bois en grume* (hewn timber with its bark on) and *bois marmenteau* (ornamental timber), it was a long time before France noticed the existence of Alderney off its coasts. And indeed Alderney plays only an imperceptible part in the history of Normandy. Rabelais, however, knew the Norman archipelago; he names Herm and Sark, which he calls Cercq. "I assure you that this land is the same that I have formerly seen, the islands of Cercq and Herm, between Brittany and England" (edition of 1558, Lyons, p. 423).

The Casquets are a redoubtable place for shipwrecks. Two hundred years ago the English ran a trade in the fishing up of cannon there. One of these cannon, covered with oysters and mussels, is now in the museum in Valognes.[31] Herm is an *eremos*.[32] Saint Tugdual, a friend of Saint Sampson, prayed on Herm, just as Saint Magloire (Maglorius) prayed on Sark. There were hermits' haloes on all these rocky points. Helier prayed on Jersey and Marculf amid the rocks of Calvados. This was the time when the hermit Eparchius was becoming Saint Cybard in the caverns of Angoulême and when the anchorite Crescentius, in the depths of the forests around Trier, caused a temple of Diana to fall down by staring fixedly at it for five years. It was on Sark, which was his sanctuary, his *ionad naomh,* that Magloire composed the hymn for All Saints, later rewritten by Santeuil, *Coelo quos eadem gloria consecrat.* It was from there, too, that he threw stones at the Saxons, whose raiding fleets twice disturbed his prayers. The archipelago was also somewhat troubled at this period by the amwarydour, the chieftain of the Celtic settlement. From time to time Magloire crossed the water to consult with the mactierne (vassal prince) of Guernsey, Nivou, who was a prophet. One day Magloire, after performing a miracle, made a vow never to eat fish again. In addition, in order to promote good behavior among the dogs and preserve the monks from guilty thoughts, he banished bitches from the island of Sark—a law that still subsists. Saint Magloire performed other services for the archipelago. He went to Jersey to bring to their senses the people of the island, who had the bad habit on Christmas Day of changing themselves into all kinds of animals in honor of Mithras. Saint Magloire put an end to this misbehavior. In the reign of Nominoe, a feudatory of Charles the Bold, his relics were stolen by the monks of Lehon-lès-Dinan. All these facts are proved by the Bollandists, the "Acta Sancti Marculphi," etc., and Abbé Trigan's "Ecclesiastical History." Victricius of Rouen, a friend of Martin of Tours, had his cave on Sark, which in the eleventh century was a dependency of the abbey of Montebourg. Nowadays Sark is a fief immobilized between forty tenants.

XII

RANDOM MEMORIES

In the Middle Ages poor people and poor money went together. One created the other. The poor improvised the sou. Rags and farthings were brothers: so much so that the former sometimes invented the latter. It was a bizarre kind of right, tacitly permitted. There are still traces of this on Guernsey. A quarter of a century ago anyone who had need of a double[33] tore a copper button off his jacket; the buttons from soldiers' uniforms were current coin; a scrap metal merchant would cut out pennies from an old cauldron. This coinage circulated freely.

The first steamship to be seen on Guernsey, on its way to somewhere else, gave the idea of having one on the island. It was called the *Medina* and had a burden of around a hundred tons. It called in at St. Peter Port on June 10, 1823. A regular service of steamers to and from England, by Southampton and Portsmouth, started only much later. The service was run by two small steamships, the *Ariadne* and the *Beresford.* Viscount Beresford was then governor of the islands.

Isolation has a long memory, and an island is a form of isolation. Hence the tenacity of memory in islanders. Traditions continue interminably. It is impossible to break a thread stretching backward through the night as far as the eye can reach. People remember everything—a boat that passed that way, a shower of hail, a fish they caught, and, still more understandably, their forebears. Islands are much given to genealogies.

A word in passing about genealogies. We shall have more to say about them. Family trees are venerated in the archipelago. They are much regarded even for cows—more usefully, perhaps, than for people. A countryman will refer to "my ancestors."

When Monsieur Pasquier was made a duke, Monsieur Royer-Collard[34] said to him: "It won't do you any harm." It is the same with genealogies: they do no harm to anyone.

Tattooing is the earliest form of heraldry. The innocence of the savage points toward the pride of nobility. And the Channel Islands are innocent, very innocent, and savage, to a certain degree. In these seaborne territories, where a kind of saltiness preserves everything, even vanities, people have a firm faith in their own antiquity. In a way this is respectable and touching. It leads to impressive claims. If these claims are made in the presence of a skeptical Frenchman he smiles; if he is polite as well as skeptical he bows. One day (May 26, 1865) I had two visitors, a Jersey man and an Englishman, both perfect gentlemen. The Jersey man said: "My name is Larbalestier." Seeing that this did not sufficiently impress me, he added: "I am a Larbalestier, of a family that went on the Crusades." The Englishman said: "My name is Brunswill. I am descended from William the Conqueror." I asked them: "Do you know a Guernsey man, Mr. Overend, who is descended from Rollo?"

There is a Granite Club in St. Sampson. Its members are stone breakers, who wear a blue rosette in their buttonhole on May 31. May is also the cricket season.

The Channel Islands are remarkable for their impassiveness. A matter that stirs passions in England seems to pass unnoticed here. The author of this book happened one day to commit a barbarism in the English language, which he did all the more readily because he knows no English. Deceived by false information given by a misprint in a pocket dictionary, he wrote "bugpipe" instead of "bagpipe." A *u* instead of an *a!* It was an enormity. "Bug" and not "bag": it was almost as bad as "shibboleth" instead of "sibboleth." Once upon a time England burned people at the stake for that. This time Albion contented itself with raising its hands to heaven. How can a man who knows no English make a mistake in English? The newspapers made this scandal headline news. Bugpipe! There was a kind of uprising throughout Great Britain; but, strange to say, Guernsey remained calm.[35]

Two varieties of traditional French farmhouse are to be seen on Guernsey. On the east side it is the Norman type, on the west side the Breton. The Norman farm has more architecture, the Breton farm more trees. The Norman farm stores its crops in a barn; the Breton farm, more primitive, shelters its crops under a thatched roof borne on rugged columns that are almost cyclopean in aspect—shapeless cylinders of undressed stones bonded with Portland cement. From these farms women, some still wearing the old Guernsey headdress, set out for the town with their baskets of vegetables and fruit on a *quériot*, a donkey cart. When a market woman earns her first money of the day she spits on it before putting it in her pocket. Evidently this brings luck.

These good countryfolk of the islands have all the old prickliness of the Normans. It is difficult to strike the right note in dealing with them. Walking out one winter day when it was raining, an acquaintance of ours noticed an old woman in rags, almost barefoot. He went up to her and slipped a coin in her hand. She turned around proudly, dropped the money to the ground, and said: "What do you take me for? I am not poor. I keep a servant." If you make the opposite mistake you are no better received. A countryman takes such politeness as an offense. The same acquaintance once addressed a countryman, asking: "Are you not Mess Leburay?" The man frowned, saying: "I am Pierre Leburay. I am not entitled to be called Mess."[36]

Ivy abounds, clothing rocks and house walls with magnificence. It clings to any dead branch and covers it completely, so that there are never any dead trees; the ivy takes the trunk and branches of a tree and puts leaves on them. Bales of hay are unknown: instead you will see in the fields mounds of fodder as tall as houses. These are cut up like a loaf of bread, and you will be brought a lump of hay to meet the needs of your cowshed or stable. Here and there, even quite far inland, amid fruit and apple orchards, you will see the carcasses of fishing boats under construction. The fisherman tills his fields, the farmer is also a fisherman: the same man is a peasant of the land and a peasant of the sea.

In certain types of fishery the fisherman drops his net into the sea and anchors it on the bottom, with cork floats supporting it on the surface, and leaves it. If a ship passes that way during the night it cuts the net, which drifts away and is lost. This is a heavy loss, for a net may cost as much as two or three thousand francs. Mackerel are caught in a net with meshes too wide for their head and too small for their body; the fish, unable to move forward, try to back out and are caught by the gills. Mullet are caught with the trammel, a French type of net with triple meshes, which work together to trap the fish. Sand eels are caught with a hoop net, half meshed and half solid, which acts as both a net and a bag.

Small ponds vary the pattern of the farms in western Guernsey, particularly in low-lying areas. Close by are the bays in which, scattered about on the turf, the fishermen's boats—the *Julia, Piety,* the *Seagull,* and so on—are beached, supported by four blocks of wood. Gulls and ducks perch fraternally on the sides of the boats, the ducks coming from the ponds and the gulls from the ocean. Here and there along the coast rocky promontories sometimes retain the sand brought in by the tide, forming a kind of basin in which the residues left by the sea accumulate; at first it is only an alluvial deposit, then it is an islet, then grass grows on it and it becomes an island. The owners of the land bordering the shore claim, in spite of latent contradiction by the government, that these formations belong to them. Monsieur Henry Marquand was good enough to sell me one of them. It is a pretty little island with rocks and grass. I paid three francs for it.

To prevent the haystacks from being carried away by the wind, chains from boats are laid over them. In the fields on the west coast, where hurricanes have freedom of action, the trees are on the defensive, bending down in unnatural attitudes, like athletes. There are no flowers in the gardens of the west, and the ingenious proprietors make good the lack with plaster statues. The yew trees in the gardens of cottages, clipped low and widening toward the foot, are like round tables, of a convenient shape for dogs to scratch their backs on. The walls are topped by lines of large round boulders.

Sometimes, on the deserted shore, there is a tower occupied by a soldier and his wife and children. These coastal towers are called Martello towers after their inventor. The tower provides comfortable accommodation for the soldier's family. The casemate serves as a bedroom; the wife does her cooking and her laundry; the cradle is next to the cannon, and the embrasure forms an alcove; from the distance smoke can be seen emerging peaceably from the top section of the tower, which has become a kitchen. In the Norman isles the main concern of domestic servants, who are seen perpetually kneeling in front of the house door, is to keep the doorstep white— an activity that wears away a lot of sandstone. The same fashion is found in Holland: on the day when the sheets are as white as the steps of the staircase a great progress will have been achieved.

The archipelago has an abundance of plants that are excellent for medicinal purposes or for cooking, though they are rather disdained by the inhabitants. They are surprised to see the French eating salads of dandelions, lambs' lettuce, and what they call *sarcle,* which they say is "as bitter as gall." It is necessary to beware of a large, squat species of mushroom found on salt meadowland known as a toadstool. All over the island, even outside cottages, you will see flagstaffs; for it is a great satisfaction to an Englishman to deck his house with a flag.

Laid out on the short turf of the untilled land to dry in the wind and sun are black cakes of peat cut from the local bog. The large fields of communal grazing at L'Ancresse have gates that half-naked children will open for you for a penny. Poor children have free schools, officially known as ragged schools. Such harsh terms are quite acceptable to the English. On some steamships you will see a notice beside the helmsman: "Do not speak to this man." In France we would say: "Please do not speak to the helmsman." If you are curious to see the gulf that separates a "man" from a "gentleman," you must go to England. In this respect the Channel Islands are England.

Any manual work makes you a "man." The duc de Caumont-La Force, an émigré who worked as a bookbinder, had become a "man."

Vicomtesse ***, who had sought refuge on Jersey, suffered the poverty of exile and swept out her own room. The old woman from whom she rented the room, a Mrs. Lamb, used to say: "She looks after herself; she does all her own work, whatever has to be done. She's not a lady; she's a woman."

Ribeyrolles[37] used to work in his garden, wearing a smock. "He's but a portioner," said the neighbors. One of the Hungarian exiles, Colonel Katona, performed for General Mezzaros all the services that an aide-de-camp performs for his general. This classed him as a lackey. When someone called at his lodging and asked for the general his landlady pointed to the colonel, saying: "There's his toady." Some nuances are almost imperceptible. A countryman named Lefèvre appeared before the registrar for the census. "Is it Lefèvre or Lefebvre?" he was asked. "Do you spell it with a *b*?" "Oh no!" he replied. "I am not a gentleman."

On Guernsey the judges wear purple robes. Surprisingly in this old Norman territory, stamped paper is unknown. Legal disputes are carried on using ordinary paper. Parliamentary discussions sometimes become quite lively. In local council meetings you will hear remarks such as these:

One speaker to another: "You are an impertinent fellow and a rogue."

The chairman: "What you are saying is quite off the point."

Some of our colloquial Parisian turns of phrase have been imperturbably adopted into the grave language of official business. For example, the case of Dobrée versus Jehan (April 5, 1866) gave rise to a judicial summing-up that said, à propos of the deposition of one Marguerite Jehan: "This witness is completely off her head." Another unusual use of language: we have in front of us a doctor's prescription for a purgative: "Take one of these pills this evening and the other tomorrow morning if the first one has not paid off."

XIII

LOCAL PECULIARITIES

Each island has its own coinage, its own patois, its own government, its own prejudices. Jersey is worried about having a French landowner. Suppose he wanted to buy up the whole island! On Jersey foreigners are not permitted to buy land; on Guernsey they may. On the other hand, religious austerity is less on the former island than on the latter; the Jersey Sunday is freer than the Guernsey Sunday. The Bible has greater mandatory force in St. Peter Port than in St. Helier. The purchase of a property on Guernsey is a complicated matter, particularly for an ignorant foreigner, and one of great peril: the buyer gives security on his purchase for twenty years that the commercial and financial situation of the seller shall be the same as it was at the precise moment when the sale took place. Other confusions arise from differences in the coinage and in weights and measures. The shilling, the old French *ascalin* or *chelin,* is worth twenty-five sous in England, twenty-six sous on Jersey, and twenty-four sous on Guernsey. The "Queen's weight" also has its whims: the Guernsey pound is not the same as the Jersey pound, which is not the same as the English pound. On Guernsey land is measured in *vergées* and *vergées* in *perches.* There are different measures on Jersey. On Guernsey only French money is used, but it is called by English names. A franc is known as a tenpenny piece. The lack of symmetry is carried so far that there are more women than men in the archipelago: six women to five men. Guernsey has had many names, some of them archaeological: to scholars it is known as Granosia, while for loyal citizens it is Little England. And indeed it resembles England in geometrical form; Sark can be seen as its Ireland, though an Ireland off the east coast. In the waters around Guernsey there are two hundred varieties of shellfish and forty species of sponges. For the Romans the island was sacred to Saturn, for the Celts to Gwyn; it did not gain much by the change, for Gwyn, like Saturn, was a devourer of children. It has an old law code dating from 1331 called the Precept of Assize. Jersey for its part has three or four old Norman courts: the Court of Inheritance, which deals with cases concerning the fiefs; the Cour de Catel, a criminal court; the Cour du Billet, a commercial tribunal; and the Saturday Court, a police court. Guernsey exports vinegar, cattle, and fruit, but above all it exports itself: its main trade is in gypsum and granite. Guernsey has 305 uninhabited houses: why? The reason, for some of them at least, is perhaps to be found in one of the chapters of this book.[38] The Russian troops who were stationed on Jersey in the early years of this century have left their memory in Jersey's horses, which are a compound of the Norman horse and the Cossack horse. The Jersey horse is a fine runner and a powerful walker; it could carry Tancred and leave Mazeppa behind.[39]

In the seventeenth century there was a civil war between Guernsey and Castle Cornet, Castle Cornet being for the Stuarts and Guernsey for Cromwell—rather as if the Île Saint-Louis declared war on the Quai des Ormes.[40] On Jersey there are two factions, the Rose and the Laurel—diminutives of the Whigs and the Tories. The islanders of this archipelago, so well called the "unknown Normandy,"[41] delight in divisions, hierarchies, castes, and compartments. The people of Guernsey are so fond of islands that they form islands in the population. At the head of this little social order are the "Sixty," sixty families who live apart; halfway down are the "Forty," forty families who form a separate group and keep to themselves; and around them are the ordinary people. The authorities of the island, local and English, consist of ten parishes, ten rectors, twenty constables, 160 douzeniers, a Royal Court with a public prosecutor and controller, a parliament called the States, ten judges called jurats, and a bailiff, referred to as *ballivus et coronator* in old charters. In law they follow the customs of Normandy. The prosecutor is appointed by commission, the bailiff by patent—a distinction of great importance in England. In addition to the bailiff, who holds civil authority, there are the dean, who is in charge of religious affairs, and the governor, who is in command of the military. Other offices are listed in detail in the "Table of Gentlemen occupying Leading Positions on the Island."

XIV

PROGRESS OF CIVILIZATION
IN THE ARCHIPELAGO

Jersey is the seventh largest English port. In 1845 the archipelago possessed 440 ships with a total burden of forty-two thousand tons, and its harbors handled an incoming traffic of sixty thousand tons and an outgoing traffic of fifty-four thousand tons, carried in 1,265 vessels of all nations, including 142 steamers. These figures have more than tripled in twenty years.

Paper money is used on a large scale in the islands, and with excellent results. On Jersey anyone who wishes can issue banknotes; and if the notes are honored when they fall due the bank is established. Banknotes in the archipelago are invariably for a pound sterling. If and when the idea of bills is understood by the Anglo-Normans, they will undoubtedly adopt them; and we should then have the curious spectacle of the same thing as a Utopian vision in Europe and as an accomplished fact in the Channel Islands. A financial revolution would have been achieved, though on a microscopic scale, in this small corner of the world. The people of Jersey are characterized by a firm, lively, alert, and rapid intelligence that would make them admirable Frenchmen if they so desired. The people of Guernsey, though just as penetrating and just as solid, are slower. These are strong and valiant people, more enlightened than is generally supposed, who afford not a few surprises. They are well supplied with newspapers in both English and French, six on Jersey and four on Guernsey—excellent, high-class papers. Such is the powerful and irreducible English instinct. Imagine a desert island: the day after his arrival Robinson Crusoe will publish a newspaper, and Man Friday will become a subscriber. To complement the newspapers there are the advertisements: advertising on a colossal, limitless scale, posters of all colors and all sizes, capital letters, pictures, illustrated texts displayed in the open air. On all the walls of Guernsey is displayed a huge picture of a man, six feet tall, holding a bell and sounding the alarm to call attention to an advertisement. Guernsey has more posters than the whole of France. This publicity promotes life; frequently the life of the mind, with unexpected results, leveling the population by the habit of reading, which produces dignity of manner. On the road to St. Helier or St. Peter Port you may fall into conversation with a passerby of unexceptionable aspect, wearing a black coat, severely buttoned up, and the whitest of linen, who talks of John Brown[42] and asks about Garibaldi. Is he a minister of the church? Not at all: he is a cattle drover. A contemporary writer comes to Jersey, goes into a grocer's shop,* and sees, in a magnificent drawing room attached to the shop, his complete works, bound, in a tall glass-fronted bookcase topped by a bust of Homer.

*Charles Asplet, Beresford Street. (Note by Hugo.)

XV

OTHER PECULIARITIES

The various islands fraternize with one another; they also make fun of each other, gently. Alderney, which is subordinate to Guernsey, is sometimes vexed by this, and would like to become the seat of the bailiff and make Guernsey its satellite. Guernsey ripostes, good-humoredly, with this popular jest:

> *Hale, Pier', hale, Jean,*
> *L'Guernesey vian.*

> Pull (the oar), Pierre, pull, Jean:
> Guernsey's coming!

These islanders, being a sea family, are sometimes cross with one another, but never feel rancor. Anyone who thinks they utter coarse insults misunderstands them. We do not believe in the proverbial exchange that is said to have taken place between Jersey and Guernsey: "You are a lot of donkeys," with the retort: "You are a lot of toads." This is a form of salutation of which the Norman archipelago is incapable. We cannot accept that two islands in the ocean play the parts of Vadius and Trissotin.[43]

In any case Alderney has its relative importance: for the Casquets it is London. The daughter of a lighthouse keeper named Houguer, who had been born on the Casquets, traveled to Alderney for the first time at the age of twenty. She was overwhelmed by the tumult and longed to get back to her rock. She had never seen cattle before; and, seeing a horse, exclaimed: "What a big dog!"

On these Norman islands people age early. Two islanders meet and chat: "The old fellow who used to pass this way is dead."—"How old was he?"—"All of thirty-six."

The women of this insular Normandy do not like to be servants: are they to be criticized or praised for this? Two servants in the same house find it difficult to agree. They make no concessions to each other: hence their service is awkward, intermittent, and spasmodic.

They have little care for the well-being of their master, though without bearing him any ill will: he must get along as best he can. In 1852 a French family who had come to Jersey as a result of events in their country took into their service a cook who came from St. Brelade and a chambermaid who came from Boulay Bay. One morning in December the master of the house, having risen early, found the front door, which opened on to the main road, standing wide open, and no sign of the servants. The two women had been unable to get on together, and after a quarrel—no doubt feeling that they had fully earned their wages—had bundled up their belongings and gone their separate ways in the middle of the night, leaving their master and mistress in bed and the front door open. One had said to the other: "I can't stay in the house with a drunkard," and the other had retorted: "I can't stay in the house with a thief."

"Always the two on the ten" is an old local proverb. What does it mean? It means that if you employ a laborer or a female servant your two eyes must never leave their ten fingers. It is the advice of a miserly employer: ancient mistrust denouncing ancient idleness. Diderot tells us how five men came to mend a broken pane of glass in his window in Holland: one was carrying the new pane, one the putty, one a bucket of water, one the trowel, and another the sponge. It took two days for the five of them to replace the pane.

These are, of course, ancient Gothic habits of idleness born of serfdom, just as Creole indolence is born of slavery, which nowadays are disappearing everywhere under the friction of progress, in the Channel Islands as in other countries, but perhaps more rapidly there than elsewhere. In these industrious island communities active work, which is an essential element of honesty, is increasingly becoming the law of labor.

In the archipelago of the Channel certain things belonging to the past can still be seen. This, for example: "Fief court held in the parish of St. Ouen, in Monsieur Malzard's house, on Monday, May 22, 1854, at noon. Presided over by the seneschal, with the provost on his right and the serjeant on his left. Also present the noble squire, seigneur of Morville and other places, who possesses part of the parish in vassalage. The seneschal called on the provost to take the oath, in these terms: 'You swear and promise, by your faith in God, that you will well and faithfully perform the duties of provost of the fief and seigneurie of Morville and preserve the rights of the seigneur.' And the said provost, having raised his hand and bowed to the seigneur, said: 'I swear so to do.' "

The Norman archipelago speaks French, but with some variants, as we shall see. *Paroisse* (parish) is pronounced *paresse*. You may have *un mâ à la gambe qui n'est pas commun* ("a sore leg, which doesn't often happen"). "How are you?" "*Petitement. Moyennement. Tout à l'aisi*": that is to say, poorly, fairly well, well. To be sad is to "have low spirits"; to smell bad is to have a *mauvais sent;* to cause damage is *faire du ménage;* to sweep your room, wash the dishes, etc., is *picher son fait;* a bucket, which is often filled with refuse, is a *bouquet.* A man is not drunk, he is *bragi.* You are not wet, you are *mucre.* To be a hypochondriac is *avoir des fixes.* A girl is a *hardelle;* an apron is a *tablier;* a tablecloth is a *doublier;* a dress is *un dress;* a pocket is a *pouque;* a drawer is an *haleur;* a cabbage is a *caboche;* a cupboard is a *presse;* a coffin is a *coffret à mort;* New Year gifts are *irvières;* the roadway is the *cauchie;* a mask is a *visagier;* pills are *boulets.* "Soon" is *bien dupartant.* If stocks are low in the market hall and there is little on sale they say that fish and vegetables are *écarts* (scarce). Early potatoes are *temprunes* on Guernsey and *heurives* on Jersey. Going to law, building, traveling, running a house, having people to dinner, entertaining friends are all *coûtageux* (costly; in Belgium and French Flanders they say *frayeux*). A girl does not allow a young man to kiss her for fear of coming home *bouquie,* with her hair disarranged. *Noble* is one of the words most frequently heard in this local variant of French. Anything that has been successfully achieved is a *noble train.* A cook brings back from the market a *noble quartier de veau.* A plump duck is a *noble pirot.* A fat goose is a *noble picot.* The language of justice and the law also has a Norman flavor. Case papers, petitions, and draft laws are "lodged with the clerk of court." A father whose daughter marries is no longer responsible for her while she is *couverte de mari.*

In accordance with Norman custom, an unmarried woman who becomes pregnant indicates the father of her child. She sometimes makes her own choice, and this may have inconvenient consequences.

The French spoken by the older inhabitants of the archipelago is not perhaps entirely their fault. Some fifteen years ago a number of Frenchmen arrived in Jersey, as we have already noted. (We may remark in passing that people could not understand why they had left their country: some of the inhabitants called them *ces biaux révoltés,* these handsome rebels). One of these Frenchmen was visited by a former teacher of French who had lived in the country, he said, for many years. He was an Alsatian, and was accompanied by his wife. He had little respect for the Norman French that is the language of the Channel. He once remarked, on entering a room: *"J'ai pien de la beine à leur abrendre le vranzais. On barle ici badois."* ("I have great difficulty in teaching them French. Here they speak a patois.")

"Comment badois?" ("What do you mean, *badois?"*), said someone.

"Oui, badois."

"Ah! Patois?"

"C'est ça, badois."

The professor continued his complaints about the Norman *badois.* When his wife spoke to him he turned to her, saying: *"Ne me vaites bas ici te zènes gonchigales."* ("Don't let us have any conjugal scenes here.")[44]

XVI

ANTIQUITIES AND ANTIQUES;
CUSTOMS, LAWS, AND MANNERS

Nowadays, let us remark at the outset, the Norman islands, which have each their college and numerous schools, have excellent teachers, some of them French, others natives of Guernsey and Jersey.

As for the patois denounced by the Alsatian professor, it is a true language and by no means to be despised. This patois is a complete idiom, extremely rich and very distinctive. It throws an obscure but profound light on the origins of the French language. A number of scholars have devoted themselves to the patois, among them the translator of the Bible into the language of Guernsey, Monsieur Métivier, who is to the Celto-Norman language what Abbé Eliçagaray was to the Hispano-Basque language. On the island of Guernsey there are a stone-roofed chapel of the eighth century and a Gallic statue of the sixth century, now serving as a jamb to the gateway of a cemetery; both are probably unique. Another unique specimen is a descendant of Rollo, a very worthy gentleman of whom we have already spoken. He consents to regard Queen Victoria as his cousin. His pedigree seems to be proven, and it is not at all improbable.

In the islands, as we have said, people are much attached to their coats of arms. We once heard a lady of the M family complaining about the Gs: "They have taken our coat of arms to put it on their tombs."

Fleurs-de-lys abound. England likes to take over fashions that France has discarded. Few members of the middle class with handsome houses and gardens are without railings ornamented with fleurs-de-lys.

People are very touchy, too, about misalliances. On one of the islands—Alderney, I think—when the son of a very ancient dynasty of wine merchants misallied himself with the daughter of a hatter of recent origin, there was universal indignation. The whole island cried out against the son, and a venerable dame exclaimed: "What a cup for parents to sup!" The Princess Palatine was not more tragically vexed when she reproached a cousin of hers who had married Prince de Tingry with lowering herself to wed a Montmorency.[45]

On Guernsey if a man offers his arm to a woman it indicates that they are engaged. A new bride does not leave her house for a week after her marriage except to go to church: a taste of prison adds spice to the honeymoon. Besides, a certain modesty is in order. Marriage involves so few formalities that it is easily concealed. Cahaigne,[46] on Jersey, once heard this exchange of question and answer between a mother, an old woman, and her daughter, a girl of fourteen: "Why do you not marry this Stevens?"—"Do you want me to get married twice, then, Mother?"—"What do you mean?"—"We were married four months ago."

On Guernsey, in October 1863, a girl was sentenced to six weeks in prison "for annoying her father."

XVII

PECULIARITIES (CONTINUED)

The Channel Islands have as yet only two statues, one on Guernsey of the Prince Consort and one on Jersey known as the Golden King, though no one knows what personage it represents and whom it immortalizes.[47] It stands in the center of the main square in St. Helier. An anonymous statue is still a statue: it flatters the self-esteem of the local people and probably celebrates the glory of someone. Nothing emerges more slowly from the earth than a statue, and nothing grows faster. When it is not an oak it is a mushroom. Shakespeare is still waiting for his statue in England; Beccaria is still waiting for his statue in Italy; but it seems that Monsieur Dupin is going to have his in France.[48] It is gratifying to see such public homage being rendered to men who have been an honor to a country, as in London, for example, where emotion, admiration, regret, and the crowds of mourners reached successive crescendos at the funerals of Wellington, Palmerston, and the boxer Tom Sayers.

Jersey has a Hangman's Hill, which Guernsey lacks. Sixty years ago a man was hanged on Jersey for taking twelve sous from a drawer—though it must be said that about the same time in England a child of thirteen was hanged for stealing cakes and in France an innocent man, Lesurques, was guillotined. Such are the beauties of the death penalty.

Nowadays Jersey, more progressive than London, would not tolerate the gallows. The death penalty has been tacitly abolished.

In prison the inmates' reading is carefully watched. A prisoner has the right to read only the Bible. In 1830 a Frenchman condemned to death, named Béasse, was allowed to read the tragedies of Voltaire while waiting for the gallows. Such an enormity would not be tolerated nowadays. This Béasse was the second-last man to be hanged on Guernsey. Tapner[49] is, and will be, let us hope, the last.

Until 1825 the salary of the bailiff of Guernsey was thirty *livres tournois*, or about fifty francs—the same as in the time of Edward III. Now he gets three hundred pounds sterling. On Jersey the royal court is called the Cohue. A woman who goes to law is called the *actrice*. On Guernsey criminals are sentenced to be flogged; on Jersey the accused is put in an iron cage.

People laugh at the relics of saints, but venerate Charles II's old boots, which are respectfully preserved in St. Ouen's Manor. Tithes are still collected: as you go about the island you will come across the tithe-collectors' stores. *Jambage* seems to have been abolished, but *poulage*[50] is still strictly enforced. The author of these lines pays two hens a year to the queen of England.

Taxes, curiously, are assessed on the total fortune, actual or surmised, of the taxpayer. This has the disadvantage of not attracting great consumers to the island. Monsieur de Rothschild, if he owned a pretty cottage on Guernsey that had cost some 20,000 francs, would pay an annual 1.5 million francs in tax. It must be added that if he lived there only five months in the year he would pay nothing. It is the sixth month that is to be dreaded.

The climate is an extended spring. Winter there may be, and of course summer, but not in excess: never Senegal, never Siberia. The Channel Islands are England's Îles d'Hyères. Albion's delicate chests are sent there. Such a Guernsey parish as St. Martin's, for example, ranks as a minor Nice. No Vale of Tempe, no Gémenos, no Val Suzon surpasses the Vallée des Vaux on Jersey or the Vallée des Talbots on Guernsey. On the southern slopes at least nothing can be greener, milder, and fresher than this archipelago.

High life is possible here; for these small islands have their own great world, their high society. They speak French, as we have noted; the best people say, for example: *"Elle a-z-une rose à son chapeau"* ("She has a rose in her hat").[51] Apart from that their conversation is charming.

Jersey admires General Don; Guernsey admires General Doyle. These were governors in the early part of this century. Jersey has a Don Street, Guernsey a Doyle Road. In addition, Guernsey dedicated to its general a tall column standing above the sea that can be seen from the Casquets, while Jersey presented its general with a cromlech. It originally stood in St. Helier, on the hill now occupied by Fort Regent. General Don accepted the cromlech, had it carted, block by block, down to the shore and loaded onto a frigate, and carried it off. This monument was the marvel of the Channel Islands: it was the only round cromlech on the islands; it had seen the Cimmerians, who remembered Tubal Cain, just as the Eskimos remember Frobisher[52]; it had seen the Celts, whose brain, compared with the brain of the present day, was in the proportion of thirteen to eighteen; it had seen those strange timber towers (*donjons*) whose carcasses are found in sepulchral mounds, and make one hesitate between Du Cange's etymology, deriving the term from *domgio,* and Barleycourt's, deriving it from *domijunctae;* it had seen clubs made from flint and the axes of the druids; it had seen the great wickerwork figure of Teutatès;[53] it existed before the Roman wall; it contained four thousand years of history. At night sailors had seen from afar in the moonlight this huge crown of standing stones on the high cliffs of Jersey: now it is a pile of stones in some corner of Yorkshire.

XVIII

COMPATIBILITY OF EXTREMES

The right of primogeniture exists; the tithe exists; the parish exists; the seigneur exists, both the seigneur of a fief and the seigneur of a manor; crying *haro* exists, as witness "The case of crying *haro* between Nicolle, esquire, and Godfrey, seigneur of Mélèches, was heard by the justices, after the court had been opened by the customary prayer" (Jersey, 1864). The *livre tournois* exists; seisin and disseisin exist; the right of forfeiture exists; feudal tenure exists; the redemption of family property exists; the past exists. There is the style of *messire*. There are the bailiff, the seneschal, *centeniers, vingteniers,* and *douzeniers.* There are the *vingtaine* at St. Savior's and the *cueillette* at St. Ouen's.[54] Every year there is the "constables' ride" to survey the state of the roads. It is headed by the viscount,[55] "bearing in his hand the royal staff." There is the canonical hour, before noon. Christmas, Easter, Midsummer, and Michaelmas are the legal quarter days. Property is not sold, it is granted on lease. A dialogue like this may be heard in court: "Provost, is this the day, the place, and the hour at which the pleadings of the court of the fief and seigneurie have been published?"—"Yes."—"Amen."— "Amen."

The case of "the villager who denies that his holding is in the enclaves" is provided for.

There are "casualties, treasure troves, marriages, etc., from which the seigneur may profit."

There is "the seigneur's entitlement as guardian until a proper party presents himself." There are adjournment and act of vassalage, record and double record; there are the court of chief pleas, enfoeffments, acts of seisin, allodial tenure, and rights of regality. All very medieval, you may say. No: this is true liberty. Come here; live; exist. Go where you will, do what you will, be what you will. No one has the right to know your name. If you have a God of your own, preach his faith. If you have a flag of your own, fly it. Where? In the street. It is white: very well. It is blue: all right. It is red: red is a color like any other. Do you want to denounce the government? Stand on a boundary stone and say whatever you want. Do you want to form an association? By all means. Of how many members? As many as you want. What limit is there? None. Do you want to hold a meeting? Carry on. Where? In the public square. Suppose I want to attack royalty? That is no concern of ours. What if I want to put up a poster? *There* are the walls. You may think, speak, write, print, make a speech on anything you like: that is your own affair. You are free to hear anything and read anything, and that implies that you are also free to say anything and write anything. And so there is absolute freedom of speech and of the press. Anyone who wants can be a printer, an apostle, a pontiff. If you want to be pope, that is up to you. For that you have only to invent a religion. Imagine a new form of God, of whom you will be the prophet. No one has any right to interfere. If necessary the police will help you. There are no restrictions. Absolute freedom: it is a magnificent spectacle. You can argue about a judicial decision. Just as you can preach to the priest, you can judge the judge. The papers can say: "Yesterday the court reached an iniquitous decision." A possible judicial error, surprisingly, has no claim to respect. Human justice is open to dispute just as is divine revelation. Individual independence can scarcely go further. Each man is his own sovereign, not by law but by custom. This is sovereignty so complete and so intrinsic to life that it is no longer felt. Law has become breathable: it is as colorless, imperceptible, and as necessary as air. At the same time people are "loyal." They are citizens who allow themselves the vanity of being subjects.

All in all, the nineteenth century rules and governs; it finds its way in through all the windows in this medieval world. The old Norman legality is shot through with liberty. This old house is full of the light of liberty. Never was an anachronism so little troublesome.

History makes this archipelago Gothic, but industry and intelligence make it modern. It avoids falling into immobility thanks to the lungs of the people—though this does not prevent there being a seigneur of Mélèches. Feudalism de jure, a republic de facto: such is the phenomenon of the Channel Islands.

There is one exception to this liberty: only one, which we have already noted. The tyrant of England has the same name as Don Juan's creditor: it is Sunday. The English are the people for whom time is money, but Sunday, the tyrant, reduces the working week to six days: that is, it deprives them of a seventh of their capital. And there is no possibility of resistance. Sunday rules by custom, which is more despotic than law. Sunday, that king of England, has as his Prince of Wales the dullness known as spleen. He has the power to create boredom. He closes workshops, laboratories, libraries, museums, and theaters, and almost closes gardens and forests, too. We must not omit to notice, however, that the English Sunday is less oppressive on Jersey than on Guernsey. On Guernsey a poor woman who keeps a tavern serves a glass of beer to a customer on a Sunday: fifteen days in prison. An exile from France, a bootmaker, decides to work on Sunday to feed his wife and children, and closes his shutters so that his hammering will not be heard: if anyone hears him, a fine. One Sunday a painter just arrived from Paris stops in the road to draw a tree; a centenier speaks to him and tells him to cease this scandalous activity, but is merciful enough not to report him to the *greffe* (record office). A barber from Southampton shaves someone on Sunday: he pays three pounds sterling to the public treasury. The reason is quite simple: God rested on that day. Fortunate, however, is a people that is free six days out of seven. If Sunday is regarded as a synonym of servitude, we can think of countries where the week has seven Sundays.

Sooner or later these last restrictions will be swept away. No doubt the spirit of orthodoxy is tenacious. No doubt the trial of Bishop Colenso, for example, is a serious matter. But consider the progress that England has made in liberty since the days when Elliott[56] was brought before the assizes for saying that the sun was inhabited.

There is an autumn for the fall of prejudices. It is the time for the decline of monarchies.

That time has now arrived.

The civilization of the Norman archipelago is moving forward and will not stop. That civilization is autochthonous, which does not prevent it from being hospitable and cosmopolitan. In the seventeenth century it felt the effects of the English revolution, and in the nineteenth century of the French revolution. It has twice felt the profound emotions of independence.

Besides, all archipelagos are free countries. It is the mysterious work of the sea and the wind.

XIX

A Place of Asylum

These islands, formerly to be dreaded, have become gentler. Once they were mere reefs: now they are refuges. These places of distress have become havens of rescue. Those who have escaped from disaster emerge here. All those who have suffered shipwreck, whether in a storm or in a revolution, come here. These men, the sailor and the exile, wet with different kinds of foam, dry themselves together in this warm sun. Chateaubriand,[57] young, poor, obscure, and without a country, was sitting on a stone on the old wharf on Guernsey, when a good woman said to him: "What do you want, my friend?" It is very sweet—almost a mysterious relief—for one banished from France to hear in the Channel Islands the language that is civilization itself, the accents of our provinces, the cries to be heard in our ports, the songs of our streets and countryside: *reminiscitur Argos.*[58] Louis XIV thrust into this ancient Norman community a valuable band of good Frenchmen speaking pure French: the revocation of the Edict of Nantes[59] revitalized the French language in the islands.

Frenchmen who have been exiled from France like to spend their time in this archipelago in the Channel, dreaming, as they walk about amid the rocks, the dreams of men who are waiting for something—drawn by the charm of hearing their native tongue. The marquis de Rivière—the same man to whom Charles X said: "By the way, I forgot to tell you that I had made you a duke"—wept at the sight of the apple trees in Jersey, and preferred Pier Road in St. Helier to London's Oxford Street. The duc d'Anville, who was a Rohan and a La Rochefoucauld, also lived in Pier Road. One day Monsieur d'Anville, who had an old basset hound, had occasion to consult a doctor in St. Helier about his health and thought that the doctor would be able to do something for his dog. He asked him, therefore, for a prescription for his basset. The doctor gave his advice, and the following day the duke received a bill in the following terms:

Two consultations:
for the duke, one louis
for his dog, ten louis.

These islands have offered shelter to men afflicted by destiny. All kinds of misfortunes have passed this way, from Charles II fleeing from Cromwell to the duc de Berry on his way to encounter Louvel.[60] Two thousand years ago Caesar, who was to meet his fate at the hands of Brutus, came here. Since the seventeenth century these islands have had fraternal feelings for the whole world; they glory in hospitality. They have the impartiality of a place of asylum.

Royalists, they welcome the vanquished republic; Huguenots, they admit the Catholic exile. They even show him the politeness, as we have observed, of hating Voltaire as much as he does. And since, in the view of many people, and particularly of state religions, to hate our enemies is the best way of loving ourselves, Catholicism should be much loved in the Channel Islands. For a newcomer escaped from shipwreck and spending some time here in the course of his unknown destiny, these solitudes sometimes bring on a profound despondency: there is despair in the air. And then suddenly he feels a caress, a passing breath of air that raises his spirits. What is this breath of air? A note, a word, a sigh, nothing. This nothing is enough. Who in this world has not felt the power of this: a nothing!

Some ten or twelve years ago a Frenchman who had recently landed on Guernsey was wandering along one of the beaches on the west coast—alone, sad, bitter, thinking of the country he had lost.[61] In Paris you stroll about; on Guernsey you roam. The island seemed to him lugubrious. Everything was covered in mist, the breakers thundered onto the shore, the sea was discharging immense quantities of foam on the rocks, the sky was hostile and black. Yet it was spring; but the spring of the sea has a wild name: it is called the equinox. It is more a hurricane than a zephyr; and there are memories of a day in May when, under this blast, the foam leapt up to twenty feet above the top of the signal mast on the highest platform of Castle Cornet. This Frenchman felt as though he was in England; he knew not a word of English; he saw an old Union Jack, torn by the wind, flying on a ruined tower at the end of a deserted promontory; there were two or three cottages nearby; in the distance there was nothing to be seen but sand, heath, moorland, and spiny furze; a few batteries, low built, with wide embrasures, showed their angles; the stone dressed by man had the same melancholy aspect as the rocks worn down by the sea. The Frenchman felt rising within him the deepening feeling of internal mourning that is the beginning of homesickness; he looked and listened; not a ray of sun; cormorants on the hunt, clouds fleeting by; everywhere on the horizon a leaden weight; a vast livid curtain falling down from the zenith; the specter of spleen in the shroud of the tempest; nothing anywhere that resembled hope, and nothing that resembled his native land. The Frenchman was pondering on all this, more and more cast down; then suddenly he raised his head. From one of the cottages, half-open, there came a clear, fresh, delicate voice, the voice of a child, and the voice was singing:

> *La clef des champs, la clef des bois,*
> *La clef des amourettes!* [62]

XX

Not all reminiscences of France in the archipelago are as happy as these. One Sunday on the charming island of Sark an acquaintance of ours heard in a farmyard this verse of an old French Huguenot hymn, very solemnly sung in chorus by religious voices with the grave tones of Calvinism:

> *Tout le monde pue, pue, pue*
> *Comme une charogne.*
> *Gniac', gniac', gniac' mon doux Jésus*
> *Qui ait l'odeur bonne.*

> Everyone stinks, stinks, stinks
> Like carrion.
> There is only my sweet Jesus
> Who smells sweet.

It is a melancholy and almost painful thought that people died in the Cévennes to the sound of these words. This verse, though involuntarily high comic, is tragic. We laugh at it: we ought to weep. At this verse Bossuet, one of the Forty of the French Academy, cried: "Kill! Kill!"

In any case, to fanaticism, hideous when it is the persecutor, august and touching when it is the persecuted, the outward hymn is nothing. It has its own grand and somber internal hymn that it sings mysteriously in its soul, whatever the words. It permeates even the grotesque with sublimity, and, whatever may be the poetry and prose of its priests, it transfigures that prose and that poetry with the immense latent harmony of its faith. It corrects the deformity of formulas by the greatness of trials accepted and torments endured. Where poetry is lacking it substitutes conscience. The libretto of martyrdom may be dull: what matter if the martyrdom is noble!

XXI

Fishermen, great eaters of fish, have large families. This law holds good in the Norman archipelago, where there may be up to seven or eight children per cottage. This gives rise to particular problems, involving true matters of conscience. What is the first duty of a pilot? He is a pilot, and he has a duty to mariners in distress. He is a father, and he has a duty to his children. He is himself in distress. Risking your life is of no consequence when you are on your own; but the question changes when you are part of a family unit. In a hurricane and in darkness, when out at sea a ship is in distress and there is a chance that anyone going to its aid may not return, the pilot finds himself caught between two shipwrecks, the shipwreck of the seamen in danger who without him will perish, and the shipwreck of his children, who without him will die. It is a fearful dilemma. He has to think of his family. This means that heroism is for sale; a man is not an angel of salvation free of charge; he has his price.

Frequently, such is the strange asperity of man, the price is negotiated at sea, in clouds, in lightning, off a reef. One party is selling life, the other is buying it. It is a question of take it or leave it. The benefit is not to be given away free. The man who is drowning finds the price proposed too high. There is a dispute over a few coppers on the threshold of this formidable good action.

It is certain at any rate that one night, in the midst of a storm, someone who was on the summit of a cliff, battered by wind and rain, heard below him, in the deep, raging sea, the following dialogue, interrupted by the sinister interventions of the wind. Two black shapes could be distinguished in the darkness, two vague shapes of vessels bobbing up and down, close together, on the foam, and speaking to one another:

"Where have you come from?"

"Take care. Don't come too close. My mizzen mast may fall on you."

"Where have you come from?"

"I don't know."

"Where are you making for?"

"I don't know."

"Do you want me to rescue you?"

"Take care. I have more than one mast. It may fall on you."

"Do you want me to rescue you?"

"How many of you are there in your boat?"

"Three men."

"If my mast fell on your boat you would be drowned. Go away."

"If I go away you are lost."

"God will preserve us!"

"Do you want me to take you in to Guernsey? I am a pilot."

"Where is Guernsey?"

"There."

"You are wrong. It is Jersey."

"I am not wrong. It is Guernsey."

"God will preserve us!"

"What ship are you?"

"La Galante."

"Where from?"

"Portrieux."

"Whither bound?"

"Newfoundland."

"What have you on board?"

"Nineteen men. Plus my cargo."

"Do you want me to rescue you?"

"Who are you?"

"Pilot Number Six."

"Your name?"

"Létivier."

"Where are you from?"

"St. Peter-in-the-Wood."

"God will preserve us!"

"Do you want me to rescue you?"

"How much?"

"Fifty pounds."

"Will you take twenty-five?"

"No. Fifty."

"No. Twenty-five."

"I'm off, then."

"Right: off you go."

"You're just off the coast: it's a stony bottom. Do you hear the alarm bell yonder? In a quarter of an hour you'll be done for."

"Will you take forty pounds?"

"No. Forty-five."

"All right: forty-five."

And so Létivier saved *La Galante*. Such is the grim bargaining process.

XXII

Homo Edax [63]

The configuration of an island changes over time. An island is a construction by the ocean. Matter is eternal; not its aspect. Everything on earth is being perpetually moulded by death: even extra-human monuments, even granite. Everything changes shape, even the shapeless. Edifices built by the sea crumble like any other. The sea, which has built them up, also demolishes them.

In fifteen hundred years, between the mouth of the Elbe and the mouth of the Rhine alone, seven islands out of twenty-three have foundered. They must be looked for under the sea. The sea created the Zuider Zee in the thirteenth century; in the fifteenth century it created the bay of Bies-Bosch, destroying twenty-two villages; and in the sixteenth century it improvised the Dollart gulf, swallowing up Torum. A hundred years ago, off Bourg-d'Ault, now perched atop a sheer cliff in Normandy, the church tower of the old village of Bourg-d'Ault could still be seen under the sea. It is said that on Écrehou you can sometimes see under the water at low tide the trees of a druidical forest that was drowned in the eighth century. Guernsey was once attached to Herm, Herm to Sark, Sark to Jersey, and Jersey to France. A child could straddle the strait between France and Jersey. When the bishop of Coutances passed that way a bundle of sticks was thrown into the gap so that he should not wet his feet.

The sea builds up and demolishes; and man helps the sea, not in building up but in destroying. Of all the teeth of time the one that works hardest is man's pickax. Man is a rodent. Everything is modified or changed at his hand, either for the better or for the worse. Here he disfigures, there he transfigures. The Brèche de Roland[64] is not so fabulous as it seems; man can carve up nature. The scar of human work can be seen on the work of God.

It seems that a certain power of achievement is granted to man. He appropriates the creation to humanity. Such is his function. He has the necessary boldness; one might also say the necessary impiety. This collaboration with nature is sometimes offensive. Man, a short-lived being who is perpetually dying, takes on the infinite. Against all the ebb and flow of nature, against elements seeking to communicate with other elements, against the vast navigation of forces in the depths man declares a blockade. He, too, can say: "Thus far and no farther." He has his idea of fitness, and the universe must accept it. Besides, has he not a universe of his own? He intends to make of it whatever he thinks fit. A universe is a mass of raw material. The world, which is God's work, is man's canvas.

Everything limits man, but nothing stops him. He responds to limits by jumping over them. The impossible is a frontier that is perpetually receding.

A geological formation that has at its base the mud of the Deluge and at its summit the eternal snows is, for man, a wall like any other: he cuts through it and continues beyond. He slashes an isthmus, subdues a volcano, cuts away a cliff, mines the rock for minerals, breaks up a promontory into small pieces. Once upon a time he did all this work for Xerxes;[65] nowadays, less foolish, he does it for himself. This diminution of foolishness is called progress. Man works on his house, and his house is the earth. He disarranges, displaces, suppresses, knocks down, levels, mines, undermines, digs, excavates, breaks up, pulverizes, effaces this, abolishes that, and rebuilds with what he has destroyed. Nothing makes him hesitate—no mass, no blockage, no obstacle, no consideration for splendid material, no majesty of nature. If the enormities of creation are within his reach he tears them down. This aspect of God that can be ruined tempts him, and he mounts an assault on immensity, hammer in hand. Globe, let this ant of yours have his way.

A child, breaking a toy, seems to be looking for its soul. Man, too, seems to be looking for the soul of the earth.

Let us not, however, exaggerate our power. Whatever man does, the great lines of creation persist; the supreme mass does not depend on man. He has power over the detail, not over the whole. And it is right that this should be so. The Whole is providential. Its laws pass over our head. What we do goes no farther than the surface. Man clothes or unclothes the earth; clearing a forest is like taking off a garment. But to slow down the rotation of the globe on its axis, to accelerate the course of the globe on its orbit, to add or subtract a fathom on the earth's daily journey of 718,000 leagues around the sun, to modify the precession of the equinoxes, to eliminate one drop of rain—never! What is on high remains on high. Man can change the climate, but not the seasons. Just try and make the moon revolve anywhere but in the ecliptic!

Dreamers, some of them illustrious, have dreamed of restoring perpetual spring to the earth. The extreme seasons, summer and winter, are produced by the excess of the inclination of the earth's axis over the plane of the ecliptic of which we have just spoken. In order to eliminate the seasons it would be necessary only to straighten this axis. Nothing could be simpler. Just plant a stake on the Pole and drive it in to the center of the globe; attach a chain to it; find a base outside the earth; have 10 billion teams, each of 10 billion horses, and get them to pull. The axis will straighten up, and you will have your spring. As you can see, an easy task.

We must look elsewhere for Eden. Spring is good; but freedom and justice are better. Eden is moral, not material.

To be free and just depends on ourselves.

Serenity is internal. Our perpetual spring is within us.

XXIII

POWER OF THE STONE BREAKERS

Guernsey is a Trinacria.[66] The queen of Trinacrias is Sicily. Sicily belongs to Neptune, and each of its three angles was dedicated to one of the three prongs of his trident. On its three capes were three temples, one dedicated to Dextra, another to Dubia, and the third to Sinistra. Dextra was the cape of rivers, Sinistra the cape of the sea, Dubia the cape of rain. In spite of the threat by Pharaoh Psammetichus to Thrasydaeus, king of Agrigentum, to make Sicily "as round as a discus," these Trinacrias are immune to reshaping by man, and will keep their three promontories until the deluge that made them unmakes them. Sicily will always have its Cape Peloros facing Italy, its Cape Pachynos facing Greece, and its Cape Lilybaion facing Africa, and Guernsey will always have its L'Ancresse Point in the north, its Pleinmont Point to the southwest, and its Jerbourg Point to the southeast.

Apart from this, the island of Guernsey is in course of demolition. This granite is good: who wants it? All its cliffs are up for auction. The inhabitants are selling the island by retail. The curiously shaped Roque-au-Diable has recently been sold off for a few pounds sterling. When the huge quarry of La Ville-Baudue has been worked out they will move on to another.

This stone is in demand all over England. For the embankments being built along the Thames alone two hundred thousand tons will be needed. Loyal citizens who like their royal statues to be solid were upset that the pedestal of the bronze figure of Prince Albert, which is in Cheesering granite, was not made of good Guernsey stone. However that may be, the coasts of Guernsey are falling to the pickax. In St. Peter Port, under the windows of the inhabitants of La Falue, a mountain has disappeared in four years.

And this is happening in America as well as in Europe. At the present time Valparaiso is engaged in selling to stone merchants by auction the magnificent and venerable hills that earned it its name of Paradise Valley.

Old Guernsey people no longer recognize their island. They would be tempted to say: "They have changed my native place." Wellington said this of Waterloo, which was his native place.

Add to this the fact that Guernsey, which used to speak French, now speaks English: another demolition.

Until about 1805 Guernsey was divided into two islands. An inlet cut across it from side to side, from the eastern Mount Crevel to the western Mount Crevel. This arm of the sea debouched at the west end opposite the Fruquiers and the two Sauts Roquiers. There were also bays reaching quite far inland, one of them going as far as Salterns; this arm of the sea was called the Braye du Valle. Last century St. Sampson had moorings for boats on both sides of an ocean street—a narrow and winding street. In the same way as the Dutch have drained the Haarlemmer Meer, making it a not very attractive plain, the people of Guernsey have filled in the Braye du Valle, which is now meadowland. The street has become a blind alley: the harbor of St. Sampson.

XXIV

KINDNESS OF THE PEOPLE
OF THE ARCHIPELAGO

Those who have seen the Norman archipelago love it; those who have lived there esteem it. The inhabitants are a noble little people, great of soul. They have the soul of the sea. These men of the Channel Islands are a race apart. They maintain a certain supremacy over the *grand'terre,* the mainland, and take a high line with the English, who are sometimes disposed to disdain "these three or four flowerpots in the pond." Jersey and Guernsey retort: "We are Normans, and it is we who conquered England." You may smile, but you can also admire. The day will come when Paris will make these islands the fashion and make their fortune; and they deserve it. A constantly increasing prosperity awaits them when they are known. They have the singular attraction of combining a climate made for idleness and a population made for work. This eclogue is also a workshop. The Norman archipelago has less sunshine than the Cyclades, but more greenery; it has as much greenery as the Orkneys, but more sun. It has no temple like the one at Astypalaea, but it has the cromlechs; it has no Fingal's Cave, but it has Sark. Moulin Huet is as good as Le Tréport; the beach at Azette is as good as Trouville; Plémont is as good as Étretat. The landscape of the archipelago is beautiful; its people are kind; it has a proud history. It has an apostle, Saint Helier; a poet, Robert Wace; a hero, Pierson.[67] Several of England's best admirals and generals were born in the archipelago. These poor fishermen are magnificent when the occasion calls for it; when collections were made to help the victims of flooding in Lyons and famine in Manchester, Jersey and Guernsey gave more, proportionately, than either France or England.* These peoples have preserved from their earlier activities as smugglers a proud liking for risk and danger. They go everywhere. They send out swarms. The Norman archipelago nowadays establishes colonies, as the Greek archipelago used to do. That is their glory. There are Jerseymen and Guernseymen in Australia, in California, in Ceylon. North America has its New Jersey and its New Guernsey, which is in Ohio. These Anglo-Normans, though a little hampered by their sects, have an incorruptible appetite for progress. A plenitude of superstitions, no doubt, but also a plenitude of good sense. Was not France once a land of brigands? Was not England once given to cannibalism? Let us be modest and remember our tattooed ancestors.

Where banditry once prospered commerce now rules: a superb transformation. It has been the work of centuries, no doubt, but also of men. This magnanimous example is given by a microscopic archipelago. Such little nations as these are the proof of civilization. Let us love them and venerate them. These microcosms reflect on a small scale the great process of development of mankind in all its phases. Jersey, Guernsey, Alderney: once the haunts of animals and bandits, now workshops. Once wild reefs, now ports.

For the observer of the series of transformations that are called history no spectacle is more moving than the sight of these nocturnal sea peoples climbing up slowly and by degrees to the sunlight of civilization. The man of the shadows has turned around and now faces the dawn. Nothing can be greater, nothing more moving. Once a pirate, now a workman; once a savage, now a citizen; once a wolf, now a man. Is he any less daring than he used to be? No: only this daring is heading toward the light. What a magnificent difference between the ship-

---

*Here, for Guernsey and for the French victims of the 1856 floods, the proportions of money subscribed: France gave, per head of population, thirty centimes; England six centimes; Guernsey thirty-eight centimes. (Note by Hugo.)

ping of the present day—coastal and inland shipping, commercial shipping, honest and fraternal shipping—and the shapeless old dromond, which had for its motto *Homo homini monstrum!*[68] The barrier has become a bridge; the obstacle has become a help. These people were pirates: now they are pilots. And they are more enterprising and bolder than ever. This country has remained the country of adventure while becoming the country of probity. The lower has been the starting point, the more impressive is the ascent. The droppings of the nest on the eggs in it arouse admiration of the bird's wingspan. We now think indulgently of the piracy formerly practiced in the Norman archipelago. In the presence of all these charming and serene vessels being triumphantly guided through these mazes of waves and reefs by the lenticular beacon and the electric lighthouse, we think, with the satisfied conscience inherent in the progress that has been achieved, of these old wild and furtive seamen who sailed their boats without a compass over dark seas lividly lighted from promontory to promontory, long distances apart, by ancient braziers with flickering flames, tormented in their iron cages by the tremendous winds of the deep.

PART I

SIEUR CLUBIN

BOOK I

The Making of a Bad Reputation

I

A Word Written on a Blank Page

The Christmas of 182– in Guernsey was unusual. On Christmas Day it snowed. In the Channel Islands a winter in which it freezes is memorable, and snow is an event.

On that Christmas morning the road that skirts the sea between St. Peter Port and the Vale was covered in white. It had been snowing from midnight until dawn. About nine o'clock, just after sunrise, since it was not yet time for the Anglicans to go to St. Sampson's Church and the Wesleyans to the Eldad Chapel, the road was practically deserted. In the whole stretch between the first and second Martello towers there were only three people—a child, a man, and a woman. These three, walking at some distance from one another, had apparently no connection with one another. The child, whose age might be about eight, had stopped and was looking curiously at the snow. The man was perhaps a hundred paces behind the woman. Like her, he was making for St. Sampson. Youngish, he looked like a workman or seaman or something of that kind. He was dressed in his workaday clothes, a jacket of coarse brown cloth and trousers with tarpaulin leggings—suggesting that, notwithstanding the holy day, he was not on his way to church or chapel. His thick shoes of rough leather, the soles studded with large nails, left prints on the snow more like the lock of a prison gate than a man's footprint. The woman for her part was evidently dressed for church: she wore a wide padded cloak of black ribbed silk, under which was a smart dress of Irish poplin striped white and pink, and but for her red stockings could have been taken for a Parisienne. She walked with a light and lively step, a gait that had not yet borne the weight of life and that revealed her to be a young girl. She had the fugitive grace of bearing that marks the most delicate of transitions—adolescence, the mingling of two twilight periods, the first emergence of a woman in the final stage of childhood. The man was paying no attention to her.

Suddenly, near a clump of holm oaks at the corner of a field, at a spot known as the Basses Maisons, she turned back, and the movement caught the man's eye. She stopped, seemed to look at him for a moment, and then bent down, and the man thought he saw her writing something in the snow with her finger. She straightened up and continued on her way, walking more quickly; then turned back again, now laughing, and disappeared off the road to the left into the path lined by hedges that leads to the Ivy Castle. When she turned around for the second time the man recognized Déruchette, a charming local girl.

Feeling no need to hasten his pace, he walked on and in a few moments came to the clump of holm oaks. He was no longer thinking of the girl, and it is possible that if at that moment a porpoise had emerged from the sea or a robin from the bushes he would have continued on his way, with eyes only for the robin or the porpoise. But as chance had it he was looking down, and his glance fell mechanically on the spot where the girl had stopped. There were two small footprints, and beside them he saw the word she had traced in the snow: "Gilliatt."

It was his own name. He was called Gilliatt.

He stood motionless for some time, looking at the name, the little footprints and the snow; then continued thoughtfully on his way.

II

THE BÛ DE LA RUE[69]

Gilliatt lived in the parish of St. Sampson. He was not liked in the parish. There were reasons for this.

In the first place, he lived in a "ghostly" or haunted house. Sometimes, on Jersey or Guernsey, either in the country or in the town, in some desolate area or in a populous street, you will come across a house whose entrance is barricaded. The doorway is blocked by a holly bush, and the ground-floor windows are closed by unsightly structures of planks nailed together; while the windows on the upper floors are both closed and open: they are bolted shut, but all the panes are broken. If there is an inner courtyard, it is overgrown by grass and the enclosing wall is crumbling. If there is a garden it is a wilderness of nettles, brambles, and hemlock, home to rare insects. The chimneys are cracked and the roof is falling in. Inside, so far as can be seen, the rooms are dismantled; the woodwork is rotten, the stonework is covered with mold. The wallpaper is peeling off the walls, and you can study old wallpaper styles—the griffins of the Empire, the swags of the Directory, the balusters and cippi of Louis XVI. The dense growth of spiders' webs full of trapped flies points to the deep peace enjoyed by the spiders. Sometimes you will see a broken jar left on a shelf. This is a haunted house—a house to which the Devil comes at night.

A house, like a man, can become a corpse: it can be killed by superstition, and then it becomes a place of dread. Such dead houses are by no means uncommon in the Channel Islands.

Country people and seagoing folk are worried by the Devil. The people of the Channel—the English archipelago and the French coastal regions—have very clear ideas about him. The Devil has agents throughout the world. It is well established that Belphegor is the ambassador of Hell in France, Hutgin in Italy, Belial in Turkey, Thammuz in Spain, Martinet in Switzerland, and Mammon in England. Satan is an emperor like other emperors: Satan Caesar. His household is well staffed: Dagon is controller of the pantry, Succor Benoth chief of the eunuchs, Asmodeus banker of the gaming house, Kobal manager of the theater, Verdelet grand master of ceremonies, Nybbas the court fool. The learned Wierus, a good strygologist and a well-informed demonographer, calls Nybbas the great parodist.

The Norman fishermen of the Channel need to take a great many precautions when they are at sea because of the illusions created by the Devil. It was long believed that Saint Maclou lived on the great square stack of Ortach, in the open sea between Alderney and the Casquets, and in the past many old seamen declared that they had frequently seen him in the distance, sitting on the rock and reading a book. And so seamen sailing past the rock made many genuflections as they passed until the fable was dissipated and gave place to the truth. It was discovered, and is now generally known, that the rock was inhabited not by a saint but by a devil. This devil, one Jochmus, had been clever enough to be accepted for several centuries as Saint Maclou. The Church itself, of course, sometimes falls into errors of this kind. The devils Raguhel, Oribel, and Tobiel were saints until 745, when Pope Zacharias, having found them out, ejected them. In order to carry out such expulsions, which are undoubtedly beneficial, it is necessary to know your way about with devils.

The oldest inhabitants of the region say—but facts of this kind belong to the past—that the Catholic population of the Norman archipelago was formerly, in spite of itself, more closely in communication with the Devil than the Huguenot population. Why? We do not know.

What is certain is that this minority was formerly much troubled by the Devil. He had taken a liking to the Catholics and sought to associate with them, which might suggest that the Devil is more Catholic than Protestant. One of his most intolerable familiarities was to pay nocturnal visits to Catholic marital beds at a time when the husband was fast asleep and the wife just falling asleep. This inevitably gave rise to misunderstandings. Patouillet believed that Voltaire was conceived in this way, and this is not at all improbable. This case is well known, and is described in books of exorcisms under the heading "De erroribus nocturnis et de semine diabolorum." The Devil was particularly active at St. Helier toward the end of the last century, probably as a punishment for the crimes of the Revolution. The consequences of the excesses of the Revolution are incalculable. At any rate this possible arrival of the Devil at night, when people cannot see clearly, when they are asleep, embarrassed many orthodox women believers. To give birth to a Voltaire is not a pleasant thought. One woman, worried, consulted her confessor about the best way to clear up misunderstandings of this kind. The confessor replied: "To be sure whether it is the Devil or your husband, feel his forehead, and if you find horns you will be sure…." "Sure of what?" asked the woman.

The house in which Gilliatt lived had been haunted but was so no longer. But this made it all the more suspect. Everyone knows that when a witch or warlock takes up residence in a house the Devil decides that the house is sufficiently well kept and obligingly gives up calling there unless he is summoned, like the doctor.

The house was called the Bû de la Rue. It was situated at the tip of a tongue of land, or rather of rock, that formed a small private anchorage in the creek of Houmet Paradis.[70] The water here is deep. The house stood by itself on the point, almost off the island, with just enough land to make a small garden. The garden was sometimes drowned by high tides. Between St. Sampson harbor and the creek of Houmet Paradis is the large hill that is crowned by the complex of towers and ivy known as Vale Castle or the Archangel's Castle, so that the Bû de la Rue could not be seen from St. Sampson.

Witches and warlocks are by no means uncommon on Guernsey. In certain parishes they still practice their profession, and the nineteenth century makes no difference. Some of their practices are decidedly criminal. They boil up gold. They gather herbs at midnight. They cast the evil eye on people's livestock. They are consulted by the local people; they ask to be brought the "water" of sick people in bottles, and are heard to murmur, "The water seems very sad." One day in March 1856 one of them found seven devils in the "water" of a sick person. They are fearsome and are feared. One of them recently bewitched a baker "along with his oven." Another is villainous enough to wafer and seal with great care envelopes "that contain nothing." Another again goes so far as to have three bottles labeled *B* on a shelf in his house. These monstrous facts are well authenticated. Some witches and warlocks are obliging and, for two or three guineas, will take over your illnesses. Then they writhe about on their bed, groaning. While they are writhing you say: "There! I'm all right again." Others will cure you of all ills by tying a handkerchief around your body: a remedy so simple that it is surprising no one has thought of it before. Last century the Royal Court of Guernsey put them on a pile of faggots and burned them alive. Nowadays it sentences them to eight weeks in prison, four weeks on bread and water alternating with four weeks in solitary confinement. *Amant alterna catenae.*[71]

The last witch-burning on Guernsey was in 1747. It took place in one of the squares in the town, the Carrefour du Bordage. Between 1565 and 1700 eleven witches and warlocks were burned in the square. As a rule they confessed their guilt, and were helped to confess by the use of torture. The Carrefour du Bordage also rendered other services to society and religion. Heretics, too, were burned there. In the reign of Mary Tudor, among other Huguenots, a mother and her two daughters were burned. The mother was called Perrotine Massy. One of the daughters was with child and gave birth while at the stake. In the words of the chronicle, "her belly burst open" and from it emerged a living infant. The newborn child rolled out of the fire and was picked up by an onlooker called House. Thereupon Bailiff Hélier Gosselin, like a good Catholic as he was, had the child thrown back into the flames.

III

"For Your Wife, When You Marry"

Let us return to Gilliatt.

There was a story among the local people that toward the end of the French Revolution a woman with a small child had come to live on Guernsey. She was English—unless perhaps she was French. She had an odd name that in the Guernsey pronunciation and the countryfolk's spelling became Gilliatt. She lived alone with the child, who some said was her nephew, others her son, others again a grandson, still others no relation at all. She had a little money—just enough to live in a poor way. She had bought a piece of grazing land at La Sergenté and a furze-brake at La Roque Crespel, near Rocquaine. At that time the house at the Bû de la Rue was haunted. It had been unoccupied for more than thirty years, and it was falling into ruin. The garden had been too frequently invaded by the sea to produce any crops. Apart from the noises that were heard and the lights that were seen at night, the most frightening thing about the house was that, if you left a ball of wool, needles, and a plateful of soup on the chimneypiece at night, in the morning you would find the soup eaten, the plate empty, and a newly knitted pair of mittens. This wretched dwelling, along with its resident demon, was for sale for a few pounds sterling. The woman bought it, evidently tempted by the Devil. Or by the low price.

She not only bought it: she moved into it along with her child; and from that moment the house quieted down. The house has got what it wants, said the local people. The haunting ceased. No cries were now heard at daybreak. No lights were seen apart from the tallow candle that the woman lit in the evening. A witch's candle is the Devil's torch, they say; and with this explanation people were satisfied.

The woman made good use of the few rods[72] of land she possessed. She had a good cow, of the kind that produces yellow butter. She grew white beans, cabbages, and Golden Drop potatoes. Like everyone else, she sold "parsnips by the barrel, onions by the hundred, and beans by the dénerel."[73] She did not go to market, but sold her produce through Guilbert Falliot, at Les Abreveurs Saint-Sampson. Falliot's ledgers show that on one occasion he sold on her behalf a dozen bushels of "three-month" potatoes, the earliest variety.

The house had been patched up—just enough to make it habitable. It was only in very bad weather that rain dripped into the rooms. It consisted of a ground floor and a loft. The ground floor was divided into three rooms, two for sleeping and one for meals. A ladder led up to the loft. The woman did the cooking and taught the child to read. She did not go to any church, which led people to conclude, all things considered, that she must be French.

Not to go "anywhere" was a bad sign.

In short, people did not know what to make of the newcomers.

That she was French is probable. Volcanoes cast out stones, revolutions people. Families are removed to distant places, destinies are transferred to other countries, groups of family and friends are scattered and broken up, and strangers fall from the clouds—some in Germany, others in England, others again in America. They surprise the people of the country. Where have these unknowns come from? They have been spewed out by the Vesuvius smoking over there. Various names are given to these aerolites, these people who have been expelled and ruined, who have been eliminated by fate: they are called émigrés, refugees, adventurers.

If they stay in their new country they are tolerated; if they move on, people are relieved. Sometimes they are completely inoffensive, strangers—at least so far as the women are concerned—to the events that have driven them from home, feeling neither hate nor anger; involuntary projectiles, astonished at their fate. They put down roots again wherever they can. They were doing no harm to anyone and do not understand what has happened to them. I have seen a wretched tuft of grass tossed into the air by the explosion of a mine. The French Revolution cast more people to great distances than any other explosion.

The woman known on Guernsey as "la Gilliatt" was perhaps one such tuft of grass. The woman grew old, the child grew up. They lived alone, avoided by their neighbors. They were sufficient unto themselves. The she-wolf and the cub groom one another. This was another of the formulas that the good feeling of their neighbors applied to them. The child became a youth, the youth became a man, and then— since the old skins of life must always be sloughed off—the woman died. She left him the field at La Sergenté, the furze-brake at La Roque Crespel, the house at the Bû de la Rue, and, in the words of the official inventory, "a hundred golden guineas in the foot of a stocking." The house was adequately furnished with two oak chests, two beds, six chairs, a table, and the necessary domestic utensils. On a shelf were a few books, and in a corner was a very ordinary trunk, which had to be opened for the inventory. The trunk was of tawny leather, ornamented with arabesques of copper nails and pewter stars, and contained a bride's trousseau, new and complete, of fine Dunkirk cloth, chemises, and skirts, together with silk dresses and a paper on which was written, in the dead woman's hand, "For your wife, when you marry."

This death was a terrible blow for the survivor. Previously unsociable, he now avoided all human contact. He had been used to isolation: now his life was a blank. When there are two people, life is possible: when one of them is left alone it seems impossible to carry on, and he gives up. This is the first form of despair. Later the realization comes that duty involves a series of acceptances. We look on life and we look on death, and we submit; but it is a submission that draws blood.

Since Gilliatt was young, the wound healed. At that age the fibers of the heart recover their strength. His sadness, gradually fading away, mingled with the nature around him and became a kind of charm, drawing him toward natural things and away from men, increasingly assimilating him to the solitude in which he lived.

IV

Unpopularity

Gilliatt, as we have said, was not liked in the parish. This antipathy was entirely natural.

There were abundant reasons for it. In the first place, as explained above, there was the house he lived in. Then there were his origins. Who was the woman? And where did the child come from? People do not like strangers about whom there is something of a mystery. Then, too, his clothes. He dressed like a workman, but—though not rich—he had enough to live on without working. Then there was his garden, which he managed to cultivate and which produced crops of potatoes in spite of the equinoctial gales. And then there were the big books that he kept on a shelf and that he actually read.

There were other reasons, too.

Why did he live such a solitary life? The Bû de la Rue was a kind of lazaretto in which Gilliatt was confined in quarantine. This explained why people were surprised by his isolation and held him responsible for the solitude that they had made around him.

He never went to chapel. He often went out at night. He held converse with witches and warlocks. He had once been seen sitting on the grass with a look of astonishment on his face. He haunted the dolmen of L'Ancresse and the fairy stones that are scattered about in the countryside. People were convinced that he had been seen respectfully saluting the Crowing Rock. He bought all the birds that were brought to him and set them free. He was polite to the good people he encountered in the streets of St. Sampson, but liked to take a long way around to avoid the town. He often went out fishing and always came back with a catch. On Sundays he worked in his garden. He had a set of bagpipes, bought from the Highland soldiers who had been stationed on Guernsey, and used to play them at nightfall amid the rocks on the seashore. He waved his arms about as if he were sowing seed. What are people to make of a man like that?

And the books that he had inherited from the dead woman, and that he read, were disturbing, too. When the Reverend Jaquemin Hérode, rector of St. Sampson's, had been in the house for the woman's funeral, he had read on the spines of the books the titles of Rosier's *Dictionary,* Voltaire's *Candide,* and Tissot's *Advice to the People on Health.*[74] A French noble, an émigré who had come to live in St. Sampson, declared that this must have been the Tissot who had carried the Princesse de Lamballe's head on a pike.

The reverend gentleman had also noticed on one of the books the daunting and threatening title *De Rhubarbaro.*

It must be said, however, that since this work, as the title indicates, was written in Latin, it was doubtful whether Gilliatt, who knew no Latin, read it. But it is just those books that a man does not read that provide evidence against him. The Spanish Inquisition considered this point and put the matter beyond doubt.

In fact the book was merely Dr. Tilingius's treatise on rhubarb, published in Germany in 1679.

There was also a suspicion that Gilliatt might be making charms, philters, and magic potions. He certainly possessed vials.

Why did he go out walking along the cliffs in the evening, sometimes as late as midnight? Evidently it was to talk to the evil beings that haunt the seashore at night, enveloped in smoke.

Once he had helped the witch of Torteval—an old woman called Moutonne Gahy—to pull her cart out of the mud.

When a census was taken on the island, he replied to a question about his occupation, "Fisherman, when there are any fish to catch." Put yourself in the place of the local people: they don't like answers of that kind.

Poverty and wealth are comparative terms. Gilliatt owned fields and a house, and, compared with people who had nothing, he was not poor. One day, to test him, and perhaps also by way of an advance—for there are women who would marry a devil if he had money—a girl asked Gilliatt, "When are you going to take a wife?" Gilliatt replied, "I will take a wife when the Crowing Rock takes a husband."

This Crowing Rock is a large stone standing erect in a field near Monsieur Lemessurier du Frie's. It is a stone to beware of. No one knows what it is there for. A cock is heard crowing there, but it cannot be seen: a very unpleasant occurrence. Then, too, it is asserted that the stone was set up in the field by *sarregousets,* who are the same as *sins.*[75]

At night, when it thunders, if you see men flying in the red of the clouds and the quivering of the air, these are sarregousets. A woman who lives at Grand Mielles knows them. One evening when there were sarregousets at a crossroads this woman shouted to a carter who did not know which road to take, "Ask them your way. They are civil creatures, always ready to talk to people." Ten to one the woman was a witch.

The learned and judicious King James I had women of this kind boiled alive: then he tasted the stock and from its taste was able to say whether the woman was a witch or not.

It is regrettable that in our day kings have lost any talent of this kind, which showed the usefulness of the institution of monarchy.

Gilliatt had a reputation for sorcery, and there were good grounds for this. One night at midnight, during a storm, when he was in a boat, alone, off the Sommeilleuses,[76] he was heard to ask, "Is there room enough for me to get through?"

Then a voice cried from the rocks, "Plenty of room! Go to it!"

Whom could he have been speaking to, if not to whoever it was that replied? This seems to us proof.

On another stormy evening, when it was so dark that you couldn't make out anything, near Catioroc[77]—a double row of rocks, where witches and warlocks, goats and spectral faces gather to dance on Fridays—people were sure they recognized Gilliatt's voice in this terrible conversation:

"How is neighbor Brovard?" (This was a building worker who had fallen off a roof.)

"Getting better."

"*Ver dia!* He fell from a bit higher than that big post. Good that he didn't break anything."

"There was good weather for the seaweed-gathering last week."

"Better than today."

"Right! There won't be much fish in the market."

"It blows too hard."

"They won't be able to put their nets down."

"How is Catherine?"

"She is a charmer."

Catherine was evidently a sarregousette.

Clearly Gilliatt was up to some dark business at night. Certainly no one doubted it.

He was seen sometimes pouring water from a jug onto the ground. And it is well known that water poured on the ground marks out the form of devils.

On the road to St. Sampson, opposite the first of the Martello towers, are three stones set in the form of steps. On the top step, which is now empty, there once stood a cross—or it may have been a gibbet. These stones are maleficent.

Worthy people and absolutely credible witnesses declared that they had seen Gilliatt talking to a toad near these stones. Now there are no toads on Guernsey: Guernsey has all the grass snakes, while Jersey has all the toads. This toad must have swum over from Jersey to speak to Gilliatt. The conversation was in a friendly tone.

These facts were clearly established; and the proof is that the three stones are still there. Anyone who doubts this can go and see them; moreover, a short distance away, there is a house on the corner of which is the sign: DEALER IN CATTLE, ALIVE OR DEAD, OLD ROPE, IRON, BONES, AND CHEWING TOBACCO; PROMPT PAYMENT AND ATTENTION TO ORDERS.

No honest man can deny that the stones and this house exist. All this was injurious to Gilliatt's reputation.

Only the ignorant are unaware that the greatest danger in the waters of the Channel is the king of the Auxcriniers. No figure in the marine world is more redoubtable. Anyone who sees him is sure to suffer shipwreck between one St. Michael and the other.[78] He is small, being a dwarf, and deaf, being a king. He knows the names of all those who have died at sea and the places where they lie. He is familiar with every part of that great graveyard, the ocean. A head, massive in the lower part and narrow at the top, a squat body, a viscous and misshapen belly, wartlike excrescences on his skull, short legs, long arms, flippers for feet, claws for hands, a broad green face: such is this king. His claws are webbed and his flippers have nails. Imagine a fish that is a specter and has a face like a man. To get the better of him you would have to exorcise him or fish him out of the sea. But as he is, he is a sinister figure. It is alarming to encounter him at sea. Above the breakers and the swell, through the dense mist, sailors glimpse the outlines of a figure: a low forehead, a snub nose, flat ears, an enormous gap-toothed mouth, a glaucous grimace, eyebrows in the form of inverted *V*s, great grinning eyes. When the lightning is red he is livid; when the lightning is purple he is pallid. He has a stiff, spreading, square-cut beard, dripping wet, over a membrane in the form of a cape, ornamented with fourteen shells, seven in front and seven behind. These shells are extraordinary even to those who know about shells. The king of the Auxcriniers is seen only in violent seas. He is the lugubrious strolling player of the storm. His figure is seen emerging from the fog, the gust of wind, the rain. His navel is hideous. A carapace of scales covers his flanks like a waistcoat. He stands erect above the heaving waves whipped up by the wind, which twist and turn like shavings from a carpenter's plane. His whole body emerges from the foam; and if there are any ships in distress on the horizon he dances, pale in the half-darkness, his face lit by the ghost of a smile, mad and terrible in aspect. He is an ill-omened figure to meet. At the time when Gilliatt was a subject of concern to the citizens of St. Sampson, the last people to see the king of the Auxcriniers declared that he now had only thirteen shells on his cape. Thirteen shells: this made him all the more dangerous. But what had become of the fourteenth? Had he given it to someone? And whom had he given it to? No one could say for certain, and people were reduced to conjectures. What is certain is that Monsieur Lupin-Mabier of Les Godaines, a man of property paying tax at the rate of eighty quarters, was ready to depose on oath that he had once seen a very unusual shell in Gilliatt's hands.

It was not uncommon to hear two countrymen talking on these lines:

"It's a fine ox I have, isn't it, neighbor?"

"A fine fat one, certainly, neighbor."

"It's a good one all the same."

"Better for tallow than for meat."

"Ver dia!"

"Are you sure that Gilliatt hasn't cast his eye on it?"

Gilliatt would sometimes stop on the edge of a field where plowing was going on, or of a garden in which gardeners were working, and make mysterious remarks, for example:

"When the devil's bit is in flower, harvest the winter rye." (The "devil's bit" is scabious.)

"The ash is putting on leaves: there will be no more frost."

"Summer solstice, thistles in flower."

"If it doesn't rain in June, the wheat will turn white. Look out for blight."

"There are berries on the wild cherry. Beware of the full moon."

"If the weather on the sixth day of the moon is the same as on the fourth, or on the fifth, it will be the same, nine times out of twelve in the first case and eleven times out of twelve in the second, for the whole of the month."

"Keep an eye on neighbors who are at law with you. Beware of malicious tricks. A pig given hot milk to drink will die. A cow that has had its teeth rubbed with a leek won't eat."

"When the smelts spawn beware of fevers."

"When frogs appear, sow your melons."

"The liverwort is in flower: sow your barley."

"The lime trees are in flower: mow the meadows."

"The poplars are in flower: take the covers off."

"The tobacco is in flower: close the greenhouses."

And the terrible thing was that those who took this advice did well out of it.

One night in June, when he was playing his bagpipes in the dunes at La Demie de Fontenelles, the mackerel fishing failed.

One evening, at low tide, a cart laden with seaweed overturned on the beach below the house at the Bû de la Rue. Gilliatt was probably afraid of being brought before the magistrates, for he went to a good deal of trouble in helping to raise the cart, and reloaded the seaweed himself.

When a little girl in the neighborhood was infested with lice he went to St. Peter Port and returned with an ointment, which he rubbed on the child; and since Gilliatt had got rid of her lice this proved that he had given her them in the first place. Everyone knows that there is a charm for giving people lice.

Gilliatt was suspected of looking into wells, which is dangerous when a person has the evil eye; and it is a fact that one day at Les Arculons, near St. Peter Port, the water in a well turned bad. The woman to whom the well belonged said to Gilliatt: "Just look at that water," and she showed him a glassful. Gilliatt admitted it was bad. "It's true," he said, "the water is thick." The woman, who mistrusted him, said: "Then put it right again for me." Gilliatt asked a number of questions: Had she a stable? Had the stable a drain? Did the gutter of the drain run close to the well? The woman replied, "Yes." Then Gilliatt went into the stable, worked on the drain, and altered the line of the gutter: whereupon the water became pure again. The local people knew what to think. A well does not become foul one moment, and then pure, without reason. The trouble with the well was clearly not natural; and indeed it is difficult not to believe that Gilliatt had cast a spell on the water.

One day he had gone to Jersey, and it was noted that he had stayed in St. Clement's, in Rue des Alleurs; and *alleurs* are ghosts.

In villages the inhabitants observe all the little details of a man's behavior; then they add them up, and the total makes a reputation.

One day Gilliatt was observed to have a nosebleed. This was thought to be a grave matter. The master of a ship who had traveled a lot—who had sailed almost around the world—affirmed that among the Tungusians all witch doctors were subject to nosebleeds. When you see a man with a bleeding nose you know what to think. Fair-minded people, however, remarked that what was true of witch doctors in Tungusia might not apply to the same extent on Guernsey.

One year around Michaelmas he was observed to stop in a field at Les Huriaux, on the highway to Les Videclins. He gave a whistle, and a moment afterward a crow flew down, followed a moment later by a magpie. The fact was attested by a worthy local citizen, who was later appointed *douzenier* in the *douzaine*,[79] which had power to make a new survey and register of tenants of the royal fief.

In Le Hamel, in the *vingtaine*[80] of L'Épine, there were some old women who were positive that one morning, at daybreak, they had heard swallows calling Gilliatt's name.

Add to all this that he was ill-natured. One day a poor man was beating a donkey that wouldn't move. The man gave it a few kicks in the belly, and the donkey fell to the ground. Gilliatt ran to pick it up, but it was dead. Thereupon he cuffed the man.

On another occasion, seeing a boy coming down from a tree with a nestful of newly hatched tree-creepers, naked and almost featherless, he took the brood from the boy and carried his malevolence so far as to return the fledglings to the tree. When passersby took him to task, he merely pointed to the father and mother birds, which were crying plaintively above the tree as they returned to their brood.

Gilliatt had a soft spot for birds—and this is, of course, a distinctive mark of a magician. The local children delight in robbing the nests of seagulls on the cliffs. They bring home quantities of blue, yellow, and green eggs, with which they make chimney ornaments. Also very pretty are screens decorated with seabirds' eggs. Since the cliffs are steep, children sometimes slip and fall to their death. There was no limit to Gilliatt's ingenuity in ill-doing. At the risk of his own life he would climb up the sheer cliff faces and hang up bundles of hay, old hats, and other objects to act as scarecrows and prevent the birds from nesting and the children from venturing there.

All this explains why Gilliatt was disliked in the neighborhood—and surely with ample cause.

V

More Suspicious Facts

Public opinion was divided about Gilliatt.

He was generally believed to be a *marcou*, but some went farther and thought he was a *cambion*. A cambion is a son begotten on a woman by the Devil.

When a woman has borne a man seven male children in a row, the seventh is a marcou. But the sequence must not be spoiled by a daughter.

The marcou has the imprint of a natural fleur-de-lys on some part of his body, and so is able to cure scrofula, just like the king of France. There are marcous in all parts of France, particularly in the Orléanais. Every village in the Gâtinais has its marcou. All that is necessary to cure sufferers is for the marcou to breathe on their sores or let them touch his fleur-de-lys. The cure is particularly successful on the night of Good Friday. Some ten years ago the marcou of Ormes in the Gâtinais, known as the *beau marcou*, who was consulted by people from all over the Beauce region, was a cooper named Foulon, who kept a horse and carriage. To put a stop to his miracles it was found necessary to call in the gendarmes. He had a fleur-de-lys under his left breast. Other marcous have it in different places.

There are marcous on Jersey, Alderney, and Guernsey—no doubt because of France's rights over the duchy of Normandy. Otherwise what is the point of the fleur-de-lys?

There are people afflicted with scrofula in the Channel Islands; and this makes it necessary to have marcous.

Some people who had been present one day when Gilliatt was bathing in the sea thought they saw the fleur-de-lys. When asked about it he merely laughed; for he laughed sometimes like other men. Since then no one had ever seen him bathing: he now bathed only in solitary and dangerous places. Probably by moonlight—which it will be agreed is in itself suspicious. Those who persisted in believing that he was a cambion—that is, a son of the Devil—were clearly wrong. They ought to have known that cambions are rarely met with except in Germany. But fifty years ago ignorance was widespread among the inhabitants of the Vale and St. Sampson.

To believe that anyone on Guernsey is a son of the Devil is evidently absurd.

The very fact that Gilliatt caused disquiet led people to consult him. The countryfolk came to him, apprehensively, to talk about their diseases. This apprehension itself contained an element of faith in his skill; for in the country the more a doctor is suspected of possessing uncanny powers, the more certain is the cure. Gilliatt had his own medicines, inherited from the dead woman, and dispensed them to anyone who asked for them, never taking any money. He cured whitlows by applications of herbs, and the liquor in one of his vials relieved a fever—the chemist in St. Sampson (who in France would be called a pharmacist) thought that it was probably a decoction of cinchona. The less well disposed readily conceded that he was a good devil enough so far as the treatment of his patients with ordinary remedies was concerned. But he would not admit to being a marcou. When someone suffering from scrofula asked if he could touch his fleur-de-lys, he merely slammed the door in his face. He obstinately refused to perform any miracles, which is a ridiculous attitude for a warlock to take. You are not obliged to be one; but if you are you should carry out the duties of the position.

There were one or two exceptions to this universal dislike. Sieur Landoys of Clos-Landès was clerk and registrar of the parish of St. Peter Port, custodian of the records, and keeper of the register of births, marriages, and deaths. He was vain of his descent from Pierre Landais, treasurer of Brittany, who was hanged in 1485. One day Sieur Landoys swam too far out to sea and was in danger of drowning. Gilliatt dived into the water, almost drowning, too, and saved him. From that day Landoys never spoke ill of Gilliatt. To those who expressed surprise at this he replied: "How can I feel dislike for a man who has never done me any harm and has rendered me such a service?" He even came to form a kind of friendship with Gilliatt. The parish clerk and registrar was a man without prejudices. He did not believe in witches and warlocks. He laughed at those who were afraid of ghosts. He had a boat in which he went fishing in his leisure hours and had never observed anything out of the ordinary, except that once, on a moonlit night, he had seen a woman clad in white leaping out of the sea; and even of this he was not absolutely sure. Moutonne Gahy, the witch of Torteval, had given him a small bag, to be worn under his cravat, which gave protection from spirits. He made fun of the bag and had no idea what it contained; but he did wear it, feeling safer when he had it hanging around his neck.

A few courageous characters, following in the footsteps of Sieur Landoys, ventured to find a number of extenuating circumstances in Gilliatt, a few signs of good qualities such as his sobriety and his abstinence from gin and tobacco, and sometimes went so far as to pay him this generous tribute: "He doesn't drink or smoke or chew tobacco or take snuff."

But sobriety only counts as a quality if it is accompanied by other qualities.

There was a general aversion to Gilliatt. Nevertheless, as a marcou, he was in a position to be of service. One Good Friday, at midnight—the day and time commonly chosen for cures of this kind—all the scrofulous people on the island flocked to the Bû de la Rue, either as the result of inspiration or by agreement among themselves, and, with clasped hands and pitiable sores, begged Gilliatt to cure them. He refused; and they saw this as another manifestation of his malevolence.

VI

THE PAUNCH

Such a man was Gilliatt.

Girls considered him ugly.

He was not ugly. He might even have been called handsome. His profile had something of the air of a barbarian of antiquity. In repose, he resembled the figure of a Dacian on Trajan's Column. His ears were small and delicate, without lobes, and excellently shaped for hearing. Between his eyes he had that proud vertical furrow that betokens boldness and perseverance. The corners of his mouth turned down, giving it an expression of bitterness. His forehead formed a serene and noble curve. His clear eyes had a firm glance, in spite of the flickering of the eyelids brought on in fishermen by the reverberation of the waves. He had a charming boyish laugh. No ivory could be of a purer white than his teeth. But tanning by the sun had given him almost the coloring of a Negro. You cannot brave the ocean, storms, and night with impunity: at the age of thirty he looked like a man of forty-five. He wore the somber mask of the wind and the sea.

People called him Gilliatt the Cunning One.[81]

There is an Indian fable that tells how Brahma asked Strength, "Who is stronger than you?" The reply was "Cunning." And there is a Chinese proverb: "What could the lion not do if he were a monkey?" Gilliatt was neither a lion nor a monkey; but his actions gave some warrant to the Chinese proverb and the Hindu fable. He was of ordinary height and ordinary strength, but was able, thanks to his inventive and powerful dexterity, to lift weights that might have taxed a giant and perform feats that would have done credit to an athlete. There was something of the gymnast about him; and he used both his right and his left hand with equal skill.

He did not go shooting, but he fished—sparing the birds but not the fish. So much the worse for these dumb creatures! He was an excellent swimmer.

Solitude produces men of talent or idiots. Gilliatt had something of both. Sometimes his face had the air of astonishment we have already mentioned, and then he might have been taken for a savage. At other times he had a look of profound thought. Ancient Chaldea had men of this kind; at certain times the blankness of the shepherd became transparent, revealing the magus.

After all, he was only a poor man who could read and write. Probably he was on the borderline between the dreamer and the thinker. The thinker wills what happens, the dreamer accepts it. Solitude adds a quality to simple people, and gives them a certain complication. They become imbued, unconsciously, with a sacred awe. The shadowy area in which Gilliatt's mind constantly dwelt was composed, in almost equal parts, of two elements, both of them obscure but very different from each other: within him ignorance and weakness; without, mystery and immensity.

By dint of climbing about on the rocks, scaling the cliffs, coming and going in the archipelago in all weathers, sailing in any kind of craft that came to hand, venturing by day or by night through the most difficult channels, he had become—without seeking any personal advantage, but merely following his fancy and pleasure—a seaman of extraordinary skill.

He was a born pilot. The true pilot is the sailor who navigates the bed of the ocean more than its surface. The waves are an external problem, continually complicated by the submarine configuration of the sea over which the boat is traveling. To see Gilliatt sailing over the shallows and amid the reefs of the Norman archipelago, you might well think that he carried in his head a map of the sea bottom. He was familiar with it all and would venture anywhere.

He knew the various buoys better than the cormorants that perched on them. The imperceptible differences between the four buoys at Les Creux, Alligande, Les Trémies, and La Sardrette were perfectly obvious and clear to him, even in foggy weather. He could distinguish at once the oval-topped post at Anfré, the three-spiked marker at La Rousse, the white ball at La Corbette, and the black ball at Longue-Pierre, and he was in no danger of confusing the cross at Goubeau with the sword set in the ground at La Platte, or the hammer-shaped marker at Les Barbées with the swallowtail marker at Le Moulinet.

His rare skill in seamanship was strikingly demonstrated one day when one of those naval tournaments known as regattas was held on Guernsey. This was a competition to navigate a four-sailed boat single-handed from St. Sampson to the island of Herm, a league away, and then back from Herm to St. Sampson. Any fisherman can work a four-sailed boat single-handed, and this does not seem a great challenge; but there were two things that made it more difficult. In the first place, the boat was one of those old broad and heavy boats of Rotterdam build, wide-bellied, that the seamen of the last century called Dutch paunches. This ancient style of Dutch craft, flat and big-bellied, which dispense with a keel and instead have wings to starboard and port that are let down on one or other side, depending on the wind, can occasionally still be met with at sea. The second difficulty was that on the return journey from Herm the boat was to have a heavy ballast of stones. Empty on the outward journey, it was to return fully laden. The prize in this contest was the boat itself, which was to be presented to the winner. It had served as a pilot boat, and the pilot who had rigged it and worked it for twenty years was the stoutest seaman in the Channel. After his death no one had been found capable of managing it, and it had been decided to make it the prize for the winner of a regatta. Although not decked, it had good seagoing qualities and would be a tempting prize for a skillful seaman. Its mast was well forward, increasing the pulling power of its sails. Another advantage of this was that the mast did not get in the way of the cargo.

It was a strongly built vessel—heavy, but roomy, and taking the open sea well: altogether, a good, serviceable craft. There was eager competition for the boat: the challenge was a tough one, but the prize was handsome. Seven or eight fishermen, the most vigorous on the island, entered the contest. One after the other they set out in the boat, but not one of them reached Herm. The last one to try was noted for having rowed a boat across the dangerous narrows between Sark and Brecqhou in heavy seas. Streaming with sweat, he brought the paunch back, saying: "It can't be done." Then Gilliatt got into the boat, took hold of the oar and then the mainsheet, and put to sea. He did not bitt the sheet, which would have been unwise, but neither did he let it go, which kept him in control of the sail, and, leaving the boom to move with the wind without drifting, he took hold of the tiller with his left hand. In three-quarters of an hour he was at Herm. Three hours later, although a strong south wind had sprung up and was blowing across the seaway, he brought the boat back to St. Sampson with its load of stones. As an extra, in a show of bravado, he had added to his cargo the little bronze cannon that the people of Herm fire off every year on the fifth of November in celebration of the death of Guy Fawkes.

Guy Fawkes, it may be noted in passing, died 260 years ago: long-continued rejoicings indeed!

And so Gilliatt, overloaded and overtaxed as he was, and in spite of the fact that he had the Guy Fawkes cannon on board and the south wind in his sails, brought the paunch back—you could almost say carried it back—to St. Sampson.

Seeing this, Mess Lethierry[82] exclaimed: "There's a bold seaman for you!" And he held out his hand to Gilliatt.

We shall have more to say about Mess Lethierry.

The paunch was awarded to Gilliatt.

This exploit did nothing to injure his reputation for cunning.

There were some who declared that there was nothing surprising about his feat, seeing that Gilliatt had hidden a branch from a wild medlar tree in the boat. But this could not be proved.

From that day on Gilliatt had no other boat than the paunch. In this heavy craft he went on his fishing expeditions. He moored it in the excellent little anchorage that he had all to himself under the very walls of the house at the Bû de la Rue. At nightfall he would throw his nets over his shoulder, walk down through his garden, step over the dry-stone wall, and jump down from one rock to another and into the paunch. Then off to the open sea.

He brought home good catches of fish, but it was said that the medlar branch was always fixed to the boat. No one had ever seen the branch, but everyone believed in its existence.

When he had more fish than he needed he did not sell them but gave them away.

The poor people of the parish took his fish, but still held it against him, because of the medlar branch. It wasn't right: you shouldn't cheat the sea.

He was a fisherman, but he was not only that. By instinct, or by way of relaxation, he had learned three or four other trades. He was a carpenter, a craftsman in iron, a wheelwright, a boat caulker, and even a bit of an engineer. No one could mend a broken wheel better than he. He made all his fishing equipment in his own fashion. In a corner of the Bû de la Rue he had a small forge and an anvil; and, finding that the paunch had only one anchor, he had made another all by himself. The anchor was first-rate. The ring had the necessary strength; and Gilliatt, without ever having been taught how to do it, had found the exact dimensions of the stock required to prevent the anchor from tripping.

He had patiently replaced all the nails in the planking of the boat by rivets, making it impossible for rust to make holes.

In this way he had greatly improved the seagoing quality of the boat, and was now able to go off occasionally and spend a month or two on some lonely islet like Chousey or the Casquets. People would say: "So Gilliatt is away again"; but no one was upset by his absence.

VII

A GHOSTLY TENANT FOR A GHOSTLY HOUSE

Gilliatt was a man of dreams. Hence his acts of daring; hence also his moments of timidity.

He had ideas that were all his own.

Perhaps there was an element of hallucination in Gilliatt, some-thing of the visionary. Hallucinations may haunt a peasant like Mar-tin[83] just as much as a king like Henry IV. The Unknown sometimes holds surprises for the spirit of man. A sudden rent in the veil of dark-ness will momentarily reveal the invisible and then close up again. Such visions sometimes have a transfiguring effect, turning a camel driver into a Mohammed, a goat girl into a Joan of Arc. Solitude brings out a certain amount of sublime exaltation. It is the smoke from the burning bush. It produces a mysterious vibration of ideas that enlarges the scholar into the seer and the poet into the prophet; it produces Horeb, Kedron, Ombos, the intoxication induced by the chewing of laurel leaves at the Castalian spring, the revelations of the month of Busios,[84] Peleia at Dodona, Phemonoe at Delphi, Trophonius at Lebadeia, Ezekiel by the river Chebar, Jerome in the Thebaid.

Usually the visionary state overwhelms a man and stupefies him. There is such a thing as a divine besottedness. The fakir bears the bur-den of his vision as the cretin bears his goiter. Luther talking to devils in his garret at Wittenberg, Pascal in his study shutting off the view of hell with a screen, the negro obi conversing with the white-faced god Bossum are all examples of the same phenomenon, diversely affecting the different minds it inhabits according to their strength and their di-mensions. Luther and Pascal are, and remain, great; the obi is a poor half-witted creature.

Gilliatt was neither so high nor so low. He was given to thinking a lot: nothing more.

He looked on nature in a rather strange way.

From the fact that he had several times found in the perfectly limpid water of the sea strange creatures of considerable size and var-ied shape belonging to the jellyfish species that when out of the water resembled soft crystal but when thrown back into the water became one with their natural element, having identical coloring and the same diaphanous quality, so that they were lost to sight, he concluded that since such living transparencies inhabited the water there might be other living transparencies in the air, too. Birds are not inhabitants of the air: they are its amphibians. Gilliatt did not believe that the air was an uninhabited desert. Since the sea is full, he used to say, why should the atmosphere be empty? Air-colored creatures would disappear in daylight and be invisible to us. What proof is there that there are no such creatures? Analogy suggests that the air must have its fish just as the sea has. These fishes of the air would be diaphanous—a provision by a wise Creator that is beneficial both to us and to them; for since light would pass through them, giving them no shadow and no visible form, they would remain unknown to us and we should know nothing about them. Gilliatt imagined that if we could drain the earth of atmosphere, and then fished in the air as we fish in a pond, we should find a multitude of strange creatures. And then, he went on in his reverie, many things would be explained.

Reverie, which is thought in a nebulous state, borders on sleep, which it regards as its frontier area. Air, inhabited by living transparencies, may be seen as the beginning of the unknown; but beyond this lies the vast expanse of the possible. *There* live different creatures; *there* are found different circumstances. There is nothing supernatural about this: it is merely the occult continuation of the infinite natural world. Gilliatt, in the hardworking idleness that was his life, was an odd observer. He went so far as to observe sleep. Sleep is in contact with the possible, which we also call the improbable. The nocturnal world is a world of its own. Night, as night, is a universe. The material human organism, living under the weight of a fifteen-league-high column of air, is tired at the end of the day, it is overcome by lassitude, it lies down, it rests; the eyes of the flesh close; then in this sleeping head, which is less inert than is generally believed, other eyes open; the Unknown appears. The dark things of this unknown world come closer to man, whether because there is a real communication between the two worlds or because the distant recesses of the abyss undergo a visionary enlargement. It seems then that the impalpable living creatures of space come to look at us and are curious about us, the living creatures of earth; a phantom creation ascends or descends to our level and rubs shoulders with us in a dim twilight; in our spectral contemplation a life other than our own, made up of ourselves and of something else, forms and disintegrates; and the sleeper—not wholly aware, not quite unconscious—catches a glimpse of these strange forms of animal life, these extraordinary vegetations, these pallid beings, ghastly or smiling, these phantoms, these masks, these faces, these hydras, these confusions, this moonlight without a moon, these dark decompositions of wonder, these growths and shrinkings in a dense obscurity, these floating forms in the shadows, all this mystery that we call dreaming and that in fact is the approach to an invisible reality. The dream world is the aquarium of night.

So, at least, thought Gilliatt.

VIII

THE SEAT OF GILD-HOLM-'UR

Nowadays you will look in vain, in the little bay of Houmet, for Gilliatt's house, his garden, and the creek in which he moored his boat. The Bû de la Rue is no longer there. The little promontory on which it stood has fallen to the picks of the cliff demolishers and has been carried, cartload by cartload, aboard the ships of the rock merchants and the dealers in granite. It is now transformed into quays, churches, and palaces in the capital city. All this ridge of rocks has long since gone off to London.

These lines of rocks extending into the sea, with their fissures and their fretted outlines, are like miniature mountain chains. Looking at them, you have the same kind of impression as would a giant looking at the Cordilleras. In the language of the country they are called banks. They have very different forms. Some are like backbones, with each rock representing a vertebra; others are in the form of herringbones; others again resemble a crocodile in the act of drinking.

At the end of the Bû de la Rue bank was a large rock that the fishing people of Houmet called the Beast's Horn. Pyramidal in shape, it was like a smaller version of the Pinnacle on Jersey. At high tide the sea cut it off from the bank, and it was isolated. At low tide it could be reached on a rocky isthmus. The remarkable feature of this rock, on the seaward side, was a kind of natural seat carved out by the waves and polished by the rain. It was a treacherous place. People were attracted to it by the beauty of the view; they came here "for the sake of the prospect," as they say on Guernsey, and were tempted to linger, for there is a special charm in wide horizons. The seat was inviting. It formed a kind of recess in the sheer face of the rock, and it was easy to climb up to it: the sea that had hewn it from the rock had also provided a kind of staircase of flat stones leading up to it. The abyss sometimes has these thoughtful ideas; but you will do well to beware of its kindness. The seat tempted people to climb up to it and sit down. It was comfortable, too: the seat was formed of granite worn and rounded by the surf; for the arms there were two crevices in the rock that seemed made for the purpose; and the back consisted of the high vertical wall of the rock, which the occupant of the seat was able to admire above his head, without thinking that it would be impossible to climb. Sitting there, it was all too easy to fall into a reverie. You could look out on the great expanse of sea; you could see in the distance ships arriving and departing; you could follow the course of a sail until it disappeared beyond the Casquets over the curve of the ocean. Visitors were entranced; they enjoyed the beauty of the scene and felt the caress of the wind and the waves. There is a kind of bat at Cayenne that sets out to fan people to sleep in the shade with the gentle beating of its dusky wings. The wind is like this invisible bat: it can batter you, but it can also lull you to sleep. Visitors would come to this rock, look out on the sea and listen to the wind, and then feel the drowsiness of ecstasy coming over them. When your eyes are sated with an excess of beauty and light, it is a pleasure to close them. Then suddenly the visitor would wake up. It was too late. The tide had risen steadily, and the rock was now surrounded by water. He was lost.

The rising sea is a fearful blockading force. The tide swells insensibly at first, then violently. When it reaches the rocks it rages and foams. Swimming is not always possible in the breakers. Fine swimmers had been drowned at the Beast's Horn on the Bû de la Rue.

At certain places and at certain times to look at the sea is a dangerous poison; as is, sometimes, to look at a woman.

The old inhabitants of Guernsey called this recess fashioned from the rock by the waves the Seat of Gild-Holm-'Ur or Kidormur. It is said to be a Celtic word, which those who know Celtic do not understand and those who know French do. The local translation of the name is Qui-Dort-Meurt, "he who sleeps dies." We are free to choose between this translation and the translation given in 1819, I think, in the *Armoricain* by Monsieur Athénas. According to this respectable Celtic scholar Gild-Holm-'Ur means "the resting place of flocks of birds."

There is another seat of the same kind on Alderney, the Monk's Seat, which has been so well fashioned by the waves, with a rock projection so conveniently placed that it could be said that the sea has been kind enough to provide a footstool for the visitor's feet.

At high tide the Seat of Gild-Holm-'Ur could no longer be seen: it was entirely covered by water.

Gild-Holm-'Ur was a neighbor of the Bû de la Rue. Gilliatt knew it well and used to sit in the seat. He often went there. Was he meditating? No. As we have just said, he did not meditate: he dreamed. He did not allow himself to be caught unawares by the sea.

"Vieux Guernesey" (1864–65).

BOOK II

MESS LETHIERRY

I

A RESTLESS LIFE, BUT A QUIET CONSCIENCE

Mess Lethierry, a leading figure in St. Sampson, was a redoubtable sailor. He had sailed far and wide. He had been cabin boy, sail maker, topman, helmsman, leading hand, boatswain, pilot, and master. He was now a shipowner. No man knew the sea as he did. He was intrepid in rescue work. In bad weather he would be out on the shore, scanning the horizon. What's that out there? Someone in trouble? It might be a small fishing-boat from Weymouth, a cutter from Alderney, a bisquine[85] from Courseulle, the yacht of some English lord, an Englishman, a Frenchman, a poor man, a rich man, the Devil himself: it made no difference.

He would jump into a boat and call on two or three stout fellows to join him; but he could do without them if necessary—crew the boat all by himself, cast off, take up the oars, and put to sea, sinking into the hollow of the waves and rising to the crest again, plunging into the hurricane, heading for danger. Then he would be seen in the distance amid the gusting winds and the lightning, standing erect in his boat, dripping with rain, like a lion with a mane of foam. Sometimes he spent his whole day in this way—in danger, amid the waves and the hail and the wind, coming alongside boats in distress, saving their crew, saving their cargo, challenging the storm. Then in the evening he would go home and knit a pair of stockings.

He led this kind of life for fifty years, from the age of ten to sixty, so long as he felt young. Then when he was sixty he noticed that he was no longer able to lift with one hand the anvil in the smithy at Le Varclin, which weighed three hundred pounds; and suddenly he was taken prisoner by rheumatism. He was compelled to give up the sea, and passed from the heroic to the patriarchal age. He was now just a harmless old fellow, rheumaticky and comfortably off. These two products of a man's labor often come together. At the very moment when you become rich you are paralyzed. That rounds off your life. Then men say to themselves: "Let us enjoy life."

On islands like Guernsey the population consists of men who have spent their life walking around their field and men who have spent their life traveling around the world. There are two kinds of laborers, the workers on the land and the toilers of the sea. Mess Lethierry belonged to the latter category. Yet he also knew the land. He had worked hard all his life. He had traveled on the continent. He had for some time been a ship's carpenter at Rochefort and later at Sète. We have just spoken of sailing around the world. He had made the circuit of France as a journeyman carpenter. He had worked on the pumping machinery of the saltworks in Franche-Comté. This respectable citizen had led the life of an adventurer. In France he had learned to read, to think, to have a will of his own. He had turned his hand to all sorts of things, and in all he had done he had gained a character of probity. At bottom, however, he was a seaman. Water was his element; he would say: "My home is where the fish are." And indeed his whole life, apart from two or three years, had been devoted to the ocean—as he used to say, he had been "flung into the water." He had sailed the great seas—the Atlantic and the Pacific—but he preferred the Channel. He would exclaim enthusiastically: "That's the real tough one!" He had been born there and wanted to die there. After sailing once or twice around the world he had returned to Guernsey, knowing what was right for him, and had never left it. His voyages now were to Granville and Saint-Malo.

Mess Lethierry was a Guernsey man: that is to say, he was Norman, he was English, he was French. He had within him that quadruple homeland, which was submerged, one might say drowned, in his wider homeland, the ocean. Throughout his life, and wherever he went, he had preserved the habits of a Norman fisherman.

But he also liked to look into a book from time to time; he enjoyed reading; he knew the names of philosophers and poets; and he had a smattering of all the world's languages.

II

A MATTER OF TASTE

Gilliatt was a kind of savage. Mess Lethierry was another. But this savage had some refined tastes.

He was particular about women's hands. In his early years, while still a lad, somewhere between seaman and cabin boy, he had heard the Bailli de Suffren[86] say: "There goes a pretty girl, but what horrible great red hands!" A remark by an admiral, on any subject, carries great weight: it is more than an oracle, it is an order. The Bailli de Suffren's exclamation had made Lethierry fastidious and exacting in the matter of small white hands. His own hand was a huge mahogany-colored slab; a light touch from it was like a blow from a club, a caress was like being grasped by pincers, and a blow from his clenched fist could crack a paving stone.

He had never married. Either he did not want to get married or he had never found the right woman. It may have been because he wanted someone with the hands of a duchess. There are few such hands to be found among the fisher girls of Portbail.[87]

It was rumored, however, that once upon a time, at Rochefort in the Charente, he had found a grisette who matched up to his ideal. She was a pretty girl with pretty hands. She had a sharp tongue, and she scratched. Woe betide anyone who attacked her! Her nails, exquisitely clean, without reproach and without fear, could on occasion become claws. These charming nails had enchanted Lethierry and then had begun to worry him; and, fearing that one day he might not be the master of his mistress, he had decided against appearing before the mayor with this particular bride.

Another time he was attracted by a girl on Alderney. He was thinking of marriage when an Alderney man said to him, "Congratulations! You will have a good dung-woman for a wife." He had to have the meaning of this commendation explained to him. It referred to a practice they have on Alderney. They collect cowpats and throw them against a wall; there is a particular way of throwing them. When they are dry they fall off the wall. The cakes of dried dung, known as *coipiaux*, are then used for heating the house. An Alderney girl will get a husband only if she is a good dung-woman. Lethierry was scared off by this talent.

In matters of love and lovemaking he had a good rough-and-ready peasant philosophy, the wisdom of a sailor who was always being captivated but was never caught, and he boasted of having been easily conquered in his younger days by a "petticoat." What is now known as a crinoline was then called a petticoat—meaning something more and something less than a woman.

These rude seafaring men of the Norman archipelago have a certain native wit. Almost all of them can read and do read. On Sundays you can see little eight-year-old cabin boys sitting on a coil of rope with a book in their hands. These Norman seamen have always had a sardonic turn of mind and are ever ready with an apt remark, what we nowadays call a *mot*. It was one such man, a daring pilot called Quéripel, who addressed Montgomery, who had sought refuge on Jersey after accidentally killing King Henry II in a tournament, with these words: "An empty head broken by a foolish one." Another—Touzeau, a sea captain of St. Brelade—was the author of the philosophical pun wrongly attributed to Bishop Camus: *Après la mort les papes deviennent papillons et les sires deviennent cirons* ("After death popes become butterflies and seigneurs become mites").

III

The Old Language of the Sea

These seamen of the Channel Islands are true old Gauls. The islands, which are now rapidly becoming anglicized, long remained independent. Countryfolk on Sark speak the language of Louis XIV.

Forty years ago the classical language of the sea could be heard in the mouths of the seamen of Jersey and Alderney. A visitor would have found himself carried back to the seafaring world of the seventeenth century. A specialist archaeologist could have gone there to study the ancient language, used in working ships and in battle, roared out by Jean Bart[88] through the loud-hailer that terrified Admiral Hyde. The seafaring vocabulary of our fathers, almost completely changed in our day, was still in use on Guernsey around 1820. A ship that was a good plyer was a *bon boulinier;* one that carried a weather helm, in spite of her foresails and rudder, was a *vaisseau ardent.* To get under way was *prendre l'aire;* to lie to in a storm was *capeyer;* to make fast running rigging was *faire dormant;* to get to windward was *faire chapelle;* to keep the cable tight was *faire teste;* to be out of trim was *être en pantenne;* to keep the sails full was *porter plain.* All these terms have fallen out of use. Today we say *louvoyer* (to beat to windward), they said *leauvoyer;* for *naviguer* (to sail) they said *naviger;* for *virer* (to tack) they said *donner vent devant;* for *aller de l'avant* (to make headway) they said *tailler de l'avant;* for *tirez d'accord* (haul together) they said *halez d'accord;* for *dérapez* (weigh anchor), *déplantez;* for *embraquez* (haul tight), *abraquez;* for *taquets* (cleats), *bittons;* for *burins* (toggles), *tappes;* for *balancines* (lifts), *valancines;* for *tribord* (starboard), *stribord;* for *les hommes de quart à bâbord* (men of the port watch), *les basbourdis.* Admiral Tourville[89] wrote to Hocquincourt, *Nous avons singlé* (sailed) instead of *cinglé.* They said *le raffal* for *la rafale* (squall); *boussoir* for *bossoir* (cathead); *drousse* for *drosse* (truss); *faire une olofée* for *loffer* (to luff); *alonger* for *élonger* (to lay alongside); *survent* for *forte brise* (stiff breeze); *jas* for *jouail* (stock of an anchor); *fosse* for *soute* (storeroom).

Such, at the beginning of this century, was the seafarers' language of the Channel Islands. If he had heard a Jersey pilot speaking, Ango[90] would have been puzzled. While everywhere else sails *faseyaient* (shivered), in the Channel Islands they *barbeyaient.* A *saute de vent* (sudden shift of wind) was a *folle-vente.* Only there were the two antique methods of mooring, *la valture* and *la portugaise,* still in use. Only there could be heard the old commands *tour et choque!* and *bosse et bitte!* While a seaman of Granville was already using the term *clan* for sheave hole, a seaman of St. Aubin or St. Sampson was still saying *canal de pouliot.* The *bout d'alonge* (upper futtock) of Saint-Malo was the *oreille d'âne* of St. Helier. Mess Lethierry, just like the duc de Vivonne,[91] called the sheer of a deck the *tonture* and the caulker's chisel a *patarasse.* It was with this peculiar idiom in their mouths that Duquesne beat Ruyter, Duguay-Trouin[92] beat Wasnaer, and Tourville, in broad daylight, put down anchors fore and aft on the first galley that bombarded Algiers in 1681. It is now a dead language. Nowadays the jargon of the sea is quite differ-ent. Duperré[93] would not understand Suffren.

The language of naval signals is likewise transformed. We have moved on a long way from the four pennants—red, white, blue, and yellow—of La Bourdonnais[94] to the eighteen flags of today, which, hoisted in twos, threes, or fours, facilitate communication at a distance with their seventy thousand combinations, are never at a loss, and, as it were, foresee the unforeseen.

IV

YOU ARE VULNERABLE IN WHAT YOU LOVE

Mess Lethierry wore his heart on his hand: a big hand and a big heart. His failing was that admirable quality, confidence in his fellowmen. He had a very personal way of undertaking to do something: with an air of solemnity, he would say: "I give my word of honor to God," and would then go ahead and do what he had undertaken. He believed in God, but not in any of the rest. He rarely went to church, and when he did it was merely out of politeness. At sea he was superstitious.

Yet he had never been daunted by any storm. This was because he was intolerant of opposition. He would not put up with it from the ocean any more than from anyone else. He was determined to be obeyed. So much the worse for the sea if it resisted his authority: it would just have to accept the fact. Mess Lethierry would not give way. He would no more be stopped by a rearing wave than by a quarrel-some neighbor. What he said was said; what he planned to do was done. He would not bend before an objection nor before a storm at sea. For him the word *no* did not exist, either in the mouth of a man or the rum-bling of a thundercloud. He pressed on regardless. He would take no refusals. Hence his obstinacy in life and his intrepidity on the ocean.

He liked to season his own fish soup, knowing the exact measure of pepper and salt and herbs required, and took pleasure in making it as well as in eating it. A man who is transfigured by oilskins and de-meaned by a frock coat; who, with his hair blowing in the wind, looks like Jean Bart, and, wearing a round hat, like a simpleton; awkward in town, strange and redoubtable at sea; the broad back of a porter, never an oath, seldom angry, a gentle voice that turns to thunder in a loud-hailer, a peasant who has read the *Encyclopédie,* a Guernsey man who has seen the Revolution, a learned ignoramus, with no bigotry but all kinds of visions, more faith in the White Lady than in the Virgin Mary, the strength of Polyphemus, the will of Columbus, the logic of the weather vane, with something of a bull and something of a child about him; almost snub-nosed, powerful cheeks, a mouth that has preserved all its teeth, a deeply marked face, buffeted by the waves and lashed by the winds for forty years, a brow like a brooding storm, the complexion of a rock in the open sea; then add to this rugged face a kindly glance, and you have Mess Lethierry.

Mess Lethierry had two special objects of affection: Durande and Déruchette.

BOOK III
DURANDE AND DÉRUCHETTE

I

CHATTER AND SMOKE

The human body is perhaps nothing more than an appearance. It conceals our reality. It solidifies over the light and shadow of our life. The reality is the soul. In absolute terms, our face is a mask. The real man is what exists under the man. If we were able to perceive that man crouching, sheltered, behind that illusion that we call the flesh, we should have many a surprise. The common error is to take the external being for the real one. Some girl we know, for example, if we were to see her as she really is, would appear in the form of a bird. A bird in the form of a girl: what could be more exquisite? Just imagine that you have one in your own home. Take, for example, Déruchette. What a charming creature! One would be tempted to say to her, "Good morning, Mademoiselle Wagtail!" You do not see her wings, but you hear her twittering. Now and then she sings. In her chattering she is below mankind; in her singing she is above it. There is a mystery in this singing; a virgin is the mortal habiliment of an angel. When she develops into a woman the angel departs; but later it returns, bringing back a small soul to the mother. While waiting for life to begin, she who will one day be a mother long remains a child; the little girl continues to exist within the young woman, and now she is a warbler. Looking at her, we think, How good of her not to fly away! This sweet familiar being moves freely about the house, from branch to branch—that is to say, from room to room—going in and out, drawing nearer and then retreating, preening her feathers or combing her hair, making all kinds of delicate little noises, murmuring ineffable things in your ears. She asks questions, and you reply; you ask her something in return, and she twitters a reply. You chat with her: chatting is a form of relaxation after serious talk. This creature has something of the sky within her. She is a blue thought mingling with your black thought. You are grateful to her for being so light, so fleeting, so evasive, so ungraspable, and for her kindness in not being invisible, when she could, it seems, be impalpable. In this world of ours, beauty is a necessity. There are few functions on earth more important than this: simply being charming. The forest would be in despair without the hummingbird. To shed joy around, to radiate happiness, to emit light amid dark things, to be the gilding on our destiny, to be harmony and grace and kindness: is not this to render a service? Beauty does me good merely by being beautiful. Occasionally we meet with someone who has this fairylike power of enchanting all around her. Sometimes she is not aware of it herself, and this makes her power all the more sovereign. Her presence lights up her surroundings; her nearness is warming. She passes on her way, and we are content; she stays, and we are happy. Merely to look at her is to feel alive; she is like the dawn with a human face. She need merely be there to make an Eden of the house; she exudes Paradise from every pore; and she distributes this ecstasy to all by doing nothing more than breathing in their presence. To have a smile that somehow lessens the weight of the enormous chain dragged behind them by all living beings in common—what else can we call it but divine? Déruchette had such a smile; indeed we might rather say that Déruchette *was* that smile. If there is one thing that has more resemblance to us than our face, it is the look on our face; and if there is one thing that has more resemblance to us than the look on our face, it is our smile. Déruchette smiling was simply Déruchette.

There is something particularly attractive about the blood of Jersey and Guernsey. The women, particularly the young girls, have a blooming and unaffected beauty, a Saxon fairness and a Norman freshness combined. Rosy cheeks and blue eyes. But the eyes lack brilliancy: English education dulls them. These limpid eyes will be irresistible when they acquire the depth of Parisiennes' eyes. Paris, fortunately, has not yet made its way among Englishwomen. Déruchette was not a Parisienne, but she was not really a Guernsey girl either. She had been born in St. Peter Port, but she had been brought up by Mess Lethierry. He had brought her up to be dainty and pretty; and so she was.

Déruchette had an indolent and an unwittingly aggressive glance. She perhaps did not know the meaning of the word *love*, but she liked people to fall in love with her. But she had no ulterior motive. She was not thinking of marriage. An old French nobleman, an émigré who had settled in St. Sampson, used to say: "That girl is flirting with powder."[95]

Déruchette had the prettiest little hands in the world and feet to match her hands—"four fly's feet," Mess Lethierry used to say. In person she was all sweetness and goodness; for her family and fortune she had Mess Lethierry, her uncle; for occupation she had the living of her life, for accomplishments a few songs, for learning her beauty, for intelligence her innocence, for heart her ignorance. She had the graceful indolence of a Creole, mingled with thoughtlessness and vivacity, the teasing gaiety of childhood with a leaning toward melancholy. She dressed elegantly but in a rather insular fashion that would not have been regarded as correct on the mainland, with flowers on her bonnet all year round. She had an open forehead, a simple and tempting neck, chestnut hair, a fair skin with a few freckles in summer, a wide, healthy mouth, and on that mouth the adorable and dangerous brightness of her smile. Such was Déruchette.

Sometimes in the evening, after sunset, when night mingles with the sea and twilight invests the waves with a kind of terror, there could be seen entering the harbor of St. Sampson, menacingly churning up the water, a shapeless mass, a monstrous form that whistled and spluttered, a hideous thing that roared like a wild beast and smoked like a volcano, a kind of hydra slavering in the foam and trailing a wake of fog, hurtling toward the town with a fearful beating of its fins and a maw belching forth flames. This was Durande.

II

THE ETERNAL HISTORY OF UTOPIA

A steamship was a prodigious novelty in the waters of the Channel in 182–. For many years it caused alarm along the whole coast of Normandy. Nowadays ten or twelve steamers sail across the horizon in both directions and no one pays any attention to them. At the most some knowledgeable observer may watch them for a moment to make out from the color of their smoke whether they are burning Welsh coal or Newcastle coal. They pass on their way: that is all. "Welcome" to them if they are coming in; "Bon voyage" if they are outward bound.

People did not accept these new inventions so calmly in the first quarter of this century, and these vessels with their smoke were particularly disliked by the Channel Islanders. In this puritanical archipelago, where the queen of England has been accused of violating the Bible by giving birth with the help of chloroform,[96] the steamship immediately became known as the devil boat. To the worthy fishermen of those days—formerly Catholics, now Calvinists, but always bigots—it was seen as hell afloat. A local preacher took as his text, "Is it right to let water and fire, which were divided by God, work together?"[97] Did not this beast of fire and iron resemble Leviathan? Were we not recreating Chaos on a human scale? This was not the first time that the advance of progress had been called a return to chaos.

"A mad idea—a gross error—an absurdity!" Such had been the verdict of the Academy of Sciences when consulted by Napoleon at the beginning of this century on the subject of steamboats; and the fishermen of St. Sampson can be excused for being no wiser in scientific matters than the mathematicians of Paris. In religious matters, too, a small island like Guernsey cannot be expected to be more enlightened than a great continent like America. In 1807, when Fulton's first boat, equipped with one of Watt's engines imported from England, captained by Livingston and manned by two Frenchmen, André Michaux and another, in addition to the crew—when this first steamship made its maiden voyage from New York to Albany it chanced to be the seventeenth of August: whereupon the Methodists gave voice and in every chapel preachers denounced this machine, declaring that the number seventeen was the sum of the ten horns and the seven heads of the beast of the Apocalypse. In America they invoked the beast of the Apocalypse against the steamship, in Europe the beast of Genesis: that was the only difference.

Learned men had rejected the steamship as impossible; the priests for their part rejected it as impious. Science had condemned it; religion damned it. Fulton was a variant of Lucifer. The simple people of the coasts and the countryside joined in this reprobation because of the uneasiness they felt at the sight of this novelty. Faced with the steamship, the religious point of view was that there was a division between water and fire, a division ordained by God. Man must not separate what God has joined; and must not join what He has disjoined. The countryfolk's point of view was: "I'm afraid of it."

No one, at that remote period, was daring enough for such an enterprise—a steamship sailing between Guernsey and Saint-Malo—except Mess Lethierry. He alone, as an independent thinker, was able to conceive the plan and, as a hardy seaman, to carry it out. The French part of his nature had the idea; the English part put it into execution.

How and when this was, we shall now explain.

III

RANTAINE

Some forty years before the events we have been relating there stood in the suburbs of Paris, near the city wall, between the Fosse-aux-Loups and the Tombe Issoire, a house of very dubious reputation. It was an isolated, tumbledown hovel, a likely setting for dark deeds. Here lived, with his wife and child, a kind of urban bandit who had once been clerk to a public prosecutor at the Châtelet and had then become a thief in real earnest, later appearing before the assize court. The name of this family was Rantaine. On a mahogany chest of drawers in their house stood two porcelain cups decorated with flower patterns; on one of them, in gilt letters, were the words A SOUVENIR OF FRIENDSHIP, on the other IN TOKEN OF ESTEEM. The child lived in this miserable home side by side with crime. Since the father and mother had once belonged to the semimiddle class, the child was learning to read; he was being properly brought up. The mother, pale-faced and almost in rags, was mechanically giving her son an "education," teaching him to spell, and interrupting his lessons from time to time to help her husband in some criminal enterprise or to prostitute herself to some passerby. While she was away *La Croix-de-Jésus*[98] lay on the table, open at the place where she had stopped; the boy sat beside it, daydreaming.

The father and mother, caught red-handed in some crime, disappeared into the night of the penal system. The child, too, disappeared.

Lethierry, in the course of his travels, encountered an adventurer like himself, helped him out of some awkward predicament or other, was of service to him, as a result felt grateful to him, took a liking to him, picked him up and brought him to Guernsey, found him quick to learn the coastal shipping trade and made him his partner. This was the Rantaine boy, now grown up.

Rantaine, like Lethierry, had a bull neck, a powerful breadth of shoulders for carrying burdens, and the loins of the Farnese Hercules. Lethierry and he had the same bearing and the same sturdy build; Rantaine was taller. Anyone who saw them from behind, walking side by side in the harbor, would take them for two brothers. From the front it was quite different. Whereas Lethierry was all openness, Rantaine was reserved and impenetrable. He was circumspect. He was an expert swordsman, played the harmonica, could snuff a candle with a bullet at twenty paces, had a tremendous punch, could recite verses from Voltaire's *Henriade* and interpret dreams. He knew Treneuil's "Les Tombeaux de Saint-Denis" by heart. He talked of having been a friend of the sultan of Calicut, "whom the Portuguese call the Zamorin." If you had been able to look through the little diary he carried you would have found among his memoranda notes such as this: "At Lyons, in a crack in the wall of one of the cells in the Saint-Joseph prison, there is a file." He spoke slowly and deliberately. He claimed to be the son of a knight of the Order of St. Louis. His linen did not match and was marked with different initials. No one was more touchy than he on a point of honor: he was ever ready to fight and kill his man. His eye had something of the watchfulness of an actress's mother.

A powerful body housing a crafty mind: that was Rantaine.

It was the beauty of his punch, applied to a *cabeza de moro*[99] at a fair, that had originally won Lethierry's heart.

No one on Guernsey knew anything of his adventures. They were varied and colorful. If men's destinies have a wardrobe, Raintaine's destiny would have worn the garb of a harlequin. He had seen the world and had seen life. He had circumnavigated the globe. He had run through a whole gamut of trades. He had been a cook in Madagascar, a breeder of birds on Sumatra, a general in Honolulu, a religious journalist in the Galapagos Islands, a poet at Oomrawuttee,[100] a freemason in Haiti. In this last capacity he had delivered a funeral oration at Grand-Gôave, of which the local newspapers have preserved this fragment: "Farewell, then, noble spirit! In the azure vault of the heavens whither you now take flight you will no doubt meet the good Abbé Léandre Crameau of Petit-Gôave. Tell him that, thanks to ten years of glorious effort, you have completed the church at L'Anse-à-Veau. Farewell, transcendent genius, model mas∴!" As can be seen, his freemason's mask did not prevent him from wearing a Catholic false nose. The former won over the men of progress, the latter the men of order. He declared himself pure-bred white, and hated the blacks; but he would undoubtedly have admired Soulouque. At Bordeaux, in 1815, he had been a Verdet. At that period the vapors of his royalism emerged from his brow like an immense white plume.[101] His whole life had been a series of eclipses—appearing, disappearing, reappearing. He was a rogue fitted with a revolving light. He knew Turkish; and instead of "guillotined" he said *neboissed*. He had been the slave of a thaleb,[102] and had learned Turkish by dint of regular beatings. His employment had been to stand at the doors of mosques in the evening and read aloud to the faithful passages of the Koran written on wooden tablets or camels' shoulder blades. He was probably a renegade.

He was capable of anything, and of worse than that.

He had a way of laughing out loud and frowning at the same time. He used to say: "In politics I esteem only those who cannot be influenced by others." He would say: "I am for decency and morality." He would say: "The pyramid must be set back on its base." His manner was cheerful and cordial rather than otherwise. The form of his mouth gave the lie to the meaning of his words. His nostrils were like those of a horse. At the corners of his eyes there were networks of wrinkles where all kinds of dark thoughts congregated. It was only there that the secrets of his physiognomy could be deciphered. His crow's-feet were like a vulture's claws. His skull was low on the crown and wide at the temples. His misshapen ear, bristling with hair, seemed to say: "Beware of speaking to the beast in this cave."

One fine day, on Guernsey, Rantaine was suddenly found to be missing.

Lethierry's partner had absconded, leaving the partnership's treasury empty. It had contained some of Rantaine's money, no doubt, but there were also fifty thousand francs of Lethierry's.

In forty years of industry and probity as a shipowner and ship-wright Lethierry had made a hundred thousand francs. Rantaine had gone off with half of it.

Although half ruined, Lethierry did not lose heart and at once set out to restore his fortunes. A stout heart can be ruined in fortune but not in courage. At that time people were beginning to talk about boats driven by steam. Lethierry conceived the idea of trying out Fulton's engine, which had been the subject of so much controversy, and linking the Norman archipelago with France by a fire-driven vessel. He staked everything on his idea and devoted his remaining wealth to the project. Six months after Rantaine's flight the astonished people of St. Sampson saw, putting out to sea from the harbor, the first steamer to sail in the Channel, belching smoke and looking like a ship on fire at sea.

This vessel, attracting general dislike and disdain and immediately christened "Lethierry's galliot," was advertised as being about to run a regular service between Guernsey and Saint-Malo.

IV

CONTINUATION OF THE HISTORY OF UTOPIA

Understandably, the project did not at first go down well. All the owners of cutters sailing between Guernsey and the French coast were loud in their outcries. They denounced this attack on the Holy Scriptures and on their monopoly. There were fulminations in some of the chapels. One reverend gentleman named Elihu called the steamship a "licentious invention." The sailing ship was declared orthodox. The devil's horns were clearly seen on the heads of cattle transported by the steamship. These protests went on for some time. Gradually, however, it was realized that the cattle arrived less tired and sold better, their meat being better; that the risks of sea travel were less for men as well as for beasts; that the crossing was shorter, cheaper, and safer; that the boat sailed at a fixed time and arrived at a fixed time; that fish, traveling faster, arrived fresher; that the surplus of the large catches so fre-

quent on Guernsey could now be sent to French markets; that the butter produced by Guernsey's fine cows traveled faster in the devil boat
than in sailing sloops and lost none of its quality, so that it was in great
demand at Dinan and Saint-Brieuc and Rennes; and that, thanks to
"Lethierry's galliot," the people of Guernsey now had safe travel, regular communications, prompt and easy passages to and fro, more traffic, wider markets for their produce, increased trade; in short, they had
to reconcile themselves to this devil boat that flew in the face of the
Bible but brought wealth to the island. One or two freethinkers even
ventured to show some degree of approval. Sieur Landoys, the registrar, thought well of the boat. This showed his impartiality, for he did
not like Lethierry. In the first place Lethierry was Mess, while Landoys
was merely Sieur. Then Landoys, though registrar in St. Peter Port,
lived in the parish of St. Sampson; and in that parish there were only
two men without prejudices, Lethierry and himself. Necessarily,
therefore, they hated one another. Two of a trade rarely agree.

Nevertheless Sieur Landoys was fair-minded enough to approve of
the steamship. Others then joined him. Gradually the thing grew; facts
are a rising tide; and in course of time, with continual and increasing
success, with the evidence of good service rendered, with the clear increase in general well-being, there came the day when everyone, with
the exception of a few wiseacres, admired "Lethierry's galliot."

It would be less admired today. This steamer of forty years ago
would make the shipbuilders of the present day smile. This marvel was
misshapen; this prodigy was a frail thing.

Our great transatlantic steamers of the present day are as far removed from Denis Papin's steam paddleboat on the Fulda in 1707 as is
the three-decker *Montebello*[103]—200 feet long by 50 wide, with a main
yard 115 feet long and a burden of three thousand tons, carrying
eleven hundred men, 120 guns, ten thousand cannonballs, and 160
rounds of grape-shot, when in action belching out thirty-three hundred pounds of iron at every broadside and when under way spreading
to the wind fifty-six hundred square meters of canvas—from the Dan-
ish dromond of the second century, discovered, laden with stone axes,
bows, and clubs, in the mud of the sea bottom at Wester Satrup and
now preserved in the town hall of Flensburg.

A space of a hundred years, from 1707 to 1807, separates Papin's
first boat from Fulton's. "Lethierry's galliot" was undoubtedly an im-

provement on these two primitive models, but it was still primitive. For all that it was a masterpiece. Every embryo conceived by science has a double aspect: as a fetus it is a monster, as the germ of something more it is a marvel.

V

THE DEVIL BOAT

"Lethierry's galliot" was not masted to make the best use of the wind. This was not a fault peculiar to her, but in accordance with the laws of naval architecture; in any event, since the vessel was driven by steam, the sails were only accessory. Besides, it makes almost no difference to a paddleboat what sails she carries. The new vessel was too short, too round, too tubby; she was too bluff and had too much beam; for shipbuilders were not yet bold enough to construct their vessels light. She had some of the disadvantages and some of the qualities of the paunch. She did not pitch much, but rolled a lot. The paddle boxes were too high. She had too much breadth of quarter for her length. The massive engines took up a lot of room, and to enable her to carry a large cargo it had been necessary to give her unusually high bulwarks, so that she had something of the same defect as the old seventy-fours, a bastard type of vessel, which had to be cut down to make it properly seaworthy and capable of fighting. Being short, she should have been able to veer quickly, since the time taken in carrying out a maneuver is related to the length of the vessel, but her weight canceled out the advantage of her shortness. Her midship frame was too broad, and this slowed her down, the resistance of the water being proportional to the greatest width below the waterline and to the square of the vessel's speed. She had a vertical prow, which would not be a fault nowadays; but in those days the invariable practice was to set the prow at an angle of forty-five degrees. All the curves of the hull were well adjusted to one another, but they were not long enough for oblique sailing, still less for lying parallel with the water displaced, which must always be thrown off to the side. In heavy weather she drew too much water, sometimes fore and sometimes aft, which showed that her center of gravity was not in the right place. The cargo not being where it ought to be because of the weight of the engines, the center of gravity often moved aft of the mainmast, and then it was necessary to depend on steam power and beware of the mainsail, for in these circumstances its effect was to cause the vessel to fall off instead of keeping her head to the wind. The best thing to do, when the ship was close to the wind, was to loose the mainsheet immediately; the wind was thus held ahead by the tack and the mainsail no longer acted as an after sail. This was a difficult maneuver. The rudder was the old-fashioned type, not the wheel-controlled rudder of our day but a bar rudder, turning on hinges fixed to the sternpost and controlled by a horizontal bar passing above the transom. Two dinghies hung from davits. The ship had four anchors—the sheet anchor, a second anchor (the working anchor), and two bower anchors. These four anchors, slung on chains, were worked, as occasion required, by the main capstan at the stern and the small capstan in the bow. At that period the pump windlass had not yet superseded the intermittent use of the handspike. Having only two bower anchors, one to starboard and one to port, she lacked the greater security of a third anchor between the two and might have some difficulty in certain winds, though she could get help in such cases from the working anchor. The buoys were of the usual type, so constructed as to carry the weight of the buoy ropes without dipping. The longboat was of serviceable size, a useful safety precaution for the vessel; it was strong enough to raise the sheet anchor. A novel feature of the ship was that she was partly rigged with chains; but this did not reduce either the ease of movement of the running rigging or the tension on the standing rigging. The masts and yards, although of secondary importance, were perfectly adequate; the top rigging, drawn taut, looked light. The ribs were solid but roughly shaped, since a steamship does not require the same delicate molding as a sailing ship. The Durande had a speed of two leagues an hour.[104] When lying to she rode well. Such as she was, "Lethierry's galliot" was a good sea boat; but she lacked the sharpness of bow to cut her way through the waves, and she could not be said to be a graceful sailer. There was a feeling that in a situation of danger, faced with a reef or a cloudburst, she would be difficult to handle. She creaked like something that had been clumsily put together. When rolling in the waves she squeaked like a new shoe.

She was mainly a freighter, and, like all ships built for commerce rather than war, was designed mainly for the stowage of cargo. She had little room for passengers. The transport of livestock made stowage difficult and awkward. In those days cattle were carried in the hold, which complicated the loading of the ship. Nowadays they are carried on the foredeck. The devil boat's paddle boxes were painted white, the hull down to the waterline red and the rest of the vessel black, in accordance with the rather ugly fashion of this century. Empty, she had a draft of seven feet; laden, of fourteen.

The engines were powerful, delivering one horsepower per three tons burden—almost the power of a tug. The paddle wheels were well placed, a little forward of the vessel's center of gravity. The engines had a maximum pressure of two atmospheres. They consumed a great deal of coal, in spite of the fact that they used the method of condensation and expansion. They had no flywheel because of the instability of their mounting, but they made up for this lack, as is still the practice in our day, by having two alternating cranks at the ends of the driving shaft, so arranged that one was always at its thrusting point when the other was at its dead point. The engines rested on a single cast-iron plate, so that even in a serious accident no battering by the waves could upset their balance and even in the event of damage to the hull the engines themselves would not be affected. To make the engines still stronger, the main connecting-rod had been set close to the cylinder, thus transferring the center of oscillation of the beam from the middle to the end. Since then oscillating cylinders have been invented that make it possible to do without connecting rods; but in those days setting the connecting rod near the cylinder was regarded as the last word in technology. The boiler was divided by partitions and had a brine pump. The paddle wheels were very large, which reduced the loss of power, and the funnel was very tall, giving a better draft; but the size of the wheels exposed them to the force of the waves and the height of the funnel exposed it to the violence of the wind. The wheels were well made, with wooden blades, iron clamps, and cast-iron hubs, and, remarkably, could be taken to pieces. There were always three paddle blades under water. The speed at the center of the blades was only a sixth greater than that of the vessel: this was the main defect of the paddle wheels. Moreover, the end of the cranks was too long, and the slide valve caused too much friction in admitting steam into the cylinder. By the standards of that time, however, the engines seemed, and indeed were, admirable.

The engines had been made in France, at the Bercy ironworks. Mess Lethierry had more or less designed them himself; the engineer who had built them according to his plans was now dead, so that they were unique and could not be replaced. The designer was still there, but the constructor had gone.

The engines had cost forty thousand francs.

Lethierry had built his ship himself on the large covered stocks beside the first Martello tower between St. Peter Port and St. Sampson. He had gone to Bremen to buy the timber for it. He had used all his skill as a shipwright in its construction, and his talent was demonstrated by the planking, with straight and even seams covered with sarangousti, an Indian mastic that is better than pitch. The sheathing had been well beaten. Lethierry had painted the lower part of the hull with a protective coat of galgal,[105] and to compensate for the roundness of the hull he had fitted a jibboom on the bowsprit, enabling him to add a false spritsail to the regular one. On the day the ship was launched he cried, "Now I'm afloat!"[106] And indeed the ship proved to be a success, as we have seen.

Either by chance or by design, the ship had been launched on the fourteenth of July, the anniversary of the taking of the Bastille. On that day Lethierry stood on the deck between the paddle wheels, gazed at the sea, and shouted to it: "It's your turn now! The people of Paris took the Bastille: now we are taking *you!*"

Lethierry's galliot sailed once a week from Guernsey to Saint-Malo, leaving on Tuesday morning and returning on Friday evening, in time for the Saturday market. She had stouter timbers than the largest sloops engaged in the coastal trade in the archipelago, and, with a cargo-carrying capacity proportionate to her size, carried as much in one voyage as the ordinary local boats did in four. As a result she brought in large profits. The reputation of a ship depends on the stowage of the cargo, and Lethierry was a skilled stevedore. When he could no longer work at sea himself, he trained up a seaman to replace him. At the end of two years the steamship was bringing in a clear 750 pounds sterling a year, or eighteen thousand francs. The Guernsey pound sterling is worth twenty-four francs, the English pound twenty-five and the Jersey pound twenty-six. These little differences are not so unimportant as they seem: the banks, at any rate, do well out of them.

VI

Lethierry's Triumph

Lethierry's galliot prospered, and Mess Lethierry saw the moment approaching when he would be called Monsieur. On Guernsey men do not automatically become Monsieur: there is a whole ladder to be climbed first. The first rung is the name by itself, let us say Pierre; then, on the second rung, Neighbor Pierre; on the third rung, Father Pierre; on the fourth, Sieur Pierre; on the fifth, Mess Pierre; then, at the top of the ladder, Monsieur Pierre.

This ladder, starting from the ground, continues into the empyrean. The whole of hierarchical England comes into it at their appropriate levels. These are the various rungs, increasingly glorious as they go up: above the gentleman (the equivalent of Monsieur) is the esquire, above the esquire the knight (with the title *Sir* for life); then, still higher up, the baronet (with the hereditary title *Sir*), then the lord (laird in Scotland), then the baron, then the viscount, then the earl (count in France, jail in Norway), then the marquis, then the duke, then the peer, then the prince of the blood royal, then the king. The ladder ascends from the common people to the middle classes, from the middle classes to the baronetage, from the baronetage to the peerage, from the peerage to royalty.

Thanks to his successful enterprise, thanks to steam, thanks to his engines, thanks to the devil boat, Mess Lethierry had become *someone.* In order to build his boat he had had to borrow; he had incurred debts in Bremen, he had incurred debts in Saint-Malo; but every year he paid off some of the money he owed.

He had also bought on credit a pretty stone-built house, entirely new, just at the entrance to St. Sampson harbor, with the sea in front and a garden behind. At one corner of the house was its name, Les Bravées. The house, whose front formed part of the harbor wall, was notable for a double range of windows: one on the north side, looking into a flower-filled garden, and one on the south, looking onto the ocean. The house thus had two fronts, one facing onto storms, the other onto roses.

These two fronts seemed made for the two occupants of the house, Mess Lethierry and Miss Déruchette.

The house was popular in St. Sampson, for Mess Lethierry had at length become popular. This popularity was due partly to his good nature, his tenacity, and his courage, partly to the number of men he had rescued, a great deal to his success, and also because he had given St. Sampson the privilege of being the port of departure and arrival of the steamship. St. Peter Port, the capital, had wanted that honor for itself, but Lethierry had held to St. Sampson. It was his native town. "That was where I was pitched into the water," he used to say. This brought him great local popularity. His position as a house owner paying land tax made him what is called on Guernsey an *habitant*. He had been appointed douzenier. This poor seaman had risen to the fifth of the six levels in the Guernsey social scale; he was Mess Lethierry; he was within reach of the dignity of Monsieur; and who could say that he might not rise even further? Who could say that they might not one day find in the Guernsey almanac, in the section headed "Gentry and Nobility," the proud and unheard-of entry "Lethierry, Esq."?

But Mess Lethierry disdained, or rather never thought of, the vanity of such distinctions. He felt he was useful, and that gave him pleasure. Being popular meant less to him than being necessary. He had, as we have said, only two objects of affection, and consequently had only two ambitions—Durande and Déruchette.

At any rate he had taken a ticket in the lottery of the sea, and he had won the first prize.

The first prize was the Durande steaming to and fro.

VII

THE SAME GODFATHER AND THE SAME PATRON SAINT

After creating his steamship Lethierry had christened it. He had called it the Durande. Henceforth we shall call it by no other name. We may be permitted also, in spite of typographical practice, not to italicize the name *Durande,* in line with the notions of Mess Lethierry, for whom the Durande was almost a living person.

Durande and Déruchette are the same name. Déruchette is the diminutive—a diminutive that is very common in the west of France.

In country areas the saints frequently bear names with all their diminutives and all their augmentatives. You might think there were several different persons when in fact there is only one. These multiple identities of patron saints under different names are by no means rare. Lise, Lisette, Lisa, Élisa, Isabelle, Lisbeth, Betsy are all Elizabeth. It is probable that Mahout, Maclou, Malo, and Magloire are the same saint: this, however, we are less sure about.

Saint Durande is a saint of the Angoumois and Charente. Is she an authentic saint? We leave that to the Bollandists. Whether authentic or not, she has chapels dedicated to her.

When he was a young seaman at Rochefort, in Charente, Lethierry had made the acquaintance of this saint, probably in the person of some pretty local girl, perhaps the grisette with the fine nails. He remembered it sufficiently well to give this name to the two things he loved—Durande to the ship, Déruchette to the girl.

He was father of one and uncle of the other.

Déruchette was the daughter of a brother of his. She had lost her father and mother, and he had adopted her, replacing both the father and the mother.

Déruchette was not only his niece: she was his goddaughter. It was he who had held her in his arms at her christening and he who had chosen her patron saint, Durande, and her name, Déruchette.

Déruchette, as we have said, had been born in St. Peter Port. Her name was entered in the parish register under the date of her birth.

While the niece was small and the uncle poor, no one paid any particular attention to the name Déruchette; but when the child became a young lady and the seaman a gentleman, the name struck people as odd. They were astonished at Lethierry's choice. They asked him: "Why Déruchette?" He replied: "It's a name like any other." Several attempts were made to change her name. He would have none of it. One day a fine lady of St. Sampson's high society, the wife of a well-to-do blacksmith who no longer worked, said to Mess Lethierry: "In the future I shall call your girl Nancy." "Why not Lons-le-Saulnier?" he retorted.[107] The fine lady did not give up, and on the following day returned to the attack, saying: "We really cannot have Déruchette. I have found a pretty name for her—Marianne." "Certainly it is a pretty name," rejoined Mess Lethierry, "but it is made up of two ugly creatures, a husband and a donkey."[108] So he held to the name Déruchette.

It would be wrong to conclude from this last remark that he did not want to see his niece married. He wanted to have her married, but in the way he wanted. He wanted her to have a husband like himself, a hard worker whose wife would have little to do. He liked black hands in a man and white hands in a woman. To prevent Déruchette from spoiling her pretty hands, he had brought her up to be a young lady. He had given her a music teacher, a piano, a small library, and a work-basket with needles and thread. She liked reading better than sewing, and playing the piano better than reading. This was what Mess Lethierry wanted. To be charming was all that he expected of her. He had brought her up to be a flower rather than a woman. Anyone who is familiar with seamen will understand this. Rough characters like delicate ones. For the niece to realize the uncle's ideal, she had to be rich. This was Mess Lethierry's firm intention. His great maritime machine was working toward that end. He had made it Durande's mission to provide a dowry for Déruchette.

VIII

"BONNY DUNDEE"

Déruchette had the prettiest room in Les Bravées, with two windows, figured mahogany furniture, a bed with curtains in a white-and-green-check pattern, and a view of the garden and the high hill on which stands Vale Castle. On the far side of the hill was the Bû de la Rue.

In her room Déruchette had her music and her piano. She accompanied herself on the piano when she sang her favorite song, the melancholy Scottish air "Bonny Dundee." All the gloom of evening is in the song, all the brightness of dawn was in her voice, making a pleasantly surprising contrast. People said: "Miss Déruchette is at her piano," and as they passed by at the foot of the hill they would sometimes stop outside the garden wall to listen to this voice of such freshness singing a song of such sadness.

Déruchette was gaiety itself as she flitted about the house, creating a perpetual spring. She was beautiful, but more pretty than beautiful, and more sweet than pretty. She reminded the good old pilots who were Mess Lethierry's friends of the princess in a soldiers' and sailors' song—

Qui était si belle qu'elle passait pour telle
Dans le régiment.

Mess Lethierry used to say: "She has a cable of hair."

She had been a charmer since her earliest days. There had been concern for many years about her nose, but the little girl—probably determined to be pretty—had held on her course. The process of growth had done her no harm; her nose had become neither too long or too short; and as she grew up she remained charming.

She always referred to her uncle as "my father."

Lethierry allowed her to develop some skill as a gardener and even as a housewife. She personally watered her beds of hollyhocks, purple mulleins, perennial phlox, and scarlet herb bennet; she grew pink hawk's-beard and pink oxalis; and took full advantage of the Guernsey climate, so hospitable to flowers. Like everyone else, she had aloes growing in the open, and—what is much more difficult—she successfully grew Nepalese cranesbill. Her little kitchen garden was well organized; she had spinach in succession to radishes and peas in succession to spinach; she sowed Dutch cauliflowers and brussels sprouts, planting them out in July, turnips for August, curly endive for September, round parsnips for the autumn, and rampion for the winter. Mess Lethierry did not interfere with these activities, provided that she did not do too much digging or raking and, above all, that she did not apply the fertilizer herself. He had given her two maids, one called Grace and the other Douce—common Guernsey names. They worked in the garden as well as in the house, and were allowed to have red hands.

Mess Lethierry's bedroom was a small room looking onto the harbor and adjoining the large low room on the ground floor in which were the main doorway of the house and its various staircases. In this room were his hammock, his chronometer, and his pipe. There were also a table and a chair. The ceiling, with exposed beams, was whitewashed, as were the four walls. Nailed to the wall on the right of the door was the Archipelago of the Channel, a handsome chart bearing the inscription W. FADEN, 5 CHARING CROSS. GEOGRAPHER TO HIS MAJESTY. To the left of the door, also suspended on nails, was one of those large cotton handkerchiefs displaying in color the naval signals used all over the globe, with the flags of France, Russia, Spain, and the

United States in the four corners and the Union Jack of England in the center.

Douce and Grace were two quite ordinary girls, in the best sense of the term. Douce was not ill natured and Grace was not plain. The dangerous names they bore had not brought them to any harm. Douce was not married but had a "gallant": the term is used in the Channel Islands, and the thing exists. The two girls provided what might be called a Creole type of service, with a slowness characteristic of Norman domesticity in the archipelago. Grace, a pretty and coquettish girl, kept scanning the horizon with the watchfulness of a cat: like Douce, she had a gallant, but also, it was said, a husband, a seaman whose return she dreaded. But that is none of our business. The difference between Grace and Douce was that, in a house less austere and less innocent, Douce would have remained a servant and Grace would have become a soubrette. Grace's potential talents were lost on an ingenuous girl like Déruchette. In any case, the love affairs of Douce and Grace were kept secret. Mess Lethierry knew nothing of them, and no word of them had reached Déruchette.

The room on the ground floor, a spacious hall with a fireplace and benches and tables around the walls, had been the meeting place in the last century of a conventicle of French Protestant refugees. The only form of decoration on the bare stone walls was a frame of black wood displaying a parchment notice recording the achievements of Bénigne Bossuet, bishop of Meaux, which some poor Protestant refugees from the diocese of this ecclesiastical eagle, who had been persecuted by him after the revocation of the Edict of Nantes and had found refuge on Guernsey, had hung up to bear witness to their trials. On this you might read, if you could decipher the awkward writing and the yellowed ink, the following little known facts: "October 29, 1685, demolition of the Protestant churches of Morcef and Nanteuil on the orders of the king at the request of the bishop of Meaux."—"April 2, 1686, arrest of the Cochards, father and son, on account of their religion, at the request of the bishop of Meaux. Released, the Cochards having abjured their faith."—"October 28, 1699, the bishop of Meaux sends Monsieur de Pontchartrain a memorandum advising him that it would be necessary to consign the Demoiselles de Chalandes and de Neuville, who are of the reformed religion, to the house of the New Catholics in Paris."—"July 7, 1703, execution of the king's order, at the request of the bishop of Meaux, to have the individual named Baudouin and his wife, bad Catholics of Fublaine, confined in a hospital." At the far end of the room, near the door into Mess Lethierry's bedroom, was a small wooden structure that had been the Huguenot pulpit and with the addition of a grille with an opening in it had become the office of the steamship company; that is, the office of the Durande, manned by Mess Lethierry in person. On the old oak reading-desk, replacing the Bible, was a ledger with pages headed "Debit" and "Credit."

IX

THE MAN WHO HAD SEEN THROUGH RANTAINE

As long as Mess Lethierry had been able to sail, he had commanded the Durande and had no other pilot or captain than himself. But, as we have said, a time had come when he had to find someone to replace him. He had chosen Sieur Clubin of Torteval, a man of few words who was reputed along the whole coast for his absolute integrity. He had now become Lethierry's alter ego and deputy.

Although Sieur Clubin looked more like a lawyer than a mariner, he was an excellent and very competent seaman. He had all the skills necessary to deal with the risks of seafaring and come safely through. He was a good stevedore, a meticulous topman, a careful and knowledgeable boatswain, a sturdy helmsman, a skilled pilot, and a bold captain. He was prudent, and sometimes carried prudence so far as to be daring, which is a great quality at sea. His fear of what was probable was tempered by his instinct for what was possible. He was one of those seamen who face danger in a proportion known to them and are able to wrest success from any adventure. He had all the certainty that the sea allows to any man.

On top of all this Sieur Clubin was a renowned swimmer; he was one of those men who are at home in the gymnastics of the waves, who can stay in the water as long as they wish, and who, on Jersey, set out from the Havre des Pas, round the Collette, continue past the Hermitage Rock and Elizabeth Castle, and return to their starting point after a two-hour swim. He came from Torteval, and was reputed to have swum several times through the dangerous waters between the Hanois and Pleinmont Point.

One of the things that had most strongly recommended him to Mess Lethierry was that, knowing or discovering what Rantaine was like, he had warned Lethierry about his dishonesty, saying, "Rantaine will rob you." And so it had turned out. More than once, though admittedly in matters of no great importance, Mess Lethierry had tested Sieur Clubin's own scrupulous honesty, and he now relied on him in his retirement. He used to say: "An honest man should be given your full confidence."

X

A MARINER'S TALES

Mess Lethierry always wore his seagoing clothes—he would have been uncomfortable in anything else—and preferred his seaman's pea jacket to his pilot's jacket. Déruchette wrinkled her little nose at this. Nothing is more charming than the face a pretty woman makes when she is displeased. She would scold him, laughing. "Father," she would say, "Ugh! You smell of tar," and she would give him a little tap on his broad shoulder.

This good old hero of the sea had brought back some surprising tales from his voyages. In Madagascar he had seen birds' feathers so large that only three were needed to roof a house. In India he had seen sorrel growing nine feet high. In New Holland he had seen flocks of turkeys and geese rounded up and guarded by a sheepdog in the form of a bird known as the agami. He had seen elephant graveyards. In Africa he had seen gorillas—half men, half tigers—seven feet tall. He knew the ways of all kinds of monkeys, from the wild macaque, which he called *macaco bravo,* to the howling macaque, which he called *macaco barbado.* In Chile he had seen a female monkey softening the hearts of her hunters by showing them her young one. In California he had seen the hollow trunk of a fallen tree through which a horseman could ride a distance of 150 paces. In Morocco he had seen Mozabites and Biskris fighting with clubs and iron bars—the Biskris because they had been called *kelb,* which means dogs, and the Mozabites because they had been called *khamsi*, which means people of the fifth sect. In China he had seen a pirate named Chanhthong-quan-larh-Quoi being cut into pieces for murdering the âp of a village. At Thu-dan-mot he had seen a lion carrying off an old woman from the middle of the town market. He had watched the arrival in Saigon of the great serpent from Canton to take part in the celebrations of the festival of Quan-nam, goddess of seamen, in the Cho-len pagoda. Among the Moi he had seen the great Quan-Sû. In Rio de Janeiro he had seen Brazilian ladies putting little balls of gauze in their hair in the evening, each containing a *vagalumes,* a beautiful firefly, so as to give them a headdress of stars. In Uruguay he had fought with anthills, and in Paraguay with bird spiders, hairy creatures the size of a child's head, covering a diameter of a third of an ell with their feet, and attacking men by firing bristles that pierce their skin like arrows and raise blisters. On the river Arinos, a tributary of the Tocantins, in the virgin forests to the north of Diamantina, he had encountered the fearsome bat men, the *murdagos,* who are born with white hair and red eyes, who live in the gloom of the woods, sleeping by day, waking at night, and fishing and hunting in the darkness, seeing better when there is no moon. Near Beirut, in the encampment of an expedition in which he had taken part, after a rain gauge was stolen from a tent, a witch doctor wearing only a few strips of leather, and looking like a man clad in his braces, had rung a bell attached to a horn with such vigor that a hyena had brought back the rain gauge. The hyena had been the thief. These true stories were so like romantic tales that they amused Déruchette.

The figurehead of the Durande was the link between the ship and the girl. In the Channel Islands the figurehead is called the *poupée,* the doll. Hence the local expression that means "being at sea," *être entre poupe et poupée* ("being between the poop and the puppet").

The Durande's figurehead was particularly dear to Mess Lethierry. He had had it made by a carpenter to resemble Déruchette. The resemblance was achieved with strokes of an ax. It was a block of wood trying to be a pretty girl.

Mess Lethierry saw this slightly misshapen block of wood with the eyes of illusion. He looked on it with the reverence of a believer. He sincerely believed that it was a perfect likeness of Déruchette—in much the same way as a dogma resembles a truth and an idol resembles God.

Mess Lethierry had two great joys during the week, one on Tuesday and the other on Friday. The first joy was seeing the Durande leaving harbor; the second, seeing it return. He leaned on his windowsill, looked on what he had created, and was content. It was something like the verse in Genesis, *Et vidit quod esset bonum.*[109]

On Friday the sight of Mess Lethierry at his window was as good as a signal. When people saw him lighting his pipe at the window of Les Bravées they said, "Ah! The steamship is on the horizon." One puff of smoke heralded another.

Entering the harbor, the Durande tied up to a large ring in the basement of Les Bravées, under Mess Lethierry's windows. On the nights after the vessel's return Lethierry slept soundly in his hammock, knowing that on one side Déruchette was asleep and on the other Durande was moored.

The Durande's mooring was close to the harbor bell. Here, too, in front of the entrance to Les Bravées, was a short stretch of quay.

This quay, Les Bravées, the house and garden, the lanes lined by hedges, and most of the surrounding houses are no longer there. The working of Guernsey's granite has led to the sale of the land in this area, and the whole site is now occupied by stone breakers' yards.

XI

CONSIDERATION OF POSSIBLE HUSBANDS

Déruchette was growing up, but was showing no sign of marrying.

Mess Lethierry, in making her a girl with white hands, had made her difficult to please. Educations of that kind later turn against you.

But he himself was even more difficult to please. The husband he wanted for her was also to some extent to be a husband for Durande. He would have liked to provide for both his daughters at once. He would have liked the master of the one to be the pilot of the other. What is a husband? He is the captain in charge of a voyage. Why should the girl and the boat not have the same master? A household is subject to the tides. If you can manage a boat you can manage a woman. They are both ruled by the moon and the wind. Sieur Clubin, being only fifteen years younger than Mess Lethierry, could be no more than a temporary master for Durande: what was wanted was a young pilot, a longtime master, a true successor to the founder, the inventor, the creator. The pilot finally chosen to be the pilot of Durande would be like a son-in-law for Mess Lethierry. Why should the two sons-in-law not be combined? He cherished this idea. He too saw a bridegroom in his dreams. A sturdy topman, rough and weather-beaten, an athlete of the sea: this was his ideal. This was not quite Déruchette's ideal. She had a rosier dream.

At any rate the uncle and the niece seemed to agree on one thing: that there was no hurry. When Déruchette had been seen to become a probable heiress there was no lack of suitors. But eager contenders of this kind are not always of good quality. Mess Lethierry realized this. He would mutter, "A girl of gold, a lover of copper." And he dismissed the suitors. He was prepared to wait; and so was she.

Strangely enough, he thought little of the aristocracy. In this respect Mess Lethierry was an unlikely Englishman. It may be difficult to believe, but he had actually turned down offers from a Ganduel of Jersey and a Bugnet-Nicolin of Sark. Some have even claimed—but we doubt whether it can be true—that he had not accepted an approach from the aristocracy of Alderney and had rejected proposals from a scion of the Édou family, which is clearly descended from Edward the Confessor.[110]

XII

AN ANOMALY IN LETHIERRY'S CHARACTER

Mess Lethierry had one fault; a serious one. He hated, not someone, but *something*—the priesthood. One day, reading—for he was a reader—Voltaire—for he read Voltaire—the words, "Priests are cats," he put down the book and could be heard muttering under his breath, "Then I'm a dog."

It must be remembered that while he was creating the local devil boat he had suffered lively opposition and mild persecution from priests, Lutheran and Calvinist as well as Catholic. To be a revolutionary in seafaring matters, to try to bring progress to the Norman archipelago, to impose on the poor little island of Guernsey the disturbance of a new invention: this—we are obliged to admit—was an act of damnable rashness. And it had, more or less, been damned. It should not be forgotten that we are here talking of the old clergy, very different from the clergy of the present day, who in almost all the local churches have a liberal attitude to progress. Every possible obstacle had been put in Lethierry's way, and he had encountered the great mass of objections that can be contained in preachings and sermons. He was hated by the men of the cloth, and hated them in return. Their hatred served as a mitigating circumstance in favor of his.

But it must be said that his aversion to priests was idiosyncratic. He did not need to be hated by them to hate them. As he said, he was the dog to these cats. He was against them as an idea, and—the most invincible ground—by instinct. He felt their hidden claws, and showed his teeth. Rather wildly, it must be admitted, and not always with reason. It is wrong not to make distinctions. Hatred should not be applied en bloc. Lethierry would not have agreed with the Savoyard vicar.[111] It is doubtful whether he would have admitted that there were any good priests. His position as a philosopher[112] brought a diminution of wisdom. Tolerant people are sometimes intolerant, as moderate people are sometimes violent in their opinions. But Lethierry was too good-natured to be a good hater. He thrust his enemies to one side rather than attacking them. He kept the churchmen at a distance. They had done him harm; he was content not to wish them any good. The difference between their hatred and his was that theirs was animosity, while his was antipathy.

Guernsey, small island as it is, has room for two religions. It accommodates both the Catholic religion and the Protestant religion. It does not, however, house both religions in the same church: each form of worship has its own church or chapel. In Germany, for example in Heidelberg, they make less fuss: they cut the church in two, one half for St. Peter and the other for Calvin, with a partition between them to prevent any quarrels. They have equal shares: three altars for the Catholics and three altars for the Huguenots; and since they have services at the same times one bell rings for both, summoning worshipers to God and the Devil at the same time. It is certainly a simplification.

German phlegm can tolerate a proximity of this kind. But on Guernsey each religion has its own home. There is the orthodox parish church and the heretical one. Everyone can choose for himself. Neither one nor the other: that had been Mess Lethierry's choice.

This seaman, this worker, this philosopher, this self-made man was simple in appearance but at bottom was not at all simple. He had his contradictions and his stubbornnesses. On priests he was unshakeable. He could have given points to Montlosier.[113]

On occasion he made jokes that were quite out of place, and he had some odd turns of phrase that nevertheless had some meaning. He called going to confession "combing one's conscience." The little learning he had—very little indeed, gleaned from books he had picked up between two squalls at sea—was subject to spelling mistakes. He also mispronounced words, not always unintentionally. When Waterloo brought peace between Louis XVIII's France and Wellington's England Mess Lethierry remarked, "Bourmont was the link between the two camps." Once he spelled *papauté* (papacy) *pape ôté* (pope removed). We do not think it was done on purpose.[114]

But Lethierry's hostility to the papacy did not win him the favor of the Anglicans. He was no more popular with the Protestant rectors than with the Catholic curés. Faced with the gravest of dogmas, his irreligion burst out almost without restraint. Chance having led him to hear a sermon on hell by the Reverend Jaquemin Hérode—a magnificent sermon filled from beginning to end with texts from Holy Writ proving the eternal punishments, the torments, the tortures, the damnations, the inexorable chastisements, the burnings without end, the inextinguishable curses, the wrath of the Almighty, the heavenly furies, the divine vengeances that inevitably awaited the wicked—he was heard to say quietly, when leaving with another member of the congregation: "Do you know, I've got an odd idea. I believe that God is merciful."

This leavening of atheism came to him from his stay in France.

Although a Guernsey man of fairly pure-bred stock, he was known on the island as the "Frenchman" because of his "improper" notions. He made no secret of them, and he was full of subversive ideas. His determination to build his steamship, his devil boat, was proof enough of that. He would say, "I was suckled on 1789." That is not a good kind of milk.

Of course he made blunders. It is very difficult to avoid error in a small society. For a quiet life in France you have to "keep up appearances"; in England you have to be "respectable." Being respectable involves a series of observances, from keeping the Sabbath holy to tying

your necktie properly. "Not to have the finger pointed at you" is another harsh law. To have the finger pointed at you is the diminutive
form of anathema. Small towns—hotbeds of gossip—excel in this type
of malignity, which, isolating its victims, is like an ecclesiastical malediction seen through the wrong end of a spyglass. The most valiant are
afraid of this *Raca*.[115] They will stand firm in the face of grapeshot, they
will stand firm in a hurricane, but they will retreat when confronted by
Mrs. Grundy. Mess Lethierry was tenacious rather than logical; but
under such pressure as this even his tenacity gave way. To use another
phrase laden with hidden and sometimes shameful concessions, he
"watered his wine." He held aloof from the clergy but did not completely close his door to them. On official occasions and at the regular
times for pastoral visits he received with adequate courtesy either the
Lutheran minister or the Popish chaplain. Very occasionally he would
accompany Déruchette to the Anglican parish church, which she attended, as we have seen, only on the four great festivals of the year.

But these compromises, which cost him a considerable effort, annoyed him, and, instead of making him more favorably disposed toward the clergy, stiffened his internal resistance. He relieved his
feelings by increased mockery. This man who was entirely without bitterness had harsh feelings only in this quarter. There was no curing
him of this.

In short, that was the way he was, and nothing could be done
about it.

He disliked all clergymen. He had preserved the irreverence of the
French Revolution. He made little distinction between different forms
of worship. He did not even appreciate the great progress that had
been made—the disbelief in the real presence. His shortsightedness in
these matters went so far as to prevent him from seeing any difference
between a minister and an abbé. He made no difference between a reverend doctor and a reverend father. He would say, "Wesley is no better
than Loyola." If he saw a Protestant clergyman walking with his wife
he would turn aside. "A married priest!" he would say, in the mocking
tone in which these words were spoken in France at that period. He
was fond of telling how, on his last visit to England, he had seen the
"bishopess of London." This kind of union roused him to anger.
"Gown does not marry gown!" he would say. To him the priesthood
was like a third sex. "Neither a man nor a woman: a priest!" he might

have said. Regardless of good taste, he applied the same disdainful epithets to both the Anglican and the Popish clergy, lumping them together in the same phraseology; and he did not take the trouble, when talking of either Catholic or Lutheran priests, to vary the military-style versions of the terms used at that period. He used to say to Déruchette, "Marry whom you please, so long as it isn't a parson!"

XIII

INSOUCIANCE—AN ADDITIONAL CHARM

A word once spoken, Lethierry remembered it; a word once spoken, Déruchette forgot it. That was the difference between the uncle and the niece.

Déruchette, brought up as we have seen, had become accustomed to having little sense of responsibility. It must be observed that there are latent dangers in an education that has been too much taken for granted. It is perhaps a mistake to want to make your child happy too soon.

Déruchette thought that as long as she was happy all was well. She felt, too, that her uncle was pleased to see her pleased. Her ideas were much the same as Mess Lethierry's. Her religious beliefs were satisfied with going to the parish church four times a year. We have already seen her dressed for the Christmas service. She knew nothing at all of life. She had all that was required to fall, some day, madly in love. In the meantime she was lightheartedly happy.

She sang when the fancy took her, chattered when the fancy took her, lived for the moment, threw out some remark and then passed on her way, did something or other and then ran off, was charming. She enjoyed, too, all the freedom of English life. In England children go out on their own, girls are their own mistresses, young people are given a free hand. Such is the English way of life. Later on these free young girls become slave wives. We take these two words in their best sense: free as they grow up, then slaves to duty.

Déruchette woke up each morning without a thought of what she had been doing on the previous day. You would embarrass her considerably if you asked her what she had done last week. Yet in spite of all this there were more troubled moments when she had a mysterious sense of disquiet, a feeling that something of the darker side of life was passing over her gaiety and her joy. Such clear blue skies have their clouds. But the clouds soon passed away. She would cast the feeling off with a laugh, not knowing why she had been sad or why she was happy again. Everything was a game to her. She teased passersby with her mischief. She played tricks on boys. If she had encountered the Devil she would have had no pity on him but would have played some prank on him. She was pretty, but was so innocent that she took undue advantage of her prettiness. She smiled as a kitten scratches. So much the worse for the person scratched: she thought no more of the matter. Yesterday did not exist for her; she lived in the fullness of today. That is what it is to be too happy. In Déruchette recollection faded as snow melts in the sun.

BOOK IV

THE BAGPIPES

I

THE FIRST RED GLEAMS OF DAWN, OR OF A FIRE

Gilliatt had never spoken to Déruchette. He knew her, having seen her at a distance, as we know the morning star.

At the time Déruchette met Gilliatt on the road from St. Peter Port to the Vale and wrote his name on the snow she was sixteen. Only the day before Mess Lethierry had said to her: "No more childish tricks: you are a big girl now."

The name "Gilliatt" that the girl had written had sunk into unplumbed depths.

What were women for Gilliatt? He himself could not have said. When he met one she was afraid of him, and he was afraid of her. He never spoke to a woman except in extreme emergency. He had never been the "gallant" of any country girl. When he was walking by himself along a road and saw a woman coming toward him he would jump over the wall into a field or disappear into a clump of scrub and make off. He avoided even old women.

He had once in his life seen a Parisienne. The sight of a Parisienne was an extraordinary event on Guernsey at that distant period. And Gilliatt had heard this Parisienne relating her troubles in these words: "What a nuisance! I have just had some drops of rain on my bonnet; it is apricot, and that's a color that is easily spoiled." Later, in the pages of a book, he found an old fashion plate representing "a lady of the

Chaussée d'Antin"[116] in all her finery and put it up on his wall as a reminder of the apparition. On summer evenings he would hide behind the rocks in the creek of Houmet Paradis to watch the country girls bathing in the sea in their slips. One day, on the far side of a hedge, he had seen the witch of Torteval putting on her garter. He was probably a virgin.

On that Christmas morning when he had met Déruchette and she had written his name and gone on her way laughing, he had returned home, having forgotten why he had gone out. That night he did not sleep. He thought of all sorts of things—that it would be a good idea to grow black radishes in his garden: the exposure was right—that he hadn't noticed the Sark boat passing: had something happened to it?—that he had seen white stonecrop in flower, unusually early. He had never known exactly what relation the old woman who had died was to him; now he said to himself that she must certainly have been his mother and thought of her with redoubled tenderness. He thought of the bride's trousseau in the leather trunk. He thought that one of these days the Reverend Jaquemin Hérode would probably be appointed dean of St. Peter Port and suffragan to the bishop, and that the living of St. Sampson would become vacant. He thought that the day after Christmas would be the twenty-seventh day of the moon, and that consequently high water would be at twenty-one minutes past three, half-tide on the ebb at fifteen minutes past seven, low water at twenty-seven minutes to ten, and half-tide on the flood at twenty-one minutes to one. He recalled in exact detail the costume of the highlander who had sold him his bagpipes: his cap with its thistle, his claymore, his close-fitting jacket with its short, square tails, his kilt or philabeg with its sporran and sneeshing-mull, his kilt pin set with a Scottish gemstone, his sash and belt, his sword and dirk, and his skean dhu, a black knife with a black hilt decorated with two cairngorms; his bare knees, his stockings, his checked gaiters, and his buckled shoes. This equipment became a specter that pursued him, threw him into a fever, and lulled him to sleep. When he awoke it was broad daylight, and his first thought was of Déruchette.

The following night he slept, but all night he saw the Scottish soldier in his dreams. While still half asleep he said to himself that the Court of Chief Pleas due after Christmas would hold its sitting on January 21. He also dreamed of the old rector, Jaquemin Hérode. When he awoke he thought of Déruchette, and was very angry with her. He wished that he were a boy again so that he could throw stones at her windows.

Then he thought that if he were a boy he would have his mother, and he began to cry.

He thought of going away for three months to Chousey or the Minquiers. But he did not go.

He kept away from the road from St. Peter Port to the Vale. He imagined that his name, Gilliatt, was still traced on the ground there and that everyone who passed that way would be looking at it.

II

GRADUAL ENTRY INTO THE UNKNOWN

But he did see Les Bravées every day. He did not do it deliberately, but he did go in that direction. It so happened that his business always took him along the path that skirted the wall of Déruchette's garden.

One morning, as he was walking that way, he heard a market woman coming from Les Bravées saying to another, "Miss Lethierry likes sea kale." Thereupon he dug a trench in his garden at the Bû de la Rue to grow sea kale—a kind of cabbage with the taste of asparagus.

The garden wall at Les Bravées was quite low and could easily be stepped over. The thought of stepping over it would have appalled him; but there was nothing to prevent him, or anyone else who was passing, from hearing people speaking in the house or in the garden.

He did not listen on purpose, but he heard. One day he heard the two maids, Douce and Grace, having an argument. It was a sound within the house. The quarrel remained in his ear like music.

Another time he heard a voice that was not like the others and must, he thought, be Déruchette's. He made off at once. But the words spoken by the voice remained graven in his memory. He kept repeating them to himself. The words were: "Would you please give me the broom?"

By degrees he became bolder. He ventured to stop by the garden wall. It happened one day that Déruchette, who could not be seen from outside, although her window was open, was sitting at her piano, singing. The song was her favorite "Bonny Dundee." He became very pale, but still found the strength to stay and listen.

Spring came, and one day Gilliatt had a vision; the heavens opened. He saw Déruchette watering her lettuces.

Soon he went further than merely stopping. He observed her habits, noted the timetable of her day, and waited for her to appear—always taking great care not to show himself.

Gradually, as the flowerbeds filled with roses and were haunted by butterflies, he became accustomed to seeing Déruchette going to and fro in the garden—staying hidden behind the wall, seen by no one, for hours at a time, motionless and silent, holding his breath. You become accustomed to taking poison.

From his hiding place he frequently heard Déruchette talking to Mess Lethierry in a densely grown arbor in which there was a garden seat. He could hear what they said quite distinctly.

What a long way he had come! He had now reached the stage of watching out for her and eavesdropping on her. Alas! The human heart is a practiced spy.

He could see another garden seat, quite close, on the edge of a path, on which Déruchette sometimes came to sit.

From watching Déruchette pick and smell her flowers he had divined her taste in perfumes. Her favorite scent was that of convolvulus, followed by pinks, honeysuckle, and jasmine. Roses came only in fifth place. She looked at lilies but did not smell them.

On the basis of this choice of perfumes Gilliatt built up a picture of her in his mind. With each scent he associated a particular perfection.

The mere idea of speaking to Déruchette made his hair stand on end.

An old huckster woman whose wandering trade brought her from time to time to the lane skirting the garden of Les Bravées had become aware, in some vague way, of Gilliatt's assiduity in visiting the garden wall and his devotion to this deserted area. Did she connect the presence of this man outside the wall with the possibility that there might be a woman behind the wall? Did she discern that vague invisible thread? Had she, in her decrepitude and poverty, remained young enough to remember something of older and happier days; and, in her winter and her night, did she still remember what the dawn was like? We cannot tell, but apparently on one occasion, passing close to Gilliatt while he was at his post, she directed toward him as much of a smile as she was still capable of and mumbled between her gums: "It's getting warmer!"

Gilliatt heard what she said and was struck by it. He murmured, with an internal question mark: "It's getting warmer? What does the old woman mean?" He repeated her words mechanically all day, but still did not understand them.

One evening when he was at his window in the Bû de la Rue five or six girls from L'Ancresse came to bathe in the Houmet creek. They played about in the water, very innocently, only a hundred paces away. He slammed his window shut. He found that a naked woman repelled him.

III

AN ECHO TO "BONNY DUNDEE"

Gilliatt spent almost the whole of that summer in a spot behind the garden of Les Bravées, at an angle of the wall overgrown with holly and ivy and covered with nettles, with a tall wild mallow and a large mullein growing in the granite rock. He sat there deep in thought— thoughts to which he could not give expression. The lizards had become accustomed to him and sunned themselves amid the same stones. The summer was luminous and caressing.

Overhead, clouds passed to and fro. Gilliatt was sitting on the grass. The air was full of the sound of birds. Putting both hands to his forehead, he wondered: why had she written his name in the snow? Out at sea the wind was gusting violently. Occasionally, in the distant quarry of La Vaudue, there was a sudden blare of the quarrymen's horn, warning passersby that blasting was imminent and they should keep clear. St. Sampson harbor was not visible, but the tips of masts could be seen above the trees. A few seagulls flew around. Gilliatt had heard his mother say that women could be in love with men; that happened sometimes. He thought to himself, Now I understand: Déruchette loves me. He felt profoundly sad. He said to himself, But she, too, is thinking of me; that is good. He thought that Déruchette was rich and he was poor. He thought that the steamship was a horrible invention. He could not remember which day of the month it was. Absentmindedly, he watched the large black bumblebees with their yellow rumps and short wings, buzzing as they made their way into crevices in the walls.

One evening when Déruchette was going to bed she went to the window to close it. It was a dark night. Suddenly her ear was caught by a sound. Out in the deep shadows there was music. Someone—probably on the slopes of the hill, or under the towers of Vale Castle, or perhaps even farther away—was playing a tune on some instrument. Déruchette recognized her favorite melody, "Bonny Dundee," played on bagpipes. She could make nothing of it. After this, the same tune was played from time to time, always at the same hour, particularly on very dark nights.

Déruchette did not like it much.

IV

> For uncle and tutor, men severe and upright,
> A serenade is mere noise in the night.
>
> (OLD COMEDY)

Four years went by.

Déruchette was approaching her twenty-first birthday and was still not married.

Someone has written: "A fixed idea is like a gimlet. Each year it goes in one turn farther. If you want to get rid of it in the first year it will pluck out your hair; in the second year, it will lacerate your skin; in the third year, it will break your bones; in the fourth year, it will tear out your brain."

Gilliatt had reached the fourth year.

He had never yet spoken to Déruchette. He thought about her a lot: that was all.

Once, finding himself by chance in St. Sampson, he had seen Déruchette talking to Mess Lethierry outside the door of Les Bravées, which opened off the harbor quay. Gilliatt had ventured to come up quite close to them. He was almost sure that as he passed she had smiled. That was certainly by no means impossible.

Déruchette still heard the sound of the bagpipes from time to time. Mess Lethierry heard them, too. After a time he had become aware of this persistent musician playing under Déruchette's windows. That the music was tender in tone made matters worse. A nocturnal gallant of this kind was not to his taste. He wanted to see Déruchette married in due time, when she wanted it and he wanted it—plainly and simply, without any romantic trappings and without music. Irritated, he kept watch, and thought that he had glimpsed Gilliatt. He combed his side-whiskers with his fingers—with him a sign of anger—and grumbled: "What has he to pipe about, that fellow? He's in love with Déruchette, it seems. You're wasting your time, young man. Anyone who wants to marry Déruchette must apply to me—and not by playing the flute."

An event of great importance, long anticipated, now came to pass. It was made known that the Reverend Jaquemin Hérode had been appointed suffragan to the bishop of Winchester, dean of Guernsey, and rector of St. Peter Port, and that he would leave St. Sampson for St. Peter Port immediately after his successor was installed.

The new rector soon arrived. He was a gentleman of Norman extraction, Mr. Joseph Ebenezer Caudray, anglicized as Cawdry.

The information that now became available about the future rector was given a very different gloss by those who were well disposed and those who were not. He was said to be young and poor, but his youth was tempered by the soundness of his doctrine and his poverty by great expectations. In the special language used in discussing inheritance and wealth, death is called expectations. He was the nephew and heir of the old and well-to-do dean of St. Asaph's, and when the dean died he would be rich. Ebenezer Caudray was well connected; he was almost entitled to the style of Honorable. As to his doctrine, there were different views. He was an Anglican, but, to use Bishop Tillotson's term, very much of a "libertine": that is to say, very strict. He repudiated pharisaism, and he believed in the presbytery rather than the episcopate. He dreamed of the primitive church, when Adam had the right to choose Eve, and when Frumentanus, bishop of Hierapolis, carried off a girl to make her his wife, saying to her parents: "She wants it and I want it. You are no longer her father and you are no longer her mother. I am the angel of Hierapolis, and she is my wife. Her father is God." If you could believe what people said, Monsieur Ebenezer Caudray thought the text "Honor thy father and thy mother" less important than that other text: "The woman is the flesh of the man. The woman shall leave her father and her mother to cleave to her husband." This tendency to circumscribe paternal authority and favor all methods of forming the conjugal bond is characteristic of all Protestant faiths, particularly in England and most notably in America.

V

Well-earned Success Always Attracts Hatred

At that time this was the state of Mess Lethierry's affairs: The Durande had fully lived up to her promise. Mess Lethierry had paid off his debts, repaired the breaches in his fortune, settled his accounts in Bremen, and paid his bills in Saint-Malo. He had cleared the mortgages on Les Bravées and redeemed all the small charges on the house. He was the owner of a valuable and productive capital asset, the Durande. The net annual income from the ship was a thousand pounds sterling and was still increasing. The Durande was in fact the sole source of his fortune. It also made the fortune of the district. Since the transport of cattle was the ship's main source of profit, it had been necessary, in order to improve the arrangements for the stowage of cargo and facilitate the loading and unloading of cattle, to dispense with the davits and the two dinghies. This was perhaps unwise. The Durande now had only one boat, the longboat—though this was an excellent craft.

It was ten years since Rantaine had made off with Mess Lethierry's money.

The weak point in the Durande's success was that people had no confidence in it; it was thought to be merely a lucky chance. Mess Lethierry's prosperity was accepted, but it was regarded as an exception. He was seen as having embarked on a crazy scheme that had turned out well. Someone who had imitated him at Cowes, on the Isle of Wight, had failed, and the shareholders in the venture had been ruined. Lethierry said that this was because the ship was badly built. But people still shook their heads. New ideas suffer from the disadvantage that everyone is against them, and the slightest thing that goes wrong discredits them. One of the commercial oracles of the Norman archipelago, a banker named Jauge who came from Paris, was once consulted about investing money in steamships. He is said to have replied, turning his back on the enquirer: "The proposition you have in mind is a conversion—the conversion of money into smoke." Sailing ships, on the other hand, could find any number of people ready to invest in them. Capital was firmly in favor of canvas as against a boiler. On Guernsey the Durande was a fact, but steam was not a principle that people were ready to accept: so strong is the prejudice against progress. People said of Lethierry: "All right, it has turned out well; but he wouldn't do it again." The example he had given did not encourage others but alarmed them. No one would have ventured on a second Durande.

VI

Shipwrecked Mariners Are Lucky in Encountering a Sloop

The equinox arrives early in the Channel. It is a narrow sea that hampers and irritates the wind. Westerly winds begin to blow in the month of February, and the waves are churned in all directions. Seafarers become apprehensive; the people of the coast keep an eye on the signal mast; there are worries about ships that may be in distress. The sea lies in ambush; an invisible bugle sounds, as if calling men to war; fierce gusts of air overwhelm the horizon; the wind increases in fury. The darkness is filled with whistling and howling. Far up in the clouds the black face of the storm puffs out its cheeks.

The wind is one danger; fog is another.

Seamen have always feared fog. Some fogs hold in suspension microscopic prisms of ice, to which Mariotte[117] attributed such effects as haloes, parhelia, and paraselenae. Fogs during a storm are composite; in them various vapors of differing specific gravity combine with water vapor, superimposed in an order that divides the fog into zones, giving it a regular structure; at the bottom is iodine, above this is sulfur, above this is bromine, and above this again is phosphorus. To some extent this structure, allowing for electrical and magnetic tension, ex-

The Vision Ship (1864–65).

plains a number of phenomena—the Saint Elmo's fire observed by Columbus and Magellan, the shooting stars raining down on ships of which Seneca speaks, the two flames called Castor and Pollux that are mentioned by Plutarch, the Roman legions whose javelins seemed to Caesar to be catching fire, the pike in Duino Castle in Friuli that sent out sparks when the sentry on duty touched it with his lance, and perhaps even the thunderings down below that the ancients called the "terrestrial lightnings of Saturn." On the equator there seems to be a permanent band of mist around the globe, the cloud ring. The function of the cloud ring is to cool down the Tropics, as that of the Gulf Stream is to warm up the Pole. Under the cloud ring are the dangerous fogs. These are the horse latitudes, in which in past centuries sailors threw horses into the sea, with the object in stormy weather of lightening the ship and in calm weather of husbanding their water. Columbus said: *"Nube abaxo es muerte,"* "Low cloud is death." The Etruscans, who were to meteorology what the Chaldeans were to astronomy, had two priesthoods, the priesthood of thunder and the priesthood of the clouds; the *fulguratores* observed lightning and the *aquileges* observed fog and mist. The college of priest-augurs of Tarquinia was consulted by the Tyrians, the Phoenicians, the Pelasgians, and all the primitive seamen of the ancient Mediterranean. They had some inkling of the way in which storms were generated; it is intimately connected with the method of generation of fog, and is indeed the same phenomenon. There are three foggy zones on the ocean: an equatorial zone and two polar zones: seamen give them the same name, the "black pot."

In all waters, and particularly in the Channel, the equinoctial fogs are dangerous. They suddenly bring night over the sea. One of the dangers of fog, even when it is not particularly dense, is that it prevents sailors from recognizing changes in the seabed from changes in the color of the water, resulting in a dangerous concealment of approaching breakers or shallows. You can suddenly come on a reef without any warning. Frequently fog leaves a vessel with no alternative but to lay to or drop anchor. Fog causes as many shipwrecks as wind.

After a heavy gale that followed one of these days of fog the mail sloop *Cashmere* nevertheless arrived safely from England. It entered St. Peter Port at first light, just as Castle Cornet was firing its cannon to greet the sun. The sky had cleared. The *Cashmere* had been eagerly awaited, since it was believed to be bringing St. Sampson's new rector.

Soon after its arrival the rumor spread in the town that during the night it had picked up a boat containing the crew of a vessel that had suffered shipwreck.

VII

A Stranger Is Lucky in Being Seen by a Fisherman

That night, when the wind died down, Gilliatt went out fishing, though without going too far from the coast.

Coming back on the rising tide about two o'clock in the afternoon, on a fine sunny day, as he was passing the Beast's Horn on his way to the creek at the Bû de la Rue, he thought he saw a shadow on the Seat of Gild-Holm-'Ur, a shadow that was not the shadow of the rock. He brought his boat closer in and saw that there was a man sitting in the seat. The tide was already high and the rock was surrounded by the sea; escape was impossible. Gilliatt waved vigorously to the man, but he remained motionless. Gilliatt drew nearer. The man was asleep.

The man was dressed in black. "He looks like a priest," Gilliatt thought. He drew closer still and saw that the man was quite young. The face was unknown to him.

Fortunately the rock fell steeply down to the sea and there was plenty of depth. Gilliatt moved close in and was able to come alongside the rock. The tide now brought the boat so high that Gilliatt, standing on the gunwale, could reach the man's feet. He stood to his full height and stretched up his hands. If he had slipped he would have had little chance of coming to the surface again. The waves were lashing the rock, and he would inevitably have been crushed between the boat and the rock.

He tugged the sleeping man's foot. "What are you doing here?"

The man woke up. "I have been enjoying the view," he said.

A moment later, now wide awake, he went on: "I have just arrived on Guernsey, and took a walk along this way. I had spent the night at sea. I thought, What a beautiful view! I was tired, and I fell asleep."

"Ten minutes more, and you would have been drowned," said Gilliatt.

"Really?"

"Jump into my boat."

Gilliatt kept the boat in position with his foot, clung to the rock with one hand, and held out the other to the young man in black, who sprang lightly into the boat. He was a very handsome young man.

Gilliatt took up the oars, and in two minutes the boat ran into the creek at the Bû de la Rue.

The young man wore a round hat and a white cravat. His long black frock coat was buttoned up to the neck. He had fair hair cut in the form of a tonsure, a rather feminine face, a clear eye, an air of gravity.

The boat had now run into land. Gilliatt passed the cable through the mooring ring and turned round, to see the young man holding out a golden sovereign in a hand of extreme whiteness.

Gilliatt put the hand gently aside.

There was a silence, which was broken by the young man.

"You have saved my life."

"Maybe," said Gilliatt.

The boat was now made fast, and they landed.

The young man continued:

"I owe you my life, sir."

"What of that?"

There was a further silence.

"Are you of this parish?" asked the young man.

"No," said Gilliatt.

"What parish do you belong to?"

Gilliatt raised his right hand, pointed to the heavens and said, "That one."

The young man bowed, and left him. After walking a few paces he stopped, felt in his pocket, drew out a book, and returned to Gilliatt, holding out the book.

"Allow me to offer you this."

Gilliatt took the book. It was a Bible.

A moment later Gilliatt, leaning on his garden wall, saw the young man turning the corner of the path leading to St. Sampson.

Gradually he lowered his head, forgot the stranger, forgot that the Seat of Gild-Holm-'Ur existed. Everything else disappeared in his immersion in the depths of his reverie. This abyss of Gilliatt's was Déruchette.

He was roused from this shadowland by a voice calling his name:

"Hey there, Gilliatt!"

Recognizing the voice, he raised his eyes.

"What is it, Sieur Landoys?"

Sieur Landoys was driving along the road, a hundred paces from the Bû de la Rue, in his phaeton, drawn by his small horse. He had stopped to call to Gilliatt, but he seemed to be preoccupied and in a hurry.

"There is news, Gilliatt."

"Where?"

"At Les Bravées."

"What is it?"

"I'm too far away to tell you about it."

Gilliatt felt a tremor.

"Is Miss Déruchette going to be married?"

"No. It's not that at all."

"What do you mean?"

"Go to Les Bravées and you'll find out."

And Sieur Landoys whipped up his horse.

BOOK V

THE REVOLVER

I

CONVERSATIONS AT THE INN

Sieur Clubin was a man who was always looking out for an opportunity.

He was small and sallow-faced and had the strength of a bull. The sea had never managed to give him a weather-beaten air. His flesh looked as if it were made of wax. He was the color of a wax candle, and there was the discreet glimmer of a candle in his eyes. He had a wonderfully retentive memory. If he had once seen a man he had him placed, as if he had made a note in a ledger. His laconic glance seized hold of you. His eye took in an image of a face and retained it; even if the face had aged, Sieur Clubin could recognize it. There was no deceiving this tenacious memory. Sieur Clubin was a man of few words, sober and cold in manner, with never so much as a gesture. His frank and open air won over everyone at once.

Many people thought he was naïve: there were creases at the corners of his eyes that gave him an extraordinarily simpleminded look. As we have said, there was no better seaman than Sieur Clubin; no one better at reefing a sail, at keeping a vessel to the wind or the sails well set. No one had a higher reputation for religion and integrity. Anyone who suspected him of any failing would himself have been suspect. He was friendly with Monsieur Rébuchet, the money changer in Rue Saint-Vincent in Saint-Malo, next door to the gunsmith. Monsieur Rébuchet used to say: "I would trust Clubin to look after my shop."

Sieur Clubin was a widower. His wife had been an honest woman as he was an honest man. She had died with a reputation for unassailable virtue. If the bailiff had tried to trifle with her she would have reported him to the king. If the good Lord himself had been in love with her she would have told the curé. The couple, Sieur and Dame Clubin, were regarded in Torteval as the very epitome of the English virtue of respectability. Dame Clubin had the whiteness of the swan, Sieur Clubin of the ermine. He would have died from any spot on his coat. If he found a pin he would try to return it to its owner. If he had picked up a box of matches he would have proclaimed the fact around the town. One day he had gone into a tavern in Saint-Servan[118] and said to the owner: "I had lunch here three years ago, and you made a mistake in the bill," handing over sixty-five centimes. He had a tremendous air of probity, with a watchful pursing of the lips.

He seemed always to be pointing like a game dog. Whom was he after? Probably rogues.

Every Tuesday he sailed the Durande from Guernsey to Saint-Malo. He arrived on the Tuesday evening, stayed there for two days to load his cargo and returned to Guernsey on the Friday morning.

In those days there was a little hostelry on the harbor at Saint-Malo, the Auberge Jean. It was pulled down when the present quays were built. At that time the sea came up to the Porte Saint-Vincent and the Porte Dinan. At low tide carts and light carriages ran between Saint-Malo and Saint-Servan, weaving their way between vessels lying high and dry, avoiding buoys, anchors, and cables and sometimes risking damage to their leather hoods from a low yard or a flying jib. Between high and low tides drivers whipped their horses over sand on which six hours later the wind was whipping up the waves. On these same sands there used to roam the twenty-four guard dogs of Saint-Malo, which in 1770 ate a naval officer—an excess of zeal that led to their demise. Nowadays you no longer hear nocturnal barking between the Grand Talard and the Petit Talard.

Sieur Clubin always stayed at the Auberge Jean, which housed the French office of the Durande.

The local customs officers and coastguards ate and drank in the Auberge Jean, where they had their own table. There the customs officers from Binic met the customs officers of Saint-Malo, to the advantage of the service.

The masters of ships also patronized the inn, but they ate at a separate table.

Sieur Clubin sometimes sat at one table, sometimes at the other; but he preferred the customs officers' table to the sea captains'. He was welcome at both.

The fare at these tables was excellent. There were all sorts of strange foreign drinks for seamen far from home. A dandyish young sailor from Bilbao could have had an *helada*. Stout was drunk as at Greenwich, and brown Gueuze beer as at Antwerp.

The captains of oceangoing vessels and shipowners sometimes appeared at the captains' table. There was much exchanging of news: "How are sugars doing?"—"You can only get refined sugar in small lots. But unrefined sugars are doing well; three thousand sacks from Bombay and five hundred barrels from Sagua."—"You'll see: the conservatives will throw out Villèle."—"And what about indigo?"—"There were only seven bales from Guatemala."—"The *Nanine-Julie* has arrived. A fine three-master from Brittany."—"The two towns on the River Plate[119] are quarreling again."—"When Montevideo grows fat Buenos Aires grows thin."—"They have had to tranship the cargo of the *Regina Coeli*, which has been condemned in Callao."—"Cocoas are brisk; sacks of Caracas are quoted at two hundred and thirty-four, Trinidad at seventy-three."—"I hear that at the review in the Champ de Mars there were shouts of 'Down with the government.' "—"Green salted Saladero hides are selling at sixty francs for ox hides and forty-eight for cow hides."—"Have they got past the Balkans? What is Diebitsch doing?"—"At San Francisco there is a shortage of aniseed. Plagniol olive oil is quiet. Gruyère cheese in keg, thirty-two francs the hundredweight."—"Well, is Leo XII[120] dead yet?"—and so on, and so on.

All these matters were discussed in a clamor of voices. At the table occupied by the customs officers and coastguards the conversation was conducted in more subdued tones. The business of policing the coasts and harbors calls for less noise and more restraint in conversation.

The captains' table was presided over by an old oceangoing master mariner, Monsieur Gertrais-Gaboureau. Monsieur Gertrais-Gaboureau was not a man: he was a barometer. His long experience of the sea had given him an extraordinary infallibility as a forecaster.

He was accustomed to decree each day what the weather would be like on the following day. He sounded the winds; he felt the pulse of the tides. He said to the clouds: "Show me your tongue"—that is, lightning. He was the physician of the waves, the breezes, the squalls. The ocean was his patient; he had gone around the world as a doctor conducts a clinic, examining each climate in its health and sickness; he thoroughly understood the pathology of the seasons. He could be heard making statements such as this: "Once in 1796 the barometer fell three lines below storm level." He was a seaman from love of the sea, and hated England in proportion to that love. He had made a thorough study of the English navy in order to discover its weak points. He would explain how the *Sovereign* of 1637 differed from the *Royal William* of 1670 and the *Victory* of 1755. He compared their various superstructures. He regretted the towers on the decks and the funnel-shaped tops of the *Great Harry* of 1514, probably because they had offered such good targets for French gunners. Nations existed for him only in terms of their maritime institutions, and he referred to them by bizarre synonyms of his own devising. For him England was Trinity House, Scotland the Northern Commissioners, and Ireland the Ballast Board. He was a mine of information—an almanac and an alphabet—a volume of tide tables and freight rates. He knew by heart the toll charges of lighthouses, particularly English lighthouses: a penny per ton for passing this one, a farthing per ton for passing that one. He would say: "The Small's Rock lighthouse, which used to use only two hundred gallons of oil, now burns fifteen hundred." One day, when at sea, he had fallen gravely ill and was thought to be dead; with the crew surrounding his hammock, he had interrupted the death rattle to tell the ship's carpenter: "It would be a good idea to have on each side of the caps a sheave hole to house a cast-iron wheel with an iron axle that the mast ropes could run over." A commanding character indeed.

The subject of conversation was seldom the same at the captains' and the customs officers' tables. But this is precisely what happened at the beginning of this month of February to which our tale has brought us. The three-master *Tamaulipas*, Captain Zuela, coming from Chile and returning there, attracted the interest of both tables. At the captains' table they discussed her cargo, at the customs men's table what she was up to.

Captain Zuela, who came from Copiapó, was a Chilean with a bit of Colombian blood who had fought in the wars of independence in an independent manner, sometimes on Bolívar's side and sometimes on Morillo's, depending on which paid him best. He had grown rich by being of service to all. No one could be more of a Bourbon supporter than he, no one more of a Bonapartist, an absolutist, a liberal, an atheist, a Catholic. He belonged to that large party that could be called the Lucrative party. He turned up in France from time to time on some commercial business; and, if rumor spoke truly, he was happy to give passage on his ship to fugitives of all kinds—bankrupts, political refugees, it was all one to him, provided they paid. The embarkation process was quite simple. The fugitive waited at a lonely spot on the coast, and when his ship sailed Zuela sent a boat to pick him up. On his last voyage he had helped a fugitive from justice in the Berton case to escape, and this time he was said to be planning to carry men who had been involved in the Bidassoa affair.[121] The police had been alerted and had their eye on him.

This was a time of flights and escapes. The Restoration[122] was a period of reaction; and while revolutions lead to migrations, restorations bring proscriptions. During the seven or eight years after the return of the Bourbons there was widespread panic—in the financial world, in industry, in commerce—when men felt the earth shaking under them and there were numerous bankruptcies. In politics there was a general *sauve-qui-peut*. Lavalette had taken flight, Lefebvre-Desnouettes had taken flight, Delon had taken flight; special tribunals were dispensing ruthless punishment; and there was the case of Trestaillon. People avoided the bridge at Saumur, the esplanade in La Réole, the wall of the Observatory in Paris, the Tour de Taurias in Avignon—dismal landmarks of history that recalled the work of reactionary forces and still show the mark of their bloodstained hands. The trial of Thistlewood in London, with its ramifications in France, and the trial of Trogoff in Paris, with its ramifications in Belgium, Switzerland, and Italy, had given rise to widespread grounds for anxiety and motives for flight, and had increased the great subterranean rout that decimated every rank, up to the highest, in the social order of the day.[123] To find a place of safety was the general care. To be suspected of rebellion meant ruin. The spirit of the special tribunals survived the tribunals themselves. Conviction was a matter of course. Suspects fled to Texas, the Rocky Mountains, Peru, Mexico. The men of the Loire—regarded as brigands then, as paladins now—had established the Champ d'Asile.[124] A song by Béranger put these words in their mouths: *Sauvages, nous sommes français; prenez pitié de notre gloire.* Self-banishment was their only resource. But nothing is less simple than to flee: this monosyllable contains abysses. Everything stands in the way of those seeking to escape. To avoid detection it is necessary to assume disguise. Men of some standing in the world, and indeed some illustrious personages, were reduced to expedients normally practiced only by criminals. Nor were they very good at it. They did not fit comfortably into their assumed identity. The freedom of movement to which they were accustomed made it difficult for them to slip through the meshes of escape. Encountering the police, a rogue on the run behaved with more propriety than a general; but imagine innocence compelled to play a part, virtue disguising its voice, glory wearing a mask! Some dubious-looking character might be a well-known figure in quest of a false passport. The aspect of a man trying to escape might be suspicious, but he might nevertheless be a hero. These are fugitive features characteristic of a particular period that are neglected by what is called regular history but to which the true painter of an age must draw attention. Behind these respectable fugitives slipped a variety of rogues less closely watched and less suspect. A rogue finding it necessary to disappear could take advantage of the confusion and lose himself among the political refugees; and frequently, as we have just said, would seem in this twilight world, thanks to his greater skill, more respectable than his respectable fellow fugitives. Nothing is more inept than integrity under threat from the law. It is totally at a loss and makes all sorts of mistakes. A forger would find it easier to escape than a member of the Convention.[125]

It is a curious thing, but it could almost be said that escape from one's country opened up the possibility of new careers, particularly for dishonest characters. The quantity of civilization that a rascal brought with him from Paris or London was a valuable resource in primitive or barbarous countries; it was a useful qualification and made him an initiator in his new country. It was not by any means impossible for him to exchange the rigors of the law for the priesthood. There is something phantasmagorical in a disappearance, and many an escape has had consequences that could not have been dreamed of. An absconding of this kind could lead to the unknown and the chimerical: thus a bankrupt who had left Europe by some illicit route might reappear twenty years later as grand vizier to the Great Mogul or as a king in Tasmania.

Helping people to escape was a whole industry, and, in view of the numbers involved, a highly profitable one. It could be combined with other kinds of business. Thus those who wanted to escape to England applied to the smugglers, and those who wanted to go to America applied to long-distance operators like Zuela.

II

Clubin Sees Someone

Zuela sometimes had a meal in the Auberge Jean. Sieur Clubin knew him by sight.

Sieur Clubin was broad-minded: he was not too proud to know some rogues by sight. He sometimes went so far as to know them personally, shaking hands with them openly in the street and passing the time of day. He spoke English to a smuggler and had a smattering of Spanish for a contrabandista. He had a variety of aphorisms to justify this: "You can get some good out of knowing evil."—"The gamekeeper can learn something from the poacher."—"The pilot must take soundings of the pirate, who is a kind of hidden reef."—"I taste a rascal as a doctor tastes poison." These statements were unanswerable. Everyone agreed that Captain Clubin was right. They thought well of him for not being absurdly overnice. Who would have dared to speak ill of him? All that he did was clearly "for the good of the service." Everything about him was straightforward. Nothing could harm his reputation: it was a crystal so pure that it could not be stained even if it tried. This confidence was the just reward for many years of honesty: that is the good thing about a well-established reputation. Whatever Clubin did or appeared to do was given a favorable interpretation; his faultlessness was an established fact. Moreover, people said, he knew what he was about; and an acquaintance with certain people, which in another man would have been suspicious, served only to enhance his reputation for integrity and cleverness. This reputation for cleverness combined happily with his reputation for naïveté without any incongruity or confusion. There is such a thing as a man who is both naïve and clever. It is one of the varieties of the respectable citizen, and one of the most valued. Sieur Clubin was one of those men who, if found in close conversation with a swindler or a thief, are accepted and understood—indeed all the more respected—and are looked on with the approving glance of public esteem.

The *Tamaulipas* had now taken on her cargo; she was ready for sea and was due to sail shortly.

One Tuesday evening the Durande arrived in Saint-Malo while it was still broad daylight. As he stood on the bridge directing his ship's entry into the harbor, Sieur Clubin saw two men engaged in conversation in a lonely spot on a sandy beach between two rocks, near the Petit Bey. Looking through his glass, he recognized one of them as Captain Zuela, and he seems also to have recognized the other.

The other man was a tall figure with graying hair. He wore the broad-brimmed hat and sober garments of the Friends. He was probably, therefore, a Quaker. He kept his eyes modestly cast down.

When he arrived at the Auberge Jean Sieur Clubin learned that the *Tamaulipas* was expected to sail in ten days or so.

It was later found that he had gathered certain other information.

That evening he called in on the gunsmith in Rue Saint-Vincent and asked, "Do you know what a revolver is?"

"Yes," said the gunsmith: "It's American."

"It's a pistol that reopens the conversation."

"Yes, it has both the question and the answer."

"And a comeback to that."

"Right, Monsieur Clubin. A revolving barrel."

"And five or six bullets."

The gunsmith half-opened his mouth and clicked his tongue, making the sound that, accompanied by a nod of the head, expresses admiration.

"It's a good little weapon, Monsieur Clubin. I think it will make its way."

"I want a six-barreled revolver."

"I haven't any of those."

"What? You call yourself a gunsmith, don't you?"

"I still haven't got that particular article. It's new, you see. It's just coming into use. In France we only have pistols."

"The devil!"

"They're not yet on the market."

"The devil!"

"I have some first-class pistols."

"I want a revolver."

"I agree that it is more useful. But just wait a bit, Monsieur Clubin."

"What do you mean?"

"I think I know of one in Saint-Malo, secondhand."

"A revolver?"

"Yes."

"For sale?"

"Yes."

"Where?"

"I think I know where. I'll enquire."

"When will you be able let me know?"

"It's secondhand. But a good one."

"When should I come back?"

"If I can get you a revolver, you can be sure it will be a good one."

"When will you let me know?"

"On your next trip."

"Don't say that it's for me," said Clubin.

III

CLUBIN TAKES SOMETHING AWAY AND BRINGS NOTHING BACK

Sieur Clubin loaded the Durande, taking on board many head of cattle and a few passengers, and left Saint-Malo for Guernsey as usual on the Friday morning.

Once the vessel was out at sea and he could leave the bridge for a few moments, Clubin went to his cabin and locked himself in, took up a traveling bag that he kept there, put some articles of clothing into the expanding compartment, and biscuit, some tinned food, a few pounds of chocolate bars, a chronometer, and a spyglass into the main compartment, padlocked the bag, and passed a rope through the handles so that it could be hoisted up if need be. Then he went down to the cable locker in the hold and was seen to bring up a length of rope with knots at regular intervals and a hook at one end, such as is used by caulkers at sea and thieves on land: it is an aid to climbing.

When he arrived in Guernsey Clubin went to Torteval, where he spent thirty-six hours. He took the traveling bag and the knotted rope, but did not come back with them.

We must make clear once and for all that the Guernsey we are talking about in this book is the old Guernsey that no longer exists and can now be found only in the country districts. There it is still alive, but in the towns it is dead. This applies also to Jersey. St. Helier is now much the same as Dieppe, St. Peter Port as Lorient. Thanks to progress, thanks to the spirit of enterprise of this gallant little island people, over the last forty years everything has been transformed in this archipelago in the Channel. Where there was shadow, there is now light.

This said, we can carry on with our story.

In those days, which distance in time has now made ancient history, smuggling was rife in the Channel. The ships carrying on this illicit trade were particularly numerous on the west coast of Guernsey. Persons who are particularly well informed, and know in precise detail what was happening just half a century ago, cite the names of some of these ships, almost all of them from the Asturias and Guipúzcoa. What is beyond doubt is that scarcely a week went by without one or two of them arriving in Saint's Bay or at Pleinmont. It had almost the air of a regular service. One sea cave on Sark was known, and still is known, as the Boutiques because it was here that customers came to buy the smugglers' wares. For the purposes of this trade a kind of smugglers' language, now forgotten—related to Spanish as Levantine is to Italian—was spoken in the Channel.

At many points on the English and French coasts there was a secret understanding between the smuggling trade and open and legitimate commerce. The smugglers had the entrée to many a great figure in the financial world—through a secret door, it must be said—and they were linked up through subterranean channels with the circulatory system of commerce and the arteries of industry. A businessman at the front door, a smuggler at the back door: this was the story of many fortunes. Séguin alleged this of Bourgain; Bourgain alleged it of Séguin.[126] We cannot vouch for the truth of what they said: perhaps they were slandering one another. However that may be, the smugglers, though hunted down by the law, certainly had close connections with the world of finance. They also had contacts with the "best people." The cavern in which Mandrin rubbed shoulders with the Comte de Charolais[127] had a respectable exterior and an impeccable façade on society; it was a prosperous and respected establishment.

All this required much connivance, necessarily concealed. These mysteries could thrive only in impenetrable obscurity. A smuggler knew many things that he was bound to keep silent; to keep strict and inviolable faith was his law. The first quality for a smuggler was loyalty. Without discretion the smuggling trade is impossible. There is a secrecy of fraud as there is the secret of the confession.

This secrecy was inviolably guarded. The smuggler swore to maintain absolute silence about the trade, and he kept his word. No one was more trustworthy in this respect than a smuggler. One day the alcalde (judge) of Oyarzún captured a smuggler of the Puertos Secos and had him put to the question to force him to reveal the name of the person who financed his enterprise. The smuggler did not name the man: it was in fact the alcalde. Of the two accomplices the judge had been obliged, in order to be seen to be obeying the law, to order the smuggler to be tortured, while the smuggler had been bound to say nothing under torture in order to keep his oath.

The two most celebrated smugglers frequenting Pleinmont at this period were Blasco and Blasquito. They were *tocayos* (namesakes). This is a form of relationship among Spanish Catholics that consists in having the same patron saint in paradise—which, it must be agreed, is no less worthy of consideration than having the same father on earth.

When you were reasonably familiar with the furtive comings and goings of the smugglers and wanted to do business with them, nothing was easier—or more difficult. It was necessary only to have no fear of venturing out at night, to go to Pleinmont, and to confront the mysterious question-mark that stands there.

IV

PLEINMONT

Pleinmont, near Torteval, is one of the three corners of Guernsey. Here, at the tip of the promontory, a high grassy hill rears above the sea.

The hill is deserted; and it is all the more deserted because there is a house on it. The house adds an element of fear to the solitude: it is said to be haunted.

Whether or not it is haunted, it is certainly strange.

The house, a two-story granite building, stands on the grassy summit of the hill. It is not by any means a ruin; it is perfectly habitable. The walls are thick and the roof is sound. Not a stone is missing from the walls, not a tile from the roof. A brick chimney-stack buttresses one corner of the roof. The house turns its back on the sea. The side facing the ocean is a blank wall; but if you look closely you can see a window that has been walled up. On the gable ends are three small windows, one on the east end and two on the west end; all three are walled up. The side facing inland has a doorway and windows. The doorway is walled up. The two ground-floor windows are walled up. On the first floor—and this is what strikes you most as you approach the house—are two open windows; but the walled-up windows are less disturbing than these. Open though they are, they look black even in full daylight. They have lost their glass, and even the frames are missing. They open on the darkness within. They are like the empty sockets of two eyes that have been torn out. There is nothing inside the house. Through the gaping windows can be seen the dilapidation of the interior. No wainscoting, no woodworking; nothing but bare stone. It is like a sepulchre with windows from which ghosts can look out. Rain is undermining the foundations on the seaward side. Nettles, shaken by the wind, caress the lower parts of the walls. On the horizon not a human habitation is to be seen. This house is an empty thing, a place of silence. But if you stop for a moment and put your ear against the wall you will now and then hear a confused fluttering of wings, scared by your presence. Above the walled-up door, on the stone that forms the architrave, are inscribed the letters ELM-PBILG and the date 1780.

At night the somber moon shines into the house.

Around this house is the whole of the sea. Its situation is magnificent, and consequently sinister. The beauty of the place becomes an enigma. Why is there no human family living in this house? The situation is beautiful; the house is a good one. Why has it been abandoned?

To the questions posed by our reason are added others suggested by our reverie. This field is suitable for cultivation: why is it not cultivated? The house has no master. The doorway is walled up. What is wrong with this place? Why do men shun it? What is going on here? If nothing is going on, why is there no one here? When everyone is asleep is there anyone awake here? The sight of this house calls up images of dark and gloomy squalls, the wind, birds of prey, lurking animals, unknown beings. What wayfarers does this hostelry cater to?

You can imagine dark shadows of hail and rain bursting in through the windows. Storms have left their traces in the marks made by water trickling down the inside walls. These rooms, whether their windows are walled up or open, are visited by the hurricane. Has some crime been committed here? Surely at night this house, abandoned to darkness, must call for help? Does it remain silent? Are voices heard coming from it? With whom does it have to do in this solitude? The mystery of the hours of darkness is entirely at home here. This house is disquieting at midday: what is it like at midnight? When you look at it you are looking at a secret. You wonder—since reverie has its own logic and the possibilities open up in your mind—what happens to this house between the twilight of evening and the half-light of morning. Has extra-human life, dispersed as it is over immense distances, a junction point on this lonely hill where it stops and is forced to become visible and descend to earth? Do the scattered elements of this other world come together to swirl and eddy here? Does impalpable matter condense here and take on form? These are enigmas. There is a sacred horror in these stones. The darkness of these forbidden rooms is more than darkness: it is the unknown. After the sun goes down the fishing boats will return to harbor, the birds will be silent, the goatherd behind the rock will go off with his goats, the first reptiles, taking courage, will slip out of crevices between the stones, the stars will begin to look down, the north wind will blow, darkness will fall, and these two windows will be there, gaping wide.

The house is now open to dreams; and popular belief, which is both simpleminded and profound, peoples the somber intimacies between this house and the darkness of night with apparitions, with evil spirits, with spectral faces dimly discerned, with masks surrounded by lurid light, with mysterious tumults of souls and shades.

The house is haunted: no further explanation is needed.

Credulous minds have their explanation; but matter-of-fact minds also have theirs. There is no mystery about this house, they say. It is an old watch house, used during the wars of the Revolution and Empire and the time when smuggling was rife. It was built for that purpose, and after the wars it was abandoned. The house was not pulled down because it might be needed again. The doorway and ground-floor windows were walled up against the deposit of human excrement and to prevent anyone from getting in, and the windows on the three sides of the house facing the sea because of the southerly and westerly winds. There was no more to it than that.

The ignorant and credulous still hold to their belief. In the first place, they say, the house was not built during the wars of the Revolution. It bears a date—1780—earlier than the Revolution. And it was not built as a watch house. It bears the letters ELM-PBILG—the initials of two families, which show that, in accordance with custom, the house had been built for a newly married couple. Thus it had clearly been inhabited at one time. Then why is it no longer occupied? If the doorway and windows were walled up to prevent anyone from getting into the house, why were two windows left open? Everything should have been walled up, or nothing. Why are there no shutters? Why are there no window frames? Why is there no glass in the windows? Why were the windows walled up on one side and not on the other? The rain is prevented from coming in on the south side but is allowed in on the north side.

The credulous are wrong, no doubt, but certainly the matter-of-fact people are not right. The problem remains.

What is certain is that the house is believed to have been more useful than harmful to smugglers.

When people are scared, they cannot see things in their proper proportions. There is no doubt that many of the nocturnal happenings that had led to the belief that the house was haunted could be explained by obscure and furtive visits, by men landing here for a short time and then reembarking, by the precaution or the boldness of men engaged in suspect activities who sought either to conceal what they were up to or allowed themselves to be seen in order to inspire fear.

At that distant period many daring deeds were possible. In those days the police, particularly in small districts, fell far short of what they are today.

Moreover, if, as is said, the house was convenient for smugglers, this was partly because they were unlikely to be disturbed there as a result of its sinister reputation, which prevented people from reporting what went on there. You do not usually apply to customs men or excisemen when you are troubled by specters. On such an occasion superstitious people make the sign of the cross; they think it more efficacious than a police report. They see something, or think they see something; then they make off and say nothing about it. There is a tacit connivance—involuntary, but real—between those who inspire fear and those who feel it. Those who are scared feel they have done wrong to be scared; they imagine they have stumbled on something secret; they are afraid of finding themselves worse off in a situation that to them is mysterious, and of angering the apparitions. This makes them discreet. And, even apart from a calculation of this kind, the instinct of credulous people is to keep silent; fear makes them dumb. Terrified people do not speak much: it is as if horror says "Hush!"

It must be remembered that this was a period when the country people of Guernsey believed that on one day each year the mystery of the manger in Bethlehem was reenacted by oxen and asses. It was a time when no one would go into a stable on Christmas Eve for fear of finding the animals on their knees.

If we are to believe local legends and the tales told by people you meet, superstition used sometimes to be carried so far as to hang on the walls of this house at Pleinmont, on nails of which some traces can still be seen, rats with their paws cut off, bats without their wings, the carcasses of dead animals, toads squashed between the pages of a Bible, sprigs of yellow lupin—strange votive offerings made by people who had been unwise enough to pass that way at night and had seen something, in the hope that these gifts would win pardon for them and appease nocturnal apparitions, evil spirits, and phantoms. There have always been people ready to believe in abacas and witches' sabbaths, including some highly placed personages. Caesar consulted Sagane; Napoleon, Mademoiselle Lenormand.[128] There are consciences so unquiet that they will seek to obtain indulgences from the Devil. "May God do and Satan not undo" was one of the Emperor Charles V's prayers. Others are more timorous still. They will even persuade themselves that one can wrong what is evil. They are concerned to behave impeccably to the Devil. Hence come religious practices directed toward the immense and obscure power of evil. It is a form of bigotry like any other.

Crimes against the Devil exist in certain diseased imaginations; to have broken the law of the underworld torments some eccentric casuists of ignorance; they have scruples in dealing with the world of darkness. To believe in the efficacy of worshiping the mysteries of the Brocken and of Armuyr,[129] to imagine that one has sinned against Hell, to perform chimerical penances for chimerical offenses, to admit the truth to the Father of Lies, to offer a mea culpa to the Father of Sin, to make one's confession widdershins: all these things happen or have happened, as is proved in the records of witch trials on every page. Human imaginings go to such extremes. When a man begins to be scared there is no stopping him. He dreams up imaginary faults, he dreams of imaginary purifications, and he cleanses his conscience with the shadow of the witch's broomstick.

However that may be, if this house has adventures, that is its own affair. Apart from a few chance visits and a few exceptions, no one goes there. The house is left alone; and no one feels like risking an encounter with infernal forces.

Thanks to the terror that guards it and keeps away anyone who might observe and bear witness, it has always been easy to get entry to this house at night with the help of a rope ladder, or even a hurdle from one of the neighboring fields. With a suitable supply of clothes and food, a man could wait here in complete safety until the time came for a furtive embarkation. Tradition has it that some forty years ago a fugitive—for reasons of politics according to some, for reasons of commerce according to others—spent some time hidden in the haunted house of Pleinmont before sailing in a fishing boat to England. And from England it is easy to get to America.

The same tradition maintains that any supplies left in the house will not be touched, since it is in the interests of Lucifer as well as the smugglers that whoever deposited them should return.

From the hill on which the house stands there is a view to the southwest of the Hanois reef, a mile offshore.

This reef is famous. It has done all the evil deeds that a rock can do. It was one of the most redoubtable killers in the sea. It lay treacherously in wait for ships sailing at night. It had extended the cemeteries of Torteval and Rocquaine.

In 1862 a lighthouse was built on the reef. Nowadays it shows a light to the ships that it formerly led astray; what used to be a trap now bears a torch. Seamen scan the horizon for this rock, now a protector and a guide, which they formerly shunned as an evildoer. It now reassures the vast nocturnal expanses in which it formerly inspired fear. It is rather like a robber turned gendarme.

There are three Hanois: the Grand Hanois, the Petit Hanois, and the Mauve. The "red light" is on the Petit Hanois.

This reef is one of a group of jagged rocks, some of them underwater, some emerging from the sea. Like a fortress, it has its outworks: on the side facing the open sea a string of thirteen rocks; to the north two shoals, the Hautes-Fourquies and the Aiguillons, and a sandbank, the Hérouée; to the south three rocks, the Cat Rock, the Percée, and the Roque Herpin; plus two underwater rocks, the South Boue and the Boue le Mouet, and off Pleinmont, just under the surface, the Tas de Pois d'Aval.

It is difficult, but not impossible, to swim from the Hanois to Pleinmont. It will be remembered that this was one of Sieur Clubin's feats. For the swimmer who knows these shallows there are two places where he can rest—the Round Rock and, beyond this, bearing a little to the left, the Red Rock.

V

THE BIRD'S-NESTERS

It was about the time of Sieur Clubin's visit to Torteval on that Saturday morning that there occurred a singular event that was at first little spoken of in the district and only transpired long afterward. For, as we have just remarked, many things remain unknown because of the alarm they cause to those who have witnessed them.

That Saturday night—we give the exact date and believe it to be correct—three boys climbed up the cliffs at Pleinmont. They were on their way back to the village, coming from the sea. They had been bird's-nesting. Wherever there are cliffs and rock crevices above the sea there are children robbing birds' nests. We mentioned this earlier: it will be remembered that Gilliatt was concerned about it, for the sake both of the birds and of the children.

These bird's-nesters are the street urchins of the ocean, not easily frightened.

The night was very dark. Successive layers of dense cloud concealed the zenith. Three o'clock in the morning had just struck in the church tower at Torteval, which is round and pointed, like a magician's hat.

Why were the boys returning home so late? The reason was very simple. They had gone in search of seagulls' eggs on the Tas de Pois d'Aval. That year the weather had been very mild, and the birds had begun to mate very early. The boys, watching the male and female birds coming and going around the nests and carried away by the eagerness of their quest, had forgotten what time it was. They had been surrounded by the rising tide and had been unable to get back in time to the little creek where they had moored their boat, and had had to wait on one of the projecting rocks on the Tas de Pois until the tide receded. Hence the lateness of their return home. Children late in returning home are waited for by their anxious mothers, who, reassured by their return, vent their joy in anger: anger, swollen by tears, which is dissipated by boxing their ears. And so the boys, anxious themselves, were hurrying home. They were hurrying with the particular kind of haste that would be glad of any delay and contains some degree of reluctance to return. They were looking forward to a reception made up of both kisses and cuffs.

Only one of the boys had nothing to fear on that head: he was an orphan. This boy was French; he had neither father nor mother, and at present was glad that he had no mother. Since no one was concerned for his welfare, he would not be beaten. The two others were Guernsey boys, belonging to the parish of Torteval.

After scaling the rocky hill the three boys arrived on the level area on which the haunted house stands.

At first they felt afraid, which is to be expected of anyone, and particularly any child, passing that way at that time of night. They felt a strong urge to make off as fast as they could, but they also felt an urge to stop and look.

They stopped. They looked at the house. It was black and terrifying.

Standing in the center of the deserted hilltop, it was a dark block, a hideous symmetrical excrescence, a tall square mass with surfaces set at right angles, resembling an enormous altar of darkness.

The boys' first thought had been to flee; the second was to go closer. They had never seen the house at this time of night. There is such a thing as the desire to experience fear. They had a French boy with them, and this emboldened them to approach the house. It is well known that the French believe in nothing. Besides, when there are several of you in danger, this is reassuring; when there are three of you afraid, this gives you courage.

And then they were hunters; they were children, with not as much as thirty years among the three of them; they were questing, they were searching, they were seeking out hidden things.

Why should they not stop and look? If you peer into one hole, why not peer into another?

When you are hunting for something, you are undergoing a course of training; when you are seeking to discover something, you are caught up in a chain of action. If you have been in the habit of looking into birds' nests, it gives you an itch to look into the nests of specters. Rummaging about in Hell: why not?

Hunting one prey after another, you eventually come to the Devil. After sparrows, hobgoblins. You have to learn to cope with all the fears that your parents have instilled in you. Tracking down old wives' tales brings you onto a very slippery slope. The idea of knowing as much as the old wives is tempting.

All this hotchpotch of ideas, in the state of confusion and the instinctive feelings in the minds of these Guernsey boys, combined to make them bold. They walked toward the house.

The boy who was their leader in this display of courage was worthy of the role. He was a resolute lad, a caulker's apprentice, one of those children who are already men; sleeping on straw in a shed at his place of work, earning his own living, loud-voiced, a great climber of walls and trees, without any prejudices about any apples he came across; he had worked on the refitting of warships; a child of chance, a cheerful orphan; born in France, no one knew where, he had two reasons for being bold; ready to give a penny to a beggar; mischievous, but good at heart; fair hair, with a reddish tinge; he had spoken to people from Paris. Just now he was earning a shilling a day caulking the fishermen's boats that put in at Les Pêqueries for repair. When he felt like it, he would take a holiday and go bird's-nesting. Such was the little French boy.

There was something funereal about the solitude of the place. Its inviolability had a menacing feel. It was eerie. The bare, silent hilltop sloped down to the cliff a short distance away. The sea, down below, was quiet. There was no wind. Not a blade of grass stirred. The bird's-nesters walked on slowly, with the French boy leading, looking at the house. Later one of them, telling their story, or what little he remembered of it, said: "The house didn't speak."

As they approached the house they held their breath, as if they were approaching a wild beast.

They had come up the steep path behind the house that starts from a small rocky and inhospitable isthmus on the coast and had reached the top quite near the house. But they could see only the south front of the house, which is completely walled up. They had not dared to turn left, which would have brought them in sight of the other side with its two terrifying windows.

Then they grew bolder, the apprentice caulker having whispered, "Let's steer to port. That's the best side of the house; we must see the two black windows."

They "steered to port" and reached the other side of the house.

There were lights in the windows.

The boys turned tail.

When they were at a safe distance the French boy turned around. "Look," he said: "the lights have gone out." And indeed the windows were now dark again. The outlines of the house stood out sharply against the livid sky.

The boys had not lost their fears, but their curiosity returned. They moved closer to the house.

Suddenly lights again appeared at both windows.

The two Torteval boys took to their heels. The little devil of a French boy stopped in his tracks but did not retreat. He remained motionless, facing the house and watching.

The lights went out, and then came on again. It was terrifying. The reflection made a vague train of fire on the grass, which was moistened by the night dew. For a moment the light outlined on the inside walls of the house tall black moving figures and the shadows of enormous heads.

Since the house had no ceilings or internal partitions, having nothing left but its four walls and the roof, if there was light at one window there was bound to be light at the other.

Seeing that the apprentice caulker was standing firm, the other two boys returned slowly, one after the other, trembling but curious. The apprentice caulker whispered: "There are ghosts in the house. I saw the nose of one of them." The two Torteval boys huddled behind the French boy; and, standing on tiptoe, sheltered by him, using him as a shield, confronting the house with him, reassured that he stood between them and the ghostly vision, they looked over his shoulder at the house.

The house for its part seemed to be looking at them. There it stood in the vast silent darkness, with two glaring eyes—the windows. The light disappeared, reappeared, and then disappeared again, as lights of that kind do. This sinister intermittence is probably the result of the coming and going of Hell: gaping open and then closing again. The window in a sepulcher acts somewhat like a dark lantern.

Suddenly a dense black shadow in the form of a man appeared at one of the windows as if coming from outside, then disappeared into the interior. It looked as if someone had entered the house. Entering a house through the window is the normal practice of ghosts.

For a moment the light was brighter, and then it went out and did not reappear. The house became black again. Then sounds were heard—sounds resembling voices. It is always the way. When you see you cannot hear; when you cannot see you hear.

Night over the sea has a quietness all its own. The silence of darkness is deeper there than anywhere else. When there are neither wind nor waves on this vast moving expanse, where normally you could not hear the beat of an eagle's wings, you could hear the wings of a fly. This sepulchral quiet set off more sharply the sounds coming from the house.

"Let's have a look," said the French boy. And he took a step toward the house. The other two were in such terror that they made up their minds to follow him. They had not courage enough to escape on their own.

They had just passed a large pile of sticks, which somehow seemed to reassure them in this solitude, when an owl flew out of a bush, amid a rustling of branches. Owls have a curious swerving flight that is vaguely disturbing. The bird flew close to the boys, staring at them out of its round eyes, which gleamed in the darkness. The two boys to the rear shuddered. The French boy addressed the owl: "Sparrow, you're too late. I'm not going to stop now. I want to see what's going on." And he went on.

In spite of the crackling sound of his heavy hobnailed shoes on the furze, the sounds from the house could still be heard, rising and falling in the measured tones and the continuity of a conversation.

A moment later he added: "Anyway, it's only stupid people that believe in ghosts."

This insolence in the face of danger rallied the laggards and urged them on.

The two Torteval boys walked on, falling into step behind the apprentice caulker.

The haunted house seemed to them to grow enormously large. This optical illusion caused by fear had a basis in reality: the house was indeed growing larger because they were drawing nearer to it.

Meanwhile the voices in the house grew steadily clearer. The boys listened. The ear also has a magnifying power. The sound was more than a murmur, more than a whisper, less than a babel of voices. Now and then a few words could be made out; but the words had a peculiar sound and the boys could not understand them. They stopped, listened, and then moved on.

"It's ghosts talking," murmured the apprentice caulker; "but I don't believe in ghosts."

The Torteval boys were tempted to retreat beyond the pile of sticks; but it was a long way back, and their friend was still walking toward the house. They were afraid to stay with him, but they did not dare to leave him.

Step by step, much troubled, they followed him.

The apprentice caulker turned to them, saying: "You know it isn't true. There are no such things as ghosts."

The house was growing increasingly tall. The voices were becoming increasingly distinct.

They drew nearer.

As they approached they realized that there was some kind of shaded light in the house. It was a very faint gleam, as if from a dark lantern, like those commonly used in witches' sabbaths.

When they were quite close they stopped.

One of the two Torteval boys ventured: "They aren't ghosts; they are ladies in white."

"What's that hanging from one of the windows?" asked the other.

"It looks like a rope."

"It's a snake."

"It's a hangman's rope," said the French boy, with an air of authority. "They always use one. But I still don't believe in them."

And in three bounds rather than three steps he was at the foot of the wall. There was something feverish in his boldness.

The other two, trembling, followed him. They huddled close to him, one on his right, the other on his left. They held their ears close to the wall. The conversation in the house was still continuing.

This was what the ghosts were saying:[130]

———

"Well, that's agreed, then?"

"Yes."

"It's settled?"

"Yes."

"A man will be waiting here, and he'll go to England with Blasquito?"

"He'll pay?"

"Yes, he'll pay."

"Blasquito will take him in his boat."

"Without asking what country he comes from?"

"That's none of our business."

"Without asking his name?"

"We don't ask for names: we weigh the purse."

"Right. The man will be waiting in this house."

"He'll need some food."

"He will get it."

"Where?"

"In this bag I've brought with me."

"Good."

"Can I leave the bag here?"

"Smugglers aren't thieves."

"And the rest of you, when are you sailing?"

"Tomorrow morning. If your man were ready he could come with us."

"He isn't ready."

"That's his lookout."

"How long will he have to wait here?"

"Two, three, four days. Perhaps less, perhaps more."

"Are you sure Blasquito will come?"

"Absolutely sure."

"Here? To Pleinmont?"

"Yes: to Pleinmont."

"How soon?"

"Next week."

"Which day?"

"Friday, Saturday, or Sunday."

"Without fail?"

"He is my tocayo."

"He will come whatever the weather?"

"Yes: whatever the weather. He's not afraid. I am Blasco; he is Blasquito."

"So he will not fail to come to Guernsey?"

"I come one month; he comes the next month."

"I see."

"Counting from next Saturday, a week today, Blasquito will arrive within five days."

"But if the sea were very rough?"

"*Egurraldia gaïztoa?*"[131]

"Yes."

"Blasquito would not come so quickly, but he would still come."

"Where will he be coming from?"

"Bilbao."

"Where will he be heading for?"

"Portland."

"Good."

"Or Torbay."

"Better still."

"Your man need not worry."

"Blasquito won't betray him?"

"Only cowards are traitors. We are brave men. The sea is the church of winter. Treason is the church of hell."

"No one can hear what we are saying?"

"No one can hear us or see us. Fear keeps people away from here."

"I know."

"Who would dare to come and listen to us here?"

"True enough."

"Besides, even if anyone were listening they wouldn't understand. We are speaking a language of our own that nobody here understands. You understand it, and that makes you one of us."

"I came here to arrange things with you."

"Right."

"Now I must go."

"All right."

"Tell me: suppose the passenger wanted Blasquito to land him somewhere other than Portland or Torbay, what then?"

"If he's got the money there will be no difficulty."

"Will Blasquito do whatever the man wants?"

"Blasquito will do whatever the money wants."

"Will it take long to get to Torbay?"

"That depends on the wind."

"Eight hours?"

"Thereabouts."

"Will Blasquito obey his passenger?"

"If the sea obeys Blasquito."

"He will be well paid."

"Gold is gold. The sea is the sea."

"That is true."

"A man with gold can do what he wants. God, with the wind, does what he wants."

"The man who wants to go with Blasquito will be here on Friday."

"Right."

"At what time of day will Blasquito arrive?"

"At night. We arrive at night. We leave at night. We have a wife who is called the Sea and a sister who is called Night. The wife is sometimes unfaithful; the sister never."

"Then it's all settled. Good-bye, lads."

"Good-bye. A drop of brandy?"

"No, thank you."

"It's better for you than medicine."

"I have your word, then?"

"My name is Pundonor."[132]

"Good-bye."

"You are a gentleman and I am a caballero."

———

Clearly only devils could speak in this way. The boys did not stay to hear any more, and this time took to their heels in earnest. The French boy, finally convinced, ran faster than the others.

On the following Tuesday Sieur Clubin was back in Saint-Malo with the Durande.

The *Tamaulipas* was still in the roads.

Between two puffs on his pipe Sieur Clubin asked the landlord of the Auberge Jean:

"Well, when is the *Tamaulipas* sailing?"

"On Thursday; the day after tomorrow," replied the innkeeper.

That evening Clubin had his meal at the coastguards' table, and, contrary to his usual habit, went out after supper. As a result he was absent from the Durande's office and lost some of the vessel's freight. This was remarked on as being unlike a man so punctual in business.

He seems to have had a few minutes' conversation with his friend the money changer.

He returned two hours after Noguette[133] had rung the curfew. This Brazilian bell rings at ten o'clock; so it was midnight.

VI

La Jacressarde

Forty years ago there was an alley in Saint-Malo called the Ruelle Coutanchez. It no longer exists, having been caught up in improvements to the town.

It consisted of a double row of houses leaning toward each other and leaving just enough room between them for a gutter that was called the street. People walked with their legs apart on either side of the water, knocking their head or their elbow on the houses to right and left. These ancient medieval houses in Normandy have an almost human aspect. A dilapidated old hovel and a witch are not unlike each other. Their slanting upper stories, their overhangs, their circumflex-shaped canopies, and their scrub of ironwork are like lips, chins, noses, and eyebrows. The garret window is the eye, half blind. The wall is the cheek, wrinkled and covered with sores. Their foreheads are close together, as if they were plotting some mischief. This architecture summons up the idea of such old words, reflections of ancient villainy, as cutthroat and cutpurse.

One of the houses in the Ruelle Coutanchez—the largest and the best-known or most ill-famed—was called La Jacressarde. It was a lodging for the kind of people who have no permanent lodging. In all towns, and particularly in seaports, there is always to be found, below the general population, a residue. Lawless characters—so lawless that even the law sometimes cannot get its hands on them—pickers and stealers, tricksters living by their wits, chemists of villainy continually brewing up life in their crucibles; rags of every kind and every way of wearing them; withered fruits of roguery, bankrupt existences, consciences that have declared themselves insolvent; the incompetents of breaking and entering (for the big men of burglary are above all this); journeymen and journeywomen of evil, rascals both male and female; scruples in tatters and out at elbow; scoundrels who have sunk into poverty, evildoers who have had little reward from their work, losers in the social duel, devourers who now go hungry, the low earners of crime, beggars and villains: such are the people who form this residue. Human intelligence is to be found here, but it is bestial. This is the rubbish heap of souls, piled up in a corner and swept from time to time by the broom that is called a police raid. La Jacressarde was a corner of this kind in Saint-Malo.

In such dens you do not find the big men of crime, bandits and robbers, the major products of ignorance and poverty. If murder is represented here it is the work of some brutal drunkard; the robbers here are mere petty thieves. This is the spittle of society rather than its vomit. Small-time crooks, yes; brigands, no. Yet you can never be sure. On this lowest level of low life there may sometimes be extremes of wickedness. When the police raided the Épi-scié cabaret—which was for Paris what La Jacressarde was for Saint-Malo—they picked up Lacenaire.[134]

Lodgings of this kind accept anybody. A fall in the social scale is a leveling experience. Sometimes honesty reduced to rags finds a home there. Virtue and integrity, we know, can suffer misadventure. We should not, out of hand, value a Louvre highly or despise a prison.

Both public respect and universal reprobation must be bestowed only after careful examination. There can be surprises. An angel in a house of ill fame, a pearl on a dung heap: there may sometimes be such somber and dazzling discoveries.

La Jacressarde was a courtyard rather than a house, and a well rather than a courtyard. It had no windows looking onto the street. Its façade was a high wall pierced only by a low doorway leading into the courtyard. You lifted the latch, pushed the door, and found yourself in a courtyard.

In the middle of the courtyard was a round hole, its margin level with the ground. It was a well. The courtyard was small; the well was large. Around the well was broken paving.

On three sides of the courtyard, which was square, were buildings. On the street side there was nothing; but facing the doorway and to right and left was the house.

If, rather at your peril, you entered the courtyard after nightfall, you would hear the sound of mingled breathing, and if there was enough moonlight or starlight to give form to the obscure shapes that confronted you, this is what you would see:

The courtyard. The well. Around the courtyard, facing the door-way, a kind of shed in the form of a horseshoe (if a horseshoe can be square), a worm-eaten gallery open to the air, roofed with wooden beams borne on stone pillars set at irregular intervals; in the center, the well; around the well, on a litter of straw, a ring of boots and shoes, worn and down-at-heel; toes sticking through holes, numbers of bare heels; men's feet, women's feet, children's feet. All these feet were asleep.

Beyond the feet, in the semidarkness of the shed, your eye might distinguish bodies, forms, sleeping heads, figures lying inert, rags of both sexes, the promiscuity of the dunghill, a strange and sinister deposit of humanity. This sleeping chamber was open to anyone and everyone. The occupants paid two sous a week. Their feet touched the well. On stormy nights rain fell on these feet; on winter nights it snowed on these bodies.

Who were these creatures? Unknowns. They came in the evening and left in the morning.

The order of society is complicated by such human debris. Some of them slipped in for a single night and made off without paying. Most of them had had nothing to eat all day.

Every vice, every form of abjection, every infection, every kind of distress; the same sleep of despondency on the same bed of mud. The dreams of all these souls were very similar to one another. It was a ghastly concourse, mingling in the same miasma all their lassitudes, their weaknesses, their bouts of drunkenness, their marches and countermarches in a day without a crust of bread or a kindly thought; livid pallors with eyes tight closed; regrets, lusts; hair mingled with streetsweepings; faces with the look of death on them, perhaps of kisses from the mouths of darkness. All this human putridity fermented in this vat. They had been thrown into this lodging by fatality, by their wanderings, by a ship that had arrived the day before, by their release from prison, by chance, by the night. Each day destiny emptied its pack here. Hither came any who would, here slept any who could, here spoke any who dared; for this was a place of whispers. Those who came here were quick to mingle in the mass; they tried to forget themselves in sleep since they could not lose themselves in the dark. They took as much of death as they could. They closed their eyes in a kind of death agony that recurred every evening. Where did they come from? From society, of which they were the dregs; from the waves, on which they were the foam.

There was not enough straw to go around. Many a naked body lay on the hard paving. They lay down in the evening exhausted; they got up in the morning stiff and sore. The well, thirty feet deep, without a parapet, without a cover, gaped open day and night. Rain fell into it, filth oozed into it, all the trickles of water in the courtyard drained into it. Beside it was the bucket for drawing water. Anyone who was thirsty drank from it. Anyone who was tired of life drowned himself in it, slipping from his sleep amid the refuse to that other sleep. In 1819 the body of a boy of fourteen was taken out of the well.

To live safely in this house you had to "belong." Outsiders were not regarded with favor. Did these people know each other? No. They scented each other.

The mistress of the house was a young woman with a wooden leg, not bad-looking, who wore a bonnet trimmed with ribbons, who washed herself occasionally with water from the well.

At dawn the courtyard emptied; the occupants scattered in all directions.

There were a cock and some hens in the courtyard that scratched about in the refuse all day long. Across the courtyard ran a horizontal beam borne on posts, the likeness of a gallows that did not seem entirely out of place there. Sometimes, on the day after a rainy evening, a bedraggled silk dress belonging to the woman with the wooden leg would be hung out on the beam to dry.

Above the shed and, like it, running around the courtyard, was an upper story, and above this a loft. A staircase of rotting wood ran up through an aperture in the roof of the shed to the upper floor—a rickety ladder up which the woman with the wooden leg stumped noisily. Casual lodgers, paying by the week or by the night, slept in the courtyard. More permanent residents lived in the house.

Windows without glass, doorways without doors, fireplaces without fires: the house was like that. You passed from one room to another either through a long square hole where there had been a door or through a triangular gap between the joists in the dividing walls. The floors were littered with fallen plaster. It was hard to see how the house held together. It was shaken by every wind. Climbing the worn and slippery steps of the staircase was a hazardous business. The whole structure was open to the air. Winter entered the house as water enters a sponge. The multitude of spiders provided some reassurance against the immediate collapse of the building. There was no furniture of any kind. Two or three straw mattresses in the corners of the rooms, gaping open and revealing more ashes than straw. Here and there a jug and an earthenware pot, serving a variety of uses. A repellent sweetish smell.

From the windows there was a view of the courtyard—a view like the view of a scavenger's cart. The things—to say nothing of the people—that lay rotting, rusting, moldering there were indescribable. All the various kinds of debris fraternized; they fell off the walls, they fell off the occupants. The rags and tatters seeded the rubble.

In addition to the floating population of the courtyard La Jacressarde had three permanent lodgers—a coal man, a ragpicker, and a maker of gold. The coal man and the ragpicker occupied two of the straw mattresses on the first floor; the gold maker, a chemist, lodged in the loft. No one knew where the woman slept. The gold maker was also something of a poet. In the roof space, under the tiles, he had a room with a narrow window and a large stone fireplace in which the wind roared. Since the window had no frame he had nailed over it a strip of scrap metal salvaged from a ship, which admitted little light but plenty of cold air. The coal man paid for his lodging with a sack of coal from time to time; the ragpicker paid with a setier of grain for the chickens once a week; the gold maker did not pay anything. In the meantime he was burning up the house. He had torn off what little woodwork there was and kept taking laths from the wall or the roof to heat his crucible. On the wall above the rag-and-bone man's bed were two columns of figures written in chalk, a column of threes and a column of fives, according to whether a setier of grain cost three liards or five centimes.[135] For his crucible the "chemist" used a broken old shell-case, promoted by him to the role of cauldron, in which he mixed his ingredients. He was obsessed with the idea of transmutation. Sometimes he talked about it to the vagrants in the courtyard, who laughed at him. Then he would say: "People like that are full of prejudices." He was determined not to die until he had thrown the philosopher's stone through the windows of science. His furnace consumed a great deal of wood. The banisters of the staircase had disappeared into its maw, and the whole of the house was going that way, little by little. The landlady used to say to him: "You will leave us nothing but the shell." Then he would disarm her by writing poetry to her.

Such was La Jacressarde.

The domestic staff consisted of a goitrous boy, or perhaps a dwarf, who might have been twelve or might have been sixty, who went about with a broom in his hand.

The lodgers entered by the doorway leading into the courtyard; the general public entered through the shop.

What was the shop?

In the high wall facing onto the street, to the right of the entrance to the courtyard, was a square opening that was both a door and a window, with shutters and a window frame—the only shutters in the whole of the house with hinges and bolts. Behind this window, opening off the street, was a small room formed by cutting off a corner of the shed around the courtyard. Scrawled in charcoal on the street door was the inscription CURIOSITY SHOP—a term that was then in use. On three shelves in the shop window could be seen a few china jars without handles, a torn Chinese parasol in figured gold-beater's skin that could be neither opened nor shut, some shapeless fragments of iron and earthenware, battered hats and bonnets, three or four ormer shells, a few packets of bone and copper buttons, a snuffbox with a portrait of

Marie-Antoinette, an odd volume of Bois-Bertrand's *Algebra*. This was the shop; these were the "curiosities" sold here. A door in the back of the shop led into the courtyard in which was the well. In the shop were a table and a stool. The shopkeeper was the woman with the wooden leg.

VII

SHADY TRANSACTIONS

Clubin had been away from the Auberge Jean for the whole of Tuesday evening, and he was away again on Wednesday evening.

That evening, as night was falling, two men walked along the Ruelle Coutanchez and stopped in front of La Jacressarde. One of them knocked on the window. The shop door was open, and they went in. The woman with the wooden leg put on the smile she kept for respectable citizens. There was a candle on the table.

The men were indeed respectable citizens.

The one who had knocked on the window said: "Good evening, mistress. I've come about you know what."

The woman smiled again and went out of the door into the courtyard. A moment later a man appeared in the half-open door. He was wearing a cap and an overall, with the bulge of some object showing under the overall. He had bits of straw in the creases in his overall, and the look of someone just roused from sleep.

He came forward. The three looked at one another. The man in the overall had a wary, cunning air. He asked: "You are the gunsmith?"

The man who had knocked on the window replied: "Yes. You are the man from Paris?"

"Name of Redskin. Yes."

"Let me see it."

"There you are."

The man drew from under his overall an object rarely seen in Europe at that time—a revolver.

It was new and shining. The two men examined it. The one who seemed to know the establishment and had been addressed as the gunsmith tried the mechanism and then passed the revolver to the other man, who looked less like a local man and kept his back turned to the light.

The gunsmith asked: "How much?"

The man in the overall answered: "I've just brought it from America. There are some who bring in monkeys and parrots and animals, as if the French were savages. That is what I bring in. It's a useful invention."

"How much?" repeated the gunsmith.

"It's a pistol that revolves."

"How much?"

"Bang! The first shot. Bang! The second shot. Bang! A whole volley of shots! It does a good job."

"How much?"

"It has six barrels."

"Well: how much?"

"For six barrels the price is six louis."

"Will you take five?"

"Can't be done. One louis per bullet. That's the price."

"Come, now: if we're to do business you must be reasonable."

"I've put a fair price on it. Just examine it, Mr. Gunsmith."

"I have examined it."

"It turns as fast as Monsieur Talleyrand. It ought to be in the *Dictionary of Weathervanes.*[136] It's a jewel."

"I've looked at it."

"The barrels are of Spanish forging."

"I can see that."

"It's rifled. I'll tell you how they do the rifling. They empty into the forge the stock of a scrap-iron dealer—a load of old iron, farriers' nails, broken horseshoes—"

"And old scythe-blades."

"As I was just going to say, Mr. Gunsmith. Then they expose the whole lot to a good sweating heat, and that gives you the finest quality of iron."

"Yes; but there can be cracks and faults in the metal."

"True enough. But they put that right by small dovetails, just as they avoid the risk of defects in soldering by heavy pounding. They weld it together with a heavy hammer and give it two more turns in the furnace. If the iron has been overheated they retemper it with strong heats and light hammering. Then the stuff is drawn out and well rolled on the lining; and with iron of that quality you get a barrel like this."

"You are in the trade, then?"

"I'm a man of all trades."

"The barrel is very light-colored."

"That's the beauty of it, Mr. Gunsmith. They get that effect with butter of antimony."

"So we are going to pay you five louis for it?"

"If you don't mind, sir, may I remind you that I said six louis?"

The gunsmith lowered his voice: "Listen to me, Mr. Parisian. Take your chance, and get rid of it. A gun like that is not a good thing for a man like you to have. It draws attention to you."

"True enough," said the man from Paris. "It is a bit conspicuous. It's better for a respectable citizen."

"Will you take five louis?"

"No: six. One for each hole."

"All right, then: six napoleons."

"I want six louis."

"You are not a Bonapartist, then? You prefer a louis to a napoleon?"

The man from Paris who called himself Redskin smiled.

"Napoleon is better," he said; "but Louis is worth more."

"Six napoleons."

"Six louis. It makes a difference of twenty-four francs to me."

"In that case there's no deal."

"All right. I'll keep this little trinket."

"Keep it, then."

"Asking for a cut price! Not likely! I'm not the man to give away a thing like that—a new invention."

"Good-bye, then."

"It's a great improvement on a pistol, which the Chesapeake Indians call Nortay-u-Hah."

"Five louis in cash is good money."

"Nortay-u-Hah means Short Gun. Not many people know that."

"Will you take five louis and an écu thrown in?"

"I said six, sir."

During this conversation the man who had kept his back to the candle and had not yet spoken had been making the mechanism revolve.

He now went up to the gunsmith and whispered in his ear, "Is it a good one?"

"First-rate."

"Then I'll pay the six louis."

Five minutes later, while the man from Paris who called himself Redskin was tucking the six louis into a secret recess under the armpit of his overall, the gunsmith and the purchaser of the revolver, carrying it in his trouser pocket, left the Ruelle Coutanchez.

VIII

Cannon Off the Red and Off the Black

On the following day, which was Thursday, a tragic event took place a little way out of Saint-Malo, near the Pointe du Décollé, at a spot where the cliffs are high and the sea is deep.

There a tongue of rock shaped like a spearhead, linked with the mainland by a narrow isthmus, reaches out to sea and ends abruptly in a sheer crag—a very common feature in the architecture of the sea. To reach level ground above the crag from the shore involves climbing up a slope that at some points is quite steep.

About four o'clock in the afternoon there was standing on a level spot of this kind a man wearing a uniform cape and probably armed, to judge from the straight, angular folds in his cape. The summit of the crag on which he stood was a level area of some size scattered with large cubes of rock like giant paving stones, with narrow fissures between them. This platform, with a dense carpet of low-growing grass, ended in an open space above a vertical rock-face, rising some sixty feet above high-water level, which looked as if it had been cut with the help of a plumb line. Its left-hand corner, however, had broken away, forming one of those natural staircases commonly found in granite cliffs, with awkwardly shaped steps that sometimes call for the strides of a giant or the agility of a clown. This tumble of rocks reached perpendicularly down to the sea and continued down into it. It was a breakneck track, but if need be a man could make his way down to embark in a boat at the foot of the cliff.

A breeze was blowing. The man, wrapped in his cape, stood firmly on his feet, holding his right elbow in his left hand and with his other hand on a telescope, through which he was looking, with one eye closed. He seemed absorbed in an intent watch. He had moved forward to the very edge of the cliff and stood motionless there, his eye imperturbably fixed on the horizon. It was high tide, and the waves were beating against the base of the cliff below him.

The object the man was watching was a ship out at sea that was behaving in a peculiar manner.

The ship, which had left Saint-Malo harbor barely an hour before, had stopped beyond the Banquetiers. It was a three-master. She had not dropped anchor but had merely lain to, perhaps because the bottom would have allowed her to bear to leeward only on the edge of the cable and because she would have strained on her anchor under the cutwater.

The man, whose uniform cape showed him to be a coastguardsman, was following all the movements of the three-master, and seemed to be taking a mental note of them. The ship was lying to a little off the wind; the fore topsail was taken aback and the wind was filling the main topsail. The mizzen had been squared and the topsail had been set as close as possible so as to work the sails against one another and to make little way either on- or offshore. Her master had evidently no wish to expose his vessel much to the wind, for he had only braced up the small mizzen topsail, so that the ship, coming crossway on, was drifting at no more than half a league an hour.

It was still broad daylight, particularly out at sea and on the top of the cliff. Lower down, on the coast, the light was beginning to fail.

The coastguardsman, engrossed in his task and conscientiously scanning the open sea, had not been watching the cliff beside him and below him. His back was turned to the rough stone staircase leading from the sea to the top of the cliff. He did not notice that something was moving there. Behind a crevice in the rocks there was someone—a man—who had evidently been hiding there before the coastguardsman's arrival. Every now and then, in the shadow of the rock, a head appeared, looking up, watching the watcher. The head, wearing a broad-brimmed American hat, belonged to the Quaker who had been seen ten days ago talking to Captain Zuela amid the rocks on the Petit Bey.

Suddenly the coastguardsman's attention seemed to redouble. Quickly he wiped the glass of the telescope with the sleeve of his cape and focused it on the three-master.

A small black dot had left the ship.

The black dot, like an ant on the surface of the sea, was a boat. It seemed to be making for the shore. It was manned by a number of seamen, rowing vigorously. It gradually altered course and headed for the Pointe du Décollé.

The coastguardsman's watch had reached a peak of intensity. He followed every moment of the boat's movement. He had drawn even closer to the edge of the cliff.

At this moment the figure of a tall man, the Quaker, appeared at the top of the rock staircase, behind the coastguardsman. The watcher did not see him.

The man stopped for a moment, his arms hanging by his sides and his fists clenched, and watched the coastguardsman's back, like a hunter watching his prey.

He was only four paces behind the coastguardsman. He took a step forward and stopped; then took another step, and stopped again. Only his legs moved; the rest of his body was as still as a statue. His footsteps made no sound on the grass. Then he took a third step, and stopped again. He was now almost touching the coastguardsman, who remained motionless, intent on his watch. The man slowly brought his clenched fists up to the level of his collarbone; then his arms suddenly shot forward, and his fists, as if released by a trigger, struck the coastguardsman's shoulders. It was a fatal blow. The coastguardsman had no time even to utter a cry. He fell head first from the cliff into the sea. There was a brief glimpse of the soles of his shoes. It was as if a stone had fallen into the sea. Then the water closed over him.

A few large circles formed on the dark water.

All that was left was the telescope that had fallen from the coastguardsman's hands and was lying on the grass.

The Quaker looked down from the edge of the cliff, watched the ripples on the sea dying down, waited for a few minutes, and then stood up, humming between his teeth:

Monsieur d'la Police est mort
En perdant sa vie.

The gentleman of the police is dead
As a result of losing his life.

He looked down again. Nothing had reappeared; but, at the spot where the coastguardsman had fallen into the water, a brown patch had formed on the surface of the water and was spreading under the movement of the waves. Probably the coastguardsman had fractured his skull on some underwater rock and his blood had risen and formed this stain on the sea.

Watching this reddish patch, the Quaker went on humming his song:

Un quart d'heure avant sa mort,
Il était encore—

A quarter of an hour before his death
He was still—

He did not finish. He heard a soft voice behind him saying: "So there you are, Rantaine. How are you? You have just killed a man."

He turned around and saw, in a crevice in the rocks, some fifteen paces away, a short man holding a revolver.

He replied: "As you see. How do you do, Sieur Clubin?"

The other man started.

"You recognize me, then?"

"You recognized me all right," said Rantaine.

The sound of oars was heard. It was the boat that the coastguardsman had been watching, now approaching the coast.

Sieur Clubin murmured, as if speaking to himself: "It was over very quickly."

"What can I do for you?" asked Rantaine.

"Not much. It is just ten years since I saw you last. You must have done well for yourself. How are you?"

"Pretty well," said Rantaine. "What about you?"

"Very well," replied Sieur Clubin.

Rantaine took a step toward Sieur Clubin.

He heard a sharp click. It was Sieur Clubin cocking the revolver.

"Rantaine, we are fifteen paces from one another. It's a good distance. Stay where you are."

"Very well," said Rantaine. "What do you want of me?"

"I have come to talk to you."

Rantaine did not move. Sieur Clubin went on:

"You have just murdered a coastguardsman."

Rantaine raised the brim of his hat and replied:

"You have already told me that."

"In rather less precise terms. I said, a man; now I say, a coastguardsman. This coastguardsman was No. 619. He was married, and he leaves a wife and five children."

"That may well be," said Rantaine.

After an imperceptible pause Clubin went on:

"These coastguardsmen are picked men; almost all of them are former sailors."

"I have noticed," said Rantaine, "that they do generally leave a wife and five children."

Sieur Clubin continued:

"How much do you think this revolver cost me?"

"It's a good little gun," said Rantaine.

"What do you think it's worth?"

"I think a lot of it."

"It cost me a hundred and forty-four francs."

"You must have bought it," said Rantaine, "in the shop in Rue Coutanchez."

Clubin went on:

"He didn't even give a cry. Falling cuts off your voice."

"Sieur Clubin, there's going to be a bit of a breeze tonight."

"I am the only one in the know."

"Do you still put up at the Auberge Jean?" asked Rantaine.

"Yes; it's a comfortable place."

"I remember having had a good dish of sauerkraut there."

"You must be very strong, Rantaine. What shoulders you have! I wouldn't like to get a tap from you. When *I* came into the world I looked so puny that they weren't sure whether they would be able to keep me alive."

"Fortunately, they managed to."

"Yes, I still put up at the old Auberge Jean."

"Do you know, Sieur Clubin, how I recognized you? It was because you recognized *me*. I said to myself, 'Only Clubin could do that.' "

And he took a step forward.

"Get back to where you were, Rantaine."

Rantaine retreated, saying to himself in an aside: "Faced with a thing like that, you're as helpless as a child."

Sieur Clubin went on:

"Now, this is the situation. To the right, in the direction of Saint-Énogat, three hundred paces from here, we have another coastguardsman, No. 618, who is alive, and to the left, toward Saint-Lunaire, a customs post. That makes seven armed men who can be here within five minutes. The rock is surrounded. The pass will be guarded. There is no way of escape. There is a corpse at the foot of the cliff."

Rantaine cast a sidelong glance at the revolver.

"As you say, Rantaine, it is a good little gun. Perhaps it is only loaded with blank, but what difference does that make? It needs only one shot to bring all these armed men to the spot. I have six shots to fire."

The sound of oars was increasingly distinct. The boat was very near now.

The tall man looked at the shorter man with a strange look in his eye. Sieur Clubin's voice was becoming increasingly tranquil and gentle.

"Rantaine, the men in the boat that is coming in would help to arrest you. You are paying Captain Zuela ten thousand francs for your passage. As a matter of fact, you could have done a better deal with the Pleinmont smugglers; but they would only have taken you to England, and you cannot risk going to Guernsey, where you are known. So the situation is this. If I fire you will be arrested. You are paying Zuela ten thousand francs to get you away, and you have given him a down payment of five thousand francs. Zuela would keep the five thousand francs and go on his way. There you are, then. You have a good disguise, Rantaine. That hat, that coat of yours, and these gaiters change you. You have lost your spectacles, and it was a good idea to let your whiskers grow."

Rantaine smiled: a smile that was more like a grimace. Clubin went on:

"Rantaine, you are wearing a pair of American trousers with two fobs. In one of them is your watch: you can keep it."

"Thank you, Sieur Clubin."

"In the other is a small box of beaten iron with a spring-loaded lid. It is an old sailor's tobacco box. Take it out of your fob and throw it to me."

"But that is robbery!"

"Call for help if you want to."

And Clubin continued to fix his eyes on Rantaine.

"Look here, Mess Clubin—," said Rantaine, taking a step forward and holding out his open hand.

The style "Mess" was an attempt at flattery.

"Stay where you are, Rantaine."

"Mess Clubin, we can come to some arrangement. I'll give you half."

Clubin folded his arms, allowing the tip of his revolver to show.

"What do you take me for, Rantaine? I am a respectable citizen."

After a moment's pause he added: "I want the lot."

Rantaine muttered between his teeth: "He's a hard man, this fellow."

A gleam came into Clubin's eye. His voice became as sharp and cutting as steel:

"I see you don't understand the position. It is you who go in for robbery: my aim is restitution. Listen to me, Rantaine. Ten years ago you left Guernsey by night, taking from the funds of a partnership of which you were a member fifty thousand francs that belonged to you but failing to leave behind fifty thousand francs that belonged to someone else. Those fifty thousand francs that you stole from your partner, the good and worthy Mess Lethierry, now amount, with compound interest over ten years, to eighty thousand six hundred and sixty-six francs and seventy centimes. Yesterday you went to a money changer. I will tell you his name: it was Rébuchet, in Rue Saint-Vincent. You gave him seventy-six thousand francs in French banknotes, for which he gave you three English banknotes, each for a thousand pounds sterling, plus some small change. You put the banknotes in the iron tobacco box and put the box in your right-hand fob. These three thousand pounds are worth seventy-five thousand francs. On behalf of Mess Lethierry, I shall be satisfied with that amount. I am leaving tomorrow for Guernsey, and I mean to hand them over to him. Rantaine, the three-master lying to out there is the *Tamaulipas*. Last night you had your baggage stowed away aboard her among the bags and trunks of the crew. You want to get away from France. You have good reason to. You are going to Arequipa.

"The boat is coming to fetch you, and you are waiting for it here. It is just coming: you can hear the sound of oars. It is up to me either to let you go or compel you to stay. But that's enough talking. Throw me the tobacco box."

Rantaine opened his fob, took out a small box, and threw it to Clubin. It was the iron tobacco box. It rolled to Clubin's feet.

Clubin bent down without lowering his head and picked the box up in his left hand, keeping his two eyes and the six barrels of the revolver trained on Rantaine.

Then he cried: "Turn around."

Rantaine turned his back.

Sieur Clubin tucked the revolver away under his armpit and pressed the spring to open the box.

It contained four banknotes, three for a thousand pounds and one for ten pounds.

He folded up the three thousand-pound notes, put them back in the tobacco box, closed the box, and put it in his pocket. Then he picked up a pebble, wrapped the ten-pound note around it, and called to Rantaine:

"Turn around again."

Rantaine turned around. Sieur Clubin went on:

"I told you I would be satisfied with three thousand pounds. You can have the ten pounds back."

And he threw Rantaine the note wrapped around the pebble.

Rantaine kicked the banknote and the pebble into the sea.

"As you please," said Clubin. "I see you must be well off. I needn't worry about you."

The sound of oars, which had become steadily closer during this exchange, now ceased, showing that the boat had reached the foot of the cliff.

"Your cab is waiting for you down there. You may go, Rantaine."

Rantaine made for the rock staircase and started to go down.

Clubin walked carefully to the edge of the cliff, bent his head, and watched Rantaine's descent.

The boat had stopped near the last step in the cliff face, at the very spot where the coastguardsman had fallen.

As he watched Rantaine going down Clubin muttered:

"Poor No. 619! He thought he was alone. Rantaine thought that there were only two of them. I was the only one who knew that there were three of us."

He noticed, lying on the grass at his feet, the telescope that had been dropped by the coastguardsman, and picked it up.

The sound of oars was heard again. Rantaine had just jumped into the boat, and it was putting out to sea.

After the first few strokes of the oars, when the boat was beginning to pull away from the cliff, Rantaine suddenly stood up, his face distorted with rage, and shook his fist, shouting:

"Oh, the Devil himself is a rascal!"

A few seconds later Clubin, standing on the cliff top and training the telescope on the boat, distinctly heard these words, shouted in a loud voice above the noise of the sea:

"Sieur Clubin, you are a respectable citizen, but you won't mind if I write to Lethierry to tell him what has happened. There is a sailor from Guernsey in the boat, named Ahier-Tostevin, one of the crew of the *Tamaulipas*, who will be coming back to Saint-Malo on Zuela's next voyage and will bear witness to the fact that I have given you, on Mess Lethierry's behalf, the sum of three thousand pounds sterling."

It was the voice of Rantaine.

Clubin liked to see things through. Standing motionless as the coastguardsman had stood, and on the same spot, his eye glued to the telescope, he kept his glance firmly fixed on the boat. He watched it growing steadily smaller amid the waves, disappearing and reappearing, drawing near the ship that was lying to and finally coming alongside, and was able to make out the tall figure of Rantaine standing on the deck of the *Tamaulipas*.

When the boat had been hauled in and slung up on the davits the *Tamaulipas* got under way. A breeze was blowing up to seaward, and she spread all her sails. Clubin kept his telescope trained on the outline of the ship, which became increasingly indistinct. In half an hour the *Tamaulipas* was no more than a black spot diminishing on the horizon against the pale twilight sky.

IX

USEFUL INFORMATION FOR THOSE EXPECTING, OR FEARING, LETTERS FROM OVERSEAS

That evening Sieur Clubin was again late in returning to his inn.

One of the causes of his lateness was that before returning he had gone to the Porte Dinan, where there were a number of taverns. In one of the taverns where he was not known he had bought a bottle of brandy, which he had put in one of the capacious pockets of his sea jacket as if he wanted to hide it. Then, since the Durande was due to sail the following morning, he had looked around the ship to make sure that everything was in order.

When Sieur Clubin returned to the Auberge Jean there was no one in the lower room but the old oceangoing captain Monsieur Gertrais-Gaboureau, sitting with his tankard and smoking his pipe. He greeted Sieur Clubin between a mouthful of beer and a puff of smoke:

"How d'you do,[137] Captain Clubin?"

"Good evening, Captain Gertrais."

"Well, there's the *Tamaulipas* away."

"Ah!" said Clubin: "I hadn't noticed."

Captain Gertrais-Gaboureau spat and went on:

"Zuela's off."

"When did he go?"

"This evening."

"Where is he off to?"

"To the Devil."

"I dare say; but where?"

"Arequipa."

"I didn't know that," said Clubin.

He added:

"I'm going to bed."

He lit his candle, walked to the door, and then came back.

"Have you been to Arequipa, Captain Gertrais?"

"Yes. Years ago."

"Where do you call in on the way there?"

"In all sorts of places. But the *Tamaulipas* won't be calling in any-where."

Monsieur Gertrais-Gaboureau knocked out the ash from his pipe on the edge of a plate and went on:

"You know the lugger *Cheval de Troie* and that fine three-master the *Trentemouzin* that set off for Cardiff? I didn't think they ought to go because of the weather. When they came back they were in a pretty state. The lugger had a cargo of turpentine. She sprang a leak, and when they started pumping they pumped out all the turpentine along with the water. As for the three-master, she suffered mainly in her topsides. The cutwater, the head rail, the bumkins, and the stock of the port anchor were all broken. The flying jibboom of the outer jib was broken off at the cap. The jib shrouds and the bobstays—what a pretty state they were in! The mizzenmast is all right, but it has had a severe shock. All the iron on the bowsprit has given way, but by a wonder the bowsprit itself was only scraped, though it is completely stripped. There's a hole three feet square in the bow on the port side. That's what happens when you don't take advice."

Clubin had put his candle down on the table and had begun taking out and replacing a row of pins he had in the collar of his jacket. Then he went on:

"Didn't you say, Captain Gertrais, that the *Tamaulipas* won't be calling in anywhere?"

"No, she won't. She's making straight for Chile."

"In that case there won't be any word from her until she gets there."

"No, you're wrong, Captain Clubin. In the first place, she can send mail by any vessels bound for Europe that she meets."

"I see."

"And then there is the post box of the sea."

"What do you mean by the post box of the sea?"

"You don't know what that is, Captain Clubin?"

"No."

"When you pass the Strait of Magellan—"

"Well?"

"Snow everywhere, always rough weather, vile winds, a foul sea."

"What then?"

"When you have rounded Cape Monmouth—"

"Then?"

"Then you round Cape Valentine."

"And then?"

"Then you round Cape Isidore."

"And then?"

"You round Cape Anna."

"All right. But what is the post box of the sea you talk about?"

"I'm coming to that. Mountains to right of you, mountains to left of you; penguins everywhere, and stormy petrels. A fearful place! *Mille saints mille singes!* What a battering you get there! What winds! The squalls don't need any help there! That's where you have to look to the wing transom. That's where you shorten sail. That's where you replace the mainsail by the jib, and the jib by the storm jib. One blast of wind after another! And then sometimes four, five, or six days under bare poles. Often a brand-new suit of sails will be reduced to rags. What a dance it leads you! Gusts that make a three-master hop like a flea. I once saw a little cabin boy on an English brig, the *True Blue*, swept off the jibboom he was working on, and the jibboom with him. You're thrown into the air like butterflies! And I saw the leading hand on the *Revenue*, a pretty little schooner, torn off the fore crosstree and killed on the spot. I have had my sheer rails smashed and my waterway in smithereens. You come out of it with all your sails in ribbons. Fifty-gun frigates take in water like a wicker basket. And what a devilish coast it is! Rugged as they come. Such jagged rocks and reefs! Then you come to Port Famine. There it's worst of all. The heaviest breakers I've seen in my life. It's a hellish place. And there you suddenly see these two words written in red: POST OFFICE."

"What do you mean, Captain Gertrais?"

"What I mean, Captain Clubin, is that immediately after you have rounded Cape Anna you see on a rock a hundred feet high a tall post with a barrel hanging from it. The barrel is the post box of the sea. The English thought fit to label it Post Office. What business was it of theirs? It is the post office of the ocean; it does not belong to that honorable gentleman the king of England. This post box is common property. It belongs to all who sail the seas, whatever flag they fly. Post Office, indeed! It's as if the Devil himself were offering you a cup of tea. And this is how it works. Every vessel that passes that way sends a boat to the barrel with her mail. Ships coming from the Atlantic post their letters for Europe, and ships coming from the Pacific post their letters for America. The officer in charge of your boat puts your letters into the barrel and takes out those he finds in it. You take these letters; and the boat that comes after you will take yours. As you are sailing in opposite directions the continent you have come from is the one I am going to. I carry your letters, and you carry mine. The barrel is made fast to the post with a chain. And it rains! And it snows! And it hails! And what a dirty sea, with the stormy petrels flying all around you! The *Tamaulipas* will pass that way. The barrel has a good hinged lid, but no lock or padlock. So you see, you can write to your friends, and the letters will be delivered."

"Curious," muttered Clubin thoughtfully.

Captain Gertrais-Gaboureau returned to his beer.

"If that rascal Zuela wanted to write to me he would put his scribble in the barrel at Magellan, and I would get it four months later.— Well, Captain Clubin, are you leaving tomorrow?"

Clubin, absorbed in a kind of daydream, did not hear. Captain Gertrais repeated his question.

Clubin woke up.

"Yes, of course, Captain Gertrais. It's my day. I must sail tomorrow morning."

"If I were you I wouldn't go, Captain Clubin. The hair on dogs' coats smells damp. For the last two nights the seabirds have been wheeling around the lighthouse. It's a bad sign. I have a storm glass that is misbehaving. We are in the moon's second quarter; the month is at its wettest. A little while ago I saw pimpernels closing up their leaves and a field of clover with the stems of the flowers standing up straight. The worms are coming out of the ground, the flies are biting, the bees are staying in their hives, the sparrows are twittering. You can hear church bells a long way off. This evening I heard the Angelus from Saint-Lunaire. And there was a dirty sunset. There will be heavy fog tomorrow. I wouldn't advise you to sail. I'm more afraid of fog than of a hurricane. It's a treacherous thing, fog."

BOOK VI

Drunk Helmsman, Sober Captain

I

The Douvres

Some five leagues out to sea, to the south of Guernsey, opposite Plein-mont Point and between the Channel Islands and Saint-Malo, is a group of rocks known as the Douvres.[138] It is a baneful spot.

There are many reefs and rocks called Douvre, in English Dover. Near the Côtes du Nord is a rock with the name of Douvre on which a lighthouse is at present being built. It is a dangerous reef, but it is not to be confused with the one we are concerned with here.

The nearest point to the Douvres on the French mainland is Cap Bréhant. They are a little farther from the French coast than the near-est of the Channel Islands. Their distance from Jersey is about the same as the distance from the northwest to the southeast of Jersey. If that island were turned on Corbière Point as on a hinge the promon-tory in St. Catherine's Bay would reach almost exactly to the Douvres. The distance is rather more than four leagues.

In the seas of the civilized world even the wildest rocks are seldom deserted. There are smugglers on Hagot, customs officers on Binic, Celts on Bréhat, oyster cultivators at Cancale, rabbit catchers on Césambre or Caesar's Island, crab gatherers on Brecqhou, trawlermen on the Minquiers, hand-net fishers on Les Écrehou. On the Douvres there is no one. Only seabirds make their home there.

No spot in the ocean is more dreaded. The Casquets, on which the

White Ship is said to have been wrecked; the Calvados Bank; the Needles on the Isle of Wight; the Ronesse, which makes the Beaulieu coast
so dangerous; the Préel shoals, which restrict the entrance to Merquel
and make it necessary to set the red-painted marker buoy twenty fathoms out; the treacherous approaches to Étables and Plouha; the two
granite Druids off the south coast of Guernsey, Old Anderlo and Little Anderlo; Corbière Point; the Hanois; the Île des Ras, whose terrors
are expressed in the saying,

> *Si jamais tu passes le Ras,*
> *si tu ne meurs, tu trembleras;*

> Should ever you pass by the Ras,
> if you do not die, you will tremble;

the Mortes-Femmes, the passage between the Boue and the Frouquie;
the Déroute between Guernsey and Jersey; the Hardent between the
Minquiers and Chousey; the Mauvais Cheval between Boulay Bay and
Barneville—none of these has such a sinister reputation as the Douvres. A seaman would rather face all these rocks, one after the other,
than the Douvres once.

In all this perilous sea that is the Channel—the Aegean of the
west—there is nothing to equal the terrors of the Douvres apart from
the Paternoster reef between Guernsey and Sark. And even from the
Paternoster you can signal for help: it is within sight of Icart Point to
the north and Gros-Nez to the south. From the Douvres you can see
nothing.

There is nothing here but squalls, water, clouds, limitless horizons,
emptiness. No one sails this way unless he has lost his bearings. The
granite rocks are huge and hideous. Cliffs everywhere. The harsh in-
hospitability of the abyss.

This is the open sea. The water here is very deep. A completely isolated rock like the Douvres attracts and provides a home for creatures
that shun the haunts of men. It is like a huge madrepore, a submarine
bank of coral. It is a labyrinth engulfed by the sea. Here, at a depth that
divers can barely reach, are hidden caves and caverns and dens, a network of dark passageways in which monstrous creatures pullulate.
They devour each other: the crabs eat the fish and are themselves

eaten. In this dark world roam fearful living shapes, created to be unseen by the human eye. Vague forms of mouths, antennae, tentacles, gaping jaws, scales, claws, and pincers float and quiver in the water, grow larger, decompose, and disappear in the sinister transparency. Fearful swarms of sea creatures swim to and fro, prowling, doing what they have to do. It is a hive of hydras.

This is horror in its ideal form.

Imagine, if you can, a teeming mass of holothurians.

To see the inmost depths of the sea is to see the imagination of the Unknown, and to see it from its most terrible side. This abyss has a likeness to night. Here, too, there is a form of sleep, of apparent sleep at least: the sleep of the consciousness of created things. Here are committed, with no fear of retribution, the crimes of the irresponsible. Here, in a fearful peace, rude forms of life—almost phantoms, but wholly demons—go about the dread business of this dark world.

Forty years ago two rocks of extraordinary form marked out the Douvres from afar to any who passed that way: two slender pillars curving toward each other and almost touching at the top. They looked like the tusks of an elephant that had been swallowed up by the sea; only, tall as towers, they were the tusks of an elephant the size of a mountain. Between these two natural towers guarding the dark city of monsters there was only a narrow passage through which the waves surged. This twisting passage, with a series of sharp bends, was like a narrow street between enclosing walls. These twin rocks were called the two Douvres, the Great Douvre and the Little Douvre; one was sixty feet high, the other forty. The constant to-and-fro movement of the waves had acted like a saw at the base of these towers, and on October 26, 1859, a violent equinoctial gale overthrew one of them. The remaining tower, the smaller one, is battered and truncated.

One of the strangest rocks in the Douvres group is known as the Homme or Man. It still stands. Last century some fishermen who had been blown off their course onto this rocky shore found the body of a man on top of this rock. Beside the body were numbers of empty seashells. The man had been shipwrecked here and had taken refuge on the rock, had lived for some time on shellfish, and then had died. Hence the name of the rock.

The solitudes of the ocean are melancholy: tumult and silence combined. What happens there no longer concerns the human race. Its use or value is unknown. Such a place is the Douvres. All around, as far as the eye can see, is nothing but the immense turbulence of the waves.

II

AN UNEXPECTED BOTTLE OF BRANDY

On Friday morning, the day after the departure of the *Tamaulipas,* the Durande sailed for Guernsey. She left Saint-Malo at nine.

The weather was fine; there was no mist. It looked as if old Captain Gertrais-Gaboureau had been maundering.

Sieur Clubin's other activities had evidently cost him most of his cargo. He had loaded only a few packages of fancy goods for shops in St. Peter Port and three crates for the Guernsey hospital, one of yellow soap, another of candles, and a third of French sole leather and fine Cordovan leather. From his previous cargo he was bringing back a case of crushed sugar and three cases of Congou tea to which the French customs had refused entry. He had embarked very little livestock; only a few bullocks, which were rather loosely stowed in the hold.

There were six passengers: a Guernsey man; two Saint-Malo cattle dealers; a "tourist" (a term that was already coming into use at that period); a Parisian of the lower middle class who was probably a commercial traveler; and an American, traveling to distribute Bibles.

The Durande had a crew of seven in addition to the captain, Sieur Clubin: a helmsman, a chief engineer, a carpenter, a cook (who could also work as a seaman if need be), two stokers, and a cabin boy. One of the stokers was also an engineer. This stoker-cum-engineer, a very brave and very intelligent Dutch Negro who had escaped from the sugar refineries of Surinam, was called Imbrancam. He understood the ship's engines and looked after them admirably. In the ship's early days his jet-black face emerging from the engine room had helped to give the Durande her diabolical reputation.

The helmsman, a Jersey man by birth but of Cotentin stock, was called Tangrouille, of a family of the higher nobility.

This was literally true. The Channel Islands, like England, are a hierarchical country. There are still castes in the islands. The castes have their own ideas, which are their defenses. The ideas of castes are the same everywhere, in India as in Germany. Nobility is won by the sword, and is lost by working. It is preserved by idleness. To do nothing is to live nobly; those who do no work are honored. To have a trade brings you down in the world.

Formerly in France an exception was made only for glass manufacturers: emptying bottles being one of the glories of a nobleman, making them did not bring dishonor. In the archipelago of the Channel, as in Great Britain, those who want to remain noble must remain rich. A workman cannot be a gentleman. Even if he has been a gentleman he is one no longer. Many a seaman is descended from knights bannerets but is now only a seaman. Thirty years ago on Alderney there was a lineal descendant of the Gorges family who would have had a claim to the seigneurie of Gorges, confiscated by King Philippe Auguste; he walked barefoot along the beaches, gathering seaweed. A Carteret is a carter on Sark. There are a draper on Jersey and a shoemaker on Guernsey named Gruchy who claim to be members of the Grouchy family and cousins of the French marshal of that name who fought at Waterloo. The old records of the diocese of Coutances mention a seigneurie of Tangroville, evidently related to Tancarville on the lower Seine, which belonged to the Montmorency family. In the fifteenth century Johan de Héroudeville, an archer and squire in the service of the seigneur of Tangroville, carried "his corslet and other equipment." In May 1371, as Bertrand du Guesclin tells us, "Monsieur de Tangroville did his devoir as knight bachelor" at Pontorson. But in the Channel Islands, if you fall into poverty, you are quickly eliminated from the nobility. It takes only a change of pronunciation. Tangroville becomes Tangrouille, and that is the end of the matter.

This had been the fate of the helmsman of the Durande.

In St. Peter Port, on the Bordage, is a scrap metal merchant named Ingrouille who is probably an Ingroville. In the reign of Louis the Fat the Ingroville family owned three parishes in the electorate of Valognes. A certain Abbé Trigan wrote the *Ecclesiastical History of Normandy*. He was priest in the seigneurie of Digoville. If the seigneur of Digoville had become a commoner he would have been called Digouille.

Tangrouille, probably a Tancarville and possibly a Montmorency, had the time-honored characteristic of a nobleman, but a grave fault for a helmsman: he drank.

Sieur Clubin had insisted on keeping him on, and had answered for his decision to Mess Lethierry.

Helmsman Tangrouille never left the ship, and slept on board.

On the day before the ship sailed, when Sieur Clubin came fairly late in the evening to look over the ship, Tangrouille was asleep in his hammock.

During the night Tangrouille woke up, according to his usual habit. Every drunkard who is not his own master has his private hiding place. Tangrouille had his, which he called his glory hole. It was in the hold. He had chosen this place as the unlikeliest he could think of, and felt sure that no one but himself knew about it. Captain Clubin, a sober man himself, was a stern disciplinarian. The small quantities of rum and gin that the helmsman could conceal from the captain's vigilant eye were stowed away in this mysterious corner of the hold, behind a sounding bucket, and almost every night he had a rendezvous with his store. The captain's surveillance was strict, so that there was little chance of any great orgy, and as a rule Tangrouille's nocturnal excesses were confined to two or three furtive mouthfuls.

Sometimes, indeed, there was nothing at all in the store. On that particular night Tangrouille had found an unexpected bottle of brandy there. His joy had been great, his astonishment greater still. From what seventh heaven had this bottle fallen? He could not recall when or how he had brought it on board. He had drunk it immediately—partly out of prudence, lest the bottle should be discovered and confiscated—and had thrown the empty bottle into the sea. When he went to the helm on the following morning he was unsteady on his feet, but he was able to steer much in his usual way.

Clubin, as we know, had returned to the Auberge Jean to sleep.

He always wore under his shirt a leather traveling belt containing a reserve of some twenty guineas, which he took off only at night. On the inside of the belt he had written his name in thick lithographic ink, which is indelible.

Before leaving the inn on the following morning he had put in his belt the iron box containing the banknotes for seventy-five thousand francs and had then, as usual, buckled it around his waist.

III

INTERRUPTED CONVERSATIONS

The Durande made a jaunty departure. The passengers, after stowing their cases and trunks on and under the benches, proceeded to inspect the ship, as passengers always do—a practice so habitual as to seem obligatory. Two of them, the tourist and the man from Paris, had never seen a steamship before, and when the paddle wheels began to turn admired the foam they produced. Then they admired the smoke. They examined, item by item and in the most minute detail, all the nautical apparatus on the deck and lower deck—the rings, the grapnels, the hooks, the bolts, which with their precision of form and carefully contrived disposition have the quality of colossal pieces of jewelry: iron jewelry gilded with rust by the tempest. They examined the little signal-gun moored on the deck: "chained like a watchdog," said the tourist; "and with a tarpaulin overall to keep it from catching cold," added the man from Paris. As the ship drew away from the land the passengers exchanged the usual comments on the view of Saint-Malo. One of them opined that views from the sea are deceptive and that at a league from the coast Ostend and Dunkirk are as like as two peas. The mention of Dunkirk was followed by the observation that the two red-painted lightships were called respectively the *Ruytingen* and the *Mardyck*.

Saint-Malo grew steadily smaller and finally disappeared.

The aspect of the sea was a vast calm. The wake behind the ship was like a long street fringed by foam that continued almost without a twist or turn until it was lost to view.

Guernsey lies on an imaginary straight line drawn between Saint-Malo in France and Exeter in England. At sea a straight line is not always the logical line to take; but steamships have, to some extent, an ability to follow a straight line that is denied to sailing ships.

The sea, in conjunction with the wind, is a composite of forces. A ship is a composite of mechanisms. The sea's forces are mechanisms of infinite power; the ship's mechanisms are forces of limited power. Between these two organisms, one inexhaustible, the other intelligent, takes place the combat that is called navigation.

Human will contained in a mechanism confronts the infinite. The infinite, too, contains a mechanism. The elements know what they are doing and where they are going. None of these forces is blind. Man must keep a watch on them and seek to discover their route.

Until the law governing these forces is discovered the struggle continues; and in this struggle steam navigation is a kind of perpetual victory of man's genius, every hour of the day, over all the forces of the sea. It also has the virtue of disciplining the ship: it reduces her obedience to the wind and increases her obedience to man.

The Durande had never sailed better than on this day. She behaved marvelously. About eleven o'clock, with a fresh north-northwesterly breeze, the Durande was off the Minquiers, under low steam, steering west on the starboard tack and keeping close to the wind. The weather was still clear and fine. But for all that the trawlers were making for home.

Gradually, as if everyone was thinking of getting back to harbor, the sea was being cleared of shipping.

It could not be said that the Durande was following her usual route. The crew were not concerned by this, having absolute confidence in the captain; nevertheless—perhaps because of a mistake by the helmsman—there was some deviation from her normal course. She seemed to be heading for Jersey rather than Guernsey. Just after eleven o'clock the captain corrected her course and turned her head toward Guernsey. Only a little time had been lost, but when the days are short it is unfortunate to lose any time. There was a fine February sun. Tangrouille, in the state he was in, had neither a firm footing nor a steady hand. As a result he frequently yawed, and this slowed down the ship's progress.

The wind had now almost died away.

The passenger from Guernsey, who had a telescope, trained it from time to time on a small patch of grayish mist that was lightly floating in the wind on the horizon to the west. It looked like a lump of cotton wool powdered with dust.

Captain Clubin had his usual austere and puritanical air. He seemed to be watching even more intently.

The atmosphere on board was tranquil and almost merry as the passengers talked together. If you close your eyes during a sea passage you can judge the state of the sea from the tremolo of conversations on board. Perfect freedom of conversation between passengers shows that the sea is absolutely calm.

For example, a conversation such as this could only take place on a very calm sea:

"Just look at that pretty green and red fly, sir."

"It must have lost its way over the sea and is having a rest on the ship."

"A fly doesn't usually get tired."

"No, they are very light. The wind carries them along."

"Do you know, sir, they once weighed an ounce of flies, and then they counted them and found that there were six thousand two hundred and sixty-eight of them?"

The Guernsey man with the telescope had joined the two cattle dealers from Saint-Malo, and their conversation went something like this:

"An Aubrac ox has a round thickset body, short legs, and a tawny hide. He is a slow worker because of the shortness of his legs."

"In that respect the Salers breed is better than the Aubrac."

"I've seen two magnificent oxen in my life, sir. The first had short legs, solid forequarters, full hindquarters, broad haunches, good length from the neck to the rump, good height to the withers, good fat, and a hide that was easy to take off. The other showed all the signs of having been properly fattened—a sturdy body, a strong neck, light legs, a white-and-red hide, sloping hindquarters."

"That's the Cotentin breed."

"Yes, but with something of the Angus or the Suffolk bull."

"You'll hardly believe this, sir, but in the south of France they have donkey shows."

"Donkey shows?"

"Yes, I assure you. The ugly ones are regarded as the best."

"Then it's the same as with mules: the ugliest are the best."

"Just so. Like the Poitevin mare: big belly, thick legs."

"The best type of mule is like a barrel on four posts."

"The standard of beauty for animals is not the same as for men."

"And certainly not the same as for women."

"That's true."

"I like a woman to be pretty."

"I like her to be well dressed."

"Yes: neat, tidy, well turned out, smart."

"Looking brand-new. A young girl should always look as if she had just come out of a bandbox."

"But about these two oxen I was talking about. I saw them being sold in the market at Thouars."

"Yes, I know the Thouars market. The Bonneaus of La Rochelle and the Babus, the grain merchants of Marans—I don't know if you have heard of them—must have been at that market."

The tourist and the man from Paris were talking to the American with the Bibles. There, too, the conversation was going well.

"Sir," said the tourist, "I will tell you the tonnage of shipping in the civilized world: France, seven hundred and sixteen thousand tons; Germany, a million; the United States, five million; England, five million five hundred thousand. Add to this the tonnage of the smaller countries, and you get a total of twelve million nine hundred and four thousand tons, distributed in a hundred and forty-five thousand ships scattered over the oceans of the globe."

The American interrupted:

"Sir, it is the United States that have five million five hundred thousand."

"I will accept that," said the tourist. "You are an American?"

"Yes, sir."

"I accept that, too."

There was a silence. The American was wondering whether to offer the man a Bible.

The tourist went on:

"Is it the case, sir, that you are fond of using nicknames in America, so much so that you apply them to all your famous people, and call your celebrated Missouri banker Thomas Benton 'Old Bullion'?"

"Yes, sir—just as we call Zachary Taylor 'Old Rough and Ready.' "

"And General Harrison 'Old Tip'—isn't that so?—and General Jackson 'Old Hickory'?"

"Because Jackson is as tough as hickory wood, and because Harrison beat the redskins at Tippecanoe."

"It's a very odd fashion."

"It's just our way. We call Van Buren the 'Little Magician'; Seward is called 'Little Billy' because he introduced small dollar bills; and Douglas, the Democratic senator for Illinois, who is four feet tall but a great orator, is the 'Little Giant.' You can go from Texas to Maine, but you will never find anyone using the name Cass: it is always the 'big man from Michigan.' And Clay is known as the 'Mill-Boy of the Slashes': his father was a miller."

"I would rather say Clay or Cass," said the man from Paris. "It's shorter."

"You would show you didn't know what was what. Corwin, who is secretary of the Treasury, is the 'Wagon Boy.' Daniel Webster is 'Black Dan.' And Winfield Scott, whose first thought after beating the English at Chippeway was to call for a plate of soup, is called 'Marshal Tureen.' "

The patch of mist that had been seen in the distance had grown in size, and now occupied a segment of about fifteen degrees on the horizon. It was like a cloud hanging low over the water for lack of wind. There was now hardly a breath of air. The sea was as smooth as a millpond. Although it was not yet noon the sun was growing pale. It gave light but not heat.

"I think the weather's going to change," said the tourist.

"We'll perhaps have rain," said the man from Paris.

"Or fog," said the American.

"The rainiest place in Italy, sir," said the tourist, "is Tolmezzo, and Molfetta has the least rain."

At midday, in accordance with custom in the archipelago, the bell rang for dinner. Those who wanted dinner went below. Some passengers who had brought food with them ate it cheerfully on deck. Clubin ate nothing.

While the passengers were having their meal the conversations continued.

The Guernsey man, feeling an interest in his Bibles, joined the American, who asked him:

"You know these waters?"

"Yes; I belong to these parts."

"And so do I," said one of the men from Saint-Malo.

The Guernsey man acknowledged this with a bow, and went on:

"Here we are in the open sea, but I would not have liked having fog when we were off the Minquiers."

The American, addressing the man from Saint-Malo, said:

"Islanders are more men of the sea than those who live on the coast."

"That's true. We coast people are only half in the water."

"What are the Minquiers?" continued the American.

"They're very nasty rocks," replied the man from Saint-Malo.

"There are also the Grelets," said the Guernsey man.

"That's true, too," said the man from Saint-Malo.

"And the Chouas," added the Guernsey man.

The man from Saint-Malo laughed. "Well, if it comes to that, there are also the Sauvages," he said.

"And the Moines,"[139] said the Guernsey man.

"And the Canard,"[140] riposted the man from Saint-Malo.

"Sir," said the Guernsey man politely, "you can always give tit for tat."

"There are no flies on us Malouins,"[141] said the man from Saint-Malo, with a wink.

"Have we got to make our way through all these rocks?" asked the tourist.

"No. We left them to the south-southeast. They're behind us now."

And the Guernsey man went on:

"Counting both the big ones and the little ones, there are altogether fifty-seven rocks in the Grelets."

"And forty-eight in the Minquiers," said the man from Saint-Malo.

The conversation now continued between the man from Saint-Malo and the Guernsey man.

"I think, sir," said the Guernsey man, "that there are three rocks you haven't counted."

"I've counted them all."

"From the Dérée to the Maître-Île?"

"Yes."

"And the Maisons?"[142]

"Yes. They are seven rocks in the middle of the Minquiers."

"I see that you know your rocks."

"If I didn't I wouldn't be a Saint-Malo man."

"It is always a pleasure to hear what a Frenchman thinks."

It was now the Saint-Malo man's turn to bow in acknowledgment. He went on:

"Then there are the Sauvages—three rocks."

"And the Moines—two."

"And the Canard—one."

"Its name shows that there is only one."

"That isn't always so, for the Suarde is four rocks."

"What do you call the Suarde?" asked the Guernsey man.

"We call the Suarde what you call the Chouas."

"It's not an easy passage between the Chouas and the Canard."

"Only birds can get through."

"And fish."

"It's difficult even for them. In rough weather they knock against the walls."

"There is sand in the Minquiers."

"And around the Maisons."

"These are eight rocks you can see from Jersey."

"That's true: from the beach at Azette. Not eight, though—seven."

"At low tide you can walk between the Minquiers."

"Yes, of course: the sand is uncovered."

"And what about the Dirouilles?"

"The Dirouilles are very different from the Minquiers."

"It's dangerous there, too."

"They are over Granville way."

"It's easy to see that you Saint-Malo people are just like us: you like sailing."

"Yes," said the man from Saint-Malo, "but the difference is that we say we are accustomed to sailing, while you say you like it."

"You are good sailors."

"I am a cattle dealer."

"What other people came from Saint-Malo, then?"

"There was Surcouf."[143]

"Anyone else?"

"Duguay-Trouin."[144]

Here the commercial traveler from Paris intervened:

"Duguay-Trouin? He was captured by the English. He was a brave man and a good fellow. A young Englishwoman fell in love with him. It was she who struck off his fetters."

At this moment a voice of thunder was heard:

"You're drunk!"

IV

IN WHICH CAPTAIN CLUBIN SHOWS
ALL HIS QUALITIES

Everyone looked round.

It was the captain addressing the helmsman.

Unusually, Sieur Clubin was using the familiar *tu* form. Normally he never addressed anyone in that way, and his use of it now showed that he must be furiously angry, or at least wanted to appear so.

A well-timed outburst of anger is a way of throwing off responsibility, and sometimes of transferring it.

The captain, standing on the bridge between the paddle boxes, glared at the helmsman, spitting out the word *Drunkard!* Honest Tangrouille hung his head.

The blanket of fog had grown in size and now covered almost half the horizon. It was advancing in all directions at the same time, for fog has something of the quality of a patch of oil. It was expanding almost imperceptibly, driven noiselessly and without haste by the wind. It was gradually taking possession of the ocean. It was coming from the northwest and blowing straight toward the ship. It was like a vast, shapeless moving cliff, coming down on the sea like a wall. There was an exact spot at which the great waste of water entered the fog and disappeared.

The point of entry into the fog was still about half a league away. If the wind changed they might still avoid being caught in it; but it would have to change immediately. The gap of half a league was visibly lessening; the Durande was moving forward, and the fog, too, was advancing. The fog was approaching the ship and the ship was approaching the fog. Clubin gave orders to put on more steam and to bear east.

The Durande now skirted the fog for some time, but it was still advancing. The ship was still in clear sunlight.

Time was being lost in these maneuvers, which were unlikely to succeed. Night falls quickly in February.

The Guernsey man, watching the fog, remarked to the two Saint-Malo men:

"This is a right nasty fog."

"A filthy bit of weather," said one of them.

"A bad thing to happen when you're at sea," said the other.

The Guernsey man went up to Clubin:

"Captain Clubin, I'm afraid we're going to be caught up in the fog."

"I wanted to stay in Saint-Malo," said Clubin, "but I was advised to go."

"Who by?"

"By old sailors."

"Well," said the Guernsey man, "I think you were right to sail. Who knows but there may be a storm tomorrow? At this time of year you must always be prepared for the worst."

A few minutes later the Durande entered the bank of fog.

It was a curious effect. Suddenly those who were in the after part of the vessel could no longer see those who were farther forward. A soft gray wall cut the Durande into two. Then the whole ship plunged into the fog. The sun was now like a great swollen moon.

Everyone shivered with cold. The passengers put on their great-coats, the sailors their oilskins. The sea, with hardly a ripple, had a cold, menacing tranquillity. An undue calm of this kind seems to hold a hidden threat. Everything had turned pale and wan. The black funnel and the black smoke that it emitted stood out boldly against the pallor in which the ship was enveloped.

There was no object now in making east. The captain turned the ship's head toward Guernsey and put on more steam.

The passenger from Guernsey, who had been standing near the engine room, heard the Negro called Imbrancam talking to his fellow stoker and listened. The Negro was saying:

"This morning, when we had sun, we were going slow; now, with this fog, we are going fast."

The Guernsey man returned to Sieur Clubin.

"Captain Clubin," he said, "are we taking enough care? Haven't we too much steam on?"

"What can I do, sir? We must make up for the time lost because of that drunkard of a helmsman."

"True enough, Captain Clubin."

And Clubin added:

"I want to make speed for harbor. It is bad enough having fog; it would be much worse with darkness as well."

The Guernsey man returned to the two from Saint-Malo, saying: "We have an excellent captain."

Every now and then great waves of fog, like carded wool, swept over the Durande, concealing the sun, which then reappeared, seeming paler and sickly. What little could be seen of the sky resembled its dirty, blotchy representation on a theater backcloth.

The Durande passed close to a cutter that had prudently dropped anchor. It was the *Shealtiel* of Guernsey. The skipper noticed the Durande's speed. It seemed to him, too, that she was not on the right course; he thought that she was bearing too much to the west. He was surprised to see her going full steam ahead in the fog.

By two o'clock the fog was so thick that the captain had to leave the bridge and stand near the helmsman. The sun had disappeared, and there was now nothing but fog. The Durande was enveloped in a kind of white darkness, and was sailing through a diffused pallor. Neither the sky nor the sea could now be seen.

There was not a breath of wind. The can of turpentine hanging from a ring below the bridge did not even quiver.

The passengers had all fallen silent. The man, from Paris, however, was humming under his breath Béranger's song "*Un jour le bon Dieu s'éveillant.*"

One of the men from Saint-Malo asked him: "You come from Paris, sir?"

"Yes, sir. *Il mit la tête à la fenêtre.*"

"What are things like in Paris?"

"*Leur planète a péri peut-être.*—Everything is going wrong in Paris, sir."

"Then it's the same on land as it is at sea."

"That's true. This is a terrible fog."

"And it can lead to some calamity."

"Why do we have all these calamities?" cried the man from Paris. "What's the point of them? What purpose do they serve? It's like the burning down of the Odéon,[145] which made whole families penniless. Is that right? I don't know what your religious beliefs may be, but I can tell you that *I* am not happy with the way the world is."

"Nor am I," said the man from Saint-Malo.

"Everything in this world of ours," said the Parisian, "seems to me to be out of order. My idea is that God isn't there anymore."

The man from Saint-Malo scratched the top of his head, like someone trying to understand.

The Parisian went on:

"God is absent from our world. They ought to pass a decree compelling him to stay in residence. He's in his country house and doesn't care about us. And so everything is going askew. It is clear, my dear sir, that God is no longer in charge; he is on holiday, and the business is being run by some deputy, some angel trained in a seminary, some imbecile with the wings of a sparrow." The word *sparrow* was pronounced in the manner of a Paris street urchin.

Captain Clubin, who had come up to the two men, put his hand on the Parisian's shoulder.

"Quiet, sir!" he said. "Take care what you are saying! We are at sea."

The passengers were struck dumb.

After a silence of five minutes the Guernsey man, who had heard this exchange, whispered to the man from Saint-Malo:

"A religious man, our captain!"

It was not raining, but everyone on board felt wet. They measured the progress the Durande was making only by their increasing discomfort. A feeling of melancholy came over them.

Fog creates a silence over the ocean; it calms the waves and stills the wind. In this silence the churning of the Durande's engines had a troubled and plaintive sound.

They met no more ships. Even if, away toward Guernsey or Saint-Malo, out of the fog, there were still a few vessels at sea, the Durande, fog-shrouded, would be invisible to them and her long trail of smoke, emerging from nowhere, would look like a black comet in a white sky.

Suddenly Clubin shouted:

"*Faichien!* You've gone wrong again! You are going to wreck the ship! You ought to be put in irons. Get out of there, you drunkard!"

And he seized the tiller.

The helmsman, shamefaced, slunk forward among the men.

"We'll be all right now," said the Guernsey man.

The Durande sailed on, full speed ahead.

About three o'clock the curtain of fog began to lift, and the sea could be seen again.

"I don't like the look of it," said the Guernsey man.

Fog can only be dispersed either by the sun or by the wind. By the sun is good; by the wind is not so good. But it was now too late for the sun. At three in the afternoon, in February, the sun is losing its strength. And if the wind rises at this critical point in the day, that is not a good sign: it will then often blow up into a hurricane.

But if there was any wind at all it was barely perceptible.

Clubin, with his eye on the binnacle, was holding the tiller and steering, muttering under his breath. The passengers heard him say:

"No time to be lost. That drunkard has held us back."

His face was completely expressionless.

The sea under the fog was now less calm, and there was something of a swell. There were patches of cold light on the surface of the sea. Seamen are concerned when they see light patches of this kind: they show where the winds at higher levels have gouged out holes in the ceiling of fog. The fog lifted from time to time and then came down again thicker than before. Sometimes it was completely opaque. The Durande was caught up in a veritable ice floe of fog. Now and again this fearful circle opened up like pincers, revealing a little bit of the horizon, and then closed again.

The Guernsey man, with his telescope, was now standing in the bow of the vessel like a lookout.

The fog lifted, then came down again.

The Guernsey man turned around in alarm:

"Captain Clubin!"

"What's the matter?"

"We're heading straight for the Hanois."

"You are wrong," said Clubin coldly.

The Guernsey man persisted. "I'm sure we are."

"We cannot be."

"I've just seen a rock on the horizon."

"Where?"

"There."

"That is the open sea. There can't be anything there."

And Clubin continued on his course toward the point indicated by the passenger.

The Guernsey man took up his telescope again.

A moment later he came rushing aft:

"Captain!"

"Well?"

"You must go about."

"Why?"

"I'm sure I saw high rocks, quite close. It's the Great Hanois."

"What you saw was a thicker patch of fog."

"It *is* the Great Hanois. For God's sake, go about!"

Clubin gave a pull on the tiller.

V

CLUBIN AT HIS MOST ADMIRED

There was a sharp grating sound. The rending of a ship's side on a sunken rock in the open sea is one of the most sinister sounds that can be imagined. The Durande stopped short. Some of the passengers were thrown sprawling on the deck.

The Guernsey man threw up his hands.

"We're on the Hanois! Just as I said!"

There was a general cry: "We're lost!"

Clubin's voice, sharp and decided, dominated the clamor:

"No one is lost! Keep quiet!"

The black figure of Imbrancam, naked to the waist, emerged from the engine-room hatch and said calmly:

"Captain, we're taking in water. The engine is about to stop."

It was a moment of dread.

The crash had been like a suicide. Had it been brought about on purpose it could not have been more terrible. The Durande had thrown itself against the reef as if attacking it. A jagged point of rock had been driven into the vessel like a nail. More than a square toise[146] of the inside planking had been shattered, the stem was broken, the rake damaged, the bow stove in; and water was pouring into the hull with a dreadful bubbling sound. The ship had suffered a wound that had brought her to shipwreck. The shock had been so violent that it had broken the pendants of the rudder, which now hung loose, beating against the hull. The bottom had been knocked out of the vessel by the reef, and nothing could be seen around her but the dense, compact fog, now almost black. Night was falling.

The Durande was down by the head. She was like a bullfighter's horse that had been gored by the bull. She was dead.

The sea was at half-tide and rising.

Tangrouille had now sobered up: no one is drunk in a shipwreck. He went down between decks and, coming up again, reported to Clubin:

"Captain, the water is filling the hold. In ten minutes it will be up to the scuppers."

The passengers were running frantically around the deck, wringing their hands, leaning overboard, looking at the engine, going through all the pointless motions of terror. The tourist had fainted.

Clubin held up his hand and they all fell quiet. He asked Imbrancam:

"How long can the engines go on working?"

"Five or six minutes."

Then he asked the Guernsey man:

"I was at the tiller. You were looking at the rocks. Which of the Hanois are we on?"

"We are on the Mauve. A few minutes ago, when the fog lifted, I had a clear view of the Mauve."

"Since we are on the Mauve," said Clubin, "we have the Great Hanois to port and the Little Hanois to starboard. We are a mile from land."

The crew and the passengers listened anxiously and intently, their eyes fixed on the captain.

There was nothing to be gained by lightening the ship, and in any case it would have been impossible: in order to get rid of the cargo it would have been necessary to open the ports and allow more water to get in. Nor would it have helped to drop the anchor, for the vessel was already firmly attached to the rock. Besides, on a bottom on which it would be difficult to get a purchase, the chain would probably have fouled. The engines were not damaged and could have been used to work the ship until the fire was extinguished—that is, for a few minutes more. It would thus have been possible to reverse the paddle wheels and back off the rock; but the Durande would then have sunk immediately. The rock was partly stopping up the holes in the ship's hull and reducing the inflow of water. It served as an obstacle to the invading sea. If the gash in the hull had been cleared of the obstruction it would have been impossible to stem the rush of water and work the pumps. If you pull out the dagger that has been plunged into a man's heart, you will kill him at once. Getting clear of the rock would have meant sinking to the bottom.

The water had now reached the cattle in the hold and they were beginning to bellow.

Clubin snapped out an order:

"Lower the longboat."

Imbrancam and Tangrouille hastened to obey and undid the lashings on the boat. The rest of the crew looked on as if petrified.

"All hands to the work!" shouted Clubin.

This time they all obeyed.

Clubin continued, impassively, to issue orders in the old language of command that the seamen of the present day would not understand:

"Haul taut!—Use a voyal if the capstan won't work.—Stop heaving!—Slack there!—Keep the blocks clear!—Lower away!—Slack away at both ends, smartly, now!—All together!—Take care she doesn't go down stern first.—It's catching on there!—Get hold of the mast tackle falls!—Watch out!"

The longboat was launched.

At that moment the Durande's wheels stopped turning and the funnel ceased belching smoke. The fires had been extinguished.

The passengers fell rather than climbed down into the boat, sliding down the ladder or clinging to the rigging. Imbrancam picked up the unconscious tourist, carried him into the boat, and returned to the ship.

After the passengers, the crew made a rush for the boat, knocking down the cabin boy and trampling on him. Imbrancam barred their way, saying: "The *moço* goes first."

He thrust the seamen aside, picked up the boy, and handed him down to the passenger from Guernsey, standing in the boat.

Seeing the cabin boy safe, Imbrancam stood aside and said to the rest of the crew: "Now you can go."

Meanwhile Clubin had gone to his cabin and gathered up the ship's papers and instruments. He then took the compass from the binnacle, handed the papers and instruments to Imbrancam and the compass to Tangrouille, and told them to get into the boat.

They went down into the boat, following the other seamen. The longboat was now full, with water almost up to the gunwale.

"Now," shouted Clubin, "off you go."

There was a general cry from the boat:

"What about you, Captain?"

"I am staying here."

People who suffer shipwreck have little time for thinking and still less time for sentiment; but those who were in the boat, and at least relatively safe, had feelings that were not entirely selfish. All of them joined in the cry:

"Come with us, Captain."

"I am staying here."

The Guernsey man, who was familiar with ships and the sea, replied:

"No, no, Captain. You are on the Hanois. From here it is only a mile's swim to Pleinmont. But for a boat the only landing is in Rocquaine Bay, and that is two miles away. We have heavy waves and fog. It will take us at least two hours to get to Rocquaine in the boat. It will be a pitch-black night. The tide is rising and the wind is freshening. There is going to be a squall. We want nothing better than to come back and fetch you, but if dirty weather blows up we shan't be able to. You are done for if you stay here. Come with us."

The man from Paris intervened:

"The boat is full—too full—and one man more will be one man too many. But there are thirteen of us, and that's unlucky for the boat. It's better to overload it with one man than one figure too many. Come along with us, Captain."

Tangrouille added:

"It is all my fault, not yours. It's not right that you should stay."

"I am staying here," said Clubin. "The ship will be torn to pieces by the storm tonight. I will not leave it. When a ship is lost the captain is dead. People will say of me, He did his duty to the end. I forgive you, Tangrouille."

Folding his arms, he cried:

"Carry out my orders. Cast off. Off you go!"

The longboat got under way. Imbrancam was at the tiller. All the hands that were not pulling an oar were raised toward the captain. From every mouth came the cry, "Hurrah for Captain Clubin!"

"There goes a brave man!" said the American.

"The finest man that sails the seas," said the Guernsey man.

Tangrouille was weeping. "If I had had the courage," he muttered to himself, "I would have stayed with him."

The boat disappeared into the fog and was lost to sight.

Nothing more was to be seen.

The sound of oars grew fainter and finally died away.

Clubin remained alone.

VI

LIGHT THROWN ON AN ABYSS

When this man found himself alone on this rock, in this fog, amid this waste of water, far from any contact with living beings, far from any sound of human life, left for dead—alone between the rising sea and the night that was now coming on—he had a feeling of intense joy.

He had succeeded.

He had realized his dream. The long-term bill of exchange that he had drawn on destiny was about to be met.

For him, to be abandoned was to be saved. He was on the Hanois, a mile from land, and he had seventy-five thousand francs. Never had any shipwreck been so skillfully arranged. No detail had been forgotten; everything had been planned. Since his earliest days Clubin had had one idea: to use honesty as his stake in the roulette game of life, to have the reputation of a man of integrity, to wait for the decisive moment, to allow his stake to accumulate, to find the winning streak, to choose the right moment; he would not fumble about but would seize his opportunity; he would make his coup, and make only one; he would scoop the pool and leave other poor fools behind him. He intended to achieve at one blow what stupid crooks failed to do twenty times in a row; and while they ended up on the gallows he would make his fortune. The meeting with Rantaine had given him the idea, and he had immediately formed his plan. He would relieve Rantaine of his money; he would frustrate any revelations by Rantaine by disappearing; to be believed dead was the best mode of concealment; and to achieve that he was prepared to destroy the Durande. The shipwreck was a necessary part of the scheme; and it had the additional advantage of leaving a good reputation behind him, making his whole life a masterpiece of contrivance. Anyone seeing Clubin in his present situation would have thought him a fiend, but a successful and contented fiend.

He had lived his whole life for this moment.

The whole of his character was summed up in the words "At last!" A frightful serenity settled palely on his dark brow. His expressionless eye, its inmost part seeming blanked off as if by a wall, became fathomless and terrible, reflecting the fire within his soul.

Man's inmost being, like external nature, has its own electric tension. An idea is a meteor: in the moment of success the accumulated meditations that have prepared the way for that success half-open and emit a spark. A man who, like some evil predator, feels a prey within his claws enjoys a happiness that cannot be concealed. An evil thought that has triumphed lights up a face. The success of some scheme, the achievement of some aim, some fierce delectation will momentarily bring to men's eyes somber flashes of illumination. It is like a joyful storm, a menacing dawn. It is an emanation of a man's consciousness, become a thing of darkness and cloud.

This was the gleam in Clubin's eye. It was like no gleam ever seen in the heavens or on earth. The villain who had been pent up within Clubin had now burst forth.

Looking into the vast darkness around him, he could not restrain a burst of low, sinister laughter.

Now he was free! Now he was rich!

His equation was coming out. He had solved his problem.

He had plenty of time. The tide was rising and supporting the Durande, and would eventually lift it off. In the meantime it was firmly lodged on the rock and in no danger of sinking. Besides he had to give the longboat time to get well away, and perhaps to be lost at sea, as Clubin hoped it would be.

Standing on the Durande, he folded his arms, savoring his isolation in the darkness.

For thirty years he had borne the burden of his hypocrisy. Being himself evil, he had coupled with integrity. He hated virtue with the hatred of a man who has married the wrong wife. All his life he had been meditating evil, but since he had reached man's estate he had worn the rigid armor of outward appearance. In his hidden self he was a monster; within his outer semblance of an honest man was the heart of a bandit. He was a pirate with the appearance of a gentleman. He was a prisoner of honesty, shut up in the mummy's casket of innocence; he was graced with the wings of an angel—a backbreaking encumbrance for a rascal. He had a heavy burden of public esteem. Keeping up the reputation of an honest man is a hard task. What a labor it is to maintain the balance between evil thoughts and fair words! He had been at the same time the phantom of uprightness and the specter of crime. This contradiction had been his destiny. He had had to maintain a good appearance, always appear presentable, while seething under the surface, concealing the grinding of his teeth under a smile. Virtue was a thing that stifled him. He had spent his life wanting to bite this hand that was held over his mouth; and, wanting to bite it, had been obliged to kiss it.

To have lied is to have suffered. A hypocrite is of necessity patient, in the double meaning of the term: he must plan the means of achieving his triumph, but while doing so he suffers torments. The long-continued premeditation of some evil deed, accompanied by and mingled with an appearance of austerity; internal infamy coupled with a good reputation; always to be pretending; never to be yourself; to be deceiving people all the time—all this is hard work. To compose an appearance of straightforwardness from all the black substances churning in your brain, to seek to devour those who respect you, to be affectionate, to restrain yourself, to repress your feelings, to be always on the alert, to watch yourself all the time, to put a fair face on your latent crime, to present your deformity as beauty, to fabricate an appearance of perfection from your vileness, to hold a dagger in your hand but use it to caress, to sugar the poison, to watch over the ease of every gesture and the tone of every word, never to have a natural glance: what can be harder than this, or more painful? The odiousness of hypocrisy is felt in some obscure way by the hypocrite himself. To be perpetually ingesting his own imposture brings on nausea. The sweetness that deceit gives to villainy is repugnant to the villain, who is continually forced to have this mixture in his mouth, and there are moments of retching when the hypocrite is on the point of vomiting up his thoughts. To swallow this saliva is revolting. Then, too, there is, deep down, the hypocrite's feeling of pride. There are times when, curiously, he thinks well of himself.

Within a deceitful rogue there is an outsized ego. The worm has the same crawling motion as the dragon, and the same way of raising its head again. The traitor is a despot in trammels, able to achieve his aims only by accepting a secondary role. He is littleness capable of any enormity. The hypocrite is a titan, but a titan who is also a dwarf.

Clubin really believed that he had been ill-used. Why had he not been born rich? He would have liked nothing better than to inherit from his parents an income of a hundred thousand pounds a year. Why had he not? It was not *his* fault. Why, because he had not been given all the pleasures of life, was he compelled to work: that is, to deceive, and betray, and destroy? Why had he thus been condemned to this torture of flattering, toadying, and trying to please others, of struggling to make himself liked and respected, and of having all the time to wear a false face over his own? Dissimulation is an act of violence against yourself. A man hates those to whom he lies. But now the time had come, and Clubin was taking his revenge.

On whom? On everyone, and on everything.

Lethierry had always treated him well. This was another grievance, and now he was avenging himself on Lethierry.

He was avenging himself on all those in whose presence he had been obliged to constrain himself. Now he was getting his own back. Anyone who had thought well of him was his enemy; he had been captive to such men.

Now he was free. He had made his escape; he had left mankind. What would be seen as his death was in reality his life; he was going to begin again. The real Clubin was shedding the likeness of the false one. He had dissolved everything at a stroke. He had kicked Rantaine into space, Lethierry into ruin, the world's justice into oblivion, men's minds into error, the whole of humanity away from himself. He had just eliminated the world.

As for God, that word of three letters meant little to him. He had been regarded as a religious man; but what did that matter?

Within the hypocrite there are hidden caverns; or rather a hypocrite is nothing but a cavern. When Clubin found himself alone his cavern opened up. He had a moment of exquisite pleasure; it was oxygen to his soul. He savored his crime to the full.

The depths of evil became visible on Clubin's face. His full personality was now revealed. At that moment, compared with the look on his face, Rantaine would have seemed as innocent as a newborn child.

What a release it was to tear off the mask! He delighted to see himself in all his hideous nakedness and to bathe ignobly in evil. The constraint of keeping up appearances over the years finally excites an intense appetite for shamelessness, a lascivious enjoyment of villainy. In these fearful moral depths, so rarely plumbed, there is a kind of appalling and pleasurable ostentation that is the very obscenity of crime. The insipidity of a false reputation for respectability creates a longing for shame. A man in this situation disdains other men so much that he wants to be despised by them. He is tired of being respected, and enjoys the freedom of action that degradation brings. He hankers after the turpitude that is so much at ease in ignominy. Eyes that have to be kept cast down often have sidelong glances of this kind. Marie Alacoque is not far removed from Messalina. Consider also Cadière and the nun of Louviers.[147] Clubin, too, had lived under a veil. Effrontery had always been his ambition. He envied the whore and the brazen brow of the declared villain; he felt himself to be more of a whore than the whore herself, and had only disgust at having passed for a virgin. He had been the Tantalus of cynicism. And at last, on this rock, in this solitude, he could be frank; and now he was so. What a pleasure it was to feel himself wholeheartedly vile! At this moment Clubin enjoyed all the ecstasies that are possible in Hell. The arrears of debt due to dissimulation had been paid in full. Hypocrisy is a loan, and Satan had paid it back. Now that there was no one else there and he was alone with the sky, Clubin gave himself up to the intoxication of his shamelessness. Saying to himself, "I am a villain!" he was content.

No human consciousness had ever conceived such a state of mind as this. No opening up of a volcanic crater is comparable to the eruption of a hypocrite.

Clubin was delighted that there was no one there, but he would not have been sorry if there had been someone. He would have liked to appear abominable in presence of a witness. He would have been happy to tell the human species to its face: "You are all fools!"

The absence of any other human being ensured his triumph, but at the same time diminished it. The only spectator of his glory was himself.

To wear the iron collar of a galley-slave has a charm of its own. It advertises to all the world that you are vile.

To compel the crowd to look at you is a manifestation of power. A galley slave standing on a trestle at a street corner with his iron collar around his neck is a despot controlling all the glances that he compels to turn toward him. The scaffolding on which he stands is a kind of pedestal. What finer triumph is there than to be the point on which all eyes converge? To compel the public to look at you is one form of supremacy. For those who see evil as their ideal, opprobrium is a halo. It is a position of dominance. They are on a summit on which they can luxuriate in their sovereignty. A pillory exposed to universal view has some likeness to a throne.

To be exposed is to be looked at.

An evil reign, too, offers the same pleasures as the pillory. Nero setting fire to Rome, Louis XIV treacherously occupying the Palatinate, the Prince Regent condemning Napoleon to a slow death, Tsar Nicholas destroying Poland under the eyes of the civilized world must have enjoyed something of the same voluptuous pleasure as Clubin was luxuriating in. The immensity of the world's contempt seems to the object of that contempt to confer greatness on him.

To be unmasked is a defeat, but to unmask oneself is a victory. It is an intoxication, an insolent and self-satisfied act of imprudence, a reckless display of nakedness calculated to insult all who behold it. It is supreme happiness.

These ideas in a hypocrite seem a contradiction, but are not so. All infamy is consistent.

Honey is gall. Escobar is close to the Marquis de Sade. The proof? Léotade.[148] The hypocrite is the complete figure of wickedness, combining within himself both extremes of perversity: he is both priest and courtesan. He is a demon of double sex, the abominable hermaphrodite of evil. He fertilizes himself; he engenders himself and transforms himself. Seen from one side, he is charming; seen from the other, he is horrible.

Clubin had within him all this dark turmoil of confused ideas. He did not perceive them very clearly, but he gloried in them. The thoughts passing through his soul were like a shower of sparks from Hell flashing in the night.

He remained for some time deep in thought, looking back on his past honesty as a snake looks at the skin it has sloughed off. Everyone had believed in his honesty, and even he had come to believe in it a little. Again he burst into laughter.

People were going to think he was dead, and he was rich. They were going to think him lost, and he was saved. What a trick to play on the universal stupidity of mankind!

And included in this universal stupidity was Rantaine. Clubin thought of Rantaine with limitless disdain: the disdain of the weasel for the tiger. Rantaine had bungled his escape; he had succeeded in his. Rantaine had departed sheepishly; he was disappearing triumphant. He had taken Rantaine's place in his criminal act, and it was he who had won the spoils.

As for the future, he had no definite plan. In the iron box concealed in his belt he had his three banknotes, and this certainty was sufficient for the moment. He would change his name. There are countries where sixty thousand francs are worth six hundred thousand. It would not be a bad idea to go to one of them and live honestly with the money taken from that robber Rantaine. To speculate, to go into big business, to increase his capital, to become a millionaire in earnest: these were also worth thinking about. In Costa Rica, for example, where coffee was becoming big business, there were tons of gold to be won. That was a possibility.

But he did not need to make his mind up yet: he had plenty of time to think about it. The most difficult part was over. The main thing had been to strip Rantaine of his money and disappear with the Durande, and that had been accomplished. The rest was simple. No obstacles now lay ahead; there was nothing to fear; nothing could go wrong. He would swim to the coast, arrive at Pleinmont after dark, climb the cliff, and make straight for the haunted house. He would have no difficulty in getting into the house with the help of the knotted rope that he had hidden in a crevice in the rock, and would find there his traveling bag containing dry clothes and provisions. He could wait there in comfort, knowing that within a week Spanish smugglers—probably Blasquito—would put in at Pleinmont, and at the cost of a few guineas he would be conveyed, not to Torbay, as he had said to Blasco to conceal his real intention, but to Pasajes or Bilbao. From there he would go on to Vera Cruz or New Orleans. But now it was time to take to the water: the longboat was far away, an hour's swim was nothing to him, and here, on the Hanois, he was only a mile from the mainland. At this point in Clubin's reflections a gap opened up in the fog, and he saw the dreaded Douvres reef.

VII

An Unexpected Turn of Fate

Clubin gazed wildly at the reef. It was indeed these terrible isolated rocks.

It was impossible to mistake their misshapen outline. The twin Douvres reared up in all their hideousness, with the passage between them like a trap, a sinister back alley of the ocean. They were quite close. They had been concealed by their accomplice, the fog.

In the fog Clubin had been on the wrong course. In spite of all his care he had suffered the same fate as two great navigators—González, who discovered Cape Blanco, and Fernández, who discovered Cape Verde. The fog had led him astray. It had seemed to serve him well in the execution of his project, but it had its dangers. He had changed course toward the west, but this had been a mistake. The passenger from Guernsey, claiming that he had recognized the Hanois, had led Clubin to change direction, in the belief that he was heading for the Hanois.

The Durande, wrecked on a sunken reef near the main rock, was only a few cable-lengths from the two Douvres.

Some two hundred fathoms farther away was a massive cube of granite. On the steep rock faces could be seen grooves and projections that would make it possible to climb to the top. The straight, right-angled corners of these rugged walls suggested that there might be a level area on the summit.

This was the Homme, which was still higher than the Douvres. The platform on the top overlooked their inaccessible twin peaks. This platform, crumbling at the edges, had a tablelike surface and a kind of sculptural regularity. It was a place of the utmost desolation and menace. The waves coming in from the open sea lapped placidly against the square sides of this huge black block of stone, which seemed a kind of pedestal for the huge specters of the sea and the night.

There was a great stillness: scarcely a breath of wind, scarcely a ripple on the sea. Under the silent surface of the water could be sensed the teeming life in its hidden depths.

Clubin had frequently seen the Douvres from a distance, and he was sure that that was where he was. There was no room for doubt.

It was sharp and devastating change of fortune. The Douvres instead of the Hanois; instead of a mile from land, five leagues. Five leagues of sea was an impossible distance for a swimmer. For a man shipwrecked and alone the Douvres are the visible and palpable presence of his last hour. From here there is no way to reach land.

Clubin shuddered. He had, by his own act, brought himself into the very maw of darkness.

There would probably be a storm in the course of the night, and the boat from the Durande, overloaded as it was, would founder. No news of the wreck would reach the mainland. No one would even know that Clubin had been left on the Douvres. There was nothing before him but death from cold and hunger. His seventy-five thousand francs would not bring him a mouthful of bread. All his carefully contrived plans had ended in this disaster. He had labored to bring about his own catastrophe. There was no way out, no hope of salvation.

His triumph had become a precipice. In place of deliverance, capture. In place of a long and prosperous future, he was faced with death. In a moment, in a lightning's flash, the whole structure he had built up had collapsed. The paradise that this fiend had dreamed of had taken on its true aspect: it was a tomb.

Meanwhile the wind had risen. The fog, driven before it and torn to pieces, was rapidly disappearing over the horizon in great shapeless masses. The whole expanse of the sea could now be seen again.

The cattle in the hold, with water flowing in ever faster, were continuing to bellow.

Night was approaching, and probably also a storm.

The Durande, lifted by the rising tide, was swinging from right to left and then from left to right and was beginning to turn on the reef as if on a pivot. It could not be long before a wave swept it off the rock and cast it adrift.

It was now not so dark as when the vessel had struck the rock. Although it was later in the day, the air was clearer. The fog in its retreat had carried off some of the darkness. There was not a cloud in the sky to the west. Twilight brings with it a vast white sky, and this was now lighting up the sea.

The Durande had run aground sloping downward toward the bow.

Clubin went up to the stern, which was almost clear of the water, and stared fixedly at the horizon.

It is characteristic of hypocrisy that it clings persistently to hope. The hypocrite is always waiting for something to turn up. Hypocrisy is a vile form of hope, and the falseness of the hypocrite is based on that virtue, which in him has become a vice.

Strangely, there is a certain confidence in hypocrisy. The hypocrite trusts in some obscure element in the unknown that permits evil.

Clubin looked out on the expanse of sea. The situation was desperate, but this sinister being was not. He said to himself that after the long period of fog, vessels that had been lying to or at anchor would be resuming their course and that one of them might pass within sight of the rock.

And a sail did appear on the horizon, traveling from east to west. As the boat drew nearer Clubin could make out its rig. It had only one mast and was schooner-rigged. The bowsprit was almost horizontal. It was a cutter.

In half an hour it would be passing close to the Douvres. Clubin said to himself: "I am saved!"

At a moment such as Clubin was experiencing a man at first thinks only of the prospect of life.

The cutter was perhaps a foreigner. Might it not be a smuggler's boat heading for Pleinmont? Might it even be Blasquito himself? In that case not only would his life be saved but his fortune as well; and his stranding on the Douvres, by bringing a quicker end to his predicament, by cutting out the period of waiting in the haunted house and by concluding his adventure out at sea, would turn out to have been a stroke of luck.

All Clubin's former certainty of success returned. It is curious how ready villains are to believe that success in their enterprises is no more than their due.

There was only one thing to be done. The Durande, aground amid the rocks, mingled her outlines with theirs and was difficult to distinguish from them. In the little daylight that remained she might not be visible to the vessel that was approaching. But a human figure on the summit of the Homme, standing out in black against the wan twilight and making distress signals, would certainly be seen, and a boat would be sent out to pick up the shipwrecked mariner.

The Homme was only two hundred fathoms away. It was an easy swim, and the rock was not difficult to climb.

There was not a moment to be lost.

Since the bow of the Durande was caught in the rock, it was from the stern, where Clubin was standing, that he would have to dive into the sea. He took soundings, and found that there was plenty of depth under the stern. The microscopic shells of foraminifera and polycystinea picked up by the tallow on the sound were intact, indicating that there were underwater caverns in which the water was always calm, however rough the sea might be on the surface.

He undressed, leaving his clothes on the deck. He would be able to get something to wear on the cutter. He kept only his leather belt.

When he had stripped he took hold of the belt, buckled it on again, checked that the iron box was still there, took a quick glance at the direction he would have to take through the rocks and the breakers to reach the Homme, and dived head first into the sea.

As he was diving from a height, he went deep, touched bottom, briefly skirted the underwater rocks, and then kicked off to return to the surface.

At that moment he felt something catching hold of his foot.

BOOK VII

The Unwisdom of Asking
Questions of a Book

I

The Pearl at the Foot of the Precipice

A few minutes after his brief conversation with Sieur Landoys, Gilliatt was in St. Sampson.

He was troubled and anxious. What could have happened?

St. Sampson was buzzing with talk like a hive of bees that had been disturbed. The whole population was at the doors of their houses. Women were talking excitedly. Some people seemed to be relating some event, with much gesticulation, to groups of listeners. The words "What a misfortune!" could be heard. On some faces there were smiles.

Gilliatt did not ask anyone what was the matter. It was not in his nature to ask questions; and in any case he was too upset to speak to strangers. He mistrusted secondhand accounts, preferring to know the whole story at once. He made straight, therefore, for Les Bravées.

His anxiety was such that he was not even afraid to enter the house. In any case the door of the ground-floor room opening off the quay was wide open and there was a swarm of men and women on the threshold. Everyone was going into the house, and he went in with them.

Standing at the door was Sieur Landoys, who whispered to him:

"You know now what's up, I suppose?"

"No."

"I didn't want to shout the news to you on the road. You don't like to be like a bird of ill omen."

"What has happened?"

"The Durande is lost."

There was a crowd in the room, with knots of people speaking in low voices as if they were in a sickroom.

All these people—neighbors, passersby, busybodies, anyone and everyone—were huddled near the door, as if afraid to go any farther, leaving clear the far side of the room, where Déruchette was sitting in tears, with Mess Lethierry standing beside her.

He had his back to the rear wall. His seaman's cap came down over his eyebrows. A lock of gray hair fell on his cheek. He was silent. His arms hung motionless by his sides; his mouth seemed to have no breath left. He looked like some inanimate object that had been set against the wall.

He had the air of a man within whom life had collapsed. With the loss of the Durande he had no longer any reason for his existence. His soul lived at sea, and now that soul had foundered. What was left to him now? To get up every morning and go to bed every night.

He would no longer be able to watch for the Durande, no longer see her leaving the harbor, no longer see her returning. What would the rest of his life be worth without an object? He could eat and drink; but beyond that, nothing. This man had crowned his life's work with a masterpiece, and his efforts had brought about progress. Now this progress had been destroyed, and the masterpiece was dead. What was the use of living on for a few more empty years? There was nothing left for him to do. At his age a man cannot start life again; and now, too, he was ruined. Poor old fellow!

Déruchette, sitting weeping on a chair beside him, held one of his hands between her two hands. Her hands were joined; his fist was clenched. It was an expression of their different sorrows. In joined hands there is hope; in a clenched fist, none.

Mess Lethierry had abandoned his arm to her to do as she pleased with it. He was completely passive. He had only the small quantity of life that might be left to a man struck by a thunderbolt.

There are certain descents into the abyss that withdraw you from the world of the living. The people coming and going in your room are confused and indistinct; they are close to you but make no contact with you. To them you are unapproachable; to you they are inaccessible. Happiness and despair do not breathe the same air. A man in despair participates in the life of others from a great distance; he is almost unaware of their presence; he has lost any consciousness of his own existence; he is a thing of flesh and blood but feels that he is no longer real; he sees himself only as a dream.

Mess Lethierry had the look of such a man.

The people in the room were whispering among themselves, exchanging such information as they had about the catastrophe. This was the substance of the story:

The Durande had been wrecked on the Douvres in the fog on the previous day, about an hour before sunset. All those on board with the exception of the captain, who had refused to leave his ship, had escaped in the ship's boat. A southwesterly squall that blew up after the fog lifted had almost brought them to shipwreck a second time and had driven them out to sea beyond Guernsey. During the night they had had the good fortune to encounter the *Cashmere,* which had picked them up and brought them to St. Peter Port. It was all the fault of the helmsman, Tangrouille, who was now in prison. Clubin had behaved nobly.

The pilots, of whom there were many among the groups of people, had a particular way of pronouncing the name of the Douvres. "A bad port of call," said one of them.

On the table were a compass and a bundle of papers—no doubt the compass and the ship's papers that Clubin had handed to Imbrancam and Tangrouille when the ship's boat left the wreck. They were evidence of the magnificent self-denial of a man who thought of saving even these bits of paper at a time when he was remaining on the wreck to die—a small detail showing greatness of mind and sublime forgetfulness of self.

All those present were unanimous in admiring Clubin, and unanimous also in believing that he might yet be safe. The cutter *Shealtiel* had arrived a few hours after the *Cashmere,* bringing the latest intelligence. She had just spent twenty-four hours in the same waters as the Durande; she had lain to in the fog and tacked about during the storm. The skipper of the *Shealtiel* was among those present.

When Gilliatt arrived the skipper had just been telling his story to

Mess Lethierry. It was a full and detailed account. Toward morning, when the squall had blown itself out and the wind had become manageable, he had heard the bellowing of cattle in the open sea.

Surprised by this rural sound amid the waves, he had headed in that direction and had seen the Durande aground on the Douvres. The sea was now calm enough to allow him to go closer. He had hailed the wreck, but the only reply was the bellowing of the cattle drowning in the hold. The skipper was sure that there was no one left on the Durande. The wreck had held together well, and in spite of the violence of the squall Clubin could have spent the night on board. He was not a man to give up easily; and since he was not on the Durande he must have been rescued. A number of sloops and luggers from Granville and Saint-Malo, getting under way again on the night before after the fog lifted, must certainly have passed close to the Douvres, and one of them must have picked up Captain Clubin. It will be remembered that the Durande's boat had been full when it left the wreck, that one man more would have overloaded it and perhaps caused it to sink, and that this must have been Clubin's main reason for staying on the wreck; but, having thus done his duty as captain, when a rescue ship appeared he would certainly have made no difficulty about taking advantage of it. You may be a hero, but you are not a fool. For him to commit suicide would have been absurd, particularly since he had nothing to reproach himself with. The guilty man was Tangrouille, not Clubin. This all seemed conclusive. The skipper of the *Shealtiel* was clearly right, and everyone expected Clubin to reappear at any moment. There was talk of giving him a triumphant reception.

Two things seemed certain from the skipper's account: Clubin was saved, and the Durande was lost.

As for the Durande, it had to be accepted that the catastrophe was irremediable. The skipper of the *Shealtiel* had seen the final stage of the shipwreck. The jagged rock on which the Durande was impaled had held on to her throughout the night, resisting the violence of the storm as if it wanted to keep her as its prey; but in the morning, when the *Shealtiel,* having ascertained that there was no one on board to be saved, had begun to move away, there had come one of those sudden heavy seas that are like the last angry outbursts of the storm. The Durande had been lifted violently upward, torn off the reef, and thrown, with the speed and directness of an arrow, between the two Douvres rocks.

There had been a "devil of a crash," said the skipper of the *Shealtiel.* The Durande, raised higher by the wave, had lodged between the two rocks as far as her midship frame. She was again held fast, but more firmly than on the underwater reef. She would remain haplessly suspended there, at the mercy of the wind and the sea.

The Durande, according to the crew of the *Shealtiel,* was already three parts broken up. She would certainly have sunk during the night had she not been caught up and held on the reef.

The skipper of the *Shealtiel* had examined the wreck through his glass and reported on its condition with seamanlike precision. The starboard quarter had been stove in, the masts snapped off, the sails blown off the bolt ropes, the shrouds torn away, the cabin skylights crushed by the falling of a yard, the uprights broken off level with the gunwale from abreast of the mainmast to the taffrail, the dome of the cuddy house beaten in, the chocks of the longboat struck away, the roundhouse dismantled, the rudder hinges broken, the trusses wrenched off, the bulwarks demolished, the bitts carried away, the cross beam destroyed, the handrail gone, the sternpost broken. All this devastation had been caused by the frenzy of the storm. Of the derrick on the foremast nothing at all was left; not a trace; it had been completely swept away, with its hoisting tackle, its blocks and falls, its snatch block and its chains. The Durande had broken her back; the sea would now begin to tear her to pieces. Within a few days there would be nothing left of her.

Remarkably, however, the engines of the Durande had remained almost unscathed—proof of the excellence of Lethierry's work. The skipper of the *Shealtiel* was sure that they had not suffered any serious damage. The masts had given way, but the funnel had held firm. The iron guards on the bridge had merely been twisted. The paddle boxes had been damaged; the casings had been crushed, but the paddle wheels had apparently not lost a single blade. The engines themselves were intact. The skipper of the *Shealtiel* was sure of it. Imbrancam, the stoker, who had mingled with the groups, was equally sure. This Negro, more intelligent than many whites, was a great admirer of the engines. He held up his arms, with black fingers spread wide, and said to Lethierry, who still stood silent: "Master, the machinery is still alive."

Since Clubin was thought to be safe and the hull of the Durande was known to be lost, conversation in the various groups turned to the engines. People were as concerned about them as if they had been a person. They were amazed by how well they had performed. "There's a stout old lady for you!" said a French seaman. "She's a good one!" said a Guernsey fisherman. "There must be good stuff in her," said the skipper of the *Shealtiel,* "to get away with two or three scratches."

Gradually the engines came to be the sole subject of conversation. There were warmly held views both for and against them; they had their friends and their enemies. Some of those present—owners of good old-fashioned sailing cutters who hoped to win back customers from the Durande—were not sorry to hear that the Douvres had put the new invention out of action. The whispering grew louder and the discussions threatened to become noisy. In general, however, conversation was restrained, and every now and then there was a sudden lowering of voices, shamed by Lethierry's sepulchral silence.

The general view that emerged from the discussions was this. The essential thing was the engines. The ship could be rebuilt; the engines could not. The engines were unique. There would not be the money to make others like them; nor would there be anyone to make them; their original builder was dead. They had cost forty thousand francs, and no one would now risk that amount of money in such a venture. Moreover, it had been shown that steamships could be lost like any other vessel; the accident to the Durande had wiped out all her earlier success. But it was terrible to think that this piece of machinery, still entire and in good condition, would be torn to pieces within five or six days as the ship had been. So long as it existed the shipwreck could not be said to be complete. Only the loss of the engines would be irreparable. Saving the engines would make good the disaster.

It was easy enough to talk of saving the engines; but who would do it? Was it indeed possible? To conceive a project and to carry it out are two different things: it is easy to have a dream but difficult to turn it into reality. And if ever a dream was impracticable and senseless it was this one—to save the Durande's engines, aground on the Douvres. To send a ship and crew to work on these rocks would be absurd; it was not to be thought of. It was the time of year when there were heavy seas; and in the first squall the anchor chains would be sawn through by the sharp edges of the underwater reef and the ship would go to pieces on the rocks. It would be sending a second wreck to the aid of the first. In the cavity on the summit of the rock on which the legendary shipwrecked mariner had died of hunger there was barely room for one man. In order to salvage the engines, therefore, a man would have to go to the Douvres, and he would have to go alone—alone in that waste of sea, alone in that solitude, alone at five leagues from the coast, alone in that place of terror, alone for weeks at a time, alone in face of dangers both foreseen and unforeseen, without hope of receiving supplies if his food ran out, without help in any emergency, without any trace of human life apart from the memory of the seaman who had starved to death there, without any other companion than the dead man. And how would he set about saving the engines? He would have to be not only a seaman but a smith as well. And what hardships he would have to put up with! Any man who ventured on the task would be more than a hero: he would be a madman. For in certain enterprises of disproportionate magnitude in which superhuman power is called for, there is a higher level above bravery—madness. And indeed would it not be folly to devote so much effort to the recovery of a collection of old iron?

No: no one should go to the Douvres. The engines must be abandoned along with the rest of the ship. No such savior as was required would present himself. Where was such a man to be found?

This, expressed in different words, was the gist of the murmured conversations among those present.

The skipper of the *Shealtiel,* who had once been a pilot, expressed the general view:

"No, there's nothing more to be done. There is no one who will go out there and bring back the Durande's engines."

"Since I am not going," added Imbrancam, "it means that no one can go."

The skipper shook his left hand in a gesture expressing his conviction that the thing was impossible, and went on:

"If there were such a man—"

Déruchette turned round:

"—I would marry him," she said.

There was a silence.

A man came forward, his face ashy pale, and said:

"You would marry him, Miss Déruchette?"

It was Gilliatt.

All eyes were turned on him. Mess Lethierry had drawn himself up to his full height. There was a strange light in his eye. He took off his seaman's cap and flung it on the ground, looked solemnly in front of him without seeing any of those who were present, and said:

"Déruchette would marry him. I give my word of honor to God."

II

GREAT ASTONISHMENT ON THE WEST COAST

The moon was due to rise at ten that night; but however favorable the night, the wind, and the sea, no fishermen meant to go out either from La Hougue la Perre, nor from Bordeaux harbor, nor from Houmet Benet, nor from Le Platon, nor from Port Grat, nor from Vazon Bay, nor from Perelle Bay, nor from Pezeries, nor from Les Tielles, nor from Saint's Bay, nor from Petit-Bô, nor from any port or harbor on Guernsey. The reason was very simple: the cock had crowed at midday.

When the cock crows at an unusual time there are no fish to be had that day.

That evening, however, as night was falling, a fisherman returning to Omptolle had a surprise. As he came past Houmet Paradis, with the Platte Fougère buoy, which is in the form of an inverted funnel, on his left and the St. Sampson buoy, in the form of a man, on his right, he thought he detected a third buoy. What was this buoy, he wondered? Who had set it at that particular point? What hidden shoal was it marking? The buoy provided an immediate answer to his questions: it was moving; it was a mast. This by no means lessened the fisherman's astonishment. A buoy would have been cause for wonder; a mast even more.

No one could be fishing that day. When everyone was coming in, someone was putting out.

Who could it be? And why was he going out to sea?

Ten minutes later the mast, moving slowly, came within a short distance of the fisherman from Omptolle. He was unable to recognize the boat. He heard the sound of oars. He could make out only two oars, so there was probably only one man on board. The wind was northerly, and the man was evidently rowing out to catch the breeze beyond

Fontenelle Point. There, probably, he would put on sail. So he was intending to round L'Ancresse and Mont Crevel. Whither was he bound?

The mast passed on its way, and the fisherman returned to port.

That same night, at different points along the west coast of Guernsey and at different times, a number of people observed a boat moving out at sea.

Just as the fisherman from Omptolle was mooring his boat, a man carting seaweed half a mile farther on was whipping his horses along the lonely Les Clôtures road, near the standing stones between Martello towers 6 and 7, when he saw a sail being hoisted some distance out at sea, in an area toward the Roque Nord and the Sablonneuse, which was little frequented because it required familiarity with these dangerous waters. He paid little heed to it, being more interested in carts than in boats.

Perhaps half an hour later a plasterer returning from his work in the town and skirting the Mare Pelée saw almost in front of him a boat daringly maneuvering amid the Quenon, Rousse de Mer, and Gripe de Rousse rocks. It was a dark night but it was light over the sea—an effect that commonly occurs—and it was possible to distinguish movements out at sea. The only craft visible was this boat.

A little later, and a little farther down the coast, a man setting his crayfish pots on the sandbank between Port Soif and Portinfer wondered why a boat was picking its way between the Boue Corneille[149] and the Moulrette. You had to be a good pilot and in a great hurry to get somewhere to venture on that passage.

As eight o'clock was striking on the Câtel church the landlord of the tavern in Côbo Bay was astonished to see a sail beyond the Boue du Jardin and the Grunettes, close to the Suzanne and the Grunes de l'Ouest.

A little way beyond Côbo Bay, on the lonely Hommet promontory that bounds Vazon Bay, two lovers were taking a lingering farewell of each other. At the moment when the girl was saying to the boy: "I've got to go; it's not because I want to leave you but because I've housework to do," they were distracted from their parting kiss by a large boat that passed close to them, making for the Messellettes.

About nine o'clock that evening Monsieur Le Peyre des Norgiots, of Le Cotillon Pipet, was examining a hole made by marauders in the hedge around his field, La Jennerotte, and his little plantation of trees. While investigating the damage he could not help noticing a boat rounding Crocq Point—a reckless thing to do at that time of night.

The course followed by the boat was a risky one on the day after a storm, when the sea had still not settled down. It was an unwise venture except for a man who knew by heart the channels between the rocks.

At half-past nine, at the Équerrier, a trawler hauling in its net paused briefly to watch what appeared to be a boat making its way between Colombelle and the Souffleresse. It was a hazardous thing to do, for in that area there are sometimes sudden gusts of wind that are very dangerous. The Souffleresse, the Blower, is so called because it directs these sudden bursts of wind against passing boats.

At the moment when the moon was rising, the tide being fully in and slack in the little strait of Lihou, the solitary watchman on Lihou Island was much alarmed by the sight of a long black shape passing between the moon and him, a tall, narrow black shape that looked like a shroud standing erect and moving forward. It glided along above the wall-like ridges of rock. The watchman thought it was the White Lady.

The White Lady inhabits the Tas de Pois d'Amont, the Gray Lady inhabits the Tas de Pois d'Aval, the Red Lady inhabits the Silleuse, to the north of the Banc Marquis, and the Black Lady inhabits the Grand Étacré, to the west of the Hommet. These ladies come out at night, in the moonlight, and sometimes meet one another.

The black shape could, of course, be a sail. The long barrier of rocks along which it seemed to be walking might be concealing the hull of a boat sailing along beyond the rocks, showing only its sail. But the watchman wondered what boat would risk the passage between Lihou and the Pécheresse and between the Angullières and L'Érée Point. And why was she sailing that way? It seemed to the watchman more likely that it was the Black Lady.

Just after the moon passed the tower of St. Peter-in-the-Wood, the sergeant in Rocquaine Castle, while pulling up the inner half of the drawbridge, saw at the mouth of the bay, beyond the Haute Canée but not so far out as the Sambule, a sailing vessel that seemed to be dropping down from north to south.

On the south coast of Guernsey, beyond Pleinmont, in a bay fringed by cliffs and rock faces falling steeply down to the sea, is a curious little harbor that a Frenchman who has lived on the island since 1855—perhaps indeed the author of these lines—has christened the "harbor on the fourth floor," a name that is now in general use. This harbor, which was originally called the Moye, is a rocky plateau, partly natural and partly shaped by man, some forty feet above the sea, communicating with the waves by two heavy beams forming an inclined plane. Boats are hauled up from the sea and launched into it on the beams, which are like two rails, with the help of chains and pulleys. For men there is a flight of steps. In those days the harbor was much used by smugglers. Being difficult of access, it suited their purposes.

About eleven o'clock a number of smugglers—perhaps the very men with whom Clubin had been expecting to travel—were gathered, along with their bales of goods, on the summit of the Moye plateau. Those who live by dishonesty need to be always on the alert; and the smugglers were keeping a good lookout. They were surprised to see a sail suddenly emerging from behind the black outline of Pleinmont Point. It was moonlight. The smugglers watched it closely, fearing that it might be a party of coastguardsmen on their way to lie in ambush behind the Great Hanois. But the sail passed beyond the Great Hanois, leaving the Boue Blondel behind it to the northwest, and disappeared into the pallid mists on the horizon.

"Where the devil can that boat be heading for?" the smugglers wondered.

That evening, just after sunset, someone was heard knocking at the door of the house at the Bû de la Rue. It was a boy dressed in brown with yellow stockings, indicating that he was a junior clerk employed by the parish. The house was closed up and shuttered. An old woman prowling about the beach with a lantern in quest of shellfish called to the boy:

"What do you want, boy?"

"The man of the house."

"He isn't there."

"Where is he?"

"I don't know."

"Has he gone away?"

"I don't know."

"The new rector of the parish, the Reverend Ebenezer Caudray, wants to come and see him."

"I don't know."

"The reverend has sent me to ask if the man who lives at the Bû de la Rue will be in tomorrow morning."

"I don't know."

III

DO NOT TEMPT THE BIBLE

For the next twenty-four hours Mess Lethierry neither slept nor ate nor drank. He kissed Déruchette on the forehead, asked after Clubin, of whom nothing had been heard, signed a declaration that he did not intend to lodge a complaint against anyone and had Tangrouille released from prison.

For the whole of the following day he remained in the Durande's office, half leaning on the table, neither standing nor sitting, answering quietly when anyone spoke to him. People's curiosity now being satisfied, no one came to Les Bravées. There is a fair measure of curiosity involved in the urge to offer sympathy. The door of the house remained closed, and Lethierry was left alone with Déruchette. The gleam that had flickered in Lethierry's eyes had been extinguished, and the gloomy air he had worn when he first heard of the catastrophe had returned.

Déruchette, anxious for him, had, on the suggestion of Grace and Douce, put beside him on the table, without saying a word, a pair of socks he had been knitting when the bad news arrived.

He gave a bitter smile, saying: "So they think I'm childish."

After a quarter of an hour's silence he added:

"These things are all very well when you are not in trouble."

Déruchette had removed the socks, and at the same time had taken away the compass and the ship's papers, on which he had been brooding too much.

That afternoon, a little before teatime, the door opened and two men dressed in black came in; one was old, the other young.

The younger man, it may be remembered, has already appeared in the course of our story.

Both men had an air of gravity, but of different kinds of gravity.

The old man had what might be called the gravity of his position, the young one the gravity of his nature. One comes from a man's dress, the other from his mind.

As their garments indicated, both were clergymen belonging to the established church. The first thing in the appearance of the younger man that might have struck an observer was that his air of profound gravity, evidently springing from his mind, was not reflected in his person. Gravity is not inconsistent with passion, which it purifies and exalts; but the most striking characteristic of this young man was his personal beauty. As he was a priest he must have been at least twenty-five, but he looked like eighteen. He showed the harmony, and also the contrast, between a soul that seemed made for passion and a body made for love. He was fair-haired, pink-complexioned, fresh, neat, and lithe in his severe attire, with the cheeks of a girl and delicate hands. He had a lively and natural manner, though repressed. He was all charm, elegance, and almost sensuousness. The beauty of his expression redeemed this excess of grace. His frank smile, revealing the small teeth of a child, was thoughtful and devout. He had the gracefulness of a page and the dignity of a bishop.

Under his full head of fair hair, so golden that it seemed overattractive for a man, was a high, frank, and well-shaped forehead. A double wrinkle between his eyebrows created something of the appearance of a bird—the bird of thought—hovering with outspread wings on his forehead.

He had the appearance of one of those generous, pure, and innocent natures that develop in the opposite direction from the ordinary run of men, gaining wisdom from illusion and enthusiasm from experience.

His appearance of youth was transparent, allowing his inner maturity to shine through. Compared with his companion, the older clergyman, he seemed at first sight the son, at a second glance the father.

His companion was none other than the Reverend Dr. Jaquemin Hérode. Dr. Hérode belonged to the High Church, which is a kind of popish system without a pope. In those days the Church of England was agitated by the trends that have since been confirmed and condensed in the form of Puseyism. Dr. Hérode was of that school of thought, which is almost a variant of the Church of Rome. He was tall, very proper, stiff, and commanding. There was little sign of his inner vision in his outward appearance. He was more concerned with the letter than with the spirit of his faith. He had a rather haughty demeanor and an imposing presence. He was more like a monsignore than an Anglican clergyman; his frock coat had something of the cut of a cassock. His true spiritual home would have been Rome: he was a born prelate of the antechamber. He seemed to have been created on purpose to adorn a papal court, to walk behind the gestatorial chair, with all the pontifical train, *in abito paonazzo*.[150] The accident of having been born an Englishman and a theological training directed more toward the Old than the New Testament had put that great destiny beyond his reach. All his splendors amounted only to being rector of St. Peter Port, dean of the island of Guernsey, and suffragan to the bishop of Winchester. This, to be sure, was glory enough.

This glory did not prevent Mr. Jaquemin Hérode from being, all in all, a good man.

As a theologian he stood high in the estimation of experts in this field, and was a man of weight in the Court of Arches, the English equivalent of the Sorbonne.[151]

He had the air of a scholar, an authoritative way of screwing up his eyes, hairy nostrils, prominent teeth, a thin upper lip and a thick lower one, several academic degrees, a good living, titled friends, the confidence of the bishop, and a Bible always in his pocket.

Mess Lethierry was so completely absorbed that his only reaction to the arrival of the two clergymen was an imperceptible frown.

Dr. Hérode came forward, bowed, said a few words about his recent promotion in a tone of sober pride, and explained that he had come, in accordance with custom, to introduce to the leading men of the parish, and to Mess Lethierry in particular, his successor, the new rector of St. Sampson, the Reverend Ebenezer Caudray, who would now be Mess Lethierry's pastor.

Déruchette rose.

The younger clergyman, who was the Reverend Ebenezer, bowed.

Mess Lethierry looked at him and muttered under his breath: "Not much of a seaman."

Grace set out chairs and the two clergyman sat down near the table.

Dr. Hérode now embarked on a speech. He had heard that a great misfortune had occurred. The Durande had been wrecked. He had therefore come, as pastor, to offer consolation and counsel. This shipwreck was unfortunate, but was also beneficial. Let us look in our hearts: were we not puffed up with prosperity? The waters of felicity are dangerous. Misfortunes must be taken in good part. The ways of the Lord are mysterious. Mess Lethierry was ruined, no doubt; but to be rich is to be in danger. You have false friends; they leave you when you fall into poverty, and you remain alone. *Solus eris.*[152] The Durande was said to have brought in a thousand pounds sterling a year. That is too much for a wise man. Let us flee temptation and disdain mere gold. Let us accept with gratitude ruin and abandonment. Isolation brings much of good; it wins us the favor of the Lord. It was in solitude that Ajah found the hot waters while leading the asses of his father Zibeon.[153] Let us not rebel against the impenetrable decrees of Providence. The holy man Job had increased in wealth after his misfortunes. Who knows but that the loss of the Durande might have compensations, even temporal compensations? For example he, Dr. Jaquemin Hérode, had invested some money in a very promising affair that was under way in Sheffield, and if Mess Lethierry were to join in the enterprise with what money remained to him he would recover his fortune: it was a large order for the supply of arms to the Tsar, who was then engaged in the repression of the revolutionary movement in Poland. There would be a profit of 300 percent.

The mention of the Tsar seemed to rouse Lethierry from his abstraction. He interrupted Dr. Hérode:

"I want nothing to do with the Tsar."

The clergyman replied:

"Mess Lethierry, princes are part of God's plan. It is written: Render unto Caesar the things which are Caesar's. The Tsar is Caesar."

Lethierry, falling back into his reverie, muttered:

"Caesar? Who is Caesar? I know nothing about him."

The Reverend Dr. Hérode resumed his exhortation. He did not pursue the Sheffield plan. A man who would have nothing to do with the Tsar must be a republican, and he realized that some people might be republicans. In that case Mess Lethierry should think of going to live in a republic. He would be able to restore his fortunes in the United States even more easily than in England. To multiply his remaining money tenfold he need only take shares in the great company that was developing plantations in Texas, employing more than twenty thousand slaves.

"I want nothing to do with slavery," said Lethierry.

"Slavery," replied Dr. Hérode, "was instituted by divine authority. It is written: If a master smites his slave he shall not be punished, for it is his money."

Grace and Douce, standing at the door, were drinking in the reverend doctor's words in a kind of ecstasy.

Dr. Hérode continued with his discourse. As we have said, he was, all in all, a good man, and in spite of all social and personal differences between him and Mess Lethierry, he had come with the sincere desire to offer him all the spiritual, and indeed also temporal, aid within his power.

If Mess Lethierry was so completely ruined that he was unable to contemplate any financial speculation, whether Russian or American, why should he not take up salaried employment under government? There were some good places to be had, and the reverend doctor was ready to put forward Mess Lethierry's name for one of them. As it happened, there was a vacancy in the office of deputy viscount[154] on Jersey. Mess Lethierry was popular and respected, and the Reverend Dr. Hérode, dean of Guernsey and suffragan of the bishop, was sure that he could secure this post for him. The deputy viscount was an officer of considerable standing; he was present, as the representative of His Majesty, at meetings of the Court of Chief Pleas, at the deliberations of the Cohue, and at executions.

Lethierry looked Dr. Hérode in the eye. "I am against hanging," he said.

The reverend doctor had hitherto spoken in the same level tone, but now his voice took on a new and sharper intonation:

"Mess Lethierry, the death penalty has been divinely ordained. God has given man the sword. It is written: An eye for an eye, a tooth for a tooth."

The Reverend Ebenezer drew his chair imperceptibly closer to the Reverend Jaquemin's chair and said, in a whisper that could be heard by no one else:

"What this man says is put in his mouth."

"By whom? By what?" asked the Reverend Jaquemin in the same tone.

"By his conscience," whispered the Reverend Ebenezer.

Dr. Hérode felt in his pocket, brought out a small, thick volume closed with clasps, laid it on the table, and said:

"*There* is your conscience."

The book was the Bible.

The reverend doctor's voice now took on a gentler tone. His wish, he said, was to help Mess Lethierry, for whom he had a great respect. As a pastor, he had the right and the duty to give counsel; but Mess Lethierry was free to decide for himself.

Mess Lethierry, who had sunk back into his absorption and depression, was not listening. Déruchette, who was sitting near him and was also deep in thought, did not raise her eyes, bringing to this conversation, not very lively in itself, the additional embarrassment of her silent presence. A witness who does not speak is a burden on any encounter. The reverend doctor, however, did not appear to notice it.

When Lethierry did not reply, Dr. Hérode continued with his exhortations. Counsel comes from man, he said, but inspiration comes from God. In the counsel given by a priest there is an element of inspiration. It is wise to accept counsel and dangerous to reject it. Sochoth was seized by eleven devils for scorning the exhortations of Nathaniel. Tiburianus was stricken by leprosy for driving the apostle Andrew from his house. Barjesus, magician though he was, was struck blind for laughing at Saint Paul's words. Elkesai and his sisters Martha and Marthena are in Hell for rejecting the admonitions of Valentianus, who proved, as clear as daylight, that their thirty-eight-league-high Jesus Christ was a demon. Aholibamah, who is also called Judith, obeyed the counsel given her. Reuben and Peniel listened to advice from on high, as their names indicate: Reuben means "son of the vision," Peniel "face of God."[155]

Mess Lethierry struck the table with his fist.

"Of course!" he cried: "it was my fault!"

"What do you mean?" asked Dr. Jaquemin Hérode.

"I mean that it was my fault."

"Why was it your fault?"

"Because I let Durande return on a Friday."

Dr. Hérode whispered in Ebenezer Coudray's ear: "The man is superstitious."

Then, raising his voice, he continued, in a didactic tone:

"Mess Lethierry, it is childish to believe that Friday is unlucky. You ought not to credit such fables. Friday is a day like any other. It is often a lucky day. Meléndez founded the town of San Agustín on a Friday; Henry VII gave John Cabot his commission on a Friday; the pilgrim fathers on the *Mayflower* landed at Provincetown on a Friday; Washington was born on Friday, the twenty-second of February, 1722; Columbus discovered America on Friday, the twelfth of October, 1492."

He stood up, and Ebenezer, whom he had brought with him, also rose.

Grace and Douce, seeing that the reverend gentlemen were about to take their leave, opened the double doors.

Mess Lethierry saw nothing and heard nothing of all this.

Dr. Hérode said, aside, to Ebenezer Caudray:

"He does not even acknowledge our presence. This is not just his distress: it is sheer mindlessness. He must be mad."

He took his pocket Bible from the table and held it clasped between his two hands, as one holds a bird to prevent it from flying away. His attitude created a feeling of expectancy among those present. Grace and Douce craned forward.

His voice took on all the solemnity he could muster:

"Mess Lethierry, let us not part without reading a page from the Holy Book. We can obtain enlightenment on the various situations in life from books. For the profane there are the *sortes vergilianae;* believers take their instruction from the Bible. The first book that comes to hand, opened at random, may give us counsel; but the Bible, opened at random, offers us a revelation. It affords benefit particularly to those in affliction. Unfailingly the holy scriptures will offer balm for their troubles. In presence of the afflicted we should consult the sacred book, not selecting any particular passage but reading with an open heart whatever page it opens at. What man does not choose, God chooses. God knows what we need. His invisible finger is on the passage that we find by chance. Whatever the page, it will unfailingly bring us enlightenment. Let us not seek any other light, but hold fast to Him. It is a message received from on high. Our destiny is mysteriously revealed to us in the text thus sought for with confidence and respect. Let us listen and obey. Mess Lethierry, you are in sorrow, and this is the book of consolation; you are sick, and this is the book of health."

Dr. Hérode undid the clasp of his Bible, slipped a finger at random between two pages, laid his hand for a moment on the open book, paused as if in prayer, and then, lowering his eyes, began to read with an air of authority.

This was the passage he had chanced on:

"And Isaac came from the way of the well Lahairoi; for he dwelt in the south country.

"And Isaac went out to meditate in the field at the eventide; and he lifted up his eyes and saw, and, behold, the camels were coming.

"And Rebekah lifted up her eyes, and when she saw Isaac she lighted off the camel.

"For she had said unto the servant, What is this man that walketh in the field to meet us? . . .

"And Isaac brought her into his mother Sarah's tent, and she became his wife; and he loved her."[156]

Ebenezer and Déruchette looked at each other.

PART II

GILLIATT THE CUNNING

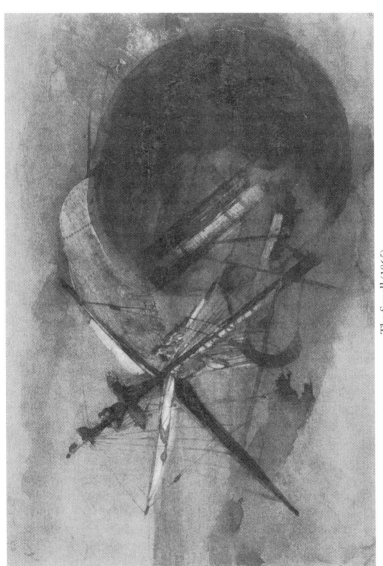

The Squall (1865).

BOOK I

THE REEF

I

A PLACE THAT IS HARD TO REACH
AND DIFFICULT TO LEAVE

The reader will have guessed that the boat seen at a series of points on the west coast of Guernsey at different times on the previous evening was Gilliatt's paunch. He had chosen to make his way down the coast through the passages between the rocks and reefs: it was a perilous route, but it was the most direct. His sole concern had been to take the quickest way of reaching the wreck of the Durande. Shipwrecks brook no delay; the sea makes urgent demands, and the loss of an hour might be irreparable. He was anxious to go to the rescue of the ship's engines as quickly as possible.

He had been concerned to get away from Guernsey without drawing attention to his departure, and had left in the manner of an escaping prisoner. It was as if he was trying to hide. Rather than pass in sight of St. Sampson and St. Peter Port, he avoided the east coast, slipping instead down the other side of the island, which is relatively uninhabited. When passing between the rocks it was necessary to use the oars. But Gilliatt worked the oars in accordance with the laws of hydraulics, entering the water without violence and leaving it without haste; and in this way he was able to proceed on his way in the darkness as rapidly and as quietly as possible. Anyone seeing him might well have thought that he was up to no good.

The truth is that, launching himself headlong on an enterprise that looked pretty nearly impossible, and risking his life with the odds heavily stacked against him, he was afraid of competition from some rival.

As day was beginning to break those unknown eyes that are perhaps open somewhere in space could have seen, at one of the spots in the middle of the sea where there is most solitude and most danger, two objects with an ever decreasing interval between them, one drawing closer to the other. One of them, almost imperceptible in the mighty surge of the waves, was a sailing boat, and in that boat there was a man: it was Gilliatt's paunch. The other—immobile, black, of colossal size—rose out of the sea in fantastic silhouette. Two tall pillars reared up from the waves into the void, supporting a kind of crosspiece that served as a bridge between their summits. This crosspiece, so shapeless when seen from a distance that it was impossible to say what it was, combined with its supporting piers to form a kind of doorway. But what was the purpose of a doorway in this waste, open in all directions, that is the sea? It was like some titanic dolmen set up there in the midst of the ocean by some magisterial imagination and erected by hands that were accustomed to build on a scale proportionate to the abyss. Its eerie outline stood out against the light sky.

The morning light was growing stronger in the east, and the whiteness of the horizon deepened the blackness of the sea. Opposite this, on the other side of the horizon, the moon was setting.

These two pillars were the Douvres. The shapeless mass caught between them, like an architrave borne on the jambs of a door, was the Durande.

This reef, holding its prey, as if showing it off, was terrible to behold. Inanimate objects sometimes display a somber, hostile ostentation directed against man. There was defiance in the attitude of these rocks. They seemed to be waiting for something.

It was a scene of pride and arrogance: the vessel defeated, the abyss triumphant. The two rocks, still dripping with water after yesterday's storm, were like two combatants sweating after their exertions. The wind had died down, there were quiet ripples on the sea, and the presence of jagged rocks just under the surface was suggested by the plumes of foam that rose and fell gracefully above them. From the open sea came a sound like the murmuring of bees. Everything around was level except the two Douvres, towering up vertically like two black columns. Up to a certain height they were hairy with seaweed. Their sheer flanks had the sheen of armor. They seemed ready to reengage in combat. It was borne in on anyone seeing them that their roots were in underwater mountains. They had an air of tragic omnipotence.

Usually the sea conceals its attacks. It maintains a deliberate obscurity. This incommensurable expanse of darkness gives nothing away. It is very rare for a thing of mystery to yield up its secrets. There is something of the quality of a monster in catastrophe, but in unknown quantity. The sea is both open and secret; it hides, and is not anxious to divulge its actions. It brings about a shipwreck and then covers it over; it swallows up its victims out of a sense of shame. The waves are hypocrites: they kill, steal, conceal stolen property, plead ignorance, and smile. They roar, and then they bleat.[157]

It was very different here. The two Douvres, raising the dead Durande above the waves, had an air of triumph. It was like two monstrous arms emerging from the abyss and displaying to the storms this corpse of a ship. It was like a murderer boasting of his achievement.

To this was added the sacred awe of the hour. The dawn has a mysterious grandeur, made up of a remnant of the dreams of night and the first thoughts of day. At this uncertain moment there are still specters about. The huge capital *H* formed by the two Douvres linked by the crossbar of the Durande stood out against the horizon in a kind of crepuscular majesty.

Gilliatt was wearing his seagoing clothes—a woolen shirt, woolen stockings, hobnailed shoes, knitted pea-jacket, trousers of rough, coarse material, with pockets, and one of the red woolen caps then worn by sailors, known last century as galley caps.

He recognized the Douvres reef and steered toward it.

The Durande was the very opposite of a ship sent to the bottom: she was a ship suspended in midair. It was a strange kind of salvage that Gilliatt was undertaking.

It was broad daylight when he arrived off the reef. As we have said, there was very little movement on the sea. The only agitation on the water came from its confinement between the rocks. In any channel, large or small, there is always some lapping of the waves. Within a strait the sea always has a covering of foam.

Gilliatt approached the Douvres with extreme caution, taking frequent soundings.

He had some cargo to unload. Accustomed as he was to frequent absences from home, he always had his emergency supplies ready for departure: a sack of biscuit, a sack of rye flour, a basket of salt fish and smoked beef, a large can of fresh water, a Norwegian chest painted with flowers containing some coarse woolen shirts, his oilskins and tarpaulin leggings and a sheepskin that he wore at night over his pea jacket. When leaving the Bû de la Rue he had quickly stowed all this in the paunch, together with a loaf of fresh bread. In his haste to get away the only tools he had taken with him were his blacksmith's hammer, his ax and hatchet, a saw, and a knotted rope with a grapnel at the end. If you have a ladder of this kind and know how to use it, you can tackle the most difficult climbs, and with it a good sailor can scale the steepest rock face. Visitors to the island of Sark can observe what the fishermen of Havre Gosselin are able to do with a knotted rope.

Gilliatt's nets and lines and other fishing tackle were also in the boat. He had taken them on board from force of habit, without thinking; for to carry out his enterprise he was going to spend some time in an archipelago of rocks and shoals where there would be no scope for using them.

When Gilliatt arrived at the reef the sea was ebbing, which was a circumstance in his favor. The falling tide had left exposed, at the foot of the Little Douvre, a number of slabs of rock, level or gently sloping, not unlike the corbels supporting the flooring of a building. These surfaces, some narrow and some broader, were set at irregular intervals along the base of the great monolith and continued to form a narrow ledge under the Durande, whose hull protruded between the two rocks, caught as if in a vise.

These rock platforms were convenient for landing and surveying the position. The stores brought in the paunch could be unloaded and kept there for a time; but it was necessary to make haste, for the rocks would be exposed only for a few hours. When the tide rose they would again be submerged.

Gilliatt brought his boat in to these slabs of rock, some of them level and some sloping down. They were covered with a wet and slippery mass of seaweed, the sloping ones being even more slippery.

Gilliatt took his shoes off, sprang barefoot onto the seaweed, and moored the paunch to a spur of rock. Then he walked along the narrow ledge of rock until he was under the Durande, looked up and examined her.

The Durande was wedged in between the two pillars of rock, suspended some twenty feet above the water. It must have been a very heavy sea that cast her up so high.

To seamen such violence of the waves is nothing new. To take only one example, on January 25, 1840, in the Gulf of Stora,[158] the last violent wave of a storm tossed a brig right over the wreck of a corvette, the *Marne,* and embedded it between two cliffs.

There was in fact only half of the Durande caught between the Douvres. She had been snatched from the waves and, as it were, uprooted from the water by the hurricane. The violence of the wind had buckled the hull, the stormy sea had held it firmly in its grasp, and the vessel, pulled in opposite directions by the two hands of the tempest, had snapped like a lath of wood. The after part, with the engines and the paddle wheels, had been hoisted out of the sea and driven by all the fury of the cyclone into the narrow gap between the two Douvres as far as her midship beam and was held fast there. The wind had struck a mighty blow; in order to drive this wedge between the two rocks the hurricane had turned itself into a sledgehammer. The forward part of the Durande, carried away and buffeted by the blast, had smashed to pieces on the rocks below.

The hold, broken open, had discharged the drowned cattle into the sea.

A large section of the forward part of the ship's side was still attached to the after part, hanging from the riders of the port paddle box on a few damaged braces that could easily be struck off with an ax. Farther away, scattered about in crevices in the reef, could be seen beams, planks, rags of canvas, lengths of chain and debris of all kinds, lying quietly amid the rocks.

Gilliatt examined the Durande carefully. Her keel made a kind of ceiling over his head.

The horizon, its limitless expanse of water barely moving, was serene. The sun was rising in its pride from this vast circle of blue.

Every now and then a drop of water fell from the wreck into the sea.

II

The Perfection of Disaster

The two Douvres differed from each other in both shape and size. The Little Douvre, which was narrower and curving, was patterned from base to summit with veins of softer brick-red rock that divided the interior of the granite into compartments. Where these veins surfaced there were cracks that would be helpful to a climber. One of these cracks, a little above the level of the wreck, had been gouged out and worn away by the breakers until it had become a kind of niche that could have housed a statue. The granite had a rounded surface and was soft to the feel, like touchstone, but was nonetheless hard for that. The Little Douvre ended in a point shaped like a horn. The Great Douvre, rising in an unbroken perpendicular mass, had a smooth, polished exterior, as if hewn by a sculptor, and looked as if it were made of black ivory. Not a hole, not an irregularity in its smooth surface. Its steep sides were inhospitable; a convict could not have used it to help in his escape, nor a bird to make its nest. The summit was flat, like that of the Homme; but it was totally inaccessible. It was possible to climb the Little Douvre, but not to find lodging on the top; the Great Douvre had room enough on the top but was unclimbable.

After his first survey Gilliatt returned to the paunch, landed her cargo on the broadest of the rock ledges above the water, rolled up his modest stores and equipment in a tarpaulin, ran a sling around the bundle, with a loop for hoisting, and pushed it into a recess in the rocks where it was out of reach of the waves. Then, clutching the Little Douvre and clinging with hands and feet to every projection and every cranny in the rock, he climbed up to the Durande, stranded in midair, and, coming level with the paddle boxes, sprang onto the deck.

The interior of the wreck was a grievous sight. The Durande bore all the marks of a frenzied attack. She had suffered a fearful rape at the hands of the storm. A tempest behaves like a band of pirates. A shipwreck is a vicious attack on a vessel's life. Cloud, thunder, rain, wind, waves, and rocks are an abominable gang of accomplices in crime.

The scene on this dismantled deck suggested that the Durande had been trampled into ruin by the furious spirits of the sea. Everywhere there were marks of their rage. Bizarrely twisted ironwork bore witness to the frantic violence of the wind. The between decks were like the cell of a madman who had broken up everything in it.

No wild beast is as ruthless as the sea in tearing its prey to pieces. Water has countless claws. The wind bites, the sea devours; waves are voracious jaws. Objects are torn off and destroyed in the same movement. The ocean strikes as smartly as a lion.

What was remarkable about the destruction of the Durande was that it was so detailed and meticulous. It was as if she had been viciously dissected. Much of the damage looked as if it had been done on purpose. Anyone observing would be tempted to think, What deliberate wickedness! The torn planking seemed to have been fretted into shape. Ravages of this kind are characteristic of the cyclone. It is the caprice of that great devastating force to shred and diminish whatever lies in its path. A cyclone has the refined cruelty of an executioner. The disasters that it brings about are like tortures. One might think it harbored a grudge against its victims; it has the intense ferocity of a savage. In exterminating its victims, it also dissects them. It torments them, it revenges itself on them, it takes pleasure in destruction—showing in all this a certain pettiness of spirit.

Cyclones are rare in our climes, and are all the more redoubtable for being unexpected. A rock in their path may become the pivot of a storm. The squall had probably formed a spiral over the Douvres and on striking the reef had turned into a whirlwind, which had tossed the Durande so high up between the rocks. In a cyclone a ship caught by the wind weighs no more than a stone in a sling.

The Durande had suffered the same kind of wound as a man cut in two; it was a torso torn open to release a mass of debris resembling entrails. Ropes swung free, trembling; chains dangled, shivering; the fibers and nerves of the vessel were exposed and hung loose. Anything that was not totally shattered was disjointed; the remaining fragments of the nail-studded casing of the hull were like currycombs bristling with points; the whole ship was a ruin; a handspike was now no more than a piece of iron, a sound no more than a piece of lead, a deadeye no more than a piece of wood, a halyard no more than an end of hemp, a strand of rope no more than a tangled skein, a stay rope reduced to a thread. All around was evidence of tragic, pointless destruction. Everything was broken off, dismantled, cracked, eaten away, disjointed, cast adrift, annihilated. It was a ghastly pile of fragments that no longer belonged together. Everywhere was dismemberment, dislocation, and disruption, in the kind of disorder and fluidity that is characteristic of all states of confusion, from the mêlées of men that are called battles to the mêlées of the elements that are called chaos.

Everything was collapsing and falling away; the flux of planks, panels, ironwork, cables, and beams had been halted just at the great fracture in the hull, from which the least shock might precipitate it all into the sea. What remained of the vessel's powerful frame, once so triumphant—the whole of the after part of the Durande, now suspended between the two Douvres and perhaps liable to fall at any moment—was split wide open at various points, revealing the dark and mournful interior.

Down below the sea foamed, spitting in contempt of this wretched object.

III

SOUND, BUT NOT SAFE

Gilliatt had not expected to find only half of the vessel. Nothing in the account by the skipper of the *Shealtiel,* which had been so exact and detailed, had given any indication that the Durande had split in two. The break had probably taken place when the skipper heard a "devil of a crash." No doubt he had been some distance away when the final blast of wind struck, and what he had thought was merely a heavy sea had in fact been a waterspout. Later, when he had drawn closer to observe the wreck, he had been able to see only the forward part of the vessel, the rest—that is, the wide break that had separated the bow from the stern—having been concealed from him by the enclosing rocks.

In other respects the skipper of the *Shealtiel* had reported the position accurately. The hull of the Durande was lost, but the engines were intact.

Such chances are common in shipwrecks, as they are in fires. The logic of disaster escapes us.

The masts had snapped off and fallen, but the funnel was not even bent; the heavy iron plating on which the engines were based had preserved them intact, in one piece. The planking of the paddle boxes had been torn apart like the slats of a venetian blind, but in the gaps thus left it could be seen that the two wheels were sound, with only one or two blades missing.

In addition to the engines, the main capstan in the stern had survived. It still had its chain, and, solidly mounted on heavy beams, could still be of service, provided that the strain on the voyal did not split the planking. The flooring of the deck was giving way almost everywhere; all this part of the structure was decidedly shaky.

The section of the hull caught between the two Douvres, however, was firmly fixed, as we have seen, and appeared to be holding together.

There was something derisory in the preservation of the engines that added to the irony of the catastrophe. The somber malice of the unknown sometimes finds expression in such bitter mockeries. The engines were saved, but at the same time they were lost. The ocean was preserving them only to destroy them at leisure, as a cat plays with a mouse. They were going to suffer a long death agony, gradually falling to pieces. They were to be a toy for the savage play of the foam. They would shrink day by day and, as it were, melt away. But what could be done to prevent this? It seemed madness even to imagine that this heavy piece of machinery, massive but also delicate, condemned to immobility by its weight, exposed in this solitude to the forces of demolition, delivered up by the reef to the discretion of the winds and the waves, could, in this implacable setting, escape gradual destruction.

The Durande was held prisoner by the Douvres. How could she be extricated? How could she be liberated? For a man to escape is difficult enough; how much more of a problem it is for a piece of machinery!

IV

A PRELIMINARY SURVEY

Gilliatt was surrounded by urgent tasks. The most immediately pressing was to find a place to moor the paunch and some kind of lodging for himself.

The Durande having settled down more to port than to starboard, the right-hand paddle box was higher than the left-hand one.

Gilliatt climbed onto the right-hand paddle box. From there he could look down on the rocks below; and, although the channel through them changed direction several times beyond the Douvres, he was able to study the plan of the reef. This was his first concern.

As we have already noted, the Douvres were like two tall gable-ends marking the narrow entrance to a lane flanked by low granite cliffs with sheer vertical faces. It is not uncommon to find singular corridors such as this, seeming as if hewn by an ax, in ancient submarine rock formations.

This very tortuous defile was never without water, even at low tide. There was always a turbulent current flowing through it from end to end. The sharpness of its turnings was good or bad, depending on the direction of the wind: sometimes it disconcerted the waves and reduced their violence; sometimes it exasperated them. The latter effect was more frequent. An obstacle infuriates the sea and drives it into excesses; the foam thus produced is an exaggerated form of the waves. In such narrow passages a storm wind is similarly compressed and feels the same malignant fury. It is a case of the tempest suffering from strangury.[159] The violent wind is still violent but is more narrowly concentrated. It is both a club and a spear. It pierces at the same time as it crushes. It is a hurricane compressed into a draft.

The two lines of rock bordering this street in the sea gradually decreased in height and disappeared together under the waves at some distance beyond the Douvres. At the far end was another gorge, lower than the one at the Douvres but still narrower, which was the eastern entrance to the defile. The two ridges of rock evidently continued under the water to the rock called the Homme, which stood like a square citadel at the far end of the reef. At low tide, as it was when Gilliatt was surveying the scene, they could be seen continuing all the way, sometimes just under the water, sometimes just emerging from it.

The whole reef was bounded and buttressed in the east by the Homme and in the west by the two Douvres. In a bird's-eye view it would be seen as a long chaplet of jagged rocks winding its way between the Douvres and the Homme.

The Douvres reef, taken as a whole, was constituted by the emergence of two gigantic sheets of granite, almost touching each other, rising vertically to form the crests of peaks in the depths of the ocean—immense offshoots of the abyss. Winds and waves had fretted out this crest and patterned it like the teeth of a saw. All that was visible on the surface was the top of the formation, the reef. What was concealed by the sea must have been enormous. The narrow passage into which the Durande had been cast by the storm was the gap between these two colossal sheets of rock.

This passage, following a zigzag course like a shaft of lightning, was of about the same width throughout its length. It had been shaped in this form by the ocean. The eternal tumult of the sea sometimes reveals bizarre regularities of this kind. There is a geometry of the waves. From one end of the defile to the other the two parallel rock walls faced each other at a distance that was almost exactly the same as the width of the Durande's midship frame. Thanks to the backward curving line of the Little Douvre, the gap between the two Douvres was wide enough to accommodate the paddle boxes: anywhere else they would have been crushed into matchwood.

The inner walls of the reef were hideous to see. When, in our exploration of the wilderness of water that we call the ocean, we encounter the unknown things of the sea, everything is surprising and misshapen. What Gilliatt could see of the defile from the wreck of the Durande was a sight of horror. In the granite gorges of the ocean there is often a strange permanent figuration of shipwreck. The defile on the Douvres reef had one such, of fearful effect. Here and there the oxides in the rock had created blotches of red, like patches of congealed blood. They resembled the bloody exudations on the walls of a slaughterhouse.

There was something of the air of a charnel house about the reef. The rough marine stone, in many shades of color—produced here by the decomposition of metallic compounds in the rock, there by molds—had patches of hideous purple, sinister greens, and splashes of vermilion, calling up ideas of murder and extermination. It was like the walls of an execution chamber, left unwashed; as if men crushed to death here had left their traces. The sheer rock walls seemed to bear the imprint of accumulated death agonies. Certain spots looked as if they were still dripping from the carnage; the rock was wet, and it seemed that if you touched it your fingers would be covered with blood. The rust of massacre was to be seen everywhere. At the foot of the parallel walls, scattered about under the water or just above it, or in hollows in the rocks, were monstrous round boulders—scarlet, black, purple—that looked like human organs; fresh lungs, rotting livers. It was as if giants had been disemboweled here. From top to bottom of the granite ran long veins of red, like blood oozing from a corpse.

All these features are common in sea caves.

V

A Word on the Secret Cooperation of the Elements

For those who, by the chances of travel, may be condemned to spend some time on a reef in the ocean, the form of the reef is not a matter of indifference. There is the pyramid-shaped reef, with a single peak emerging from the sea; there is the circular reef, rather like a ring of large stones; and there is the corridor-shaped reef. The corridor type is the most alarming: not only on account of the anguish of the waves caught between its walls and of the tumultuous movements of the sea to which this gives rise but also because of the obscure meteorological properties that appear to result from the parallelism of two rocks in the open sea. These two sheets of rock form a regular voltaic pile.

A corridor-shaped reef has a certain orientation, and its particular orientation is important. It has an immediate effect on the surrounding air and water. The corridor shape acts on the waves and on the wind—mechanically by its form and galvanically by the magnetization, which may differ between one side and the other, of its vertical planes, which are juxtaposed and opposed to each other.

Reefs of this type attract to themselves all the wild forces dispersed in the hurricane and have a remarkable ability to concentrate the storm. Hence the greater violence of the tempest around them.

It must be remembered that wind is composite. It is believed to be simple but is by no means so. It is not only a dynamic force, it is also a chemical force; it is not only a chemical force, it is also a magnetic force. There is something inexplicable in this force. Wind consists of electricity as well as air. Some winds coincide with the aurora borealis. On the Eel Bank the wind whips up waves a hundred feet high, as Dumont-d'Urville[160] noted with astonishment. The corvette, he says, "did not know whose orders to take." In a storm in southern latitudes the waves swell up in malignant tumors and the sea becomes so terrifying that savages flee to escape the sight of it. Storms in northern seas are different; they carry needles of ice, and the wind takes men's breath away and blows the Eskimos' sledges backward on the snow. Other winds are burning hot, like the African simoon, which is the Chinese typhoon and the samiel of India. Simoon, Typhoon, Samiel: they sound like the names of demons. They melt the summits of mountains; the volcano of Toluca[161] was vitrified by a storm. This hot wind, a whirl of inky black hurling itself against scarlet clouds, is referred to in the Vedas: "Behold the black god who has come to steal the red sheep." In all these facts we feel the pressure of the mystery of electricity.

Wind is full of this mystery. So, too, is the sea. Like wind, it is composite in nature; under the waves of water, which we can see, are waves of force, which we cannot see. Its constituents are—everything. Of all the jumbles of matter in the world the sea is the most indivisible and the most profound.

Try, if you can, to imagine this chaos, so enormous that it reduces everything to the same level. It is the universal container, a reservoir in which fertilizations can take place, a crucible in which transformations are achieved. It amasses and then disperses; it accumulates and then inseminates; it devours and then creates. It receives all the waste waters of the earth and stores them up. It is solid in the ice floe, liquid in the waves, fluid in the cloud, invisible in the wind, impalpable in its emanations. As matter it is a mass, and as a force it is an abstraction. It equalizes and unites all phenomena. It simplifies itself by its infinite capacity for combination. By mingling and churning up its many elements it achieves transparency. It dissolves all differences and absorbs them into its own unity. Its elements are so numerous that it attains identity. One drop is equivalent to the whole. Because it is full of tempests it reaches equilibrium. Plato saw the dancing of the spheres. Strange to say, but true: in the vast orbit of the earth around the sun the ocean, with its ebb and flow, becomes the pendulum of the globe.

In any phenomenon in the sea all phenomena are present. The sea is sucked up by a whirlwind as if by a siphon; a storm operates like a pump; lightning issues from the sea no less than from the air. In a ship at sea a dull shock is sometimes felt, and there is a smell of sulfur from the chain locker. The sea is boiling. "The Devil has put the sea in his cauldron," said de Ruyter.[162] In certain tempests at the turn of the seasons, when the generative forces of nature come into balance, ships battered by the waves seem to emit a kind of light and sparks of phosphorus run up and down the rigging, coming so close to the crew that the sailors reach out and try to capture these fire birds in flight. After the Lisbon earthquake[163] a blast of hot air, as from a furnace, drove a sixty-foot-high wave toward the city. The oscillations of the ocean are connected with the convulsions of the earth.

These incommensurable energies make possible all kinds of cataclysms. At the end of the year 1864, a hundred leagues from the coasts of Malabar, one of the Maldive Islands sank beneath the waves. It went to the bottom like a ship. The fishermen who had left the island in the morning found nothing there when they returned in the evening; they were barely able to get an uncertain glimpse of their villages under the sea. On this occasion it was boats that saw the shipwreck of houses.

In Europe, where nature seems to feel constrained by civilization, such events are rare—so rare as to be presumed impossible. Yet Jersey and Guernsey were once part of Gaul; and as we write these lines an equinoctial gale has just blown down a cliff in the Firth of Forth, on the frontier between England and Scotland.[164] Nowhere do these terrifying forces appear so formidably combined as in that extraordinary northern strait known as the Lysefjord, the most redoubtable of the rocky intestines of the ocean. Here the demonstration is complete.

The Lysefjord is Norway's sea, near the inhospitable Gulf of Stavanger, in the fifty-ninth degree of latitude. The water is heavy and black, with a fever of intermittent storms. In these waters, in the midst of this solitude, is a great somber street. It is a street for no human feet. No one passes that way; no ship ventures there. It is a corridor ten leagues long between two rock walls three thousand feet high. This is the passage that gives admission to the sea.

The passage has corners and angles like all the streets in the sea, shaped as they are by the torsion of the waves. In the Lysefjord the sea is almost always calm and the sky serene: it is a place of ill omen. Where is the wind? It is not up above us. Where is the thunder? It is not in the sky. The wind is under the sea; the thunder is in the rocks. From time to time the water quakes. At certain moments, when there is not a cloud in the sky, about halfway up the sheer cliff, a thousand or fifteen hundred feet above the sea, more usually on the south than on the north side, the rock suddenly thunders and emits a flash of lightning, which shoots out and then withdraws again, like those toys that children can cause to reach out and then spring back again. It too has contractions and enlargements; it strikes the opposing cliff, returns into the rock, then reemerges and continues flashing, shooting out numerous heads and tongues; it bristles with points of flame, strikes at will and then begins flashing again, before finally dying down into sinister blackness. Flocks of birds fly off in terror. Nothing is more mysterious than this artillery emerging from the invisible. It is a case of one rock attacking another, of two reefs thundering at each other. This is not a war that concerns men: it is the hostility of two walls of rock in the abyss.

In the Lysefjord the wind turns into an emanation, the rock performs the function of a cloud, and the thunder emerges as if from a volcano. This extraordinary defile is a voltaic pile whose plates are the two cliffs facing each other.

VI

A STABLE FOR THE HORSE

Gilliatt was sufficiently familiar with reefs to take the Douvres very seriously indeed. His first necessity, as we have said, was to find a safe place for the paunch.

The double ridge of rocks that extended beyond the Douvres like a winding trench linked up at various points with other rocks, within which there were no doubt dead ends and cellars opening off the main defile and attached to it like the branches on the trunk of a tree. The lower parts of the rocks were covered with seaweed, the upper parts with lichens. The uniform level of the seaweed on all the rocks marked the height of high tide and slack tide. Projections on the rock that the water did not reach had the silver and gilt coating that marine granites acquire from the mingling of white and yellow lichens.

At certain points on the rock there was a leprous growth of cone-shaped shells, like the granite's rotting teeth. Elsewhere, in crevices in the rock in which layers of fine sand had accumulated, with ripple marks caused by the wind rather than the waves, were clumps of blue thistles.

In sheltered spots less battered by the waves could be seen the lairs drilled from the rock by sea urchins. These porcupines of the sea, living balls that move around by rolling on their spines, whose protective armor is made up of more than ten thousand pieces, intricately adjusted and welded together, and whose mouth is known, for some unknown reason, as Aristotle's lantern, carve out holes in the granite with their five teeth, which eat away the rock, and then install themselves in the holes. Here the gatherers of seafood find them, cut them in four, and eat them raw, like oysters. Some of them dip their bread in the sea urchins' soft flesh. Hence their name of "sea eggs."

The summits of the peaks rising from the depths of the ocean, now exposed by the ebbing tide, led to just under the sheer crag of the Homme, where there was a kind of creek, almost completely enclosed by the reef, which seemed to offer a possible mooring. Gilliatt observed it carefully. It was in the shape of a horseshoe open on only one side, which was exposed to the east wind, the least bad of the winds in these parts. There the sea was enclosed and almost without motion. It would be a tolerably safe place for the paunch. In any case Gilliatt had little choice. If he wanted to take advantage of the low tide he had to act quickly.

The weather was still fine and mild. The insolent sea was now in a good humor.

Gilliatt climbed down, put on his shoes, untied his boat, got into it, pushed off, and rowed around the outside of the reef. Reaching the Homme, he examined the entrance to the creek.

The channel was marked by a fixed undulating line amid the movement of the waves, a wrinkle imperceptible to anyone but a seaman.

Gilliatt studied this almost invisible line for a moment, then held off a little in order to have room to turn and enter the channel cleanly, and quickly, with one stroke of the oars, he took his boat into the creek.

Once inside, he took a sounding. It would be an excellent place to anchor. Here the paunch would be protected from almost all the chances of the season.

The most redoubtable reefs have quiet little corners of this kind. The harborages to be found in a reef are like the hospitality of the Bedouin—straightforward and reliable.

Gilliatt brought the paunch as close as he could to the Homme, but far enough out to avoid grazing the rock, and dropped her two anchors. Then he folded his arms and reflected on his position.

The paunch was now safely housed. That was one problem solved. But the next one immediately presented itself. Where was he himself to find a lodging?

There were two possibilities: the paunch itself, with its tiny cabin, which was more or less habitable, and the level top of the Homme, which could easily be climbed.

From either of these lodgings it would be possible to reach the gap between the two Douvres where the Durande was suspended, almost dryshod, by jumping from rock to rock at low water.

But low water did not last long, and for most of the time he would be separated either from his lodging or from the wreck by more than two hundred fathoms. Swimming in the waters of a reef is difficult; if there is any sea going it is impossible.

He would have to give up the idea of finding shelter either in the paunch or on the Homme. There was no other suitable place in the neighboring rocks; the lower points were covered twice a day by the high tide, and the higher points were constantly swept by the foam, promising an unwelcome drenching.

There remained the wreck itself. Would it be possible to lodge there? Gilliatt hoped that it might.

VII

A Lodging for the Traveler

Half an hour afterward Gilliatt, returning to the wreck, climbed onto the deck and went down to the between decks and from there to the hold, examining more carefully what he had only briefly surveyed on his first visit.

With the aid of the capstan he had hoisted onto the deck of the Durande the bundle of stores and equipment he had unloaded from the paunch. The capstan had behaved well. There was no lack of handspikes to turn it: Gilliatt had plenty of choice among the wreckage.

Among the debris he found a cold chisel that had evidently fallen from the carpenter's tool kit, and added it to his little stock of tools. In addition—for in such poverty of resources everything is of value—he had his own knife in his pocket.

Gilliatt spent the whole day working on the wreck, clearing up, repairing, simplifying.

At the end of the day he took stock of the position. The entire wreck was quivering in the wind. It shook at his every step. The only part of it that was stable and firm was the section of the hull caught between the two Douvres, which contained the engines. There the crosspieces were strongly braced against the granite.

It would not be wise to make his lodging on the Durande. It would have overloaded the wreck; and it was essential to lighten it rather than add to the weight on board. To burden it further was the very opposite of what was required. This ruin required the most tender care. It was like a sick man on his deathbed. It would get quite enough maltreatment from the wind.

It was bad enough that he was going to have to work on board the Durande. The amount of work that the wreck would necessarily have to endure would undoubtedly distress it, perhaps beyond its strength.

Besides, if any accident should happen at night with Gilliatt asleep on board, he would perish along with the ship. There was no possibility of rescue; and all would then be lost. If he was to save the wreck he must find a lodging outside it.

He had to be outside the wreck and yet close to it: that was the problem. His difficulties were increasing. Where, in these circumstances, could he find a lodging?

Gilliatt reflected. There remained only the two Douvres, and they did not seem to offer much prospect of shelter.

From below a kind of protuberance, a bulging mass of rock, could be seen on the summit of the Great Douvre.

Tall rocks with flat tops, like the Great Douvre and the Homme, are peaks that have been decapitated. There are many such rocks in the mountains and in the ocean. Some rocks, particularly in the open sea, have gashes down the side, like trees that have been attacked: they look as if they have been slashed by a felling ax. And indeed they are exposed to the violent comings and goings of the hurricane, that axman of the sea.

There are other, deeper rooted, causes of cataclysms. Hence the many wounds suffered by these old granite rocks. Some of the giants have had their head cut off.

Sometimes, for no apparent reason, the head does not fall off but remains, mutilated, on the truncated summit. This singularity is not particularly rare. Two examples of this bizarre geological enigma, in highly unusual circumstances, are the Roque au Diable on Guernsey and the Table in the Annweiler valley.[165]

Something similar had probably happened to the Great Douvre. If the protuberance that could be seen on the top was not a natural irregularity in the rock, it must be a surviving fragment of the shattered summit. Perhaps there might be some cavity in this piece of rock—a hole into which a man could creep for shelter? That was all that Gilliatt asked for.

But how could he reach the summit of the Great Douvre? How could he scale that vertical rock face, as solid and as polished as a water-worn boulder and half covered with a mat of viscous confervae,[166] which looked as slippery as a surface freshly soaped?

The summit was at least thirty feet from the deck of the Durande.

Gilliatt took the knotted rope out of his toolbox, hooked it to his belt with the grapnel, and set out to scale the Little Douvre. The higher he climbed the harder it became. He had not taken his shoes off, and this increased the difficulty of the climb. Finally, with great effort, he reached the summit and stood up. There was room for his two feet, but little more. It would be difficult to establish his lodging here. A stylite might have found it adequate; but Gilliatt, more exigent than a stylite, wanted something better.

The Little Douvre leaned toward the Great Douvre, so that, seen from a distance, it seemed to be bowing to it; and the distance between the two, which was some twenty feet at the base, was only eight or ten feet at the top.

From the point to which he had climbed Gilliatt had a clearer view of the mass of rock on the summit platform of the Great Douvre. The platform was at least three fathoms above his head, and he was separated from it by a precipice. The overhang of the Little Douvre concealed the steeply scarped rock face beneath him.

Gilliatt took the knotted rope from his belt, quickly measured the distance with his eye, and hurled the grapnel toward the summit of the Great Douvre.

The grapnel grazed the rock and then slipped away. The rope, with the grapnel at the end, fell to the foot of the Little Douvre.

Gilliatt tried again, throwing the rope farther forward and aiming at the mass of rock on the summit, on which he could see various cracks and crevices.

This time the throw was so skillful and so accurate that the grapnel lodged in the rock.

Gilliatt pulled on the rope. The rock broke away, and the rope returned to dangle against the Little Douvre under Gilliatt's feet.

He threw the grapnel for the third time, and this time it did not fall. He tried the rope again. It held. The grapnel was firmly anchored. It had lodged in some crevice on the summit platform that Gilliatt could not see. He would have to trust his life to this unseen means of support.

Gilliatt did not hesitate. Time was pressing. He had to take the quickest way to achieve his aim.

In any case it was almost impossible to get back to the Durande and reconsider his plans. He would probably slip, and almost certainly fall. It was possible to climb up; it was impossible to climb down.

Gilliatt, like all good seamen, was precise and careful in his movements. He never wasted his strength. His effort was always proportionate to the work in hand. Hence the prodigies of strength that he achieved with muscles of merely ordinary power. His biceps were no stronger than anyone else's, but he had a heart that others lacked. To strength, which is a physical quality, he added energy, which is a moral quality.

He was faced with a redoubtable challenge. He had to cross the space between the two Douvres, suspended from this slender rope.

Often, in acts of devotion or of duty, we find question marks— questions that seem to come from the mouth of Death. A voice from the shadows says: "Are you going to do that?"

Gilliatt gave another pull on the rope. The grapnel still held firm. He wrapped his handkerchief around his left hand and grasped the rope with his right hand, which he covered with his left; then, holding one foot out in front of him, he kicked off sharply with the other foot so that the impetus would prevent the rope from twisting and launched himself from the top of the Little Douvre against the face of the Great Douvre.

He banged heavily against the other rock. In spite of the care he had taken, the rope twisted and he hit the rock with his shoulder. He rebounded, and this time it was his fists that struck the rock. His handkerchief had come adrift, and his hands were badly grazed; but at least there were no bones broken.

Gilliatt hung for a moment, dazed by the shock, but was sufficiently in command of himself not to relax his hold on the rope. He swung free, jerking to and fro, and it was some time before he managed to get a grip on the rope with his feet.

Recovering himself, and holding on to the rope with both hands and feet, he looked down. He was not worried about the length of the rope, which he had used to climb greater heights in the past; and it now reached right down to the deck of the Durande. Reassured that he would be able to get down again, he began to climb, and in a few moments had reached the top.

No creature without wings had ever before found a footing there. The summit platform was covered with bird droppings. It was an irregular trapezoid in shape, the broken-off top of the colossal prism of granite called the Great Douvre. The center had been hollowed out by the rain into the form of a basin.

Gilliatt had been right in his guess. At the southern corner of the trapezoid was a pile of rocks, probably fragments left by the fall of the summit. There was sufficient room between these rocks, which looked like gigantic paving-stones, to provide a refuge for any wild creature that might stray onto this summit. They were heaped up in disorder, leaving gaps and crannies, like a pile of builder's rubble. There was nothing in the nature of a cave within the rocks, but rather a series of cavities like the holes in a sponge.

One of these lairs was large enough to admit Gilliatt. It was floored with grass and moss. Gilliatt would fit into it as if in a sheath. It was two feet high at the mouth and narrowed toward the back. There are stone coffins of this shape. Since the other side of the pile of rocks faced southwest, the recess was sheltered from rain but was exposed to the north wind.

Gilliatt decided that it would serve his purpose. Thus two problems were solved; the paunch had a safe haven and he had a lodging. The great advantage of this lodging was that it was within easy reach of the wreck.

The grapnel attached to the knotted rope had fallen between two rocks and was firmly lodged. Gilliatt made sure that it would not come loose by laying a large stone on top of it.

He had now established a means of regular communication with the Durande. The Great Douvre was his home and the Durande was his workplace. He was able to come and go, to climb up and down, without difficulty.

He dropped down quickly on the knotted rope to the deck of the Durande.

The day was going well; he had made a good beginning; he was content. He realized that he was hungry.

He undid his basket of provisions, opened his knife, cut a slice of smoked beef, ate a piece of brown bread, drank from his can of fresh water, and altogether had a good supper.

To do good work and have a good meal are two of the joys of life. A full stomach is like a good conscience.

After he had eaten his meal there was still a little daylight left. He used it to begin the next very urgent task of lightening the wreck.

He had spent part of the day in sorting through the debris on the Durande. He put aside in the stoutest part of the wreck containing the engines anything that might be of use—timber, iron, ropes, canvas—and flung everything else into the sea.

The stores from the paunch that he had hoisted onto the wreck with the capstan, modest though they were, were an encumbrance. Gilliatt noticed a kind of recess in the wall of the Little Douvre, at a height within reach of his hand. Rocks often have such natural cupboards, though they are cupboards without doors. He thought that he could keep things in this one. At the back of the recess he put his two boxes, one containing tools and the other clothing; then he put in the sacks of rye flour and biscuit, and finally—perhaps rather too near the edge, but there was nowhere else to put it—the basket of provisions.

He had been careful to take out of the box of clothing his sheepskin, his oilskins, and his tarpaulin leggings.

In order to prevent the knotted rope from blowing in the wind, he tied its lower end to a rider on the Durande. Since the Durande had been badly stove in the rider was much bent, and held the rope as tightly as a closed fist.

The upper end of the rope also required attention. Tying the lower end was good as far as it went, but at the top of the rock face, where the rope hung over the edge of the summit platform, there was a danger that it would be gradually frayed by the sharp edge of the rock. Gilliatt rummaged through the pile of debris he had collected and picked out a few fragments of sailcloth and some long strands of rope yarn from a length of old cable, which he stuffed into his pockets. A seaman would have known that he was going to use these pieces of cloth and strands of yarn to protect the rope at the point where it passed over the sharp edge of the rock so as to prevent it from chafing: the process known in sailors' language as keckling.

He then put on his leggings and oilskins, pulled the hood down over his seaman's cap, tied the sheepskin around his neck and, thus attired in full panoply, grasped the rope, now firmly secured along the side of the Great Douvre, and set out on the assault of that somber citadel of the sea.

In spite of the abrasions to his hands he quickly reached the summit of the rock. The last pale glimmers of the setting sun were now dying away. It was dark over the sea, but there was still a little light on the top of the Great Douvre. Gilliatt used this last remnant of daylight to keckle the knotted rope. At the point where it passed over the edge of the summit platform he applied a bandage consisting of several thicknesses of sailcloth, each one tightly tied with a strand of yarn. It was rather like the padding that actresses put on their knees in preparation for the deaths and pathetic appeals of the fifth act.

The keckling completed, Gilliatt stood up again. For the last few minutes, while he had been engaged in this work, he had been vaguely conscious of a curious fluttering sound. In the stillness of the evening it sounded like the beating of the wings of some gigantic bat. He looked up. A great black circle was revolving in the deep white sky of twilight above his head.

In old pictures there are sometimes circles of this kind around the heads of saints. But in such cases they are golden against a dark ground; this circle was dark against a light ground. It was like the Great Douvre's halo of darkness.

The circle came closer to Gilliatt and then moved away, contracting and then enlarging. It was made up of a flock of seabirds—gulls, sea mews, frigate birds, cormorants—evidently excited and upset.

Probably the Great Douvre was their usual lodging and they were coming back to it for the night. Gilliatt had taken a room in it, and they were alarmed by this unexpected fellow lodger. A man on the Great Douvre: they had never seen such a thing before.

This agitated flight lasted for some time. They seemed to be waiting for Gilliatt to go away. Gilliatt watched them with a thoughtful air.

Finally they appeared to make up their mind; the circle suddenly broke up and turned into a spiral, and the whole flock flew off and settled on the Homme, at the other end of the reef. There it sounded as if they were discussing and deliberating on the matter. For a long time, as Gilliatt lay down in his granite sheath, taking a stone for his pillow, he heard the birds chattering to one another, each in turn. Then they fell quiet, and everyone slept, the birds on their rock and Gilliatt on his.

VIII

Importunaeque Volucres[167]

Gilliatt slept well. But he was cold, and this woke him from time to time. He had naturally put his feet at the far end of the recess and his head at the entrance; but he had not taken the trouble to remove from his bed a quantity of sharp-edged pebbles that did little to improve his sleep. Occasionally he half opened his eyes. Every now and then he heard a deep boom: it was the rising tide entering sea caves on the reef with a noise like the discharge of a cannon.

All the circumstances of his present position had the unnatural effect of a vision; he was surrounded by chimeras. In the state of bewilderment that comes with the night, he felt himself plunged into a world of impossibilities. He thought: "It is all a dream."

Then he would fall asleep again and, now really dreaming, found himself at the Bû de la Rue, at Les Bravées, at St. Sampson; he heard Déruchette singing; he was back in the real world.

While he was asleep he thought that he was awake and living his life; when he woke up he thought he was asleep. And indeed he was now living in a dream.

In the middle of the night there was a great rumbling in the sky, of which Gilliatt was dimly conscious in his sleep. Probably it was the wind rising.

Once when he awoke, feeling cold, he opened his eyes rather wider than he had done so far. There were great clouds at the zenith; the moon was fleeing, and a large star was running after her.

Gilliatt's mind was full of the diffused perceptions of a dream, and this enlargement of his dreams was mingled in confusion with the eerie landscapes of the night.

At daybreak he was frozen, but he was sound asleep.

The suddenness of dawn roused him from this sleep, which was perhaps dangerous. The recess in which he was lying faced the rising sun.

Gilliatt yawned, stretched, and emerged quickly from his hole. He had been sleeping so soundly that he did not at first realize where he was. Gradually the feeling of reality returned, and he exclaimed: "Time for breakfast!"

The weather was calm, the sky cold and clear. There were no clouds; the winds of the night had swept the horizon clean, and the sun was rising. Another fine day was beginning. Gilliatt had a feeling of elation.

He took off his oilskins and leggings, rolled them up in the sheepskin, with the fleece inside, tied the bundle up with a length of rope, and pushed it to the back of his lair, out of reach of any rain that might fall.

He made his bed: that is to say, he removed the pebbles. Then he slid down the rope to the deck of the Durande and went to the recess in the rock where he had left his basket of provisions.

The basket was not there. It had been just at the edge of the recess, and the wind that had risen during the night had blown it off and cast it into the sea.

The elements had declared their intention of defending themselves. In seeking out the basket the wind had shown both deliberate purpose and ill will.

Hostilities had begun. Gilliatt realized this at once.

To those who live with the surly familiarity of the sea, it is difficult not to regard the wind as a person and the rocks as living creatures.

Now Gilliatt's only resource, in addition to his stock of biscuit and rye flour, was the shellfish that had been the only nourishment of the man who had died of hunger on the Homme. There was no prospect of catching fish, which dislike turbulence and avoid rocks. There is no profit for fishermen in fishing amid reefs, whose sharp-edged rocks merely tear holes in their nets.

Gilliatt ate a few sea lice, which he prized off the rock with great difficulty, almost breaking his knife in the process.

While he was eating this scanty meal he became aware of a curious commotion on the sea, and looked around. A flock of gulls had swooped down on one of the lower rocks, beating their wings, knocking each other over, screaming and shrieking. They were all swarming noisily at the same spot. This horde of beaks and talons was pillaging something.

That something was Gilliatt's basket. It had been cast by the wind on a sharp-edged rock and had burst open, and the birds had flocked to the scene. They were carrying off in their beaks all kinds of fragments of food. Gilliatt recognized in the distance his smoked beef and his salt fish.

The birds, too, were joining battle and were carrying out their own reprisals. Gilliatt had taken their lodging; they were taking his supper.

IX

THE REEF, AND HOW TO MAKE USE OF IT

A week passed.

Although it was a rainy time of year there was no rain, and for this Gilliatt was thankful. What he was undertaking was, in appearance at least, beyond human strength. Success was so unlikely that the attempt seemed madness.

It is only when you get down to a task that the obstacles and dangers become apparent. You have to begin in order to see how difficult it is going to be to finish. Every beginning is a battle against resistance. The first step you make in an enterprise inexorably reveals what it entails. The difficulty to which we set our hands pricks like a thorn.

Gilliatt was at once faced with obstacles. To raise the Durande's engines from the wreck, in which they were three parts buried—to attempt, with any prospect of success, such a task of salvage, in such a place and at such a season of the year—seemed to call for a whole team of men, and Gilliatt was alone; it called for a whole range of woodworking and engineering equipment, and Gilliatt had only a saw, an ax, a chisel, and a hammer; it called for a good workshop and shed to work in, and Gilliatt had not even a roof over his head; it called for a supply of provisions, and Gilliatt had not even a loaf of bread.

Anyone who had seen Gilliatt working on the reef during this first week would not have understood what he was about. It looked as if he was no longer thinking about the Durande or the two Douvres. He was concerned only with what was lying about on the rocks; he seemed to be absorbed in salvaging small items of wreckage. He took advantage of every low tide to scour the reef for anything that the shipwreck had left there. He went from rock to rock collecting whatever the sea had deposited—scraps of sailcloth, ends of rope, pieces of iron, fragments of paneling, shattered planking, broken yards; here a beam, there a chain, elsewhere a pulley.

At the same time he was studying every recess and crevice on the reef. None of them was habitable; to his great disappointment, for he had been cold in his hole among the rocks on the summit of the Great Douvre, and he would have been glad to find a better garret to lodge in.

Two of these recesses were of some size. Although the rock floors were almost all sloping and uneven, it was possible to stand upright and to walk about in them. The wind and the rain had unrestricted access, but they were out of reach of the highest tides. They were near the Little Douvre, and could be entered at any time of day. Gilliatt decided that one of them would be a storeroom and the other a forge.

With all the lacings and earings that he could collect he parceled up the smaller fragments of wreckage, tying the pieces of wood and iron into bundles, making parcels of canvas, and lashing everything carefully together. As the rising tide floated these bundles off the rocks, he dragged them to his storeroom. In a crevice in the rock he had found a mast rope with which he was able to haul even large pieces of timber. In the same fashion he recovered from the sea the many lengths of chain scattered about among the rocks.

He worked at these tasks with astonishing tenacity. He was successful in all that he wanted to do. Nothing withstands the determination of an ant.

By the end of the week Gilliatt had brought together in his granite shed and arranged in order all the miscellaneous bric-a-brac of the storm. There was a corner for tacks and a corner for sheets; bowlines were kept separate from halyards; ribs were arranged according to the number of holes in them; puddings, carefully detached from the broken anchor rings, were tied in bunches; clump blocks, without sheaves, were separated from pulley blocks; belaying pins, bull's-eyes, preventer shrouds, downhauls, snatch blocks, pendants, kevels, trusses, stoppers, sail booms—those, at any rate, that had not been so damaged as to be useless—occupied different compartments; all the timber—stretchers, posts, stanchions, caps, port lids, fish pieces, binding strakes—was piled up separately; so far as he could he had fitted the fragments of planks from the ship's bottom into one another; reef points were not confused with robands, crowfeet with stern lines, backstay pulleys with hawser pulleys, fragments from the waist with fragments from the stern; in one corner was a section of the Durande's cat harpings, which serve to brace the top shrouds and futtock shrouds. Every bit of debris had its place. The whole of the wreck was here, classified and labeled. It was like chaos deposited in a storehouse.

A staysail, held in place by large stones, covered—though with many holes—anything that might be damaged by rain.

Badly damaged as the fore part of the Durande had been, Gilliatt was able to salvage the two catheads with their three pulley wheels.

He had recovered the bowsprit, though he had great difficulty in unrolling its gammoning. It held closely together, since, as usual, it had been put on, using the windlass, in dry weather. He managed, however, to detach it. This thick rope might come in very useful.

He also found the smaller anchor, lodged in a rock crevice that was uncovered at low tide.

In the remains of Tangrouille's cabin he found a piece of chalk, which he preserved carefully. It might be useful for marking things.

A leather fire bucket and a number of other buckets in reasonably good condition completed his stock of equipment.

All that remained of the Durande's supply of coal was also deposited in the storeroom.

Within a week the work of salvaging the remains of the wreck had been completed; the reef was swept clean, and the Durande was lightened. All that was left on the wreck was the engines.

The fragment of the fore part that remained attached to the after part did not put any strain on the hull. It hung without dragging, supported by a projection in the rock. It was large and thick, and would have been very heavy to haul away; and it would have taken up too much room in the storeroom. This section of the ship's side had the look of a raft. Gilliatt left it where it was.

During all this labor Gilliatt had been much preoccupied. He had looked in vain for the "doll," the figurehead of the Durande. He would have given his two arms to find it, if he had not had such great need of them.

At the entrance to the storeroom and just outside it were two piles of useless fragments: a heap of iron for forging and a heap of wood for burning.

Gilliatt was at work from the first crack of dawn. Apart from his hours of sleep he did not take a moment's rest.

The cormorants flying to and fro watched him as he went about his work.

X

THE FORGE

His storeroom completed, Gilliatt set to work on constructing his forge. The second cavity in the rock that he had selected was a kind of long passage of some depth. He had at first thought of making his lodging here; but the wind blew so incessantly and so strongly through it that he had had to give up the idea. This constant stream of air gave him the notion of making it his forge. Since this cavern could not be his bedroom, it would be his workshop. To bend obstacles to your will is a great step toward success. The wind was Gilliatt's enemy: he would make it his servant.

What is said of certain men—fit for anything, good for nothing—can be said also of cavities in rocks. They show promise, but do not fulfill their promise. One hollow in the rock looks like a bath, but the water leaks away through a crevice; another is a bedroom, but a bedroom without a ceiling; another again is a bed of moss, but the moss is wet; still another is an armchair, but an armchair of stone.

The forge that Gilliatt planned had been rough-hewn by nature;

but to make himself master of nature's work and turn it to use, to transform this cavern into a laboratory, was a difficult and daunting task. With three or four large rocks shaped in the form of a funnel and ending in a narrow fissure chance had created a kind of ventilation shaft of infinitely greater power than those old bellows used in forges, fourteen feet long, that produced ninety-eight thousand inches of air with every puff. This was a very different kind of thing. The dimensions of a hurricane are beyond calculation.

This excess of power was a problem; it was difficult to regulate the strength of the blast.

The cavern had two disadvantages: it was traversed from end to end by air, and also by water. The water did not come in waves but in a continual trickle that oozed rather than flowed like a stream. The foam that was continually cast over the rocks by the surf, sometimes to a height of over a hundred feet, had filled a natural basin in the high rocks above the cavern with seawater, and the overflow from this reservoir ran over the edge of the rock in a slender waterfall about an inch in breadth, with a drop of four or five fathoms. The supply was supplemented from time to time by rain, deposited by a passing shower into this inexhaustible reservoir that was always overflowing. The water was brackish and unfit to drink, but clear. It dripped gracefully down from the tips of the confervae as if from tresses of hair.

Gilliatt conceived the idea of using this water to discipline the wind. By means of a funnel and two or three pipes quickly knocked together from planks, one of them fitted with a tap, and a large tub to serve as a lower reservoir, without checks or counterweight, but with a narrow neck above and draft tubes below, Gilliatt—who, as we have said, was a bit of a blacksmith and a bit of an engineer—devised, in place of the forge bellows that he lacked, a blower, a piece of equipment that was less perfect than what is now known as a *cagniardelle,* but less rudimentary than the *trompe*[168] once used in the Pyrenees.

He had some rye flour, which he used to make paste, and he had some untarred rope, which he teased out to make tow. With the tow and the paste and odd bits of wood he stopped up all the crevices in the rock, leaving only a narrow passage for air made from a fragment of a powder flask, used for firing the signal gun, which he had found in the Durande. This directed the air horizontally onto a large flat stone that Gilliatt made the hearth of his forge. A stopper made from an end of rope could close the air passage when required. Then Gilliatt heaped wood and coal on the hearth, struck his steel against the rock, caught the spark on a handful of tow, and when the tow blazed up used it to ignite the wood and coal.

He tried out the blower. It worked perfectly.

Gilliatt felt the pride of a Cyclops, master of air, water, and fire. He was master of the air, for he had given the wind a kind of lung, created a breathing apparatus in the granite, and converted the blast of wind into a bellows. He was master of water, for he had used the trickle of water to make a *trompe*. He was master of fire, for from this damp rock he had produced a flame.

Since the cavern was almost completely open to the sky, the smoke escaped freely, blackening the overhanging rock face. The rocks that had seemed forever destined to be lashed by foam now became acquainted with soot.

Gilliatt selected as his anvil a large and densely grained waterworn boulder of roughly the shape and size he wanted. It was a very dangerous base for his work, since it was liable to shatter under the blows of his hammer. One end, which was rounded and ended in a point, could serve as the cone-shaped end of a regular anvil, but there was nothing corresponding to the pyramid-shaped end. It was the ancient stone anvil of the troglodytes. The surface, polished by the waves, was almost as hard as steel.

Gilliatt was sorry that he had not brought his own anvil with him. Not knowing that the Durande had been cut in two by the storm, he had hoped to find the carpenter's kit of tools and the equipment that was normally kept in the forward part of the hold, but by ill luck it was the forward part of the vessel that had been carried away.

The two rock chambers that Gilliatt had won from the reef were close together. His storeroom and his forge communicated with each other.

Each evening, when his day's work was done, Gilliatt made his supper of a piece of biscuit softened in water, a sea urchin, a crab, or a few sea chestnuts—the only type of game to be found on the rocks—and then, shivering like the knotted rope, climbed up to go to bed in his hole on the Great Douvre.

The kind of abstraction in which he lived was increased by the very materiality of his occupations. Reality is an alarming thing when taken in large doses. His physical labor, with its endless variety of detail, did nothing to reduce his stupor at finding himself where he was and doing what he was doing. As a rule physical tiredness is a line that draws a man down to earth; but the very singularity of the task that Gilliatt had undertaken kept him in a kind of ideal twilight zone. He felt at times as if he were hammering away at clouds. At other times it seemed to him that his tools were weapons. He had a strange feeling that he was the object of a hidden attack that he was repelling or anticipating. In twisting strands of rope together, in unraveling threads of yarn from a sail, in joining two beams, he saw himself as fashioning engines of war. The innumerable intricate tasks involved in this salvage operation were now beginning to seem like precautions against aggression by intelligent beings that were barely concealed and highly transparent. Gilliatt did not know the words required to express ideas, but he was aware of the ideas themselves. He felt less and less like a workman and more and more like a gladiator.[169] He was indeed a tamer of the elements. He almost had a perception of this. It was a strange enlargement of his spirit.

Moreover he had all around him, as far as the eye could see, the whole vast sense of wasted labor. Seeing the operation of the forces of nature in the unfathomable and the limitless, man is bewildered. He tries to divine the objects of these forces. Space, forever in motion; the tireless sea; the clouds that seem to be hurrying about their business; the whole immense, obscure effort: all these convulsions present us with a problem. What are these perpetual tremors about? What are these squalls constructing? These blasts, these sobbings, these howlings of the storm: what are they creating? What is all this tumult trying to do? The flow and ebb of these questions is as eternal as the tide. Gilliatt knew what he was doing; but he was obsessed, without understanding why, by the enigma of this agitation in the great expanse surrounding him. Unknown to himself, mechanically, imperiously, by the mere pressure of external things, and with no other effect than an unconscious and almost sullen bewilderment, Gilliatt, in his dreamy mood, assimilated his own labors to the prodigious wasted labors of the sea. For how can a man, situated as Gilliatt was, help being exposed to and seeking to understand the mystery of the dread ocean, eternally laboring? How can he help meditating, in so far as meditation is possible, on the vacillation of the waves, the furious determination of the foam, the imperceptible wearing away of the rock, the raging of the four winds? What a terrifying thought it is to contemplate this perpetual recommencement, this bottomless well the ocean, these Danaids[170] the clouds, all this labor for nothing!

No, not for nothing. But only you, the Unknown, know why.

XI

A Discovery

Men sometimes visit a reef near the coast, but never one in the open sea. Why should anyone go there? It is not an island; there is no food to be found there, no fruit trees, no pastureland, no livestock, no springs of fresh water. It is a place of nakedness set in a solitude. It is an expanse of rock, with steep scarps rising out on the sea and sharp-edged ridges under the water. There is nothing to be found here but shipwreck.

Reefs of this kind are strange places. There the sea is alone, and can do whatever she wants. There is no terrestrial life to trouble her. The sea is terrified of man; she mistrusts him; she conceals from him what she is and what she is doing. In a reef she feels safe; man will not come there. The monologue of the waves will not be disturbed. She works away on the reef, repairs any damage it suffers, sharpens its edges; she equips it with jagged points, renovates it, keeps it in good condition. She pierces holes in the rock, breaks up the soft rock and exposes the hard rock, strips off the flesh and leaves the bones, excavates, dissects, drills, cuts holes and channels, links up its guts, fills the reef with cells, imitates a sponge on a larger scale, hollows out the interior and sculpts the exterior. In this secret mountain that belongs to her, she constructs her caves and shrines and palaces. She has her own hideous and splendid vegetation, composed of floating grasses that bite and monsters that take root; and she hides this terrible magnificence in the darkness of the water. On an isolated reef there is no one watching her, spying on her, disturbing her; she can develop at her ease the mysterious side of her being that is inaccessible to man. There she deposits her horrible, living secretions. All the unknowns of the sea are to be found there.

Promontories, capes, land's ends, nazes, shoal rocks, and reefs are constructed features. Their formation by geology counts for little compared with their formation by the ocean. Reefs—those habitations of the waves, those pyramids and syrinxes[171]—are examples of a mysterious form of art that the author of this book has elsewhere called the art of nature, and have a kind of enormous style of their own. What is in fact the result of chance appears deliberate. These structures are of many forms. They have the intricate pattern of a colony of polyps, the sublimity of a cathedral, the extravagance of a pagoda, the vastness of a mountain, the delicacy of a jewel, the horror of a sepulchre. They have as many cells as a wasps' nest, as many dens as a menagerie, as many tunnels as a warren of moles, as many ambuscades as an army camp. They have gates, but the gates are barricaded; columns, but they are truncated; towers, but they are out of true; bridges, but they are broken. Their various compartments are strictly reserved: this one for birds, that one for fish, with no admission for outsiders. Their architectural forms are in constant transformation, they contradict each other, they affirm the laws of statics or repudiate them, they break off sharply, they stop short, they begin as an archivolt and end as an architrave; block is piled on block; the builder at work here is Enceladus.[172] Here an extraordinary dynamic force displays its problems, all resolved. Terrifying pendentives threaten to fall, but do not fall. It is difficult to see how these vertiginous structures stand at all. Everywhere there are overhangs, imbalances, gaps, masses hanging crazily in the air. The laws governing this architectural Babelism cannot be discerned; the Unknown, that tremendous architect, calculates none of its effects, but succeeds in everything it does. The rocks, built up in confusion, form a monstrous monument; there is no logic in its structure, but it achieves a vast equilibrium. Here there is more than stability: there is eternity. But there is also disorder. The granite seems to have taken on the tumultuous movement of the waves. A reef is the tempest turned to stone. Nothing is more awe-inspiring than this wild architecture, forever on the point of collapse, forever holding firm. All these features support one another, and at the same time act against one another. It is a conflict between opposing lines that results in the construction of an edifice; a work created by collaboration between two hostile forces, the ocean and the hurricane.

This architecture sometimes produces masterpieces, of dread ef-

fect. One such was the Douvres reef. It had been constructed and per-
fected by the sea with formidable love, and was now being groomed by
the jealous waves. It was hideous, treacherous, dark, and full of cavities.
It had a whole venous system of underwater holes ramifying to unfathomable depths. Several of the entrances to this labyrinth of passages were exposed at low tide. They could be entered; but anyone
who entered did so at his own risk.

For the purposes of his salvage operation Gilliatt found it necessary
to explore these caverns. Each one he entered was terrifying. In all of
them he found, reproduced on the exaggerated scale of the ocean, the
atmosphere of a slaughterhouse and of butchery that was so strangely
marked in the gap between the two Douvres. Only those who have
seen these ghastly frescoes painted by nature on the eternal granite
walls of such caverns can have any idea of what they are like. These
cruel caverns, too, were deceitful; it was unsafe to linger in them. The
high tide filled them up to their roofs.

There was an abundance of sea lice and other seafood in these caverns. They were obstructed by waterworn boulders, piled up to the
vaulting of the roof. Many of them weighed over a ton. They were of
all sizes and colors. Most of them appeared bloodred; some of them,
covered with hairy, sticky confervae, were like large green moles bur-
rowing into the rock.

Several of the caverns came to a dead end in a kind of apse. Others,
arteries for some mysterious traffic, continued into the rock in black
and tortuous fissures: these were the streets of the abyss. These fissures
grew steadily narrower, at length leaving no room for a man to pass. A
lighted torch revealed only dark rock walls dripping with moisture.

Once Gilliatt, ferreting about in the cavern, ventured into one of
these fissures. The tide was at a level that made it safe to do so. It was a
fine, calm, sunny day. No disturbance in the sea that might have made
it more dangerous was to be feared.

As we have said, two necessities led Gilliatt to undertake these ex-
plorations: he wanted to look for any pieces of wreckage that might be
useful in the work of salvage and to find crabs and crayfish to supple-
ment his food supply. The shellfish on the Douvres were beginning to
run out.

The fissure was very narrow, and it was almost impossible to make
his way through it. But he saw light at the far end. He redoubled his ef-

forts, made himself as small as possible, and, with much contortion, managed to inch his way forward.

Gilliatt was now, without knowing it, in the interior of the rock onto which Clubin had driven the Durande. He was under the point where the ship had struck. Though sheer and inaccessible on the outside, it was hollowed out within. It had passages, shafts, and chambers like the tomb of an Egyptian king. This system of caverns and tunnels was one of the most complicated of the labyrinths carved out by water, undermined by the tireless sea. The ramifications of this warren under the sea probably communicated with the immense expanse of water outside through a number of openings, some gaping open on the surface of the sea, others deep down and invisible. It was near here, though Gilliatt did not know this, that Clubin had dived into the sea.

Through this fissure, which seemed fit for a crocodile's lair—though there was no danger from crocodiles here—Gilliatt made his way painfully forward, twisting and turning, crawling, striking his head on the rock, crouching down and then straightening up, losing his footing and recovering himself. Gradually the passage opened out; he saw a dim light ahead, and suddenly he found himself in an extraordinary cavern.

XII

The Interior of an Edifice Under the Sea

It was fortunate that Gilliatt had this glimmer of light, for if he had taken one step more he would have fallen into a pool of water, which might well be bottomless. The water in such sea caves is so cold and brings on paralysis so quickly that it is often fatal to even the strongest swimmers. And there was no way of getting out of the water or even getting a hold on the sheer rock faces by which he was surrounded.

Gilliatt stopped short. The crevice from which he had emerged ended on a narrow, slippery ledge, a kind of corbeled projection on the sheer rock face. With his back against the wall, he surveyed what was in front of him.

He was in a large cavern. Above his head was what looked like the underside of a huge skull, which had the appearance of having just been dissected. The veins in the rock on the roof of the cave, dripping with water, imitated the branching fibers and jagged sutures of a cranium. The chamber had rock for a ceiling and water for a floor; the waves created by the tide, caught between the four walls of the cave, were like large quivering paving stones. The cave was closed in on all sides; no roof lights, no windows; not a breach in the wall, not a crack in the roof. The cave was lit from below through the water: a strange dark radiance.

In this dim twilight Gilliatt, whose eyes had dilated during his passage through the dark corridor, could make out every detail.

He was familiar with the Plémont caves on Jersey, the Creux Maillé on Guernsey, and the Boutiques on Sark, so called because they were used by smugglers to store their goods; but none of these marvelous caves was comparable with the subterranean and submarine chamber that he had just entered.

On the far side of the pool, under the water, was a kind of drowned arch. This arch, a natural pointed arch fashioned by the waves, glowed with light between its two black uprights, which reached deep down into the water. It was through this submerged porch that the light of the open sea entered the cavern: a strange kind of daylight engulfed by the sea.

The light flared out under the waves like a wide fan and was reflected from the rock. Its rectilinear radiance, broken up into long straight shafts of light over the opacity of the depths, growing lighter or darker from one crevice in the rock to another, looked as if it were divided by sheets of glass. There was light in this cavern, but light of an unknown kind. It had nothing of the quality of our everyday light. It was as if one had found one's way onto another planet. This light was an enigma; it was like the glaucous gleam in the eye of a sphinx. The cavern resembled the interior of an enormous and magnificent skull; the vault was the cranium, the arch was the mouth; the sockets for the eyes were missing. The mouth, swallowing and disgorging the inflow and outflow of the sea, wide open to catch the full light of midday, drank in light and vomited forth bitterness. There are some beings, intelligent and evil, like that. The rays of the sun, passing through this porch obstructed by a vitreous mass of seawater, became green, like the glimmering light from Aldebaran. The water, filled with this moist light, appeared like molten emerald. The whole cavern had a soft aquamarine tinge of extraordinary delicacy. The vault of the cavern, with its lobes resembling those of a brain and its intricate ramifications like a network of nerves, was bathed in a tender shade of chrysoprase. The shimmering ripples on the water were reflected on the roof of the cavern, where they dissolved and re-formed endlessly, forming a golden mesh that was now wider and now narrower, in a mysterious dance movement. It had a spectral aspect; observing it, one might well wonder what prey secured or expectation to be realized gave rise to this joyously magnificent network of living fire. From the projections in the vault and the irregularities in the rock there hung long thin trails of vegetation, their roots probably bathed in some deposit of water higher up in the granite, with drops of water trickling like pearls, one after the other, from their tips. These pearls dropped into the gulf below with a gentle splash. The effect of the scene was indescribable. It was charming beyond all imagination and at the same time melancholy beyond all expression.

This was a palace of death in which Death was content.

XIII

WHAT CAN BE SEEN THERE AND WHAT CAN BE MERELY GLIMPSED

An extraordinary place: a darkness that dazzled the eye.

The palpitation of the sea could be felt within the cavern. The oscillation outside it swelled and reduced the level of the water inside with the regularity of breathing. It seemed that some mysterious soul dwelled within this great green diaphragm that rose and fell in silence.

The water had a magical limpidity, and Gilliatt saw at varying depths submerged levels, projecting rock surfaces of an increasingly darker green. There were, too, dark recesses, probably of unfathomable depth.

On either side of the submarine porch were rough-hewn flattened arches, areas of deep shadow, marking the entrance to small side caves, lateral aisles of the central cavern that could no doubt be entered at particularly low tides. These recesses had sloping roofs at angles of varying degree. Reaching back and disappearing into them were small beaches, only a few feet wide, laid bare by the scouring of the sea.

Here and there trails of vegetation more than a fathom in length waved to and fro under the water, like tresses of hair blowing in the wind. Lower down could be glimpsed forests of seaweed.

The walls of the cavern, both under water and above water, were covered from top to bottom, from the vault of the roof to their disappearance in invisible depths, with those prodigious florescences of the ocean, so rarely seen by the human eye, which were known to the old Spanish navigators as the *praderías del mar,* the meadows of the sea. A luxuriant growth of moss in every shade of olive concealed and enlarged the protuberances in the granite. From every projection hung slender goffered ribbons of varech, a seaweed used by fishermen as a form of barometer, their glistening strands swaying in the mysterious breathing of the cavern.

Under these various types of vegetation—partly concealed, partly revealed—were the rarest gems in the jewel casket of the ocean: ivory shells, strombs, miter shells, helmet shells, murexes, trumpet shells, struthiolarias, turreted cerites. Everywhere, clinging to the rocks, were limpets, like microscopic huts, forming villages along whose streets prowled chitons, those beetles of the sea. Since few pebbles found their way into the cavern, it offered a refuge for shellfish. Shellfish, in their embroidered and braided splendor, are the *grands seigneurs* of the ocean, avoiding rough and uncivil contact with the common sort of pebbles. The glittering accumulations of shells at certain spots under the water gave out ineffable irradiations through which could be glimpsed a medley of azures, mother-of-pearls, and golds in all the hues of the water.

On the wall of the cavern, just above the level of the water, a strange and magnificent plant formed a fringe on the hangings of varech, continuing and rounding them off. This plant—fibrous, close-growing, inextricably intertwined, and almost black—formed dark, confused masses, spangled with innumerable small flowers of the color of lapis lazuli. In the water these flowers seemed to light up, like glowing blue embers. Out of the water they were flowers, under the water they were sapphires; and as the rising tide engulfed the lower levels of the cavern where these plants grew, it covered the rock with fiery carbuncles.

When the tide swelled, like a lung filling with air, these flowers, bathed in water, were resplendent, and when it fell they were extinguished—offering a melancholy likeness to human destiny. It was a process of breathing in, which is life, and breathing out, which is death.

One of the marvels of the cavern was the rock itself. Forming here a wall, there an arch, there again a buttress or a pilaster, in some places it was rough and bare and then, close by, carved into the most delicate natural patterns. Some quality of intelligence and sensibility was mingled with the massive stupidity of the granite. What an artist is the abyss! One stretch of wall, cut into a square shape and carved into rounded forms suggesting the attitudes of figures, had something of the appearance of a bas-relief: contemplating it, one might think of a roughly sketched piece of sculpture prepared by Prometheus for the chisel of Michelangelo. It seemed as if human genius, with a few strokes of a hammer, might complete what the giant had begun. Elsewhere the rock was damascened like a Saracen breastplate or nielloed like a Florentine bowl. There were panels that looked like Corinthian bronze, arabesques such as are found on the doorway of a mosque, and obscure and improbable scratch marks like those on a runic stone. Plants with twisted ramuscules and tendrils, crisscrossing on the groundwork of golden lichens, covered the rock with filigree ornament. This cavern was more than a cavern: it was an Alhambra. It was a union of the wildness of nature and the delicacy of goldsmith's work in the awe-inspiring and misshapen architecture of chance.

The magnificent molds deposited by the sea covered the angles of the granite with velvet. The steep scarps were festooned with large-flowered lianas, adept at clinging to the rock, which ornamented the walls so effectively that they seemed the result of intelligent design. Pellitories with bizarre clusters of flowers presented their clumps of greenery, well and tastefully placed. All the grace and style that a cavern is capable of was on display. The astonishing Edenic light that came from under the water—the twilight of the submarine depths and at the same time a paradisiac radiance—softened the lineaments of the rock in a kind of visionary diffusion. Each wave was a prism. In these iridescent undulations the contours of things had the chromatism of overconvex optical lenses; under the water floated solar spectra. It looked as if broken pieces of drowned rainbows were turning and twisting in this auroral transparency. Elsewhere, in other corners of the cavern, there was a kind of moonlight in the water. All these splendors seemed to have been brought together here for some mysterious nocturnal purpose. The magnificence of the cavern had an extraordinarily disturbing and enigmatic effect. There was a predominant sense of enchantment. The extraordinary vegetation and the amorphous stratification were matched to one another and had a feeling of harmony. It was a happy marriage between two forms of wildness. The ramifications of the vegetation clung firmly to the rock, though appearing to be only grazing it, in an intimate caress between the savage rock and the untamed vegetation. Massive pillars had capitals and ligatures in the form of frail, perpetually quivering garlands, like fairies' fingers tickling the feet of behemoths; the rock supported the plants and the plants clasped the rock with a monstrous grace.

These deformities, mysteriously adapted to one another, combined to create a strange sovereign beauty. The works of nature, no less supreme than the works of genius, contain a quality of the absolute and have an overwhelming presence. Their unexpectedness impresses itself powerfully on the mind; they have a feeling of premeditation, and they are never more striking than when they suddenly produce something exquisite out of the terrible.

This unknown cave was, as it were—if the expression may be permitted—astralized. It aroused a feeling of astonishment, the stronger because it was totally unexpected. This crypt was filled with the light of apocalypse. One could not be sure that it actually existed. This appearance of reality had an element of the impossible. You saw it, you touched it, you were in it; but it was still difficult to believe in it.

Was it daylight coming in through that window under the sea? Was it really water quivering in this dark basin? Were not these arches and doorways merely shaped by celestial clouds in the likeness of a cavern? What kind of stone was it under one's feet? Was not this pillar about to disintegrate and dissolve into smoke? What was this jeweled ornament of shells glimpsed under the water? How far away was one from life, from the world, from men? What was the enchantment mingled with this darkness? It created a feeling of almost sacred awe, enhanced by the gentle restlessness of the weeds that grew in the depths of the water.

At the far end of the cavern, which was oblong in shape, there could be seen, under a cyclopean archivolt of remarkably exact design, in an almost indistinguishable recess, a kind of cave within the cave, a tabernacle within the shrine, behind a curtain of green light like the veil in a temple, a square slab of stone emerging from the waves, surrounded on all sides by water, with something of the appearance of an altar, from which it seemed that a goddess had just stepped down. It called up a vision, under this crypt and on this altar, of some naked celestial being, eternally sunk in contemplation, whom the approach of a man had caused to disappear. It was difficult to believe that this august cellar should not house a vision. The apparition summoned up in the abstraction of reverie began to take on form. A flood of chaste light on barely glimpsed shoulders, a forehead bathed in the brightness of dawn, the oval of an Olympian face, mysterious rounded breasts, modestly protective arms, hair falling loose in auroral light, ineffable loins showing palely in a sacred mist, the forms of a nymph, the glance of a virgin, a Venus rising from the sea, an Eve emerging from chaos: such was the vision that forced itself on the mind. It was surely impossible that there should not be such a phantom there. A naked woman, containing within her a star, must have been on this altar a moment ago. On this pedestal, with its sense of inexpressible ecstasy, one could not but imagine a white figure, standing erect and imbued with life. The mind called up an image, surrounded by the mute adoration of this cavern, of an Amphitrite, a Tethys, a Diana with the capacity for love, a statue of the ideal shaped by a glow of light, looking out mildly on the surrounding darkness. This dazzling phantom was no longer there; this figure, made to be seen only by the invisible, could not be seen, but its presence could be felt; one experienced the tremors of supreme delight. The goddess was no longer there, but the sense of divinity lingered.

The beauty of the cavern seemed designed to house this presence. It was on account of this deity, this fairy of mother-of-pearl, this queen of the breathing air, this grace born of the waves—it was on her account, or so one imagined, that the cave had been so religiously walled in, so that nothing might ever disturb, in the sanctuary of this divine phantom, the darkness that expresses respect and the silence that expresses majesty.

Gilliatt, who had a kind of visionary insight into nature, stood lost in thought, moved by confused emotions.

Suddenly, a few feet below him, in the delightful transparency of this water that seemed like a solution of gemstones, he saw an unidentifiable object. What looked like a long rag of cloth was moving amid the oscillation of the waves. It was not merely floating, it was swimming purposefully; it had an object, it was going somewhere, it forged swiftly ahead. It had the form of a fool's bauble, with points, and these flaccid points quivered in the water. The thing seemed to be covered with a kind of dust that was resistant to water. It was more than horrible; it was foul. It had something of the character of a chimera; it was a living creature—or was it merely the appearance of one? It seemed to be heading for the dark end of the cavern and disappearing into it. The water grew darker above this sinister shape as it glided away and disappeared.

BOOK II

THE LABOR

I

THE RESOURCES OF A MAN WHO HAS NOTHING

The cavern did not let people go easily. The entrance had been difficult, and the exit was even more restricted. Gilliatt succeeded in getting out, however, and had no thought of returning. He had not found anything he was looking for, and he had not the leisure to be merely curious.

He set his forge to work at once. Lacking tools, he had to make them himself.

For fuel he had the wreck; for motive power, water; for bellows, the wind; for anvil, a stone; for craftsmanship, his instinct; for power, his will.

Gilliatt entered on his somber task with ardor.

The weather seemed inclined to help him. It continued to be dry, and had little of an equinoctial feel about it. The month of March had come, but it had come in quietly. The days were growing longer. The blue of the sky, the vast gentle movements of the great expanse of space, the serenity of high noon—all this seemed to exclude any idea of evil intention. The sea looked cheerful in the sun. A preliminary caress gives piquancy to acts of betrayal; and the sea is lavish with such caresses. When you are dealing with a woman you must beware of her smiles.

There was very little wind, and the water-driven bellows worked all the better for that. Too much wind would have been a hindrance rather than a help.

Gilliatt had a saw, and he made himself a file; with the saw he attacked the timber, with the file he attacked the metal. Then he added the blacksmith's two iron hands, his tongs and his pliers. The tongs hold the metal fast, the pliers work it, the one acting as a fist, the other as a finger; for a workman's tools form an organism. Gradually Gilliatt provided himself with other useful tools and built up his armament. He constructed a hood for his forge with a piece of sheet iron.

One of his principal tasks was the sorting and repair of the pulleys. After he had repaired the blocks and the sheaves, he trimmed off all the broken joists and reshaped the ends. As we have seen, he had all he needed for his carpenter work and a considerable store of timbers, arranged according to their shape and size and type of wood: oak on one side, deal on the other, curved members such as riders separated from straight ones like binding strakes. This formed his reserve supply of supports and levers, of which he might at any moment stand in need.

Anyone who proposes to make a hoist must have beams and pulley blocks; but he needs more than that, he must also have rope. Gilliatt repaired the cables and hawsers. He frayed out the tattered sails and managed to extract from them some excellent yarn that he formed into rope and spliced onto the old rigging. But this new rope was liable to rot and would have to be used quickly; for Gilliatt had no tar to give it a protective coat.

After repairing the ropes he set to work on the chains.

With the help of the pointed end of the rock he used as his anvil, which served in place of the horn of a regular anvil, he contrived to make links, crudely shaped but sufficiently strong, with which he joined together the broken pieces of chain so as to produce suitable lengths.

To work at a forge on your own, without anyone to help, is difficult in the extreme; but Gilliatt managed it. True, he was making only small items, which he could hold in one hand with his tongs while he hammered with the other.

He cut the round iron bars from the bridge into sections, fashioning one end into a point and the other into a broad flat head so as to produce large nails about a foot long. Nails of this kind, which are much used in the construction of bridges, are good for driving into rock.

Why was Gilliatt taking all this trouble? We shall see presently.

He had several times to put a fresh edge on his ax and the teeth of his saw. For this latter purpose he had made himself a saw file.

Sometimes he used the Durande's capstan. When the hook on the chain broke he forged a new one.

With the help of his tongs and pincers, using his chisel as a screwdriver, he contrived to dismantle the two paddle wheels. It will be remembered that the wheels had been so constructed that they could be taken to pieces. With the planking of the paddle boxes in which they had been housed, Gilliatt made two crates in which he deposited the pieces of the wheels, all carefully numbered. For the numbering process he found his piece of chalk very useful. Then he set the two crates on the soundest part of the Durande's deck.

After completing these preliminaries Gilliatt was faced with the supreme problem—what to do about the engines. He had managed to dismantle the paddle wheels, but he could not dismantle the engines.

In the first place, he was not familiar with the mechanism. If he set about the task without knowing what he was doing, he might well cause irreparable damage. And even if he had, unwisely, contemplated dismantling the engines piece by piece, he would have needed other tools—tools that could not be made with a cavern as forge, the wind as bellows, and a rock as anvil. If he tried to take the engines to pieces he might well destroy them altogether.

It looked as if Gilliatt was faced with an impossibility.

What could he do?

II

IN WHICH SHAKESPEARE AND AESCHYLUS MEET

Gilliatt had an idea.

Since the time of the mason-carpenter of Salbris who, in the sixteenth century—when science was still in its infancy, many years before Amontons discovered the first law of friction, Lahire the second, and Coulomb[173] the third—without anyone to advise him, with no one to guide him, with only his son, a child, as his assistant, and with the clumsiest of tools, contrived, in taking down the great clock of the church of La Charité-sur-Loire, to solve in one go five or six problems of statics and dynamics, bound up together like an entanglement of carts blocking the thoroughfare—since the time of that extraordinary and superb workman who found means, without breaking a single brass wire and without dislodging a single gearwheel, in a magnificently simple operation, to lower from the second to the first story of the clock tower, in one piece, this massive cage of the hours constructed of iron and copper, "as big as the watchman's lodge," so it was said, with its movement, its cylinders, barrels, hooks, and counterweights, its spindles for the hour and minute hands, its horizontal balance wheel, its anchor escapement, its tangles of chains large and small, its stone weights, one of which weighed five hundred pounds, its striking mechanism, its carillons, its jack-of-the-clocks—since the man who performed this miracle,[174] whose name is unknown, nothing comparable to what Gilliatt was contemplating had been undertaken. The operation that Gilliatt had in mind was harder still, perhaps: that is to say, even more remarkable. The weight, the delicacy, and the complication of the difficulties were no less in the case of the Durande's engines than they had been in the case of the clock at La Charité-sur-Loire.

The Gothic carpenter had had an assistant in the form of his son; Gilliatt was alone. There were considerable numbers of people—from Meung-sur-Loire, Nevers, and even Orleans—to help the mason of Salbris if necessary and to encourage him with the sympathetic hubbub of a crowd; Gilliatt had no other noise around him than the wind and no crowd but the waves.

There is nothing equal to the timidity of ignorance unless it be its temerity. When ignorance becomes bold, it has within it a compass—an intuition of what is true and right that is sometimes clearer in a simple mind than in a complicated one.

Ignorance incites a man to endeavor; for ignorance is a dreamlike state, and a dream fed by curiosity is a powerful force. Knowledge sometimes disconcerts a man, and frequently discourages action. If Vasco da Gama had been a man of learning, he would not have rounded Cape Horn. If Columbus had been a cosmographer, he would not have discovered America.

The second man to climb Mont Blanc was a scientist, Saussure; the first was a shepherd, Balmat.[175]

Such cases, it must be said in passing, are the exception, and in no way detract from the role of science, which remains the rule. The ignorant may be discoverers; only a man of science can be an inventor.

The paunch was still at anchor in the creek at the Homme, where the sea had left it in peace. Gilliatt, it will be remembered, had made arrangements to ensure access to it. One day he went to it and carefully measured its breadth of beam in several places, particularly at its broadest point. Then he returned to the Durande and measured the greatest width of the engine-room floor. This—excluding the paddle wheels—was two feet less than the greatest breadth of the paunch; so the boat was large enough to take the engines.

But how was he to get them there?

III

GILLIATT'S MASTERPIECE COMES
TO THE RESCUE OF LETHIERRY'S MASTERPIECE

Some time after this, if any fisherman had been mad enough to sail around these parts at this time of year, he would have been rewarded for his boldness by the sight of something strange between the two Douvres.

He would have seen four stout beams, at equal distances apart, extending from one Douvre to the other and tightly jammed between the two rocks so as to give them a secure hold. On the Little Douvre the ends of the beams were supported on and buttressed by the irregularities in the rock; on the Great Douvre the ends had had to be driven violently into the rock face by blows of a hammer wielded by the powerful hand of a workman standing on the very beam he was driving in. The length of the beams was slightly greater than the distance between the two rocks: hence the firmness with which they were fixed, and hence, too, their slope from one side to the other, forming an acute angle with the Great Douvre and an obtuse angle with the Little Douvre. The slope was only a slight one, but it varied from one beam to another, which was a defect. But for this, they would have seemed admirably designed to support the roadway of a bridge. To these beams were attached four hoists, each with its pendant and tackle-fall, but with the unusual and daring feature of having the block with two sheaves at one end of the beam and the single pulley at the other. The distance between the two was undoubtedly dangerous, but was probably necessitated by the task for which they were designed. The blocks were strong and the pulleys stout. To these hoists were attached cables, which from a distance appeared mere threads; and below this aerial structure of pulleys and beams the massive bulk of the Durande seemed to be suspended from these threads.

She was not yet suspended, however. Directly under the beams eight apertures had been cut in the deck, four on the starboard and four on the port side of the engines, and under these, in the lower part of the hull, were four others. Cables descending vertically from the four pulley blocks entered the openings in the deck, emerged from the hull on the port side, passed under the keel and under the engines, entered the openings on the starboard side, and continued up through the deck to the pulleys on the beams. Here a tackle held them together, bound to a single cable that could be handled by one man. The final elements in the structure were a hook and a deadeye, through which the single cable could be paid out or, if necessary, checked. This combination compelled the four hoists to work together, and by serving as a brake on the force of gravity and as a controlling tiller under the hand of the pilot in charge of the operation, kept the whole mechanism in balance. This very ingenious arrangement had some of the simplifying qualities of the Weston pulley of the present day and of Vitruvius's polyspaston. Gilliatt had discovered it for himself, knowing nothing of either Vitruvius, who no longer existed, or Weston, who did not yet exist. The length of the cables varied according to the different slopes of the beams and helped to correct this inequality. The ropes were dangerous, for the untarred sections spliced in by Gilliatt might give way; chains would have been better, but chains would not have passed easily over the hoists.

The whole thing was full of faults, but it was a remarkable achievement for one man.

This is, of course, a much-abridged account of Gilliatt's work, omitting many details that would make the matter clear to other professionals but obscure to everyone else.

The top of the Durande's funnel fitted between the two central beams.

Unwittingly, Gilliatt had become the unconscious plagiarist of the unknown, re-creating after the lapse of three centuries the mechanism devised by the carpenter of Salbris—a rudimentary and unorthodox mechanism that was hazardous for anyone venturing to operate it.

It may be remarked that even the grossest faults will not prevent a mechanism from operating after some fashion or other. It works clumsily, but it works. The obelisk in St. Peter's Square in Rome was set up in defiance of the rules of statics. Tsar Peter's carriage was so built that it seemed likely to overturn at any moment, but for all that it went along fairly. How many faults there were in the Marly waterworks![176] The whole thing was out of true, but it still supplied Louis XIV with drinking water.

Gilliatt at any rate had confidence in his plans. He had indeed been so sure of success that he had fixed two pairs of iron rings on the sides of the paunch, opposite one another, at the same distance apart as the four rings on the Durande to which the chains of the funnel were attached.

Gilliatt had evidently worked out a very complete and definite plan. With all the odds against him, he was determined to take all possible precautions. He made various arrangements that seemed unnecessary—a sure sign that he had thought carefully about what was required.

As we have already noted, his method of working would have puzzled any observer, even one who understood the business. Thus anyone seeing him, with immense effort and at the risk of breaking his neck, driving eight or ten of the large nails that he had forged into the lower parts of the two Douvres at the mouth of the narrow channel into the reef would have found it hard to understand the reason for the nails and would no doubt have wondered what was the use of all this labor.

If the observer had then seen Gilliatt measuring the section of the forward part of the Durande's side that had remained attached to the wreck, fastening a stout rope to its upper edge, hacking off with his ax the broken timbers that held it in place, dragging it out of the channel, with the falling tide pushing the lower part forward while Gilliatt hauled on the upper part, and finally, with great difficulty, using the cable to tie this heavy mass of planks and beams—wider than the entrance to the channel—to the nails driven into the base of the Little Douvre, he would have been still more puzzled, thinking that if Gilliatt wanted, for the purpose of the operation he was planning, to clear the channel of this encumbrance he had only to let it fall into the sea and leave it to be swept away on the receding tide.

No doubt, however, Gilliatt had his own reasons.

In fixing the nails in the base of the Douvres he had taken advantage of every crack and crevice in the granite, widening them if necessary, and inserting wedges of wood into which he drove his nails. He proceeded in the same way at the other end of the channel, to the east, fitting wedges into all the crevices as if to prepare for the insertion of spikes; but this seemed to be merely a precaution, for he did not drive in any nails. Understandably enough, with his shortage of materials, he did not want to use them unless this was absolutely necessary and only when this necessity was obvious. It was an additional complication on top of all his other difficulties.

His first task completed, he was now faced with another. Unhesitatingly, Gilliatt moved on from the one to the other, resolutely taking this giant's stride.

IV

Sub Re[177]

The man who was doing all this was now in a fearful state.

In this immense and varied labor Gilliatt was using up all his strength, and had little means of restoring it. Suffering from privations on one hand and weariness on the other, he had grown thin. His hair and beard had grown. He had only one shirt left that was not in tatters. He went about barefoot, for the wind had carried off one of his shoes and the sea the other. Splinters of rock from his rudimentary and dangerous anvil had covered his hands and arms with cuts and scratches: grazes rather than open wounds, they were superficial but were rendered painful by the sharp air and salt water.

He was hungry, he was thirsty, he was cold. His can of fresh water was empty. His rye flour had been eaten or used for other purposes. He was left with only a small amount of biscuit, which he broke with his teeth, having no water to soak it in. Gradually, day by day, his strength was declining. This redoubtable rock was consuming his life.

Drinking was a problem; eating was a problem; sleeping was a problem. He ate when he caught a sea slater or a crab. He drank when he saw a seabird alighting on a rock; then he would clamber up to the spot and find a crevice containing a little fresh water. He drank after the bird, and sometimes along with the bird; for the gulls had grown used to him and did not fly away at his approach. However hungry he felt, Gilliatt did not harm them. It will be remembered that he was superstitious about birds. The birds, for their part, were not afraid of this man with shaggy, unkempt hair and a long beard. The change in his appearance had given them confidence: they now regarded him not as a man but as a wild animal.

The birds and Gilliatt were now good friends. Suffering poverty and hardship together, they helped one another. While Gilliatt's rye flour lasted he had given the birds crumbs from his baking; and now they in their turn were showing him where to find water.

He ate the shellfish he collected raw; and shellfish help to quench thirst. He cooked the crabs: having no pot, he roasted them between two stones brought to red heat in his fire, as the wild people of the Faroes do.

Meanwhile, the weather had taken an equinoctial turn. Rain had come; but it was a hostile rain. There were no showers, either light or heavy, but long, thin, icy, penetrating, sharp needles that cut through Gilliatt's clothing to the skin and through the skin to the very bone. The rain brought him little water for drinking, but more than enough to drench him. Niggardly in providing assistance but prodigal in adding to his woes, the rain was unworthy of the sky. For more than a week Gilliatt endured it all day and all night. This rain was a malicious act on the part of the powers above.

At night, in his recess in the rock, he could sleep only because he was utterly exhausted by his work. He was stung by the large gnats that live by the sea and awoke covered with blisters.

He suffered from fever, which kept him going; but while fever can be a help, it is a help that can kill. Instinctively he chewed lichens or sucked leaves of wild cochlearia, the meager growths inhabiting dry crevices in the rock. He thought but little, however, of his own sufferings. He had no time to be distracted from his task by concern for himself. The engines of the Durande were in good shape, and that was enough for him.

In carrying on his work he was constantly in and out of the sea. He went into the water and came out again as a man goes from one room to another in his house.

His clothes were now never dry. He was soaked with rainwater, which continued to pour down ceaselessly, and with seawater, which never dries out. Gilliatt lived constantly drenched.

This is a condition you can get used to. Those groups of poor Irish people—old men, mothers, young girls who are almost naked, children—who spend the winter in the open air, in rain and snow, huddling together at street corners in London, live and die soaked to the skin.

It was a bizarre form of torture that Gilliatt endured: drenched to the skin and yet always thirsty. Every now and then he sucked the sleeve of his pea jacket. The fires that he lit did little to warm him. A fire in the open air is of limited help: you are scorched on one side and frozen on the other. Even when he was sweating, Gilliatt shivered.

On all sides he was faced by forces resisting all his efforts in a fearful kind of silence. He felt himself to be the enemy they were attacking.

Material things declare a somber *Non possumus*. Their very inertia is a melancholy warning.

Gilliatt was surrounded by an immense cloud of hostility. He suffered from burns and shivered with cold. The fire bit into his flesh; the water froze him; thirst threw him into a fever; the wind tore at his clothes; hunger gnawed at his stomach. He was oppressed by an exhausting combination of forces ranged against him. A vast silent complex of obstacles, with all the irresponsibility of fate but with a kind of terrible unanimity, was converging on Gilliatt from all sides. He felt it bearing inexorably down on him. There was no way of escaping it. It was almost like a personal enemy. Gilliatt was conscious of a mysterious force rejecting him, a hatred seeking to diminish him. He could escape from it by flight, but since he had resolved to remain he must face up to this impenetrable hostility. Since these forces were unable to expel him, they were seeking to defeat him. Who were they? The Unknown. He was in the grip of the Unknown, which pressed down on him, hemmed him in, took his breath away. He was being crushed by the invisible. Each day the mysterious screw was given another turn.

Gilliatt's situation in these disquieting circumstances was like an unfair duel with a treacherous opponent.

He was surrounded by a coalition of obscure forces. He sensed a determination to get rid of him, as a glacier expels an erratic boulder. Almost without seeming to touch him, this hidden coalition was reducing his clothes to tatters, scarifying his flesh, holding him at bay, and, as it were, putting him *hors de combat* before the fight. In spite of it all he kept on working without remission, but as the work was being done the worker was being undone. It seemed that these wild forces of nature, fearing the man's spirit, were seeking to exhaust his body. Gilliatt held firm, and waited. The abyss had begun by wearing him down. What would it do next? The double Douvre—that granite dragon lying in wait in midocean—had admitted Gilliatt to its lair. It had allowed him in and let him get on with his work. This acceptance was the hospitality of a gaping maw.

The empty waste, the boundless expanse, the space in which there are so many forms of rejection for man, the mute inclemency of natural phenomena pursuing their regular courses, the great general law of things, implacable and passive, the ebb and flow of the tides, the reef, this black constellation of stars in whirling movement, the focal point of an irradiation of currents, the mysterious conspiracy of things against the temerity of a living being, the winter, the clouds, the besieging sea—all this enveloped Gilliatt, surrounded him, seemed to be closing in on him, separating him from living beings in the manner of a dungeon building up around a man. Everything was against him, nothing was for him; he was isolated, abandoned, enfeebled, broken down, forgotten. His stores gone, his tools broken and defective, he suffered thirst and hunger by day and cold at night; covered with rags, his clothes threadbare—rags over festering sores; holes in his clothing and in his flesh, his hands torn, his feet bloody, his limbs emaciated, his face pallid; but there was a flame in his eyes. A proud flame; a man's will made visible. A man's eye reveals his quality. It shows how much of a man there is within us. We declare ourselves by the light that gleams under our eyebrows. Petty spirits merely wink; great spirits emit a flash of lightning. If there is no brilliance under the eyelid, there is no thought in the brain, no love in the heart. A man who loves exerts his will, and a man who exerts his will radiates light and brilliance. Resolution puts fire in the glance: a noble fire that results from the combustion of timid thoughts.

Sublime characters are stubborn. A man who is merely brave has only one method of action, a man who is merely valiant has only one temperament, a man who is merely courageous has only one virtue; greatness is reserved for the man who is stubborn in pursuing the right course. Almost the whole secret of men of great heart is contained in one word: *Perseverando.*

Perseverance is to courage what the wheel is to the lever; it is a perpetual renewal of the fulcrum. Whether the objective be on earth or in heaven, the only thing that matters is to make for that objective; the former case is for Columbus, the latter for Jesus. The cross is mad: hence its glory. To achieve suffering and triumph, it is necessary to leave no room for argument with one's conscience and to allow no relaxation of one's will. In the sphere of morality a fall does not exclude the possibility of soaring. A fall is the starting point of a rise. The second-rate allow themselves to be put off by apparent obstacles; the strong do not. For them the prospect of perishing is merely a possibility; the prospect of conquering is a certitude. You can offer Stephen all sorts of good reasons for not allowing himself to be stoned. Disdain for reasonable objections engenders that sublime victory in defeat that is called martyrdom.

All Gilliatt's efforts seemed to be concentrated on the impossible. Success was meager or slow in coming, and much effort was required to obtain very little result. This was what showed his greatness of spirit; this was what was so poignant about his situation.

That so much preparation, so much work, so much fumbling effort, so many nights of uncomfortable sleep, so many days of labor had been necessary to rig up four beams over the wreck of a ship, to cut up and set aside all that was worth saving in the ship, and to suspend this wreck within a wreck from four hoists with their cables: this was the terrible thing about his solitary labor. Fatality in the cause; necessity in the effect. Gilliatt had not only accepted this: he had wanted it. Fearful of a competitor, since a competitor might have been a rival, he had not sought any assistant. The whole crushing enterprise, the risk, the danger, the toil that was daily increasing, the possibility that the salvager might be engulfed in his salvage, the hunger, the fever, the nakedness, the distress—in his egotism he had chosen all these things for himself.

It was as if he were in a terrifying bell-glass from which the air was being withdrawn. His vitality was gradually leaving him, though he was barely aware of this.

The exhaustion of a man's strength does not exhaust his will. To believe in something is only the second power; to will something is the first. The proverbial mountains that can be moved by faith are nothing compared with what can be achieved by will. The ground that Gilliatt was losing in vigor he was regaining in tenacity. The diminution of the physical man under the attack of these wild natural forces strengthened his moral force.

Gilliatt was not aware of his tiredness, or rather he refused to recognize it. The refusal of the soul to yield to the weakness of the body is a source of immense power.

He saw the progress he was making in his work, and saw nothing else. He was wretched, but he did not know it. He was hallucinated by his objective, which he was within reach of achieving. He put up with all his sufferings, thinking only of one thing: forward! His work was going to his head. The human will is intoxicating. A man's soul can make him drunk. Drunkenness of this kind is known as heroism.

Gilliatt was a kind of Job of the ocean. But he was a Job who struggled, a Job who fought and faced up to his trials, a Job who conquered, and—if such terms are not too grandiose for a poor seaman who fished for crabs and crayfish—a Job who was also a Prometheus.

V

SUB UMBRA[178]

Sometimes Gilliatt opened his eyes at night and looked at the darkness. He felt a strange sensation.

The eye opened on blackness. A dismal situation; anxiety.

The pressure of darkness can be felt. An unspeakable ceiling of shadows; a depth of obscurity that no diver can fathom; light mingled with the obscurity, a strange somber vanquished light; brightness reduced to powder; seeds or ashes? millions of torches that give no light; a vast ignition that keeps its secret hidden; a diffusion of light into dust, like a shower of sparks halted in midflight; the turbulence of the whirlpool and the immobility of the tomb; the problem that opens up a precipitous gulf; an enigma that both shows and conceals its face; the infinite masked in blackness: such is the night. All this weighs heavily on man.

This amalgam of all mysteries in one, the cosmic mystery as well as the mystery of fate, overwhelms the human mind.

The pressure of darkness acts in inverse proportion on different kinds of souls. Man confronting night recognizes his incompleteness. He sees the darkness and feels his frailty. The black sky is a blind man. Man, face-to-face with night, bows down, kneels, prostrates himself, grovels, crawls toward a hole, or seeks for wings. Almost always he tries to flee from this formless presence of the Unknown. He wonders what it is; he trembles, he bows his head, he acknowledges his ignorance. Sometimes, too, he wishes to go there.

Go where?

There.

There? What is that? What is there out there?

This curiosity is evidently a curiosity about forbidden things, for in this direction all the bridges around man are broken. The arch leading to infinity is missing. But what is forbidden has a drawing power; it is a gulf. Where man's feet cannot take him his eyes can reach, and when the eyes can go no farther, the mind can reach beyond. There is no man who will not make the effort, however weak and inadequate he may be. Depending on his nature, man is always either drawn or repelled by the night. Some minds are repressed by it; others are enlarged. It is a somber spectacle. It contains an element of the undefinable.

When the night is serene it is a depth of shadow; when it is stormy it is a depth of smoke. This limitless expanse withholds itself from man, and at the same time offers itself to him; closed to experimentation, but open to conjecture. Innumerable points of light make the bottomless darkness blacker still. Gemstones, scintillations, stars. Presences identified in the Unknown; fearful challenges to those who would approach these lights. They are landmarks of creation in the Absolute; marks of distance in an expanse where there are no distances; a numbering system, impossible but nevertheless real, for measuring the depths of space. First one shining microscopic point, then another, then another, then another; an imperceptible presence, but vast. The light we see is a spark; the spark is a star; the star is a sun; the sun is a universe; the universe is nothing. Any number is zero when compared with infinity.

These universes, which are nothing, nevertheless exist. In observing them we feel the difference between being nothing and not being at all.

The inaccessible added to the inexplicable: that is the sky.

This contemplation gives rise to a sublime phenomenon: the enlargement of the soul by wonder.

Sacred awe is peculiar to man; animals have no such fears. The human mind finds in this august terror its eclipse and its proof.

Darkness is one and indivisible: hence the horror we feel. At the same time it is complex: hence the awe we feel. Its unity is a mass weighing on our spirit, which destroys any urge to resist it. Its complexity leads us to look all around ourselves, as if we feared some unexpected arrival. We submit, but remain on our guard. We are in the presence of a single Whole—hence our submission—and of diversity: hence our wariness. The unity of darkness contains something that is multiple: a mysterious multiplicity that can be seen in matter and sensed in thought. This creates silence: one reason the more for being on the watch.

Night—as the author of these lines has written elsewhere—is the proper and normal state of the particular creation of which we are part. Day, brief in duration and in space, is only a period of proximity to a star.

This universal prodigy of night is not accomplished without some friction, and the frictions of such a mechanism are contusions on our life. The frictions of the mechanism are what we call Evil. In this darkness we sense evil, a latent denial of the divine order, an implicit blasphemy by things hostile to the ideal. The vast cosmic whole is complicated by a mysterious thousand-headed teratology. Evil is present in everything as a protest against things as they are. It is a hurricane that harries a ship at sea; it is chaos, which hinders the emergence of a world. Good has unity; Evil has ubiquity. Evil upsets the pattern of life, which is a logical system. It causes a fly to be devoured by a bird and a planet by a comet. Evil is an erasure on the page of creation.

The darkness of night is vertiginous. Those who plunge into it become submerged in it and struggle to survive. No fatigue is comparable to this study of the shadows. It is the study of an obliteration.

There is no firm ground on which the spirit can find a footing. Points of departure with no arrival point. The intersection of contradictory solutions, all the ramifications of doubt presenting themselves at the same time, the embranchment of phenomena flaking off endlessly under some undefined pressure, all laws running into one another; an unfathomable promiscuity in which minerals grow like plants, in which vegetation lives, in which thought has weight, in which love radiates, in which gravitation has the power of love; the immense battlefront attacking all the questions that develop in boundless obscurity; things barely glimpsed suggesting things unknown; the simultaneity of the cosmos in full view, not for the eye but for the intelligence, in this great indistinguishable space; the invisible as a vision. This is Darkness. Man lies under it.

He knows nothing of the detail, but he bears within him, in a quantity proportionate to his mind, the monstrous weight of the Whole. This obsession led the shepherds of Chaldea to discover astronomy. The pores of creation secrete involuntary revelations; there is a kind of automatic exudation of knowledge that is conveyed to the ignorant. Every solitary, exposed to this mysterious impregnation, becomes a natural philosopher unawares.

Darkness is invisible. It is inhabited; inhabited by the Absolute, which takes up no space, and inhabited also by things that do take up space. Disquietingly, there is movement in it. In it some sacred formation is passing through its phases. In it, premeditated plans, powers, deliberately selected destinations carry out in common some immense scheme. It contains life—a terrible and horrible life. There are vast movements of heavenly bodies, the family of the stars, the family of the planets, the pollen of the zodiac, the *quid divinum* of currents, emanations, polarizations, and attractions; there are embraces and antagonisms, the magnificent flow and ebb of a universal antithesis, the imponderable at liberty amid the centers; there is sap in the globes, light outside the globes, there are wandering atoms, scattered seeds, fertilization curves, meetings for coupling and for combat, unimagined profusions, distances that are like dreams, dizzying movements, worlds plunging into the incalculable, prodigies pursuing one another in the shadows, a mechanism in permanent operation, the breathing of spheres in flight, wheels that can be felt turning; scholars make conjectures, the ignorant believe and tremble; things are there, and then withdraw; they are unassailable, they are out of reach, they cannot be approached. We are convinced to the point of oppression. We are faced with some mysterious dark reality. We can grasp nothing. We are crushed by the impalpable.

Everywhere there is the incomprehensible. Nowhere is there the unintelligible.

And to all this is added the redoubtable question: Is this immanent universe a Being?

We are in the shadows. We look. We listen.

Meanwhile, the somber earth continues on its course. Flowers are aware of this gigantic movement: the catchfly opens at eleven o'clock at night, the daylily at five in the morning. Striking regularities!

At other depths the drop of water becomes a world, infusoria pullulate, a giant fecundity emerges from the animalcule, the imperceptible displays its grandeur, the opposite extreme from immensity is seen: within a single hour a diatom will produce 1,300 million diatoms.

What a presentation of all the enigmas at once! Here we are faced with the irreducible.

We are constrained to have faith. The result is that we believe by compulsion. Faith has a strange need for form: hence man's various religions. Nothing is more distressing than a belief without shape.

Whatever we think, whether we will or no, whatever resistance we may have within us, we cannot merely look at darkness: looking inevitably leads to contemplation.

What are we to make of these phenomena? Exposed to their converging forces, in what direction are we to move? To break down this pressure is impossible. How can we adjust our thoughts to all these mysterious influences? How many revelations—abstruse, simultaneous, faltering, obscuring one another by their very mass: like stammerings of the Word! Darkness is a form of silence; but that silence says everything. There is one conclusion that emerges majestically from all this: God. God is an incompressible idea, which is immanent in man. All the syllogisms, the disputes, the negations, the systems, the religions pass over it without diminishing it. This idea is affirmed by all darkness. But everything else is unclear. A formidable immanence! The inexpressible agreement of all these forces is made manifest by the maintenance of all this darkness in equilibrium. The universe is suspended; but nothing falls. The whole incessant and enormous movement is performed without hitch and without interruption. Man participates in this movement, and the degree of oscillation he suffers is known to him as destiny. Where does destiny begin? Where does nature end? What difference is there between an event and a season, between a sorrow and a fall of rain, between a virtue and a star? Is not an hour the same as a wave? The interlocking gears, in constant motion, continue their impassive revolutions without responding to man. The star-spangled sky is a vision of wheels, pendulums, and counterweights. It is the supreme contemplation, and at the same time the supreme meditation. It is the whole of reality, as well as the whole of abstraction. There is nothing beyond. We feel trapped. We are at the discretion of this darkness. There is no escape. We see ourselves caught up in this mechanism; we are an integral part of a Whole that is unknown to us; we feel the unknown that is within us fraternizing mysteriously with an unknown that is outside of us. This is the sublime annunciation of death. What anguish, and at the same time what delight! To adhere to the infinite, to be led by this adherence to attribute to oneself a necessary immortality— or, who knows?, a possible eternity—to feel, within the prodigious swell of this deluge of universal life, the insubmersible persistency of the Self! to look at the stars and say, I am a soul like you! to look at the darkness and say, I am an abyss like you!

These vastnesses are Night.

All this, magnified by solitude, weighed on Gilliatt.

Did he understand it? No.

Did he feel it? Yes.

Gilliatt was a great spirit, unclear about himself, and a great, unsubdued heart.

VI

GILLIATT GETS THE PAUNCH INTO POSITION

The salvage of the Durande's engines that Gilliatt had planned was, as we have already said, like the escape of a prisoner; and it is well known what endless patience is required for an escape. It is well known also what industry is required. The industry can sometimes be miraculous; the patience can amount to a mortal agony. A prisoner like Thomas, for example, confined on Mont Saint-Michel, contrived to conceal half his prison wall in his straw mattress. Another, at Tulle, in 1820, cut off a quantity of lead from the roof that served as an exercise yard— where he got a knife from we do not know—and melted down the lead—how he made a fire we do not know—and then cast it in a mold—which we do know was made of breadcrumbs—to make a key enabling him to open a lock of which he had seen no more than the keyhole. Gilliatt had extraordinary skills of this kind. He would have scaled Boisrosé's cliff and climbed down again. He was the Trenck of a wreck and the Latude[179] of a piece of machinery.

The sea, his jailer, was watching him.

But however unpleasant and uncomfortable the rain had been, it had brought him one benefit. He had been able to top up his supply of fresh water; but his thirst was insatiable, and he emptied his can almost as fast as he filled it.

One day—the last day in April, or it may have been the first of May—all his preparations were complete. The floor of the engine room was framed between the eight cables from the hoists, four on one side and four on the other. The sixteen openings in the deck and under the hull through which the cables passed had been linked with one another by sawing. The planking had been cut with the saw, the timbers with the ax, the ironwork with the file, the sheathing with the chisel. The part of the keel immediately under the engines was cut away square and was ready to slip out along with the engines, supporting them. All this huge dangling mass depended on a single chain, which itself awaited only a cut with the file. At this stage of completion, so near the end of an operation, it is wise to act quickly.

The tide was at ebb—the right time to go ahead with Gilliatt's plan.

He had managed to dismantle the axle of the paddle wheels, which might have hindered and checked the lowering of the engines, and had lashed this heavy item vertically within the engine room.

It was time to finish the operation. Gilliatt, as we have said, was not tired—was determined not to be tired—but his tools were worn out. The forge was gradually becoming unusable.

The stone that served as an anvil was split. The bellows were no longer working properly. Since they were actuated by seawater, deposits of salt were forming on the joints and interfering with their operation.

Gilliatt went to the creek by the Homme rock and inspected the paunch. Satisfied that everything was in good shape, particularly the four rings to port and starboard, he hoisted the anchor and rowed back to the two Douvres.

The gap between the two rocks was wide enough to admit the paunch, and there was enough depth. Gilliatt had seen on the first day that he would be able to bring the paunch into position there under the Durande.

It was, however, a very awkward maneuver, calling for the precision of a jeweler; and running the boat into the reef was rendered all the more delicate by the necessity, for the purpose of Gilliatt's plan, of going in stern first, with the rudder leading, so that the mast and rigging of the paunch remained clear of the wreck, toward the mouth of the inlet.

These complications made the operation a difficult one for Gilliatt. It was not like entering the creek at the Homme, where only a touch on the tiller was required: here it was necessary for him to push, to haul, to row, and to take soundings, all at the same time. It took fully a quarter of an hour, but at last he succeeded.

In fifteen or twenty minutes the paunch was moored under the Durande; firmly held by its two anchors, it was almost wedged in. The larger of the two was placed so as to hold against the strongest wind to be feared, the west wind. Then, with the help of a lever and the capstan, Gilliatt lowered into the paunch the two crates containing the dismantled paddle wheels, the slings for which were ready. The crates would then serve as ballast.

Having disposed of the two crates, Gilliatt fastened the sling of the controlling tackle gear, which was intended to put a check on the hoists, to the hook on the capstan chain.

For what Gilliatt had in mind, the defects of the paunch became qualities. It had no deck, and the cargo would thus be lower down, resting on the bottom. Its mast stood well forward—perhaps too far forward—so that there would be plenty of room for the cargo; and since the mast was clear of the wreck, it would not hinder the boat's exit. And the tubby shape of the paunch was all to the good: no craft is so stable or holds the sea so well as a tub.

Suddenly Gilliatt noticed that the sea was rising. He looked to see what direction the wind was coming from.

VII

SUDDEN DANGER

There was little wind, but what wind there was came from the west. It is a disagreeable habit that the wind tends to have at the equinox.

The rising tide behaves differently in the Douvres reef according to the wind that is blowing. Depending on the squall that drives it, the sea enters the corridor between the two rocks either from the east or from the west. If it comes in from the east it is gentle and benevolent. If it comes in from the west it is a raging fury. This is because the east wind, blowing off the land, has little force, while the west wind, traversing the Atlantic, carries with it all the force of that immensity. Even a seemingly light wind coming from the west is cause for alarm. It rolls in great billows from that boundless expanse and drives too heavy a sea at the same time into the narrow passage.

Water surging into a narrow passage is always dangerous. Water is like a crowd; a multitude is like a liquid; when the quantity that can get in is less than the quantity that wants in, the crowd is crushed and the water is convulsed. Whenever the west wind—even the lightest breeze—is blowing, the Douvres are exposed twice a day to this assault. The sea rises, the waves press forward, the rocks resist, the channel between them offers only a restricted passage, the water, driven violently forward, rages and roars, and a frenzied swell beats against the walls of the channel. And so when there is the least breath of wind from the west the Douvres offer an unusual sight: outside, on the open sea, there is calm, while within the reef there is a storm. This local, circumscribed tumult cannot be called a tempest: it is merely a rebellion by the waves, though a terrifying one. The north and south winds, on the other hand, blow across the reef and stir up only a little surf within the channel. The entrance from the east, it will be remembered, is beside the Homme rock; the formidable western entrance is at the opposite end, between the two Douvres.

At this western entrance was Gilliatt, with the stranded Durande and the paunch moored beneath it. A catastrophe seemed imminent and inevitable. There was just sufficient wind—not much, but enough—to bring it about. Within a few hours the swelling of the rising tide would pour in full force into the channel between the two Douvres. The first waves were already breaking. This swell, a tidal wave from the whole of the Atlantic, would have the full force of the sea behind it. It was not a storm; the sea was not angry: there was merely a single sovereign wave containing within it a driving force that, starting from America and making for Europe, had two thousand leagues of thrust. This wave, a gigantic bar reaching across the ocean, would encounter the gap in the reef and crash against the two Douvres, those watchtowers at the entrance, buttresses of the channel; then, swollen by the tide, swollen by the obstacle, repulsed by the rock, driven hard by the wind, it would do violence to the reef and would penetrate, with all the torsions resulting from the clash with the obstacle and the frenzies of the obstructed wave, between the two walls; it would find the paunch and the Durande and would destroy them.

What was needed was a shield to protect them against this eventuality. Gilliatt had one. It was necessary to prevent the tide from bursting straight in, to ensure that it did not strike with full force while allowing it to rise, to bar its passage without refusing it entry, to resist it and give way to it, to avoid the compression of the wave in the narrow channel that was the great danger, to replace irruption by insertion, to strip the waves of their rage and brutality, to tame this fury into gentleness. The obstacle that irritated had to be replaced by the obstacle that calmed.

Gilliatt, displaying the agility he possessed that was stronger than strength, performing feats worthy of a chamois in the mountains or a sapajou in the forests, taking dizzy and unsteady strides between the least projections on the reef, jumping into the water and emerging again, swimming in the eddies, clambering up the rock with a rope between his teeth and a hammer in his hand, untied the cable that held the forward part of the Durande's side hanging against the base of the Little Douvre, used ends of rope to make, as it were, hinges tying the panel to the long nails he had driven into the granite, and turned it on the hinges to form a kind of sluice gate, presenting it sideways, as one does a rudder, to the waves, which drove one end against the Great Douvre, while the rope hinges held it fast to the Little Douvre. He then used the nails he had driven into the Great Douvre to fasten that end in the same way as the other, and made this great sheet of timber fast to the two pillars at the entrance to the channel, drawing a chain across it, like a sword belt on a cuirass; and in less than an hour this barrier stood guard against the tide, and the passage into the reef was closed as if by a gate.

This substantial structure, a heavy mass of beams and planking that would have been a raft if laid horizontally and, vertically, was a wall, had been handled by Gilliatt with all the dexterity of a conjuror. It could almost be said that he had performed his trick before the rising tide had had time to notice.

It was one of those cases in which Jean Bart[180] would have used the words he used to address to the sea each time he escaped shipwreck: "Cheated you, Englishman!" It is well known that when Jean Bart wanted to insult the ocean he called it the "Englishman."

Having barred the entrance to the channel, Gilliatt's thoughts turned to his boat. He slackened the anchor cables sufficiently to allow it to rise with the tide—what old sailors used to call anchoring with bearings. In all of this Gilliatt had not been taken unawares: he had foreseen what might be required. A seaman would have known this from the two pulleys of the top ropes cut into the shape of snatch blocks and fixed to the stern of the boat, on which ran two ropes tied to the rings of the anchors.

The tide had now risen to half-flood—a time when, even in calm weather, the force of the waves may be considerable. What Gilliatt had planned for now happened. The waves hurled themselves against the barrier, encountered it, swelled up, and then passed underneath it. Outside the barrier was a heavy swell; within it was a gentle infiltration. Gilliatt had devised what might be called the Caudine Forks of the sea. The tide had been vanquished.

VIII

An Achievement, but Not the End of the Story

The dread moment had arrived. The problem now was to get the engines into the paunch. Gilliatt thought briefly, holding his left elbow in his right hand and his forehead in his left. Then he climbed onto the wreck, part of which—the engines—was to be removed and part—the hull—to be left. He cut the four slings that fastened the four chains of the funnel to the port and starboard sides. The slings were only of rope, so that he had no difficulty in severing them with his knife; and they now hung free beside the funnel.

From the wreck he climbed to the tackle he had constructed, stamped his foot on the beams, inspected the pulley blocks, looked at the pulleys, touched the cables, examined the splices, made sure that the untarred rope was not soaked through, checked that nothing was missing and nothing was giving way; then he jumped from the binding strakes onto the deck and took up his position near the capstan, on the part of the Durande that was to remain wedged between the Douvres. This was his workstation.

Grave, with no more emotion than was required for his task, he had one last glance at his tackle; then he took a file and set about sawing through the chain that held the whole thing suspended. The grating of the file could be heard above the roaring of the sea. The chain of the capstan, which was attached to the main tackle, was within reach of Gilliatt's hand.

Suddenly there was a crack. The link of the chain, which had been more than half cut through by the file, had given way, and the whole apparatus began to swing about. Gilliatt had only just time to catch hold of the main tackle.

The broken chain whipped against the rock, the eight cables took the strain, and the whole mass that had been sawn and cut free tore itself away from the wreck, the belly of the Durande opened, and the iron flooring of the engine house, weighing heavily on the cables, appeared under the keel.

If Gilliatt had not so promptly grasped the main tackle, the whole load must have fallen. But his powerful hand was there, and it was lowered steadily.

When Jean Bart's brother Pieter Bart, that powerful and sagacious drunkard, that poor fisherman of Dunkirk who spoke familiarly to the Grand Admiral of France, saved the galley *Langeron,* in distress in Ambleteuse Bay, when in order to draw that heavy floating mass through the breakers in the raging bay he reefed the mainsail with marine reeds, with the idea that the reeds would break off of themselves and unfurl the sail to the wind, he trusted in the breaking of the reeds as

Gilliatt trusted in the breaking of the chain, showing the same extra-ordinary boldness and achieving the same surprising success.

The main tackle, controlled by Gilliatt, held firm and worked admirably. Its function, it will be remembered, was to take the shock of the separate forces, now combined into one and reduced to a single operation. It was rather like the bridle of a bowline, except that instead of trimming a sail it was keeping a mechanism in balance.

Gilliatt, standing with his hand on the capstan, was, as it were, keeping his hand on the pulse of the whole operation.

The plan he had devised had proved a brilliant success, and a remarkable coincidence of forces had been achieved. As the Durande's engines, cut free in a single block, descended toward the paunch, the paunch rose toward the engines. The wreck and the boat that had come to salvage it, aiding each other as they moved in opposite directions and, meeting each other halfway, spared themselves half the labor.

The rising tide, swelling noiselessly between the two Douvres, raised the paunch, bringing it closer to the Durande. The waves were not only vanquished: they were tamed. The ocean had become part of the mechanism.

The swell lifted the boat smoothly and gently, taking as much care as if it had been made of porcelain.

Gilliatt combined and kept in proportion the two parts of the operation, the work of the water and the working of his apparatus, and, standing motionless at the capstan, like a redoubtable statue obeyed by all the various movements at the same time, regulated the slowness of the descent to match the slowness of the ascent.

There was no sudden shock from the waves, no jerkiness in the working of the hoists. It was a strange collaboration of all the natural forces, now submitting to Gilliatt's control. On one side was gravity, bringing the engines down; on the other the tide, bringing the boat up. The attraction of the heavenly bodies, which brings about the flow of the tide, and the attraction of the earth, which is weight, seemed to combine in the service of Gilliatt. There was no hesitation or pause in their subordination, and, under the pressure of a human soul, these passive powers were becoming active auxiliaries. From minute to minute the work went steadily ahead, and the gap between the paunch and the wreck diminished insensibly. The conjunction was being achieved in silence, as if in terror of the man who was standing there. The elements were being given orders and were carrying them out.

Almost at the precise moment when the tide stopped rising, the cables stopped unwinding. Suddenly, but without any commotion, the pulley blocks ceased to work. The engines settled into the boat, as though put there by a powerful hand. They stood there, upright, erect, motionless, solidly fixed. The iron flooring lay level with its four corners resting squarely on the bottom of the boat.

The job was done. Gilliatt gazed at the scene, as if stunned. The poor fellow was not overcome by joy. He was bowed down by an immense happiness. He felt his limbs giving way; and faced with his triumph, this man, hitherto quite untroubled, began to tremble. He looked at the paunch below the wreck and at the engines in the paunch. It seemed as if he could not believe what he had done, as if he had not been expecting to succeed. He had performed a miracle, and he looked on the result with astonishment.

This feeling did not last long. Then, as if waking from sleep, he seized the saw, cut the eight cables, and, now, thanks to the rising tide, standing only some ten feet above the paunch, jumped into it. Taking a coil of rope, he made four slings, passed them through the rings he had fixed on the paunch's sides, and fastened on each side the four chains of the funnel that an hour before had been attached to the sides of the Durande. The funnel once secured, he freed the upper part of the engine house. A square section of planking from the Durande's deck was still attached to it. He stripped it off, relieving the paunch of this encumbrance of planking and joists, and threw it onto the reef, usefully lightening the boat.

The paunch remained steady under the additional weight of the engines, as he had expected she would. Although she sat lower in the water, she still had adequate freeboard. The engines of the Durande were heavy, but not so heavy as the load of stones and the cannon he had brought back from Herm in the paunch.

And so it was all over. Nothing now remained but to return to Guernsey.

IX

SUCCESS ACHIEVED BUT LOST IMMEDIATELY

It was not yet all over.

The immediate need was clearly to reopen the channel closed by the section from the side of the Durande and move the paunch away from the reef. At sea every minute is urgent. There was little wind and barely a ripple on the surface of the water; and it was a very fine evening, holding the promise of a fine night. It was slack tide, but the ebb was beginning to be felt: it was a good time to leave the reef. There would be a falling tide for leaving the Douvres and a rising tide for returning to Guernsey, making it possible to reach St. Sampson by daybreak.

But now an unexpected obstacle presented itself. There had been an oversight in Gilliatt's plans. The engines were free, but the funnel was still held prisoner. The tide, by bringing the paunch nearer to the wreck suspended above it, had reduced the dangers of the descent and the time required for the salvage operation; but this shortening of the distance between the two had left the top of the funnel within the square opening in the hull of the Durande. The funnel was caught, as if between four walls.

The assistance given by the waves had involved this little piece of deceit. It seemed that the sea, compelled to obey, had had an *arrière-pensée*.

True, what the flood tide had done the ebb was going to undo. The funnel was rather more than three fathoms in height, and eight feet of this was caught inside the Durande. The tide would have a fall of twelve feet; and the funnel, falling down with the paunch on the ebb tide, would clear the wreck by four feet and would be free to go.

But how long would it be before this happened? It would take six hours, and in six hours it would be almost midnight. How could Gilliatt possibly try to get away at that time of night? How could he trace the passage between the rocks, so inextricable even in daylight, and how could he risk sailing through the surrounding shoals in total darkness?

He would have to wait until the following morning. The loss of these six hours meant the loss of at least twelve.

He could not even hope to speed things up by reopening the channel into the reef. The barrier he had erected would be required at the next high tide.

There was nothing for Gilliatt to do but rest from his labors: the one thing he had not done since he had been on the reef. This enforced rest annoyed him, and made him almost indignant, as if it had been his own fault. He thought to himself: "What would Déruchette think of me if she saw me sitting idly here?"

Perhaps, however, this opportunity to recover his strength was not altogether a bad thing. The paunch was now at his disposal, and he decided to spend the night in her. He climbed up the Great Douvre and brought down his sheepskin, supped on a few limpets and sea chestnuts and, feeling very thirsty, drank the last few mouthfuls of fresh water from his almost empty can. Then he wrapped himself up in the sheepskin, which had a comforting feel, and lay down like a watchdog beside the engines, drew his cap over his eyes, and fell asleep.

He slept soundly. After such labor men sleep well.

X

WARNINGS FROM THE SEA

Suddenly, in the middle of the night, Gilliatt awoke with a start, as if a spring had been released. He opened his eyes. The Douvres, above his head, were illuminated as if by the light from a huge mass of glowing white embers. It was like the reflection of a great fire, covering the whole black face of the rock.

Where was this fire coming from?

It came from the water.

The sea was an extraordinary sight. It looked as if the water was on fire. As far as the eye could reach, within the reef and outside it, the whole sea was aflame. But the flames were not red; they were quite unlike the great living flames of craters and furnaces. There was no sparkle, no heat, no trace of purple, no noise. Trails of bluish light over the sea looked like the folds of a winding-sheet. A wide swathe of pale light trembled on the water. It was not a fire: it was the specter of a fire.

It was like the hideous illumination of the interior of a tomb by a flame seen in a dream. It was as if the shadows were lit up.

The night—the great dim, spreading night—seemed to be the fuel feeding this icy fire. It was a strange light created from darkness. Shadow was one element in the composition of this phantom light.

The seamen of the Channel are familiar with these indescribable phosphorescences, so full of warnings for the mariner. Nowhere are they more astonishing than in the Grand V, near Isigny.

In this light things lose their reality. Penetrated by this spectral illumination, they seem to become transparent. Rocks become mere outlines. Anchor cables look like iron bars brought to white heat. Fishermen's nets look like knitted patterns of fire under the water. One half of an oar is made of ebony; the other half, under the water, of silver. Drops of water falling off the oars into the water spangle the sea with stars. Every boat has a comet trailing behind it. The sailors, drenched and luminous, appear like men on fire. Dip your hand into the water, and it comes out gloved in flame—a dead flame, which you do not feel. Your arm becomes a firebrand. You see the forms of creatures under the water bathed in fire. The foam sparkles. The fish are tongues of fire and flashes of lightning darting about in the pallid depths.

It was this light that had passed through Gilliatt's eyelids and wakened him.

His awakening came just in time. The tide had ebbed and had begun to rise again. The Durande's funnel, which had fallen clear of the wreck while Gilliatt had been sleeping, was about to be caught up again in the hole in the vessel's hull, toward which it was slowly returning. It was now only a foot short of the wreck.

The tide would take about half an hour to rise a foot. Gilliatt had thus only half an hour to complete the deliverance of the Durande— a deliverance that was in danger of being frustrated. He stood up sharply. But urgent as the situation was, he could not help standing for a few moments contemplating the phosphorescence and thinking.

Gilliatt was thoroughly familiar with the sea. Whatever her mood, and however many times she had maltreated him, he had long been a companion of hers. That mysterious being whom we know as the Ocean could have nothing in her mind that Gilliatt could not discern. By dint of observation, reflection, and solitude he had become a diviner of the weather—he was what is known in English as weather-wise.

Gilliatt made straight for the top ropes and paid out some cable; then, when the paunch was no longer held by the anchors, he took up the boat hook and, bracing himself against the rocks, pushed the boat some fathoms away from the Durande, near the barrier he had erected. In less than ten minutes the paunch was clear of the stranded carcass of the Durande. There was no longer any danger that the funnel would be caught in a trap. The tide might now rise as fast as it liked.

Yet Gilliatt did not look like a man who was about to leave. He looked again at the phosphorescence, and weighed the anchors; it was not a preparation for departure, but merely in order to anchor the paunch again, still more firmly, near the mouth of the channel. So far he had used only the paunch's two anchors, but had not yet made use of the Durande's small anchor, which it will be remembered he had found among the rocks. He had laid it in a corner of the paunch, ready for any emergency, together with a supply of hawsers and pulleys and its cable, which had large knots in it to prevent it from running too freely. Gilliatt lowered this third anchor, taking care to fasten a warp to the cable with one end tied to the ring of the anchor and the other to the windlass of the paunch. In this way he contrived a kind of triple anchorage, much stronger than with only the two bower anchors. This reflected his lively concern with the situation and a redoubling of pre-cautions. A seaman would have recognized in this operation some-thing akin to an anchorage of refuge, when there is danger from a current that might carry the vessel under the wind.

The phosphorescence, which Gilliatt had been watching carefully, was perhaps a threat, but it had also helped him. Without it he would still have been a prisoner of sleep and at the mercy of the night. It had wakened him, and it gave him light.

A sinister light hung over the reef; but this illumination, threaten-ing as it appeared to Gilliatt, had at any rate the advantage that it had revealed the danger to him and enabled him to act. Whenever he should wish to set sail the paunch, laden with the engines, was free to go.

But now Gilliatt seemed to be thinking less and less of departure. With the paunch safely anchored, he fetched the strongest chain in his store and, fastening it to the nails he had driven into the two Douvres,

stretched it across the inner side of the rampart of beams and planking, already protected on the outside by the other chain, so as to fortify
it still further. Far from opening up the exit from the channel, he was
closing it still more firmly.

The phosphorescence was still giving him light, but it was dying
away. The first signs of dawn were now appearing.

Suddenly Gilliatt pricked up his ears.

XI

THE VALUE OF A GOOD EAR

He thought he heard, at an immense distance, a faint, indistinct sound.

At certain times there is a rumbling in the depths of the ocean.

He listened again. The distant sound was repeated. Gilliatt shook
his head, like a man who knew what it was.

A few minutes later he was at the other end of the channel in the
reef, at the eastern entrance, which was still open, and, with great
blows of his hammer, was driving large nails into the granite on either
side of the channel mouth, near the Homme rock, just as he had done
at the Douvres end.

The crevices in these rocks had already been prepared and fitted
with wedges of wood, almost all heart of oak. This part of the reef was
much weathered, with many fissures, and Gilliatt was able to drive in
even more nails than in the two Douvres.

Suddenly the phosphorescence disappeared, as if it had been blown
out, giving place to the dawn, which every moment became brighter.

After driving in the nails Gilliatt dragged along beams, then ropes,
and finally chains, and, without pausing for a moment, set about constructing at the mouth of the channel at the Homme, using beams laid
horizontally and secured with cables, one of those openwork barriers
known as breakwaters that are now a recognized technique.

Anyone who has seen, for example in Rocquaine Bay on Guernsey
or at Bourg-d'Ault in France, the effect produced by a few stakes
planted among the rocks will understand the power of such simple
arrangements. A breakwater is a combination of what is known in
France as a groyne and in England as a dike.[181] Breakwaters are the

chevaux-de-frise of the fortifications set up against tempests. The only way to fight against the sea is to take advantage of the divisibility of its power.

Meanwhile the sun had risen in perfect purity. The sky was clear, the sea was calm. Gilliatt worked quickly. He, too, was calm, but his haste betrayed some anxiety. He strode from rock to rock, from the barrier to his storeroom and from the storeroom to the barrier, dragging with him now a rider and now a binding strake. The value of his reserve store of timber was now demonstrated. Clearly he had foreseen the eventuality with which he was now dealing.

He used a stout iron bar as a lever for moving the beams.

The work was done so quickly that it was more like a natural growth than a work of construction. Only those who have seen military engineers constructing a bridge can have any idea of Gilliatt's speed.

The east end of the channel was narrower than the west end, only five or six feet across, and this made Gilliatt's task easier. Since the space to be fortified and closed was less, the structure would be more solid and could be simpler. Thus horizontal beams would be sufficient: no vertical members were necessary.

After the first crosspieces of the breakwater were in position, Gilliatt climbed onto it and listened. The distant rumbling was now becoming fuller of meaning.

Gilliatt continued with his work, buttressing it with the Durande's two catheads, bound to the tangle of beams with ropes passing through their three pulley wheels, and securing the whole thing with chains.

The whole structure was little more than a colossal hurdle, with stout beams for the horizontal bars and chains in place of osiers. It seemed interwoven as much as built. Gilliatt fastened numbers of additional ties and added more nails where necessary. Having salvaged plenty of iron bars from the wreck, he had been able to build up a considerable stock of nails.

While working he crunched biscuit from his store. He was thirsty, but had no fresh water left to drink, having drained the can at his supper the night before.

He added another four or five pieces of timber; then climbed up onto the barrier again and listened. The noise on the horizon had ceased. All was quiet.

The sea was calm and beautiful, meriting all the complimentary phrases that people use when they are pleased with her: "a mirror," "a lake," "smooth as oil," "child's play," "quiet as a lamb." The deep blue of the sky formed a counterpart to the deep green of the ocean—a sapphire and an emerald that could admire each other, each finding no fault in the other. Not a cloud above, not a trace of foam below. And amid this splendor the April sun was rising in all its magnificence. A finer day could not be imagined.

On the farthest horizon a long file of birds of passage traced a black line against the sky. They were traveling fast, making for land. Their flight had something of the air of an escape.

Gilliatt continued increasing the height of the breakwater. He raised it as high as he could, as high as the curve of the rocks would allow.

Toward noon the sun seemed to him to be hotter than it should be. Midday is the critical hour of the day. Standing on the sturdy framework he had erected, Gilliatt looked out again at the vast expanse of sea.

The sea was not merely calm: it was stagnant. There was not a sail to be seen. The sky, all over, was limpid; but the blue had now turned to white—a white that had a strange look.

On the horizon to the west there was a small unwholesome-looking stain. It remained motionless in the same place, but was growing in size. Near the rocks fringing the reef the waves quivered very gently.

Gilliatt had done well to erect his breakwater. A storm was approaching. The abyss was making up its mind to do battle.

BOOK III

THE STRUGGLE

I

EXTREMES MEET AND CONTRARY
FORESHADOWS CONTRARY

Nothing is more threatening than a late equinox.

There is an alarming phenomenon on the sea that could be called the arrival of the winds from the ocean. At any time of year, but particularly at the time of the syzygies,[182] when it is least to be expected, a strange tranquillity comes over the sea. The tremendous perpetual movement subsides; there is an air of somnolence; the sea becomes languid; it seems about to take a respite; it looks tired. All the flags worn by shipping, from the fishing boat's streamer to the warship's ensign, hang limply on the masts. The admiral's pennant and royal and imperial banners all sleep.

Suddenly the flags begin to flutter gently. This is the time, if there are clouds, to watch for the formation of banks of cirrus—if the sun is setting, to observe the reddening evening sky—if it is night and there is a moon, to study its haloes.

This is the time, too, when the captain or squadron commander, if he is fortunate enough to possess one of those storm glasses whose inventor is unknown, looks at his glass under the microscope and takes precautions against the south wind if the solution has the appearance of melted sugar and against the north wind if it breaks down into crystallizations resembling fern brakes or fir woods. And this is the time when, after consulting some mysterious gnomon engraved by the Romans, or by demons, on one of those enigmatic standing stones known in Brittany as menhirs and in Ireland as cruachs, the poor Irish or Breton fisherman hauls his boat ashore.

Meanwhile, the serenity of the sky and of the ocean persists. Day breaks radiantly and the dawn smiles. This was what filled the ancient poets and seers with religious horror, appalled as they were that the sun should be thought to be false. *Solem quis dicere falsum audeat?*[183]

The somber vision of a latent possibility is denied to man by the fatal opacity of material things. The most redoubtable and most perfidious of aspects is the mask of the abyss. We say "an eel under a rock":[184] we should say "storm under calm."

Hours—sometimes days—may pass in this way. Pilots train their telescopes this way and that. The faces of old sailors take on an air of severity, reflecting their hidden anger as they wait in suspense.

Suddenly a great confused murmuring is heard. There is a kind of mysterious dialogue in the air, but nothing is to be seen. The vast expanse remains impassive.

Meanwhile the noise increases, becomes louder, rises in tone. The dialogue becomes more distinct.

There is someone beyond the horizon.

Someone terrible: the wind.

The wind: that is to say, the rabble of titans that we call sea breezes. The immense canaille of the shadows.

They were known in India as the marouts, in Judaea as the cherubim, in Greece as the aquilons. They are the invincible birds of prey of the infinite. These northerly winds are coming up fast.

II

THE WINDS FROM THE OCEAN

Where do they come from? From the incommensurable. Their wingspan takes up the whole expanse of the gulf of ocean. Their giant wings need the illimitable distances of the solitary wastes. The Atlantic, the Pacific, those vast blue open spaces: that is what suits them

best. They darken the skies. They fly there in great troupes. Commander Page once saw seven waterspouts at the same time on the open sea.
They are there in all their wildness. They premeditate disasters. Their
business is to foment the ephemeral and eternally continuing swelling
of the waves. What they can do is unknown; what they want is hidden
from us. They are the sphinxes of the abyss, and Vasco da Gama is
their Oedipus. They appear in the obscurity of the ever-moving expanse of ocean, the faces of the clouds. Those who catch sight of their
pale lineaments in that wide dispersion that is the horizon of the sea
feel themselves in presence of an irreducible force. It seems as if
human intelligence upsets them, and they bristle with hostility to it.
Intelligence is invincible, but this element is impenetrable. What can
be done against this impalpable ubiquity? Wind turns into a club, and
then becomes wind again. The winds fight an enemy by crushing him
and defend themselves by vanishing. Those who encounter them, disconcerted by their varied plan of attack and swiftly repeated blows, are
reduced to expedients. They withdraw as much as they attack. They
are impalpable, but tenacious. How can they be overcome? The prow
of the *Argo,* carved from an oak tree from Dodona, was both prow and
pilot: it spoke to them. But they maltreated it, goddess though it was.
Columbus, seeing them approaching the *Pinta,* stood up on deck and
addressed the first verses of Saint John's Gospel to them. Surcouf[185]
insulted them, saying: "Here comes the gang!" Napier[186] fired his cannon at them. They exercise a dictatorship of chaos.

They possess this chaos. What do they do with it? Implacable deeds:
we know not what. The den of the winds is more monstrous than a
lions' den. How many corpses there are in its deep recesses! The winds
drive this great obscure and bitter mass pitilessly onward. We hear
them always, but they listen to no one. They commit acts resembling
crimes. We know not whom they are attacking with these white flecks
of foam. What impious ferocity there is in bringing about a shipwreck!
What an affront to Providence! They seem sometimes to be spitting on
God. They are the tyrants of the unknown places. *Luoghi spaventosi,* as
the seamen of Venice used to murmur.

The trembling expanses of sea suffer assault and battery at their
hands. What happens in these great wastes cannot be expressed. Some
mysterious horseman is concealed amid the shadows. There is the
noise of a forest in the air. Nothing can be seen, but the sound of

horses galloping is heard. It is midday, and all at once it is night; a tornado sweeps past; it is midnight, and suddenly it is broad daylight; the emanations of the Pole are illuminated. Whirlwinds pass to and fro, reversing their direction in a kind of hideous dance: the trampling of plagues on the water. An overheavy cloud breaks in two and falls in pieces into the sea. Other clouds, purple-tinged, flash and rumble, then turn dark and somber; the cloud, emptied of its thunder, blackens like an extinguished ember. Sacks of rain burst open and dissolve into mist. Here there is a furnace amid falling rain, there a wave emitting flame. The white gleam of the sea beneath the rain reflects light on astonishing distant vistas; in the depths, constantly changing, can be seen vaguely recognizable forms. Monstrous navels open up in the clouds. Vapors swirl around, the waves pirouette; naiads, drunk, tumble about; as far as the eye can see the massive sluggish sea is in movement, but moving nowhere; everything is livid; from the pallor emerge desperate cries.

In the depths of the inaccessible darkness great sheaves of shadow quiver. Every now and then there is a paroxysm. The noise grows into a tumult, as the waves grow into a swell. The horizon, a confused superposition of waves, an endless oscillation, murmurs in basso continuo; there are weird outbreaks of noise; there are sounds like the sneezing of hydras.

Cold winds blow up, then hot winds. The shuddering of the sea reflects a fear of some terrible happening. Disquiet; anguish; the profound terror of the waters. Suddenly the hurricane comes, like a wild beast, to drink in the ocean; there is an extraordinary suction; the water rises to the invisible mouth, a sucker takes shape, the tumor swells; there is a waterspout, the fiery whirlwind of the ancients, a stalactite above and a stalagmite below, a double upturned cone revolving, one point balanced on another, a kiss between two mountains, a mountain of foam rising and a mountain of cloud descending; a fearful coitus between the waves and the shadows. The waterspout, like the column of fire in the Bible, is dark during the day and luminous at night. In the face of the waterspout the thunder is silent, as if afraid.

There is a whole gamut in the vast confusion of the solitudes, a redoubtable crescendo: the shower of rain, the blast, the squall, the gale, the storm, the tempest, the waterspout; the seven strings in the lyre of the winds, the seven notes of the abyss. The sky is a wide expanse, the sea a rounded surface; a breath of wind passes, then there is a sudden change, and all is fury and confusion.

Such are these harsh regions.

The winds run, fly, swoop down, die away, rise again, whistle, roar, laugh; frantic, lascivious, unbridled, taking their ease on the irascible waves. They howl, but their howling has a certain harmony. They fill the sky with sound. They blow on the clouds as on a brass instrument, they raise space to their lips, and they sing in the infinite, with all the mingled voices of clarions, horns, oliphants, bugles, and trumpets, in a kind of Promethean fanfare. Any who hear them are listening to Pan. The fearful thing is that they are playing. They are filled with a colossal joy made up of shadows. In these solitudes they hunt down ships. Unceasingly, day and night, at any time of year, in the Tropics as at the Pole, blowing their wild trumpets, they pursue through the entanglements of clouds and waves the great black hunt after shipwrecks. They are the masters of hounds. They are enjoying themselves. They urge on their hounds to bark at the rocks and the waves. They drive the clouds together and tear them apart. They knead, as with millions of hands, the supple immensity of water.

Water is supple because it is incompressible. When pressed it slips away again. Put under compulsion on one side, it escapes on the other. It is thus that water becomes waves. The waves are its form of freedom.

III

EXPLANATION OF THE SOUND HEARD BY GILLIATT

The great descent of the winds on the earth takes place at the equinoxes. At these times the balance between the Tropics and the Pole swivels and the colossal tide of the atmosphere directs its flow on one hemisphere and its ebb on the other. There are constellations that symbolize these phenomena, the Balance and the Water Carrier.

This is the season for storms.

The sea waits, and keeps silent.

Sometimes the sky has an unhealthy look. It is pale, and a dark veil obscures its face. Seamen are worried when they see the ill humor of the shadows.

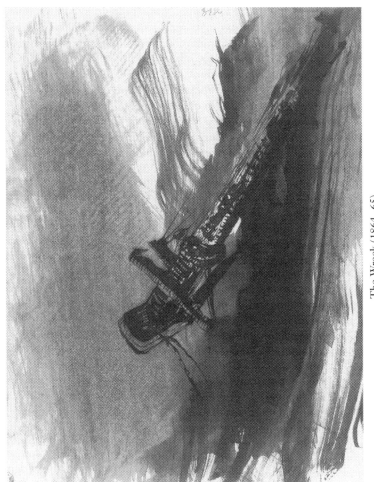

The Wreck (1864–65).

But they are most afraid when the shadows seem contented. A smiling sky at the equinox is a storm concealing its iron hand in a velvet glove. When the sky was in this mood the Weepers' Tower[187] in Amsterdam was filled with women scanning the horizon.

When the spring or autumn storms are late in coming they accumulate greater force. They are storing up greater resources for creating havoc. Beware of arrears! Ango[188] used to say: "The sea is good at settling her accounts."

When there is too long a wait the sea betrays its impatience only by greater calm; but the magnetic tension is shown by what might be called the inflammation of the water. Lights are emitted by the waves; the air is electric, the water phosphoric. Seamen feel harassed. This moment is particularly perilous for ironclads; their iron hull can produce wrong compass directions and lead them to destruction. The transatlantic steamer *Iowa* perished in this way.

For those who are on familiar terms with the sea, its aspect at such moments is strange; it is as if it desired and at the same time feared the cyclone. Some nuptials, though strongly desired by nature, are received in this fashion. The lioness in heat flees from the lion's pursuit. The sea, too, is in heat: hence its trembling motion.

This immense union is about to be consummated. And this mating, like the marriages of the ancient emperors, is celebrated by immolations. It is a festival given piquancy by disasters.

Meanwhile, from over yonder, from the open sea, from those unreachable latitudes, from the livid horizon of these solitary wastes, from the depths of the ocean's boundless freedom, the winds are approaching.

Beware! This is the equinox.

A tempest is the result of a conspiracy. Ancient mythology glimpsed these indistinct personalities mingled with the whole diffused substance of nature. Aeolus was seen as conspiring with Boreas. Agreement between the one element and the other is necessary.

They share out the task between them. Impulses have to be given to the waves, to the clouds, to the emanations; night is an auxiliary, and use must be made of it. There are compasses to be led astray, beacons to be extinguished, lighthouses to be masked, stars to be hidden. The sea must cooperate in all this. Every storm is preceded by a murmuring. Beyond the horizon there are the preliminary whisperings of hurricanes.

This is the sound that is heard in the darkness, far away, over the terrified silence of the sea. It was this dread whispering that Gilliatt had heard. The phosphorescence had been the first warning, the murmuring the second.

If the demon Legion exists, it is he, undoubtedly, that is the Wind.

The wind is multiple, but air is of one substance. In consequence all storms are mixed. The unity of air requires it.

The whole of the abyss is involved in a tempest. The entire ocean is in a squall. All its forces are mobilized and take part in the action. A wave is the gulf below, a gust of wind the gulf above. In facing a gale you are facing the whole of the sea and the whole of the sky. Messier,[189] the great naval expert, the thoughtful astronomer in his cottage at Cluny, said: "The wind from everywhere is everywhere." He did not believe that winds could be imprisoned, even within landlocked seas. In his view there were no purely Mediterranean winds. He claimed to be able to recognize them in their passage. He declared that on one day, at such and such an hour, the foehn of Lake Constance, the ancient Favonius of Lucretius, had crossed the horizon of Paris; on another day the bora of the Adriatic; on another the gyratory Notus that is said to be confined to the circle of the Cyclades. He specified their various emanations. He did not think that the autan that blows between Malta and Tunis and the autan that blows between Corsica and the Balearics were unable to escape from these bounds. He did not accept that winds could be confined in cages like bears. He said: "All rain comes from the Tropics and all lightning comes from the Poles." For winds become saturated with electricity at the intersection of the meridians of the celestial sphere, which mark the ends of the earth's axis, and with water at the equator, bringing liquid from the Line and fluid from the Poles.

Ubiquity is the name of wind.

This does not mean, of course, that there are no particularly windy zones. Nothing has been more clearly demonstrated than the existence of such continuously blowing currents of air; and one day aerial navigation, using ships of the air—which in our mania for Greek terms we call aeroscaphs—will make use of the principal lines of this kind. The canalization of the air by the winds is beyond doubt; there are rivers of wind, streams of wind, and brooks of wind. But the ramifications of the air operate in the inverse way from the ramifications of water: the brooks branch off from the streams and the streams from the rivers rather than flow into them—producing dispersion in place of concentration.

It is this dispersion that creates the solidarity of the winds and the unity of the atmosphere. One molecule out of place will displace another. The whole of wind moves together. To these deeper causes of amalgamation are to be added the relief pattern of the globe, intruding into the atmosphere with all its mountains, creating knots and torsions in the course of the wind, and giving rise to countercurrents in all directions: boundless irradiation. The phenomenon of wind is the oscillation of two oceans, one upon the other: the ocean of air, superimposed on the ocean of water, rests on this constant motion and wavers over the trembling element below.

The indivisible cannot be broken up into compartments. There is no intervening wall between one wave and another. The Channel Islands feel impulses coming from the Cape of Good Hope. Shipping throughout the world is confronting a single monster. The whole of the sea is one hydra. The waves cover the sea with a kind of fish's skin. The Ocean is Ceto.[190] On this unity swoops down the innumerable.

IV

Turba, Turma[191]

The compass recognizes thirty-two winds; that is, thirty-two directions; but these directions can be indefinitely subdivided. Wind, classified according to direction, is incalculable; classified by types, it is infinite. This is a numbering at which Homer himself would flinch.

The polar current encounters the tropical current; cold and hot are combined; the shock between the two creates a balance; the wave of the winds is formed, swollen, scattered, tattered in all directions into wild streams of water. The dispersal of the winds tosses to the four quarters of the horizon the prodigious dishevelment of the air.

All the points of the compass are there: the wind of the Gulf Stream that discharges so much fog on Newfoundland; the wind of

Peru, a region of silent sky where no man has ever heard thunder; the wind of Nova Scotia, the haunt of the great auk, *Alca impennis,* with its striped beak; the whirlwinds of Fer in the China Seas; the wind of Mozambique that handles canoes and junks so roughly; the electric wind of Japan of which warning is given by strokes on a gong; the African wind whose home is between Table Mountain and the Devil's Peak and which ranges freely from there; the equatorial wind that passes above the trade winds and describes a parabola whose highest point is always to the west; the Plutonian wind that emerges from craters in a fierce burst of flame; the strange wind peculiar to Mount Awu, which perpetually gives rise to an olive-tinted cloud in the north; the monsoon of Java, as a protection from which the casemates known as hurricane houses are built; the many-branched wind known to the English as the bush wind; the curving squalls of the Strait of Malacca that were observed by Horsburgh; the mighty southwest wind known in Chile as the pampero and in Buenos Aires as the rebojo, which carries the condor out to sea and saves it from the trench in which the savage is waiting for it, lying on his back on a freshly flayed bull's hide, bending his great bow with his feet; the chemical wind that, according to Lémery,[191] forms thunder stones in the clouds; the harmattan of the Kaffirs; the snow-blower of the polar regions that harnesses itself to the ice floes and draws after it the eternal ice; the wind in the Bay of Bengal that reaches far north to Nizhny Novgorod and wreaks havoc on the triangle of timber huts in which the Asian Fair is held; the wind of the Cordilleras, stirrer-up of great waves and great forests; the wind of the archipelagos of Australia, where honey gatherers tear down the wild hives hidden under the armpits of the branches of the giant eucalyptus; the sirocco, the mistral, the hurricane; winds that bring drought; winds that bring floods, diluvian winds; torrid winds; those that deposit dust from the plains of Brazil in the streets of Genoa; those that follow a diurnal rotation and those that run counter to it and cause Herrera to remark: *Malo viento toma contra el sol*;[193] those that run in couples, conspiring to do mischief, one undoing what the other does; the old winds that assailed Columbus on the coast of Veraguas; those that for forty days, from October 21 to November 28, 1520, threatened to prevent Magellan from reaching the Pacific; and those that dismasted the Armada and blew against Philip II. Others still there are, but how shall they all be told? The winds carrying toads and grasshoppers that transport swarms of these creatures over the ocean; those that bring about a sudden change in the wind, whose function is to finish off shipwrecked seamen; those that, with a single gust, displace the cargo of a ship and compel it to continue on its way with a list; the winds that construct circumcumuli, and those that construct circumstrati; the heavy, blind winds swollen with rain; winds bearing hail; winds carrying fever; those that spark off the solfataras and fumaroles of Calabria; those that bring a sparkle to the coats of African panthers prowling in the scrub on the Cap de Fer;[194] those that shake out of their clouds, like the tongue of a trigonocephalus, the fearful forked lightning; those that bring black snow. Such is the army of the winds.

Their distant gallop was heard on the Douvres reef as Gilliatt was constructing his breakwater.

As we have said, Wind is all winds. The whole of this horde was now coming.

On one side was this legion.

On the other, Gilliatt.

V

GILLIATT HAS A CHOICE

The mysterious forces had chosen their moment well.

Chance, if it exists, is shrewd.

So long as the paunch was moored in the creek at the Homme rock, so long as the engines were still in the wreck, Gilliatt was impregnable. The paunch was secure and the engines were safe; the Douvres, which had the engines in their keeping, were condemning them to slow destruction but were protecting them against surprise. Whatever happened, Gilliatt still had a resource. Even if the engines were destroyed this did not destroy him. He still had the paunch to escape in.

But by waiting until the paunch was taken out of the mooring where it could not be reached, by allowing it to enter the channel at the Douvres rocks, by doing nothing until it, too, was caught by the reef, by allowing Gilliatt to salvage, lower, and tranship the engines, by avoiding any interference with the tremendous effort that had loaded everything into the paunch, by permitting Gilliatt to succeed in his endeavor, a trap had been set. All this revealed in its sinister lineaments the somber trick practiced by the abyss.

Now the engines, the paunch, and Gilliatt were all together in the rock channel. They were all one. It required only a single effort, directed to the same point, to break up the paunch on the reef, send the engines to the bottom, and drown Gilliatt. Everything could be finished off in a single action, at the same time, and without any dispersal of effort; everything could be destroyed in a single blow.

Gilliatt was now in a most critical situation. The sphinx that was imagined by dreamers to be lurking in the shadows seemed to be presenting him with a dilemma: should he stay where he was or should he leave? To leave was the act of a madman; to stay was a dread alternative.

VI

THE COMBAT

Gilliatt climbed to the summit of the Great Douvre. From there he could see the whole of the sea.

The view to the west was surprising. A wall was building up; a great wall of cloud, barring the whole expanse from one side to the other, was rising slowly from the horizon to the zenith. Rectilinear, vertical, without a crack or crevice in its whole height, without a break in its coping, it seemed to have been constructed with the aid of a set square and a plumb line. It was a cloud with the appearance of granite. The steep face of the cloud, which was absolutely perpendicular at the south end, sloped a little toward the north like a bent sheet of iron, with the gradual slant of an inclined plane. The bank of fog grew wider and increased in height, its entablature always remaining parallel to the line of the horizon, which was almost indistinguishable in the gathering darkness. This wall of air rose all in one piece, in silence. Not an undulation, not a wrinkle, not a projection moving or altering its shape: an immobility in movement that gave it an aspect of gloom. The sun, shining palely through a strange sickly transparency, threw a dim light on this apocalyptic vision. The clouds were already invading almost half the space, shelving like a terrifying slope into the abyss. It was like the emergence of a mountain of shadow between earth and sky. It was the ascent of night in the full light of day.

The air was like the hot breath of an oven. The mysterious accumulation of cloud gave off the misty vapors of a steam bath. The sky, which from blue had become white, had now changed from white to gray and taken on the look of a gigantic slate. The sea, below, was dull and leaden, like another great slate. There was not a breath of wind, not a wave on the sea, not a sound. As far as the eye could reach stretched an empty waste. Not a sail in any direction. The birds had gone into hiding. There was a smell of treason in the infinite. The enlargement of this great area of shadow was proceeding imperceptibly.

The moving mountain of vapors that was heading for the Douvres was one of those clouds that could be called battle clouds; sinister clouds, too. Through these obscure masses a mysterious squinting eye seemed to be watching. This slow advance was terrifying. Gilliatt stared at the cloud, muttering under his breath: "I'm thirsty: you're going to give me something to drink."

He remained motionless for some moments, his eye fixed on the cloud. He looked as if he was sizing up the storm.

His cap was in the pocket of his pea jacket; he took it out and put it on. From the recess in the rock where he had slept for so many nights he took out his store of clothes and put on his leggings and oilskin coat, like a knight buckling on his armor at the moment of action. It will be remembered that he had lost his shoes, but his feet had been hardened on the rocks.

Having thus prepared for war, he looked down at his breakwater, grasped the knotted rope, descended from the Great Douvre to the rock below, and made straight for his storeroom. A few moments later he was at work. The huge silent cloud could now hear the blows of his hammer. What was he doing? With his remaining stocks of nails, ropes, and timber he was constructing at the east end of the channel a second openwork barrier some ten or twelve feet to the rear of the first one.

There was still a profound silence. The tufts of grass growing in crevices in the rock were not moving.

Suddenly the sun disappeared. Gilliatt raised his head.

The rising cloud had just reached the sun. It was as if daylight had been extinguished, to be replaced by confused and pallid reflections.

The wall of cloud had changed its aspect. It had lost its unity. It had formed horizontal wrinkles as it reached the zenith, from which it overhung the rest of the sky. It had broken down into different levels, and the formation of the storm was displayed like the cross section of a trench. Layers of rain and beds of hail could be distinguished. There was no lightning, but a horrible diffused light—for the idea of horror can be attached to the idea of light. The vague breathing of the storm could be heard. In this silence there was an obscure palpitation. Gilliatt, no less silent, watched as all these blocks of fog formed above his head and the deformity of the clouds took shape. On the horizon lay, steadily expanding, a band of ash-gray mist, and at the zenith a band the color of lead; over the mists below hung livid rags from the clouds above. The whole background—the wall of cloud—was wan, milky, sallow, gloomy, indescribable. A thin, whitish patch of cloud, coming from who knows where, cut obliquely across the high dark wall from north to south. One end of this cloud hung down into the sea. At the point where it touched the confusion of waves, a dense red vapor was discernible in the darkness. Under the long pale swathe of cloud, low down, smaller dark-colored clouds were flying in different directions as if uncertain which way to go. The massive cloud that formed the background was growing in all directions at the same time, increasingly eclipsing the sun, on which it maintained its lugubrious hold. To the east, behind Gilliatt, there remained only one patch of clear sky, and this was closing in rapidly. Though there seemed to be no wind, strange flecks of grayish down, scattered and fragmented, were sailing across the sky, as if some gigantic bird had just been plucked behind the wall of darkness. A ceiling of compact blackness had formed and on the distant horizon was touching the sea and mingling with the night. There was a feeling as if something was moving forward—something vast and ponderous and sinister. The darkness was growing denser. Suddenly there was an immense peal of thunder.

Gilliatt himself felt the shock. There is something dreamlike in thunder. This brutal reality in the region of visions is terrifying. It is like the upsetting of some piece of furniture in the abode of giants.

The crash was not accompanied by any electric flash: it was like black thunder. Then silence returned. There was a kind of interval, as when hostile forces are taking up their ground. Then there appeared, slowly, one after the other, great shapeless flashes. They were quite noiseless, unaccompanied by any roll of thunder. At each flash the whole scene was illuminated. The wall of cloud had now become a cavern, with arches and vaulted halls. Outlines of figures could be descried—monstrous heads, necks stretching forward, elephants with their howdahs, glimpsed and then vanishing. A column of fog, straight, round, and black, surmounted by a puff of white vapor, simulated the funnel of some colossal steamer engulfed by the sea, still with steam up and smoking. Sheets of cloud, waving, were like the folds of huge flags. In the center, under a vermilion mass, a nucleus of dense fog hung inert and motionless, impenetrable to electric sparks—a kind of hideous fetus in the womb of the tempest.

Suddenly Gilliatt felt a breath of wind ruffling his hair. Three or four large spiders of rain splashed down on the rock around him. Then there was a second peal of thunder. The wind rose.

The expectancy of darkness was at its peak. The first peal of thunder had shaken the sea; the second split the wall of cloud from top to bottom, a rent opened up, the shower hanging in the air turned in that direction, the crevice turned into an open mouth filled with rain, and the vomiting of the tempest began.

It was a fearful moment.

Rain, hurricane, fulgurations, fulminations, waves reaching up to the clouds, foam, detonations, frantic torsions, roars, hoarse cries, whistling—all at the same time. Monsters unleashed.

The wind was blowing like thunder. The rain was not falling: it was tumbling down.

For an unfortunate man, caught up like Gilliatt, with a heavily laden boat, between two rocks in the midst of the sea, it was a moment of desperate crisis. The danger from the tide, which Gilliatt had overcome, was as nothing compared with the danger from the tempest.

Gilliatt, surrounded on every side by precipices, now revealed, at the last moment and in face of supreme peril, a well-conceived strategy. He had taken up his stance in the very territory of the enemy; he had made the reef his partner; the Douvres, hitherto his adversary, were now his second in this immense duel. He had made them his base. Instead of a sepulchre, they had become his fortress. He had entrenched himself in this formidable dwelling in the sea. He was under siege, but strongly defended. He was, as it were, with his back to the wall of the reef, face-to-face with the hurricane. He had barricaded the channel through the reef, that street amid the waves. It was all he could do. It seems that the ocean, which is a despot, can, like other despots, be brought to reason by barricades. The paunch could be regarded as secure on three sides. Tightly wedged between the two inner walls of the reef, firmly held by three anchors, it was sheltered on the north by the Little Douvre and on the south by the Great Douvre—two wild rock faces more accustomed to causing shipwrecks than to preventing them. On the west it was protected by the framework of beams moored and nailed to the rocks, a tried and tested barrier that had withstood the rough assault of the rising tide—a fortress gate with the two pillars of the reef, the Douvres, as its jambs. There was nothing to be feared on that side. The point of danger was to the east.

At the east end there was only the breakwater. A breakwater is a device for breaking up the force of the waves. It ought to have at least two openwork frames. Gilliatt had had time only to make one, and he was now building the second in the teeth of the tempest.

Fortunately the wind, which is sometimes ill-judged in its assaults, was coming from the northwest. This—the wind once known as the *galerne*—had little effect on the Douvres. It blew across the reef, and thus did not drive the sea against either end of the defile that cut through it, so that instead of entering a street it came up against a wall. The storm's attack was ill directed.

But the wind's attacks tend to curve around, and it was necessary to be prepared for a change in its direction. If it should veer to the east before the second panel of the breakwater was constructed, there would be grave danger. The tempest would then be able to invade the channel between the rocks, and all would be lost.

The storm was still increasing in violence. A tempest heaps blow on blow: that is its strength, but it is also its weakness. Its very fury makes it vulnerable to human intelligence, and man is able to defend himself. But what force, what monstrous power, is directed against him! No respite, no interruption, no truce, no time to draw breath. There is some cowardice in this prodigality with inexhaustible resources. It is surely the lungs of the infinite that are breathing.

All this tumultuous immensity was hurling itself against the Douvres reef. Voices without number could be heard. Whose cries were these? The panic fear of the ancients had come again. At times it sounded like talking, as if someone were issuing commands. Then came clamors, the sound of clarions, strange trepidations, and that great majestic roar that seamen term the call of the ocean. The indefinite, fleeting spirals of the wind whistled as they churned up the sea; the waves, shaped into disc form by this whirling movement, were hurled against the rocks like gigantic quoits thrown by invisible athletes. Great masses of foam whipped wildly against the rocks. Torrents above; spittle below. Then the roaring redoubled. No sound from either human or animal throats could give any idea of the din mingled with these dislocations of the sea. The clouds were thundering, the hailstones were firing salvoes, the waves were surging to the attack. At some points there seemed to be no movement; elsewhere the wind was traveling at twenty fathoms a second. As far as the eye could reach the sea was white; the horizon was lined with ten leagues of lather. Gates of fire were opening up. Some clouds looked as if they were being burned by others; lying on heaped-up reddish clouds that seemed like red-hot embers, they had the appearance of smoke. Floating formations of cloud ran into one another and amalgamated, each altering the shape of the other. Incommensurable quantities of water were streaming down. The rattle of musketry was heard in the firmament. In the center of the ceiling of darkness there was a kind of vast upturned basket from which fell at random whirlwinds, hail, clouds, purple tinges, phosphoric lights, night, light, thunder—so formidable are these tiltings of the abyss!

Gilliatt appeared to pay no attention to all this. His head was bent over his work. The second openwork frame was beginning to rise. He responded to each peal of thunder with a blow of his hammer; this regular beat could be heard above the surrounding chaos. He was bareheaded, for a gust of wind had whipped off his cap.

He had a burning thirst. He probably had a touch of fever. Pools of rainwater had formed around him in holes in the rock, and from time to time he took up a mouthful of water in his palm and drank it. Then, without even looking to see how the storm was getting on, he returned to his task.

A moment might decide on success or failure. He knew what was awaiting him if he did not finish his breakwater in time. What was the use of wasting even a minute in watching the face of the death that was approaching?

The turmoil around him was like a boiling cauldron. There was noise and tumult on every side. Every now and then there was a roll of thunder, sounding as if it was descending a staircase. The electric shocks returned incessantly to the same points on the rock, where there were probably veins of diorite. There were hailstones as big as a man's fist. Gilliatt had repeatedly to shake out the folds in his pea jacket. Even his pockets were filled with hail.

The storm had now veered around to the west and was beating against the barrier between the two Douvres; but Gilliatt had confidence in his barricade, and with reason. Constructed from the large section of the forward part of the Durande, it yielded to the shock of the waves. Elasticity is a form of resistance; and the calculations of Stevenson[195] have shown that as a defense against waves, which themselves are elastic, a timber structure of appropriate size, fitted together and secured in the right way, is a more effective obstacle than a masonry breakwater. The barrier at the Douvres met these requirements; and it was so ingeniously anchored that a wave striking it acted like a hammer driving in a nail, pushing it against the rock and consolidating it; it could be demolished only by overturning the Douvres. All that the storm could do to the paunch, therefore, was to cast a few flecks of foam onto it over the obstacle. On that side of the reef, thanks to the breakwater, the tempest was reduced to spitting in impotent rage. Gilliatt turned his back on it, happy to feel this ineffectual fury behind him.

The flecks of foam flying on all sides were like wool. The vast angry ocean poured over the rocks, mounting onto them, entering into them, penetrating into the network of fissures within them, and emerged from the granite masses through narrow crevices—inexhaustible mouths that formed small tranquil fountains amid the deluge. Here and there threads of silver fell gracefully from these holes into the sea.

The additional frame reinforcing the barrier at the east end of the channel was now almost complete, requiring only a few knots in the ropes and chains, and the moment was approaching when this barrier would be able to play its part in the struggle.

Suddenly the sky brightened, the rain ceased, the clouds broke up. The wind had changed; a kind of tall crepuscular window opened at the zenith, and the lightning stopped. It looked like the end. It was the beginning.

The wind had veered from southwest to northeast.

The tempest was about to begin again, with a new troop of hurricanes. The north was moving to the attack, and it would be a violent assault. The south wind has more water, the north wind more thunder.

Now the attack, coming from the east, was going to be directed against the weak spot in Gilliatt's defenses. This time he interrupted his work and looked around him.

He took up his position on a projecting rock to the rear of the second openwork frame, now almost completed. If the first part of the breakwater were to be carried away it would destroy the second part, which was not yet consolidated, and would crush Gilliatt along with it. In the position that he had chosen he would be destroyed before seeing the paunch and the Durande's engines and the whole of his work engulfed and lost. This was the eventuality that had to be faced. Gilliatt accepted it and, defiantly, willed it.

In this shipwreck of his hopes all that he wanted was to die first—to be the first to die, for to him the engines were like a person. Brushing off with his left hand the hair that had been plastered over his eyes by the rain, he seized hold of his stout hammer with his right, leaned back, as if threatening the storm as the storm was threatening him, and waited.

He had not long to wait.

The signal was given by a peal of thunder; then the pallid opening in the zenith closed, there was a deluge of rain, the whole sky darkened, and the only illumination left was the lightning. The dread attack had begun in earnest.

A massive swell, visible in the repeated flashes of lightning, mounted in the east, beyond the Homme rock. It was like a great rolling cylinder of glass. Glaucous, without a fleck of foam, it stretched across the whole of the sea. It was advancing on the breakwater, and as it approached it grew in size; it was like a huge cylinder of darkness rolling over the ocean. The thunder rumbled dully on.

The great wave reached the Homme rock, broke in two, and swept on beyond it. The two portions joined up again to form a single mountain of water, which was no longer parallel to the breakwater but at right angles to it. It was a wave in the form of a massive timber beam. This battering ram hurled itself against the breakwater in a thunderous shock. Nothing could be seen for the shower of foam.

Only those who have seen them can imagine these avalanches in which the sea shrouds itself and with which it engulfs rocks more than a hundred feet in height, like the Grand Anderlo on Guernsey and the Pinnacle on Jersey. At Sainte-Marie in Madagascar it leaps over Tintingue Point.

For some moments everything was obscured by the mountainous sea. Nothing could be seen but a furious accumulation, an immense blanket of froth, the whiteness of a winding-sheet whirling in the wind of a tomb, a piled-up mass of noise and storm under which extermination was at work.

The foam cleared. Gilliatt was still standing erect.

The barrier had held firm. Not a chain was broken, not a nail dislodged. Under the onslaught of the sea it had shown the two qualities of a breakwater: it had been as flexible as a wicker hurdle and as solid as a wall. The swell had been dissolved into rain. A rivulet of foam, coursing along the zigzags of the channel, died away under the paunch at the far end.

The man who had put this muzzle on the ocean allowed himself no rest. Fortunately, for a short space, the storm turned aside. The fury of the waves turned back against the rock walls of the reef, offering a respite. Gilliatt took advantage of it to complete the rear openwork panel of the breakwater.

This labor occupied the rest of the day. The storm continued its violent assault on the flanks of the reef with lugubrious solemnity. The urn of water and the urn of fire contained within the clouds continued to pour out their contents without ever running dry. The undulations of the wind, upward and downward, were like the movements of a dragon.

When night fell, it was already there; no difference was perceptible.

The darkness, however, was not total. Tempests, which are both illuminated and blinded by lightning, are intermittently visible and invisible. Everything is white, and then everything is black. Visions depart and darkness returns.

A swathe of phosphorus, red with the redness of the northern lights, floated like a rag of spectral flame behind the dense layers of cloud, creating a vast area of pallor. The great sheets of rain were luminous.

This light helped Gilliatt and directed his work. At one point he turned around and addressed the lightning: "Just hold the candle for me." He was able, with its aid, to build the rear openwork panel even higher than the outer one. The breakwater was now almost complete.

Just as Gilliatt was making fast the topmost beam with a cable the gale blew straight into his face, making him raise his head. The wind had suddenly veered to the northeast. The assault on the eastern end of the channel was now beginning again. Gilliatt looked out to sea. The breakwater was facing a further attack. Another heavy sea was on the way.

The oncoming wave broke with a great shock against the barrier, and it was followed by another, then another and another—five or six in turmoil, almost at the same time; then a final tremendous wave.

This last wave was like a summing-up of the hostile forces, with a strange resemblance to a living creature. It would not have been difficult to imagine, in this tumescence and this transparency, the likeness of gills and fins. The wave flattened and broke up against the breakwater, its almost animal-like form torn to pieces in a splash and surge of water. It was like the crushing to death of a hydra on this rock and timber barrier. As the swell died it wrought devastation; it seemed to cling on and bite its victim. The reef was shaken by a profound tremor, in which were mingled the growlings of a wild beast. The foam was like the spittle of a leviathan.

As the foam subsided the damage inflicted by the wave could be seen. This last assault had had its effect. This time the breakwater had suffered. A long, heavy beam had been torn from the forward barrier and tossed over the one to the rear onto the overhanging rock on which Gilliatt had earlier taken up position. Fortunately he had not returned to the spot: had he done so he would have been killed out of hand.

The remarkable thing about the fall of the beam was that it did not bounce and thus saved Gilliatt from being hit on the rebound. Indeed, as we shall see, it served his purposes in another way.

Between the overhanging rock and the inner surface of the defile there was a large gap, rather like the cut made by an ax or the cleft opened up by a wedge. One end of the beam thrown into the air by the wave had lodged in this gap, widening it still further.

Gilliatt had an idea—to apply pressure to the other end.

The beam, with one end held in the gap in the rock, emerged from it in a straight line, like an outstretched arm. It ran parallel to the inner walls of the defile, its free end reaching out from the rock for some eighteen or twenty inches: a good distance for what Gilliatt had in mind.

He braced himself with his feet, knees, and fists against the surface of the rock and backed his shoulders against what was now in effect an enormous lever. The great length of the beam increased the force he was able to exert. The rock was already loosened, but Gilliatt had still to strain against the beam four times, until there was as much sweat as rain streaming from his hair. The fourth try involved a fearful effort. There was a hoarse crack, the gap, now extended into a fissure, opened up like a gaping jaw, and the heavy mass fell into the narrow defile with a tremendous crash that echoed the peals of thunder.

The rock fell straight down without breaking. It was like a standing stone thrown down in one piece. The beam that had served as a lever followed the rock, and Gilliatt, with his foothold giving way under him, narrowly escaped falling after it.

At this point there was an accumulation of stones and shingle on the seabed, and there was little depth of water. The monolith, in a great swirl of foam that splashed Gilliatt, settled down between the two parallel rock faces of the defile, making a transverse wall, a kind of hyphen between the two sides. Its two ends touched the rock face on both sides; it was a little too long, and the tip, which was of friable rock, broke off as it fell into place. The result was to form a curious kind of blind alley, which can still be seen today. Behind this stone barrier the water is almost always calm.

This was a still more impregnable rampart than the forward section of the Durande between the two Douvres. It had been created just in time.

The buffeting by the sea had been continuing. The obstinacy of the waves is always increased by an obstacle. The first openwork frame, which had been damaged, was now beginning to break up. Damage to one section of a breakwater is serious. The hole will inevitably become wider, and it cannot be repaired on the spot: the workman would be carried away by the waves.

An electric discharge that illuminated the reef revealed the damage that was being done to the breakwater. The beams were twisted out of shape, the ends of the ropes and chains were dangling in the wind, and there was a great rent in the center of the structure. The second openwork panel was intact.

The lump of rock that Gilliatt had hurled into the gap behind the breakwater with such force was the most substantial of the barriers, but it had one defect: it was too low. The sea could not break it up, but it could surge over it.

There was no question of increasing its height. It would have been necessary to add further masses of rock; but how could they be broken off, how could they be dragged to the right place, how could they be lifted and piled on top of one another and fixed in position? Timber structures can be added to easily enough, but not piles of rock. Gilliatt was no Enceladus.[196]

Gilliatt was worried by the lack of height of this little granite isthmus, and it was not long before the effects of this fault made themselves felt. The assault on the breakwater by the squalls was continuing. They were not merely crashing ferociously against it: it looked as if they were doing it deliberately. There was a sound like the tramping of feet on the much buffeted structure.

Suddenly part of a binding strake broke off, sailed over the second openwork frame and the transverse mass of rock, and landed in the defile, where the water seized hold of it and carried it off along the windings of the channel. Gilliatt could no longer see it. Probably it would end up by striking the paunch. Fortunately the water in the interior of the reef, being enclosed on all sides, was barely affected by the tumult going on outside. There was little wave movement, and the impact was unlikely to be severe. In any case Gilliatt had no time to concern himself with damage to the paunch, if there was damage. He was surrounded by dangers on all sides: the tempest was concentrating on the most vulnerable point, and he was faced with imminent peril.

There was a moment of profound darkness. In sinister connivance, the lightning ceased; the clouds and the waves became one; there was a dull clap of thunder.

The thunder was followed by a crash. Gilliatt peered out. The openwork frame that was the forward part of the barrier had been stove in. The ends of the beams could be seen whirling about in the waves. The sea was using the first breakwater to batter down the second one.

Gilliatt felt as a general would feel seeing his advance guard pulled back.

The second breakwater withstood the shock. The rear section of the defenses was firmly bound together and buttressed. But the shattered frame was heavy; it was in the hands of the waves, which hurled it forward and then drew it back; the remaining ropes and chains prevented it from falling apart and preserved its full bulk; and the very qualities that Gilliatt had given it as a defensive structure made it a terrible engine of destruction. No longer a buckler, it had become a bludgeon. Moreover it bristled with the ends of the broken timbers that emerged from it on all sides, covering it, as it were, with teeth and spurs. No blunt weapon could have been more redoubtable or more suitable for wielding by the tempest. It was a projectile, and the sea was a catapult.

Blow followed blow with a kind of tragic regularity. Gilliatt, standing anxiously behind the gateway that he had barricaded, listened to this knocking at the door by the death that was seeking to enter.

He thought bitterly that had not the Durande's funnel been fatally trapped in the wreck he would have been back in Guernsey and in harbor that morning, with the paunch in safety and the engines saved.

But the thing he had feared had come to pass. The sea had broken in. It was like a death rattle. The whole structure of the breakwater, both parts of it mingled and crushed together, now hurled itself in a tremendous surge of foam against the stone barrier, like a landslide on a mountain, and stopped there. It all formed a great tangle, a shapeless mass of beams, which could be penetrated by the waves but still dashed them to pieces. The protective rampart had been vanquished but was dying a heroic death. The sea had wrecked it, but it was breaking up the sea. Although it had been overthrown, it was still to some extent effective. The rock barrier—an obstacle that could not be driven back—was still holding off the waves. At this point, as we have seen, the defile was at its narrowest; the victorious storm had thrown back, broken, and heaped up in this bottleneck the whole structure of the breakwater; but its very violence, by crushing the whole mass together and driving the broken fragments into one another, had formed by its demolition work a solid mass of debris. Though destroyed, it was still unshakeable. A few pieces of timber broke free and were dispersed by the waves. One of them flew through the air quite close to Gilliatt. He felt the wind of its passing on his forehead.

But some of the waves—those great waves that during a storm return with imperturbable periodicity—were surging over the ruin of the breakwater. They fell back into the defile and, in spite of its turns and angles, raised a swell. The water within the channel was beginning to become dangerously agitated. The obscure kiss of the waves on the rocks was growing more vigorous.

How could this agitation be prevented from reaching the paunch? It would not take long for these squalls to whip up all the water within the reef, and with a few buffets from the sea the paunch would be ripped apart and the engines would sink to the bottom.

Gilliatt pondered, shuddering. But he was unabashed. His was a soul that had no thought of defeat.

The hurricane had now found the way forward and was surging frantically between the two walls of the defile.

Suddenly there sounded and reverberated in the defile, some distance to Gilliatt's rear, a crash more terrifying than any he had yet heard.

It came from the direction of the paunch. Some dire event was taking place in that quarter. Gilliatt hurried to the spot.

From the eastern end of the channel, where he was, he could not see the paunch because of the zigzags of the defile. Coming to the last turning in its course, he paused and waited for a flash of lightning.

A flash came and illuminated the scene.

The inrush of the sea from the eastern end of the defile had been met by a squall of wind at the western end. A disaster was on the way.

There was no sign of damage on the paunch: securely anchored as she was, she afforded little hold to the tempest; but the carcass of the Durande was in distress. The ruin of the vessel offered a considerable surface to the storm. Suspended in the air, entirely out of the water, it was offered up to its violence. The hole that Gilliatt had made in the hull to extract the engines had weakened it still further. The main beam of the keel had been cut. The Durande was a skeleton whose spinal column had been broken.

The hurricane had merely blown on it; but that was enough. The deck planking had folded like an opening book, and the vessel had been dismembered. This was the crash that Gilliatt had heard over the noise of the storm.

What he saw when he came closer seemed almost irremediable. The square incision he had made in the hull had become a gaping wound. The wind had enlarged the cut into a fracture, and this transverse break had divided the wreck into two. The after part, nearer the paunch, was still solidly fixed in the rock, but the forward part, facing Gilliatt, was hanging loose. A fracture, so long as it holds together, is like a hinge. The broken mass was swinging on its fractures, as if on hinges, and was being blown about by the wind, with a fearful noise.

Fortunately, the paunch was no longer under the wreck.

But this swaying to and fro was shaking the other half of the hull, still caught tight and immobile between the two Douvres. From shaking to falling is a short step. Exposed as it was to the determined onslaught of the wind, the dislocated part might suddenly drag with it the other part, which was almost touching the paunch, and everything—the paunch containing the engines—would be swallowed up in this collapse.

Gilliatt saw it all. A catastrophe was imminent. How could it be averted?

Gilliatt was the type of man who can draw aid from the very danger with which he is faced. He thought for a moment. Then he ran to his storeroom and took his ax. The hammer had done its work well; now it was the turn of the felling ax.

Gilliatt climbed up onto the wreck. Standing on the part of the deck that still held firm, he bent over the precipice between the two Douvres and began to cut away the broken beams, severing the remaining links with the hanging section of the hull.

The object of the operation was to complete the separation of the two parts of the wreck, to save the half that was still solid and consign to the waves the section that had fallen prey to the wind—conceding partial victory to the storm. The task was not particularly difficult, but it was dangerous. The portion of the wreck that was hanging down, pulled downward by the wind and by its own weight, was held only at a few points. The wreck was like a diptych with one panel half detached and liable to beat against the other. Only five or six pieces of the structure, bent and twisted but not broken off, were still holding. The breaks creaked and widened at every gust of the north wind, and the ax had to do no more than help the wind. The few remaining joins between the two parts eased Gilliatt's work but added to its danger. The whole thing could give way at any moment under his feet.

The storm was now reaching its paroxysm. Hitherto terrible, it had become terrifying. The convulsion of the sea now reached up into the sky. Up till now the clouds had been dominant; they seemed to do whatever they wanted; they gave the main impulsion; they conveyed their fury to the waves, while preserving a strange sinister lucidity. Below was madness; above was wrath. The sky had the wind; the ocean had only foam. Hence came the authority of the wind. The hurricane was a powerful spirit. The intoxication of its own horror, however, had disturbed it. It was now only a whirlwind. It was blindness giving birth to night. In whirlwinds there is a moment of madness; for the sky it is like something going to its head. The abyss no longer knows what it is doing. It fumbles with its thunderbolts. It is a fearful situation, a moment of horror.

The tumult on the reef was now at its peak. Every storm has a mysterious orientation of its own, and at a certain moment it loses its sense of direction. This is the worst phase of the tempest. At that moment "the wind," said Thomas Fuller,[197] "is a raving madman." It is at that moment in a storm that there is the continuous discharge of electricity that Piddington[198] calls a cascade of lightning. It is at that moment, too, that there appears, for no apparent reason, amid the blackest clouds, as if to spy on the universal terror, the circle of blue light known to the old Spanish navigators as the eye of the storm, *el ojo de la tempestad.* This lugubrious eye was on Gilliatt.

Gilliatt for his part was looking at the clouds. Now he was keeping his head up. After every stroke of his ax he stood proudly erect. He was, or seemed to be, too near destruction not to feel some pride. Did he despair? No. Faced with the ocean's supreme access of fury, he was prudent as well as bold. He stood only on the parts of the wreck that were still solid. He was risking his life, but was also careful of it. He, too, was in a state of paroxysm. His vigor had multiplied tenfold. He was all intrepidity. His ax strokes rang like challenges. He seemed to have gained in lucidity what the tempest had lost. It was a dramatic conflict: on one side the inexhaustible, on the other the indefatigable. It was a contest to see which side would compel the other to give in. In the immensity of the sky the lowering clouds had the form of gorgon faces; the air was full of menace. The rain was coming from the waves, the foam from the clouds. The phantoms of the wind bent low; meteor faces flushed crimson and then disappeared, and after their disappearance there was a monstrous darkness. Everything was pouring down, coming from every side at the same time; it was all boiling up; the massed darkness was overflowing; the cumulus clouds, laden with hail, ragged and torn, ash-gray in color, seemed to be possessed by a kind of gyratory frenzy; the air was filled with a noise like dried peas being shaken in a riddle; the inverse movements of electricity observed by Volta were flashing from cloud to cloud; the continuing rolls of thunder were terrifying; the flashes of lightning came close to Gilliatt. It looked as if he had astonished the abyss. He went to and fro on the shaky wreck of the Durande, with the deck quivering under his feet—striking, hacking, cutting, slicing with his ax, a pale figure lit by the lightning, disheveled, barefoot, clad in rags, his face spattered by the sea, standing tall amid this cesspool of thunder.

Against the delirium of natural forces man's only weapon is skill. And skill brought about Gilliatt's triumph. He wanted the whole shattered mass of debris to fall in one piece. With that in mind, he was weakening the fractures that acted as hinges without cutting them right through, leaving a few fibers to sustain the rest. Suddenly he stopped, his ax held high. The operation was complete. The whole section broke away together.

The loose half of the Durande's carcass sank between the two Douvres, below Gilliatt, who, standing on the other half, bent down and watched. It fell perpendicularly into the water, splashing the rocks, and was caught in the narrow channel before reaching the bottom, standing more than twelve feet above the waves. The deck planking, now vertical, formed a wall between the two Douvres. Like the rock that had fallen across the channel higher up, it allowed only a bare trickle of foam to slip past its two ends; and so it formed the fifth barricade improvised by Gilliatt against the tempest in this street of the sea. The hurricane, blind to what it was doing, had worked on the creation of this final barricade.

It was fortunate that the narrow gap between the two walls of the defile had prevented this barrier from sinking to the bottom. This made it stand higher out of the water; and in addition it allowed the water to pass under the obstacle, which reduced the force of the waves. What passes underneath does not surge over the top. This is part of the secret of a floating breakwater.

Now, whatever the clouds did, there was nothing to fear for the paunch and the engines. The water could no longer disturb them.

Lying between the barrier at the Douvres that protected them at the west end and the new barricade to the east, they were out of reach of attack by either the sea or the wind.

From the catastrophe Gilliatt had drawn salvation. At the end of the day the storm clouds had helped him.

Then, taking up in the hollow of his hand a little water from a pool of rainwater, he drank it and cried to the clouds: "Fooled you!"

It is a source of ironic joy for human intelligence engaged in conflict to see the boundless stupidity of the furious forces ranged against it actually rendering it a service, and Gilliatt felt the immemorial need to insult an enemy that goes back to the heroes of Homer.

Gilliatt went down to the paunch and took advantage of the flashes of lightning to examine it. It was fully time that help had come to the long-suffering vessel, which had been badly shaken during the past hour and was beginning to warp. At a quick glance he could see no serious damage, though he was sure that it had endured some violent shocks. Once the sea had grown calmer the hull had righted itself; the anchors had behaved well; and the engines had been well secured by their four chains.

As Gilliatt was completing his review something white passed close to him and disappeared into the darkness. It was a seagull.

No sight is more reassuring in a storm. When birds appear it means that the tempest is on the way out.

Another good sign was that the thunder was redoubling. The full violence of the tempest puts the thunder out of countenance. As all seamen know, the final stage of a storm is fierce, but brief. Particularly violent thunder is a harbinger of the end.

Suddenly the rain ceased. Then there was only a surly rumble in the clouds. The storm died down with the suddenness of a plank falling to the ground. It was as if it had broken up. The immense buildup of clouds fell apart. A chink of clear sky split the darkness. Gilliatt was astonished: it was broad daylight.

The storm had lasted almost twenty hours. The wind that had brought it had carried it away again. The horizon was obscured by scattered fragments of darkness. Broken and fleeting patches of mist gathered in tumultuous masses; from one end of the line of clouds to the other there was a movement of retreat; a long dying murmur could be heard; a few last drops of rain fell; and all the darkness with its thunders withdrew like a retreating host of war chariots. Suddenly the sky was blue.

Gilliatt realized that he was tired. Sleep swoops down on fatigue like a bird of prey. Gilliatt sank down into the boat without choosing where to lie, and fell asleep. For several hours he remained inert, barely distinguishable from the beams and joists among which he was lying.

BOOK IV

Obstacles in the Path

I

Not the Only One to Be Hungry

When he awoke he felt hungry.

The water was now becoming calmer, but there was still enough agitation out at sea to make immediate departure impossible. Moreover, it was too late in the day. With the load that the paunch now had on board, it would be necessary to leave in the morning in order to arrive in Guernsey before midnight.

In spite of his pressing hunger, Gilliatt began by stripping naked—the only way to warm himself up. His clothes had been soaked by the storm, but the rain had washed out the seawater, so that they could now dry off. He kept nothing on but his trousers, which he rolled up to the knee.

He spread out his shirt, his pea jacket, his oilskins, his leggings, and his sheepskin on the rocks around him, keeping them in place with small stones.

Then he thought about eating.

He used his knife, which he had been careful to sharpen and keep in good condition, to detach from the granite a few sea lice, of about the same species as the clams of the Mediterranean, which can be eaten raw—meager fare after all his toils. He had no biscuit left. There was now, however, no shortage of water. He had not merely had enough to quench his thirst: he was awash with it.

He took advantage of the falling tide to ferret among the rocks in quest of crayfish. There was enough exposed rock to allow him to hope for a good catch.

He did not reflect, however, that he could not cook anything. If he had taken the time to go to his storeroom he would have found it shattered by the rain. His wood and coal were under water, and of his stock of tow, which he used in place of tinder, every fragment was soaked. He had no means of lighting a fire.

Moreover, his blower was out of order; the hood over the hearth of his forge had been broken off; the storm had pillaged his laboratory. With such tools as had escaped damage Gilliatt could, at a pinch, work as a carpenter but not as a smith. At the moment, however, he had no thoughts for his workshop.

Drawn in another direction by his stomach, he had set out, without further reflection, in pursuit of his meal. He wandered about, not in the channel through the reef but outside, on the fringing rocks. It was in this quarter that the Durande, ten weeks ago, had struck the reef.

For the quest on which Gilliatt was engaged the outside of the reef offered better prospects than the interior. At low tide crabs are accustomed to take the air; they like to warm themselves in the sun. These misshapen creatures are happiest at midday. Their emergence from the water in the full light of day is a curious sight. Swarming in such numbers, they arouse a feeling almost of disgust. When you see them, with their awkward sidelong walk, clambering heavily from crevice to crevice up the lower parts of the rocks as if they were climbing a staircase, you are compelled to admit that the ocean has its own type of vermin.

For the last two months Gilliatt had been living on this vermin.

On this particular day, however, the hermit crabs and crayfish had made themselves scarce. The storm had driven these solitary creatures back into their hiding places, and they had not yet felt able to venture out. Gilliatt held his knife open in his hand and from time to time scraped up a shellfish from under the seaweed, eating it as he walked.

At this point he cannot have been far from the spot where Sieur Clubin had perished.

Just as Gilliatt was making up his mind to content himself with sea urchins and sea chestnuts there was a splash at his feet. A large crab, scared off by his approach, had leapt into the water. It did not go so deep as to conceal it from his sight, and he ran after it along the base of the reef. The crab continued to flee, and suddenly it disappeared: it had found its way into some crevice under the rocks.

Gilliatt clung on to some projections in the rock with one hand and bent down to look under the overhang.

There was indeed a crevice in which the crab must have taken refuge.

It was more than a crevice. It was a kind of porch. The sea made its way in through this porch, but it was not deep, and the bottom, covered with stones and shingle, could be seen. The stones were glaucous and covered with confervae, showing that they were always under water. They looked like children's heads covered with green hair.

Gilliatt took his knife between his teeth, climbed down the steep rock face, and jumped into the water. It reached almost to his shoulders. He went through the porch and found himself in a rough kind of passage with crudely shaped pointed vaulting above his head. The walls were smooth and polished. He had lost sight of the crab. He was still within his depth. As he walked on the light increasingly faded, and soon he could make out nothing in the darkness. After he had advanced for some fifteen paces the vaulting above his head came to an end. He had emerged from the passage. There was more space, and therefore more light; and the pupils of his eyes had now dilated, so that he could see quite well. Then he had a surprise.

He had entered the strange cavern that he had visited a month ago; only this time he had come in from the sea. He had just passed through the sunken arch that he had seen on his earlier visit; it could be traversed at certain particularly low tides.

His eyes gradually accustomed themselves to the dim light, and he saw better and better. He was filled with wonder. He was back in the extraordinary palace of darkness that he had discovered before, with its vaulting, its pillars, its bloodreds and purples, its vegetation of gemstones and, to the rear, the crypt that was almost a sanctuary and the stone that was almost an altar. He had little recollection of these details, but he had preserved the whole scene in his mind and he now saw it again. Facing him, at some height on the rock face, was the crevice through which he had entered the first time, and that from the point where he now was seemed inaccessible.

Near the pointed arch he saw the low, dark cavities—caves within the cavern—which he had previously seen from a distance. Now he was quite close to them. The one nearest to him was out of the water and easily accessible.

Still nearer, within reach of his hand, he noticed a horizontal fissure in the granite, above the water level. This was probably where the crab had found shelter. He thrust his hand in as far as he could and began to feel about in this hole of darkness.

Suddenly he felt something seizing hold of his arm. He was struck with undescribable horror.

Something in the dark cavity—something thin, rough, flat, ice-cold, slimy, living—had coiled around his bare arm and was creeping up toward his chest. It felt like the pressure of a belt drawn tight and the clinging grasp of a tendril. In less than a second an unseen spiral had invaded his wrist and elbow, with its tip reaching up to his armpit.

Gilliatt threw himself backward, but found that he was barely able to move. With his left hand, which remained free, he grasped the knife that he had been carrying in his teeth and with this hand holding the knife he braced himself against the rock, making a desperate effort to withdraw his arm. He succeeded only in slightly loosening the thong holding his arm, which immediately tightened again. It was as supple as leather, as hard as steel, and as cold as night.

A second thong, narrow and pointed, now emerged from the crevice in the rock, like a tongue issuing from a gaping jaw. It licked, appallingly, Gilliatt's naked chest and, suddenly becoming enormously longer and thinner, clung to his skin and coiled around his whole body. At the same time a terrible pang of pain, like nothing he had previously experienced, tensed Gilliatt's straining muscles. He felt horrible round prongs digging into his skin. It was as if innumerable lips were clinging to his flesh and seeking to drink his blood.

Then a third undulating thong emerged from the rock, felt Gilliatt's body, lashed his ribs like a whip, and settled there.

Anguish, reaching its paroxysm, is mute. Gilliatt did not utter a cry. There was enough light for him to see the repulsive forms that were latching onto him. A fourth thong, swift as an arrow, darted toward his belly and wound around it.

It was impossible to cut or to tear off the viscous bands that were adhering to Gilliatt's body so closely and at so many points. Each of these points was a source of strange and fearful pain. He had the feeling that he was being swallowed by a host of mouths that were too small for the task.

A fifth tentacle now came out of the hole. It settled on top of the others and then coiled over Gilliatt's diaphragm. This compression increased his anxiety: now he could scarcely breathe.

The thongs were pointed at the tip and widened toward the base as a sword does toward the hilt. All five evidently came from a common center. They kept moving and crawling all over Gilliatt. He felt these obscure pressures, which seemed to him like mouths, shifting from place to place.

Suddenly a large round, flat, viscous mass emerged from below the crevice. This was the center from which the five tentacles radiated like spokes from the hub of a wheel. On the opposite side of this foul disc were the beginnings of three other tentacles that were still under the rock. From the middle of the viscous mass two eyes looked out. They were looking at Gilliatt.

Gilliatt recognized the devilfish.[199]

II

THE MONSTER

To believe in the existence of the devilfish, you must have seen one. Compared with the devilfish, the hydras of old bring a smile to the lips.

At some moments we may be tempted to believe that the intangible forms that haunt our dreams encounter, in the world of the possible, magnets on which their lineaments are caught, and that these obscure dream images become living creatures. The Unknown has the power to produce marvels, and uses it to create monsters. Orpheus, Hesiod, and Homer could create only the chimera; God has created the devilfish.

When God so wills it, He excels in the creation of the execrable. Why He should have such a will is a question that troubles religious thinkers.

All ideals being admitted as valid, if causing terror is an objective, then the devilfish is a masterpiece. The whale is enormous, the devilfish is small; the hippopotamus is armor-plated, the devilfish is naked; the jararaca[200] has a whistling call, the devilfish is mute; the rhinoceros has a horn, the devilfish has none; the scorpion has a sting, the devilfish has none; the buthus[201] has pincers, the devilfish has none; the howler monkey has a prehensile tail, the devilfish has no tail; the shark has sharp-edged fins, the devilfish has no fins; the vampire bat has clawed wings, the devilfish has no wings; the hedgehog has spines, the devilfish has none; the swordfish has a sword, the devilfish has none; the torpedo fish emits an electric discharge, the devilfish emits nothing; the toad has a virus, the devilfish has none; the viper has poison, the devilfish has none; the lion has claws, the devilfish has none; the lammergeyer has a beak, the devilfish has none; the crocodile has jaws, the devilfish has no teeth.

The devilfish has no mass of muscle, no threatening cry, no armor, no horn, no sting, no pincers, no tail to seize or batter its enemies, no sharp-edged fins, no clawed fins, no spines, no sword, no electric discharge, no virus, no poison, no claws, no beak, no teeth. And yet of all animals the devilfish is the one that is most formidably armed.

What, then, *is* the devilfish? It is a suction pad.

On reefs in the open sea, where the water displays and conceals all its splendors, in hollows among unvisited rocks, in unknown caverns with an abundance of vegetation, crustaceans, and shellfish, under the deep portals of the ocean, a swimmer who ventures in, attracted by the beauty of the scene, runs the risk of an encounter. If you have such an encounter, do not give way to curiosity but make your escape at once. Those who enter there bedazzled emerge terrified.

This is the encounter that you may have at any time among rocks in the open sea. A grayish form the thickness of a man's arm and about half an ell[202] long can be seen quivering in the water. It looks like a rag of cloth, like a rolled-up umbrella without a handle. This rag gradually draws closer to you. Suddenly it opens up, and eight rays dart out around a face containing two eyes. These rays are alive; undulating, they flash like fire. It is like a wheel; fully deployed, it has a diameter of four or five feet: a terrifying expansion. Then it launches itself at you. It is a case of a hydra harpooning a man.

The creature curls itself around its prey, covering it and knotting its long tentacles around it. Its underside is yellowish, its upper side earth-colored. It is impossible to render this color, the hue of dust; this sea creature looks as if it were made of ashes. It is spiderlike in form and chameleon-like in coloring. When disturbed it becomes purple. And, horrifyingly, it is soft and yielding.

The knots it ties strangle its prey, which is paralyzed by its very contact.

It has something of the aspect of scurvy and of gangrene. It is disease shaped into a monstrosity.

It cannot be shaken off; it clings firmly to its prey. How does it do this? By the power of a vacuum. The eight antennae are broad at the root but taper to a sharp point. On their undersides are two parallel rows of pustules, decreasing in size from the base to the point. There are twenty-five in each row; thus there are fifty on each antenna, and a total of four hundred in all.

These pustules are suckers: cartilaginous substances, cylindrical in shape, horny, pallid in color. In the largest species they range in size from a five-franc piece to a split pea. These short tubes can be thrust out and withdrawn at will. They can penetrate their prey to a depth of over an inch.

This suction apparatus has all the delicacy of a keyboard. It rises up and then disappears. It obeys the creature's least intention. The most exquisite sensibility cannot match the contractility of these suckers, which are always proportioned to the internal movements of the creature and to circumstances outside it. This dragon is a sensitive plant.

This monster is the creature that seamen call the octopus, scientists call a cephalopod, and which in legend is known as a kraken. English sailors call it the devilfish or the bloodsucker. In the Channel Islands it is called the *pieuvre*. It is rarely found on Guernsey; it is quite small on Jersey, and of great size and fairly common on Sark.

A print in Sonnini's edition of Buffon depicts a cephalopod grappling a frigate; and Denys Montfort believes that the octopus found in high latitudes is capable of sinking a ship. Bory de Saint-Vincent doubts this, but notes that in our waters it will attack a man. If you go to Sark they will show you, near Brecqhou, a hollow in the rocks where some years ago an octopus seized, held on to, and drowned a lobster fisher. Péron and Lamarck[203] are in error in their belief that an octopus, having no fins, cannot swim. The writer of these lines has seen with his own eyes, in the sea cave on Sark known as the Boutiques, an octopus swimming in pursuit of a bather. It was killed and when measured was found to be four English feet across. Its four hundred suckers could be counted; they were thrust out of the creature's arms in the convulsions of its death agony.

According to Denys Montfort, one of these observers whose powerful intuition leads him to descend, or to ascend, into Magism, the octopus has almost human passions: it can hate. And indeed, in the absolute, to be hideous is to hate.

Misshapen creatures struggle under a necessity of elimination that makes them hostile. When swimming the octopus stays, as it were, within its sheath. It swims with all its parts tucked up under it. It resembles a sleeve containing a closed fist. This fist, which is the head, cleaves through the water and advances with a vague undulating movement. Its two eyes, though large, are difficult to distinguish, being of the same color as the water.

When in pursuit of its prey or lying in wait the octopus conceals itself: it makes itself smaller, it condenses itself, it reduces itself to its simplest expression. In the half-light of the sea it is barely discernible. It looks like a furrow in the waves. It in no way resembles a living creature.

The octopus is a hypocrite. You pay no attention to it; then suddenly it opens up: a viscous mass with a will of its own: what could be more horrible? It is like birdlime imbued with hate.

In limpid water of the most brilliant blue this hideous and voracious star of the sea suddenly appears. The horrible thing is that you do not see it approach. Almost always, by the time you see it you are already caught.

At night, however, and particularly during its rutting season, it is phosphorescent. Horror though it is, it has its love affairs. It goes in quest of union. It beautifies itself, it lights up, it illuminates itself; then, standing on a rock, you can see it in the deep shadow below you, unfolding in a pallid irradiation like a spectral sun.

The octopus swims, but it can also walk. Something of a fish, it is also something of a reptile. It crawls about on the sea bottom, using its eight feet and dragging itself along like the caterpillar of a geometer moth.

It has no bones, no blood, no flesh. It is flaccid. There is nothing inside it: it is no more than a skin. Its eight tentacles can be turned inside out like the fingers of a glove.

It has only one orifice, in the center, from which the tentacles radiate. Is this single opening the anus? Is it the mouth? It is both. The same opening serves both functions. The entrance is also the exit.[204]

The whole creature is cold.

The sea nettle of the Mediterranean is repulsive. One is disgusted by contact with this animated mass of gelatin that envelops a swimmer, into which his hands sink, at which his nails scratch in vain, which he can tear apart without killing it, which he can pull off without getting rid of it, a fluid and tenacious creature that slips through his fingers; but no horror can equal the sudden appearance of the octopus—a Medusa served by eight serpents. No grasp is comparable in strength with the embrace of this cephalopod.

You are attacked by a pneumatic machine. You are dealing with a vacuum that has feet. What you suffer is not scratches or bites: it is an unspeakable scarification. A bite is fearful, but less so than a suction. A claw is harmless compared with a sucker. With a claw it is the beast entering into your flesh; with a sucker it is you who are entering into the beast. Your muscles swell, your fibers are twisted, your skin bursts open under this loathsome pressure, your blood spouts out and mingles horribly with the mollusc's lymph. The creature forces itself on you by a thousand foul mouths; the hydra incorporates itself in the man; the man is amalgamated with the hydra. You both become one. You are caught up in a hideous dream. The tiger can but devour you; the octopus, horrifyingly, breathes you in. It draws you to it and into it; and you feel yourself—bound, limed, powerless—slowly being emptied into the fearful sack that is the monster.

Beyond the horrific—being eaten alive—there is the unspeakable—being drunk alive.

Such strange animals as these are at first rejected by science, in accordance with her habit of excessive prudence, even when presented with the facts; then she makes up her mind to study them; she dissects them, classifies them, catalogues them, labels them; she acquires specimens; she exhibits them under glass in museums; she describes them as molluscs, invertebrates, radiates;[205] she assigns them a place among their neighbors—a little beyond the squids, a little short of the cuttlefish; she finds these saltwater hydras a freshwater counterpart, the argyroneta; she divides them into larger, medium-sized, and smaller species; she is readier to accept the smaller rather than the larger species, for that is, in all fields, her natural bent, which is microscopic rather than telescopic; she studies their structure and calls them cephalopods, counts their antennae and calls them octopods. Having done all this, she forgets about them; and when science abandons them philosophy takes them up.

Philosophy in her turn studies these beings. She goes both less far and farther than science. She does not dissect them: she meditates on them. Where the scalpel has been at work she brings the hypothesis to bear. She seeks the final cause: the profound torment of the thinker. These creatures almost cause her concern about the Creator. They are hideous surprises. They are the killjoys of the contemplator: he observes them in dismay. They are deliberately created forms of evil. In face of these blasphemies of creation against itself what can be done? Who can be blamed for them?

Possibility is a formidable matrix. Mystery takes concrete form in monsters. Fragments of darkness emerge from the mass we call immanence, tear themselves apart, break off, roll, float, condense, borrow matter from the surrounding blackness, undergo unheard-of polarizations, take on life, compose themselves into curious forms with darkness and curious souls with miasma, and go on their way, like masks, among living and breathing beings. They are like darkness made into animals. What is the point of them? What purpose do they serve? We return to the eternal question.

These animals are phantoms as much as monsters. They are proved to exist and yet are improbable. They do in fact exist, but they might well not exist. They are the amphibians of death. Their improbability complicates their existence. They touch on the frontier of human consciousness and populate that chimerical boundary region. You deny the existence of the vampire, and the octopus appears. Their teeming numbers are a certainty that disconcerts our assured belief. Optimism, though it is itself truth, almost loses countenance in their presence. They are the visible extremity of black circles. They mark the transition from our reality to some other reality. They seem to belong to those embryos of terrible beings that the dreamer glimpses confusedly through the window of night.

These developed forms of monsters, first in the invisible and then in the possible, were suspected and perhaps actually perceived by the austere ecstasy and the sharp eye of magi and philosophers. Hence the conjectured existence of a hell. The Devil is the tiger of the invisible. The wild beast that devours souls was revealed to mankind by two visionaries, one called John and the other Dante.

For if the circles of darkness continue indefinitely, if after one ring there is yet another, if this aggravation persists in limitless progression, if this chain—the existence of which we for our part are resolved to doubt—does in fact exist, it is certain that the octopus at one extremity proves the existence of Satan at the other.

It is certain, too, that an evil thing at one end proves the existence of evil at the other.

Any evil beast, like any perverse intelligence, is a sphinx. A terrible sphinx propounding a terrible enigma: the enigma of evil.

It is this perfection of evil that has sometimes led great minds to incline toward belief in a double god, the redoubtable two-faced god of the Manichaeans.

A piece of Chinese silk, stolen from the palace of the emperor of China during the recent war, depicts a shark eating a crocodile, which is eating a snake, which is eating an eagle, which is eating a swallow, which is eating a caterpillar.

The whole of the natural world that we have under our eyes eats and is eaten. Prey bites prey.

Meanwhile, scholars who are also philosophers, and consequently are well disposed toward the created world, find, or think they have found, the explanation. Among those to whom the final end occurred was Bonnet of Geneva, that mysterious exact thinker, who was opposed to Buffon, as, later, Geoffroy Saint-Hilaire was opposed to Cuvier. The explanation put forward was that death, occurring everywhere, involves burial everywhere. The devourers are also gravediggers.

All beings enter into one another. Putrefaction is nutriment. A fearful cleansing of the globe. Man, being carnivorous, is also a burier. Our life is made up of death. Such is the terrifying law. We are all sepulchres.

In our crepuscular world this fatality in the ordering of life produces monsters. You say, What is the point? This is it.

Is that the explanation? Is that the answer to the question? But then, why is there not some different order of things? And the question remains unanswered.

Let us live, by all means. But let us try to ensure that death is a progress. Let us aspire to worlds that are less dark. Let us follow the conscience that leads us there. For, let us never forget, the best is attained only by way of the better.

III

ANOTHER FORM OF COMBAT IN THE ABYSS

Such was the creature to which Gilliatt had for some moments belonged. This monster was the inhabitant of the cavern, the dreadful *genius loci;* a kind of somber water demon.

At the center of all these splendors was horror.

When Gilliatt had found his way into the cave for the first time a month ago the dark shape that he had glimpsed in the turbulence of the secret water had been the devilfish. This was its home.

When he entered the cave for the second time in pursuit of the crab and saw the crevice in which he thought the crab had taken refuge the devilfish was there, lying in wait for its prey.

Can we imagine such a lying in wait? Not a bird would dare to sit on her eggs, not an egg would dare to hatch, not a flower would dare to open, not a breast would dare to give suck, not a heart would dare to love, not a spirit would dare to take flight, if they thought of the sinister patience of the creatures lying in wait in the abyss.

Gilliatt had thrust his arm into the hole and the devilfish had seized it. It held him in its power. He was the fly caught by this spider.

Gilliatt was up to his waist in the water, his feet strained against round, slippery pebbles, his right arm embraced and held prisoner by the flat coils of the devilfish's tentacles and his chest almost hidden under the folds and interlacings of this horrible bandage. Of the devilfish's eight arms three were clamped on the rock and five on Gilliatt. Thus, clinging on one side to the granite and on the other to the man, it chained Gilliatt to the rock. He was held by 250 suckers, in a mingling of anguish and disgust. He was caught in the grasp of a huge fist with elastic fingers almost three feet long, the undersides of which were covered with living pustules digging into his flesh.

As we have said, you cannot break free from a devilfish. If you try to you are still more securely bound: it merely tightens its grip. As you increase your efforts it matches its effort to yours. Greater exertion leads to greater constriction.

Gilliatt had only one resource, his knife. He had free movement only of his left hand; but we have seen that he could make powerful use of it. It could be said of him that he had two right hands.

His clasp knife, open, was in that hand.

You cannot sever the antennae of a devilfish: they are of a leathery substance that is impossible to cut; the knife slips off them; and besides they have such a close hold that you cannot cut them without cutting your own flesh.

The octopus is a formidable opponent; but there is a way of tackling it. The fishermen of Sark know it, as does anyone who has seen them carrying out certain sharp movements at sea. Porpoises know it, too; they have a way of biting a cuttlefish that cuts off its head. That is why so many headless squids, cuttlefishes, and octopuses are to be seen floating at sea.

The octopus is vulnerable only in the head; and Gilliatt was well aware of this. He had never seen a devilfish of such a size before, and now that he had been caught by one it turned out to be one of the largest species. Anyone else would have been worried about this.

With a devilfish as with a bull you have to choose the right moment for the kill. It is when the bull lowers its head, it is when the devilfish thrusts its head forward—a moment that passes very quickly. If you miss your chance you are lost.

All that we have described had lasted only a few minutes; but Gilliatt felt the suction of the 250 suckers increasing.

The devilfish is a cunning creature. It tries first to stupefy its prey—seizing it and then waiting as long as possible.

Gilliatt held his knife ready. The suction continued to increase. He looked at the devilfish, which looked at him.

Suddenly it detached its sixth antenna from the rock and, lashing it out at Gilliatt, tried to seize his left arm.

At the same time it thrust its head quickly forward. A second more and its mouth/anus would have been fastened on his chest. Bleeding from his sides, with both arms caught in a stranglehold, Gilliatt would have been a dead man.

But he was alert. Closely watched by his opponent, he, too, was watching.

He evaded the antenna, and at the moment when the devilfish was about to bite his chest his left hand, armed with the knife, struck down on it. There were two convulsions in opposite directions, the devilfish's and Gilliatt's. It was like a conflict between two flashes of lightning.

Gilliatt plunged his knife into the flat viscous mass and, with a turning movement like the coiling of a whip, cut a circle around the two eyes and drew out the head as one draws a tooth.

It was all over in an instant. The creature fell in one mass, like a piece of cloth torn off. Now that the pump sucking out the air was destroyed, the vacuum was released. The four hundred suckers released their hold both on the rock and on the man, and the rag of cloth sank to the bottom.

Gilliatt, panting with his efforts, could see on the pebbles at his feet two gelatinous heaps, the head on one side, the rest of the creature on the other. We say the rest of the creature, for it could not be called a body.

Fearing some last convulsion in its death agony, however, Gilliatt withdrew out of reach of its tentacles.

But the beast was dead all right. Gilliatt closed his knife.

IV

NOTHING CAN BE HIDDEN AND NOTHING GETS LOST

Gilliatt had killed the devilfish just in time. He was almost suffocated; his right arm and his chest were purple; more than two hundred swellings were beginning to appear on his skin, and some of them were bleeding. The best cure for such wounds is salt water, and Gilliatt plunged into it. At the same time he rubbed himself with the palms of his hands, and under this treatment the swellings began to die down.

Drawing back, farther into the water, he had, without realizing it, come closer to the kind of vault that he had noticed before near the crevice where he had been harpooned by the devilfish. This vault continued obliquely, out of the water, under the high walls of the cavern.

The pebbles that had accumulated in it had raised its floor above the level of normal tides. It had a low vaulted roof, and a man could enter it by stooping. The green light of the underwater cavern reached into it, giving weak illumination.

While rubbing his swollen skin Gilliatt raised his eyes mechanically and looked into the vault. He shuddered: he thought he saw, in the darkness at the far end of the cavity, what looked like a grinning face.

Gilliatt had never heard the word *hallucination,* but he had had experience of the thing itself. The mysterious encounters with the improbable that for want of a better name we call hallucinations occur in nature. Whether illusion or reality, visions do appear, and anyone who happens to be there may see them. As we have said, Gilliatt was a dreamer. He had the greatness of soul to be on occasion hallucinated like a prophet. This commonly happens to those accustomed to dream in solitary places.

He thought this was one of the mirages by which, as a man of nocturnal habits, he had sometimes been bewildered.

The cavity had all the appearance of a limekiln. It was a low recess with a rounded roof, whose steep sides grew steadily lower toward the far end, where the pebble-covered floor and the roof came together, closing off the passage.

Gilliatt entered the vault and, keeping his head down, walked toward what he had seen at the far end.

There was indeed something grinning there. It was a skull.

There was not only a skull, but a whole skeleton. The occupant of the vault was the skeleton of a man.

In such encounters as this a bold man seeks for an explanation. Gilliatt looked around him.

He was surrounded by a multitude of crabs. There was no movement in the multitude. It was like a dead anthill. All the crabs were inert. They were empty.

Groups of the crabs, scattered about on the pebbles that littered the floor of the vault, formed misshapen constellations. Gilliatt, his eyes fixed elsewhere, had walked over them without noticing.

At the end of the crypt, which Gilliatt had now reached, the crabs lay thicker on the ground, bristling in their immobility with antennae, feet, and mandibles. Open pincers stuck up, never to close again. Shells, under their crust of spines, did not move; some lay upside down, showing their livid interior. This accumulation of bodies resembled a host of enemies besieging a castle, with the appearance of a tangle of brushwood.

The skeleton lay under this pile. Under the confusion of tentacles and scales could be seen the skull with its striations, the vertebrae, the femurs, the tibias, the long knotted fingers with their nails. The rib cage was full of crabs. In there someone's heart had once beaten. The eye sockets were covered with marine molds. Limpets had left their slime in the nasal cavities. Within this recess in the rocks, however, there were no seaweeds, no vegetation of any kind, not a breath of air. No movement anywhere. The teeth were set in a grin.

What is disturbing about laughter is the imitation of it by a death's head.

This marvelous palace of the abyss, embroidered and encrusted with all the gemstones of the sea, was now at last revealing itself and giving up its secret. It was a den, the habitation of the devilfish; and it was a tomb, in which there lay a man.

The spectral immobility of the skeleton and the crabs quivered gently under the impact of the subterranean waters on this petrifaction. The horrible mass of crabs looked as if they were finishing their meal. Their carapaces seemed to be eating the carcass. It was a strange sight, the dead vermin on their dead prey. A somber sequence of death.

Gilliatt had under his eyes the devilfish's food store. A lugubrious vision, revealing the profound horror of what had happened, caught in the act. The crabs had eaten the man and the devilfish had eaten the crabs.

There were no remains of clothing around the skeleton. The man must have been naked when he was caught.

Gilliatt, examining the remains carefully, set about removing the crabs from the remains of the man. Who had he been? The corpse had been skillfully dissected, like a cadaver prepared for an anatomy lesson. All the flesh had been removed; not a muscle was left; not a bone was missing. Had Gilliatt been a doctor he would have been able to confirm this. The periostea, denuded of their covering, were white, polished, as if specially furbished. But for some green patches left by confervae, they might have been ivory. The cartilaginous septa were delicately thinned down and smoothed. The tomb can create such sinister pieces of jewelry.

The corpse had been, in effect, buried under the dead crabs. Gilliatt was unearthing it.

Suddenly he bent forward quickly. He had seen something encircling the spinal column. It was a leather belt that had evidently been buckled around the man's waist. The leather was mildewed and the buckle was rusty.

Gilliatt drew the belt toward him. The vertebrae resisted, and he had to break them in order to remove it. The belt was intact, though a crust of shells was beginning to form on it. He felt it: inside it was a hard, square object. There was no question of undoing the buckle, and he split the leather with his knife.

The belt contained a small iron box and a few gold coins. Gilliatt counted twenty guineas. The iron box was an old sailor's tobacco box, with a spring catch. It was much rusted and very firmly closed. The spring was completely oxidized and no longer worked. Once again Gilliatt's knife served him well. A little pressure with the point and the lid flew open.

There was nothing in the box but paper: a few very thin pieces of paper, folded in four. They were damp, but not damaged. The hermetically sealed box had preserved them. Gilliatt unfolded them.

They were three banknotes, each for a thousand pounds sterling, amounting in total to seventy-five thousand francs.

Gilliatt folded them up again and put them back in the box, taking advantage of the remaining space to add the twenty guineas, and closed the box as best he could.

Then he examined the belt. The outer surface had originally been varnished, but the other side was rough. On this yellow-brown background were some letters in thick black ink. Gilliatt deciphered them and read the name *Sieur Clubin*.

V

In the Gap Between Six Inches and Two Feet There Is Room for Death

Gilliatt put the box back in the belt and the belt in his trouser pocket. He left the skeleton to the crabs, with the dead devilfish beside it.

While Gilliatt had been engaged with the devilfish and the skeleton the rising tide had engulfed the entrance passage, and he could get out only by diving under the arch. This gave him no trouble: he knew the way out, and he was a master of these sea gymnastics.

The drama that had taken place ten weeks before can now be pictured. One monster had seized the other. The devilfish had taken Clubin to his death. It had been, in the inexorable darkness, what might almost be called an encounter between two hypocrisies. There had been a meeting in the depths of the abyss between these two existences of watchfulness and darkness, and one, which was the animal, had executed the other, which was the soul. A sinister act of justice.

The crab feeds on carrion, the devilfish on crabs. The devilfish seizes any animal that swims by—an otter, a dog, a man if it is able to—drinks its blood, and leaves the dead body on the sea bottom. Crabs are the burying beetles of the sea. The putrefying flesh attracts them; they make for the corpse; they eat it, and the devilfish eats them. The dead things disappear into the crab, and the crab disappears into the devilfish. We have already noted this law.

Clubin had been the bait that attracted the devilfish. It had seized hold of him and drowned him, and the crabs had devoured him. Some wave had then swept him into the cavern and the crevice where Gilliatt had found him.

Gilliatt retraced his footsteps, hunting among the rocks for sea urchins and limpets. He no longer wanted crabs: it would have been like eating human flesh.

Now he was thinking only about getting the best supper he could before leaving. There was nothing to hold him back. Great storms are always followed by a calm that sometimes lasts several days. There was now no danger from the sea. Gilliatt was determined to leave the next morning. It would be necessary, because of the rising tide, to keep the barrier between the two Douvres during the night; but Gilliatt planned to remove it at daybreak, push the paunch out from between the Douvres, and set sail for St. Sampson. The gentle breeze that was blowing from the southeast was exactly the wind he needed. The May moon was just entering its first quarter, and the days were long.

By the time Gilliatt returned to the channel between the two Douvres where the paunch was moored, his hunt for shellfish among the rocks over and his stomach more or less satisfied, the sun had set and the twilight was accompanied by that dim moonlight that might be called crescent light; the tide had reached full and was beginning to ebb. The funnel of the Durande, rising erect out of the paunch, had been covered by the foam of the storm with a coating of salt that shone white in the moonlight. This reminded Gilliatt that a great deal of rainwater and seawater had been thrown into the paunch by the tempest and that if he wanted to leave the following morning, he would have to bale it out.

On leaving the paunch to hunt for crabs he had noticed that there was about six inches of water in the bottom of the boat, which he would have no difficulty in emptying out with his baling scoop.

Returning to the boat, he was struck with terror. There was almost two feet of water in her. This was an alarming discovery: the paunch was leaking. She had gradually been filling during his absence. Heavily laden as she was, twenty inches of water was a dangerous addition. It would take only a little more to sink her. If Gilliatt had come back an hour later he would probably have found only the funnel and the mast above water.

He could not take even a minute to think what to do. He must find the leak, stop it, and then empty the boat, or at least lighten it. The Durande's pumps had been lost in the shipwreck: all he had was the paunch's baling scoop.

The most urgent thing was to find the leak. Without giving himself time to get dressed, Gilliatt set to work at once, quivering with anxiety. He no longer felt hunger or cold. The paunch was still taking in water. Fortunately there was no wind. The least wave would have sunk the boat.

The moon now set. Gilliatt, feeling his way, crouching down, more than half under water, searched for a long time before finally discovering where the mischief lay. During the storm, at the critical moment when the paunch had been thrown up into the air, the sturdy vessel, falling back, had struck the rock with some violence, and a projection on the Little Douvre had ripped a hole in the hull on the starboard side.

Unfortunately—it almost seemed maliciously—the hole was at the meeting point of two riders. This, combined with the confusion caused by the squall, had prevented Gilliatt from seeing the damage in his very cursory inspection at the height of the storm.

The alarming thing about the break was that it was so wide; the reassuring thing was that, although the paunch was floating lower than usual because of the increasing weight of water in the hull, she was still above the normal waterline.

At the moment when the damage had been done the water in the channel was violently disturbed and there was no waterline; the sea had entered through the hole, and under this overload the paunch had sunk several inches. Even after the waves had calmed down the weight of liquid that had found its way in, by raising the waterline, had kept the hole under water. Hence the imminence of the danger. The height of water in the boat had risen from six inches to twenty. But if the leak could be stopped it would be possible to empty the paunch; and once she had been made watertight she would rise to her normal waterline, the hole would be out of the water, and the necessary repair would be easy, or at least possible. As we have seen, Gilliatt still had his carpenter's tools in reasonably good condition.

But how many uncertainties there were before that stage could be reached! how many dangers! how many unlucky chances! Gilliatt heard the water inexorably trickling in. The slightest shock, and the paunch would founder. It was a wretched situation. Perhaps, indeed, it was already too late.

Gilliatt bitterly reproached himself. He should have seen the damage at once. The six inches of water in the hull should have warned him. He had been foolish to attribute these six inches to the rain and the foam. He blamed himself for having slept, for having eaten; he blamed himself for his tiredness; he almost blamed himself for the storm and the darkness. It was all his fault.

While he was heaping these reproaches on himself he still went about his work, which did not prevent him from considering what had to be done.

The leak had been located: that was the first step. The second was to stop it. That was all that could be done for the moment. You cannot do carpentry under water.

One favorable circumstance was that the damage to the hull was in the space between the two chains that made the Durande's funnel fast on the starboard side. The oakum used to stop the hole could be fixed to these chains.

Meanwhile the water was gaining. It was now over two feet deep, reaching above Gilliatt's knees.

VI

DE PROFUNDIS AD ALTUM[206]

Among the stores in the paunch Gilliatt had a fair-sized tarpaulin with long lanyards at the four corners.

He took the tarpaulin, fastened the lanyards on two of the corners to the two rings of the chains holding the Durande's funnel on the side where the leak was, and threw it overboard. It fell between the paunch and the Little Douvre and sank into the water, where it was held over the hole in the hull by the pressure of the water seeking to enter through the hole. The greater the pressure, the more firmly the tarpaulin adhered to the hull, being held in place over the hole by the waves themselves. The wound in the vessel's side was stanched, and, with the tarpaulin interposed between the interior of the hull and the water outside, not a drop could enter.

The leak was blocked but not closed. It was at any rate a respite.

Gilliatt took the baling scoop and began to empty water out of the paunch. It was high time to lighten her. The work warmed him up a little, but he was extremely tired. He was compelled to admit to himself that he might not be able to complete the task and make the hull watertight. He had had very little to eat and was humiliated to feel himself exhausted. He measured the progress of his work by the falling of the water level below his knees; but the fall was very slow.

Besides, the leak was only temporarily stopped: the mischief had been alleviated but not put right. The tarpaulin, driven into the hole by the pressure of the water, was beginning to swell into the hull like a tumor. It looked as if a fist were thrusting into the canvas and trying to burst through it. Strong and thickly coated with tar, it was holding out, but the swelling and the pressure were increasing and it was by no means certain that it would not give way: at any moment the tumor might burst, and water would again surge in.

In such a case, as the crews of vessels in distress know, the only solution is to stop the hole with whatever scraps of canvas and oakum are available and force as much as possible of this material into the hole to reduce the tumor. But Gilliatt had no material of this kind. All that he had salvaged from the wreck and stored up had either been used in his work or scattered by the storm. As a last chance he might have been able to find some fragments of material by scavenging among the rocks. The paunch was now sufficiently lightened to allow him to leave it for a quarter of an hour; but how could he look for anything without any light? He was in utter darkness: there was no moon—nothing but a somber sky studded with stars. Gilliatt had no dry rope to make a wick, no tallow to make a candle, no fire to light it, no lantern to shelter it. In the paunch and on the reef everything was confused and indistinct. He could hear the water swirling around the wounded hull; he could not even see the hole, and could only feel the growing pressure on the tarpaulin with his hands. There could be no question of looking for fragments of canvas and rope among the rocks in the prevailing darkness. How could he glean such scraps without seeing what he was doing? Gilliatt looked gloomily into the night. All these stars, and not a single candle!

Now that there was less water in the hull the pressure from outside was increasing. The swelling in the tarpaulin was growing in size: it was increasingly ballooning into the interior of the hull. The situation, after a brief improvement, was again becoming threatening.

It was of the utmost importance to plug the hole. Gilliatt's only remaining resource was his clothes, which he had laid out to dry on projecting rocks on the Little Douvre. He went to pick them up and laid them on the bulwarks of the paunch. He took his oilskins and, kneeling in the water, thrust them into the hole, pushing out the tumor in the tarpaulin and emptying it. The oilskins were followed by the sheepskin, the sheepskin by the woolen shirt, the shirt by the pea jacket. All these went into the hole. He had only one item of clothing left, his trousers: he took them off and used them to enlarge and strengthen the plug. This seemed sufficient to stop the hole.

The plug went right through the hole, enclosed within the tarpaulin. The water seeking to find a way into the hull pressed against this obstacle and spread it out over the hole, strengthening the plug. It was like an external compress.

Inside the boat only the center of the swelling had been pushed out, and there remained all around the hole and the plug a circular pad of tarpaulin that the very inequalities of the breach held firm.

The leak was sealed; but the position was still extremely precarious. The sharp edges of the breach that held the tarpaulin in place might cut through it and let the water in. In the darkness Gilliatt would not even see it happening. It was unlikely that the plug would hold out until daylight. Gilliatt's anxiety was changing in form, but he felt it growing at the same time as he felt his strength failing. He had returned to his work of emptying out the water, but his arms were so exhausted that he could hardly raise the scoop when it was full of water. He was naked and shivering with cold. He felt the sinister approach of the last extremity.

One possible chance occurred to him. There might be another vessel out at sea. Perhaps some fisherman sailing in the waters off the Douvres might come to his aid. The moment had come when it was absolutely necessary to have someone to help him. One man and a lantern, and the situation could still be saved. Two men could easily bale out the paunch, and when she was empty she would rise to her normal waterline, the hole in the hull would be above the water, and it would be possible to make good the damage. The plug could be replaced by a piece of planking, the makeshift arrangement for stopping the leak by a permanent repair. But if there was no hope in that direction it would be necessary to wait until daylight—to wait throughout the whole long night: a delay that could be fatal. Gilliatt was in a fever of impatience. If by chance some vessel's light were within sight he could signal to it from the top of the Great Douvre. The weather was calm; there was no wind and the sea was quiet. A man waving against the background of the starlit sky had a good chance of being noticed. The captain of a ship or the skipper of a fishing boat sailing at night in these waters would certainly, as a necessary precaution, keep his telescope trained on the Douvres. Gilliatt hoped that he would be seen.

He climbed onto the wreck, seized hold of the knotted rope, and scaled the Great Douvre. Not a sail on the horizon. Not a light anywhere. As far as the eye could reach, the sea was empty. There was no hope of assistance, no hope of further resistance. For the first time Gilliatt felt helpless and at a loss. An obscure fatality was now his mistress. With his boat, with the engines of the Durande, with all his toil, with all his success, with all his courage, he was now at the mercy of the abyss. He had no means of continuing the struggle; he was now purely passive. How could he stop the incoming tide, stop the water from rising and the night from continuing? His only hope now lay in the temporary plug he had constructed, exhausting himself and stripping himself naked in the process. He could neither strengthen it nor make it any firmer; such as it was, it must stay that way; there was nothing further to be done. The makeshift contrivance for stopping the leak was now within the power of the sea. How would this inert obstacle behave? The fight was now to be carried on by this contrivance, not by Gilliatt; by a scrap of material, not by human will. The swelling of a wave could reopen the breach. It all now turned on a greater or lesser degree of pressure.

The matter was now to be determined by a struggle between two mechanical quantities. Gilliatt could no longer either help his ally or resist his enemy. He was now merely a spectator of his fate—his life or his death. He had hitherto been the directing intelligence; now, at this supreme moment, he had given place to a mindless resistance. None of the trials and the terrors he had passed through was the equal of this.

When he had arrived at the Douvres he had found himself surrounded and, as it were, caught up by solitude, which not only encompassed him but enveloped him. He had been confronted by a thousand threats, all at the same time. The wind was there, ready to blow; the sea was there, ready to roar. There was no means of gagging that mouth, the wind; no means of blunting those jaws, the sea. And yet he had struggled; a man, he had fought hand to hand with the ocean; he had wrestled with the storm.

He had faced up to other anxieties and still other necessities. He had coped with every kind of distress. He had had to work without tools, move heavy weights without aid, solve problems without the necessary knowledge, eat and drink without food supplies, sleep without a bed and without a roof over him. On the reef—that tragic torturer's rack—he had been successively put to the question by the various fatalities of nature, henchmen in the service of that nature who is a mother when she wills, an executioner when she thinks fit.

He had vanquished isolation, vanquished hunger, vanquished thirst, vanquished cold, vanquished fever, vanquished toil, vanquished sleep. He had encountered a variety of obstacles leagued against him to bar his progress. After lack of resources there had been the sea; after the sea, the storm; after the tempest, the devilfish; after the monster, the specter. And now there was this final lugubrious irony. On this reef from which Gilliatt had hoped to depart in triumph Clubin's skull had stared at him with a sardonic grin. The grin on the specter's face was justified. Gilliatt realized that he was lost; he was no less dead than Clubin.

Winter, hunger, fatigue, the dismantling of the wreck, the transfer of the Durande's engines to the paunch, the equinoctial gales, the wind, the thunder, the devilfish: all these counted for nothing compared with the leak. There were resources for dealing with these various difficulties, and Gilliatt had possessed them. Against cold there was fire; against hunger, the shellfish on the reef; against thirst, rain; against the difficulties of salvaging the wreck, industry and energy; against the tides and the storm, the breakwater; against the devilfish, his knife. Against the leak there was nothing.

The hurricane was taking this sinister farewell of him: a final assault, defenses that were failing him, a treacherous attack by the conquered on the conqueror. The tempest, fleeing in defeat, was firing this last Parthian shot. The rout was turning and striking back. It was a stab in the back by the abyss.

You can fight the tempest, but how can you fight a trickle of water?

If the plug gave way and the leak opened up again the paunch would certainly founder. It would be like undoing a ligature on an artery. And once the paunch was on the bottom, with the heavy load of the Durande's engines, there was no possibility of raising her. The tremendous effort of two months' titanic labor would end in nothing. There could be no question of starting again. Gilliatt now had no forge and no materials. Perhaps at daybreak he would see all his work sinking slowly and irremediably into the abyss. It was terrible to feel the somber force beneath him. The abyss was drawing him into its grasp.

With his boat engulfed by the sea, he would be left to die of hunger and cold, like the man on the Homme rock.

For two long months the consciousnesses and providences that exist in the invisible world had watched the contest. On one side were ranged the vast expanses of the ocean, the waves, the winds, the lightning, the meteors, on the other one man; on one side the sea, on the other a human soul; on one side the Infinite, on the other an atom. There had been a battle. And now perhaps this prodigious effort was to be wasted. This extraordinary heroism was to be reduced to impotence; this formidable combat, the challenge to which had been accepted, this struggle between Nothing and Everything, this one-man Iliad was to end in despair.

Gilliatt, at a loss, gazed into space. He had not a single garment left: he was naked in face of immensity.

Then, despondent in face of all this unknown enormity, no longer knowing what was wanted of him, confronting the darkness, in presence of this irreducible obscurity, amid the noise of the water, the waves, the swell, the foam, and the squalls, under the clouds, under the winds, under these vast scattered forces, under this mysterious firmament of wings, stars, and tombs, subject to the unknown intentions of these vast presences, with the ocean around him and below him and the constellations above him, oppressed by the unfathomable, he sank down, gave in, and lay down at full length with his back on the rock, looking up to the stars, vanquished, and, raising his joined hands in face of these terrible depths, cried to the Infinite: "Have mercy!" Defeated by the immensity, he was making his submission.

He lay there, alone in the night on this rock in the middle of the ocean, prostrated by exhaustion, like a man struck by lightning, as naked as a gladiator in the circus, with in place of a circus the abyss; in place of wild beasts, the darkness; in place of the watching eyes of spectators, the glance of the Unknown; in place of the vestal virgins, the stars; in place of Caesar, God.

He felt his whole being dissolving in the cold, in fatigue, in impotence, in prayer, in darkness, and his eyes closed.

VII

THERE IS AN EAR IN THE UNKNOWN[207]

Some hours passed.

The sun rose in all its brilliance. Its first ray lit up a motionless form on the summit of the Great Douvre. It was Gilliatt.

He was still stretched out on the rock. This naked body, cold and rigid, no longer shivered. The closed eyelids had a pallid hue. It would have been difficult for an observer to decide whether it was a living body or a corpse.

The sun seemed to be looking at him.

If this naked man was not dead, he was so close to death that the least cold wind would be enough to carry him off.

The wind began to blow, a mild, life-giving wind: the spring breath of May.

Now the sun was rising higher in the deep blue sky; its rays, falling less horizontally, took on a tinge of red. Its light became heat. It enveloped Gilliatt.

Gilliatt did not move. If he was breathing it was with a faint respiration that would barely tarnish a mirror.

The sun continued its ascent, now shining less obliquely on Gilliatt. The wind, which had originally been merely mild, was now warm.

The rigid naked body was still without movement, but the skin now seemed less pallid.

The sun, approaching the zenith, fell vertically on the summit of the Great Douvre. A prodigality of light streamed down from the sky, and was joined by the vast reverberations from the serene ocean. The rock began to warm up, and conveyed some of its warmth to the man.

A sigh stirred Gilliatt's chest: he was alive.

The sun continued its caresses, which were now almost ardent. The wind, which was already the wind of midday and of spring, drew close to Gilliatt, like a mouth breathing gently on him. He moved.

The sea was ineffably calm. Its murmur was like the lullaby of a nurse cradling a child. The waves seemed to be rocking the reef to sleep.

The seabirds, now familiar with Gilliatt, fluttered anxiously above him—no longer with their former wariness but with an air of tenderness and sympathy. They uttered little cries, as if calling to him. A seagull, which seemed fond of him, was tame enough to perch near him and began to talk to him. He seemed not to hear. It jumped onto his shoulder and gently pecked at his lips.

Gilliatt opened his eyes. The birds, pleased but still shy, flew off.

He stood up, stretched like a lion awakened from sleep, ran to the edge of the summit platform, and looked down at the defile between the two Douvres. The paunch was still there, intact. The plug had held: the sea had probably not troubled it much. All was saved.

Gilliatt was no longer tired. He had recovered his strength. His faintness had been merely a sleep. He baled out the paunch, bringing the breach in the hull above the waterline; then he dressed, ate and drank, and was happy.

The leak, inspected in daylight, required more work to repair it than Gilliatt had thought. The damage had been serious and took the whole of the day to put right.

On the following morning, at daybreak, he took down the barrier he had constructed and opened up the way out of the defile. Then, clad in the rags that had mastered the leak and wearing Clubin's belt with its seventy-five thousand francs, standing erect in the paunch, now fully seaworthy, with the Durande's engines beside him, with a favorable wind and a tranquil sea, Gilliatt left the Douvres reef and set his course for Guernsey.

As he left the reef he might have been heard—if anyone had been there to hear him—humming under his breath the tune of "Bonny Dundee."

PART III

DÉRUCHETTE

BOOK I

Night and Moonlight

I

The Harbor Bell

The St. Sampson of our day is almost a town; the St. Sampson of forty years ago was almost a village.

When the long nights of winter were over and spring had come, people cut their evenings short and went to bed when night fell. The parish of St. Sampson had formerly been subject to a curfew, and it still maintained the habit of blowing out its candles early. People went to bed and rose from bed with daylight. These old Norman villages tend to be like chicken roosts.

Apart from a few well-to-do families of townsfolk St. Sampson has a population of quarrymen and carpenters. The harbor is a boat repair yard. All day long the men of St. Sampson are engaged in extracting stone and shaping wood: here the pickax is at work, there the hammer. The day is spent working oak timber and granite. In the evening the men are dead tired and sleep like logs: heavy work makes for heavy slumbers.

One evening in early May, after briefly watching the crescent moon amid the trees and listening to Déruchette walking by herself in the garden of Les Bravées in the evening coolness, Mess Lethierry had withdrawn to his room overlooking the harbor and gone to bed. Douce and Grace were already in bed. Except for Déruchette the whole house was asleep. In St. Sampson, too, everyone was asleep. Everywhere doors and shutters were closed. No one was moving in the streets. A few lights, like winking eyes about to close, shone here and there through dormer windows, showing that the servants were going to bed. It was some time since nine o'clock had struck on the old ivy-covered Norman belfry that shares with St. Brelade's church on Jersey the peculiarity of having a date consisting of four ones (IIII), for the year eleven hundred and eleven.

Mess Lethierry's popularity in St. Sampson had depended on his success; and when his success was taken from him his popularity had declined. Bad luck seems to be contagious, and unlucky people seem to be stricken with plague, so quickly are they put into quarantine. The eligible sons of good families now avoided Déruchette. The isolation of Les Bravées was so complete that the household knew nothing of the great event—great by local standards—which that day had been the talk of St. Sampson. The rector of the parish, the Reverend Ebenezer Caudray, was now rich. His uncle, the magnificent dean of St. Asaph's, had died in London, and the news had been brought from England that very morning by the mail sloop, the *Cashmere,* whose mast could be seen in the anchorage at St. Peter Port. The *Cashmere* was due to leave for Southampton on the following day at noon, and, it was said, would have among its passengers the rector, recalled to England at short notice for the official reading of the will, to say nothing of other urgent matters concerned with the inheritance of a large estate. All day there had been much confused discussion of the event. The *Cashmere,* the Reverend Ebenezer, his late uncle, his wealth, his departure, his future prospects had kept the town in a buzz of interest. Only one house, Les Bravées, knew nothing of the news and remained silent.

Mess Lethierry had thrown himself down on his hammock, fully dressed. Since the catastrophe that had hit the Durande this was all he felt like doing. Prisoners regularly resort to their wretched pallet, and Lethierry was a prisoner of his chagrin. He went to bed each night: it was a truce, a breathing space, a suspension of thought. Did he sleep at night? No. Did he lie awake? No. It would be true to say that for the past two and a half months—it was two and a half months since the catastrophe—Mess Lethierry had been living like a sleepwalker. He had not yet regained possession of his faculties. He was in the cloudy and confused state of mind of those who have suffered great afflictions. His reflections did not amount to thought; his sleep did not bring him repose. During the day he was not a man in a waking state, and during the night he was not a man asleep. He was up, and then he was lying down: that was all. When he was in his hammock he had some moments of forgetfulness that he called sleep; chimeras floated over him and within him, and the cloud of night, filled with blurred faces, passed through his brain; the emperor Napoleon dictated his memoirs to him; there were several Déruchettes; strange birds perched in trees, the streets of Lons-le-Saunier turned into snakes. Nightmares offered a respite from despair. He spent his nights in dreaming, his days in daydreams.

Sometimes he would spend a whole afternoon, motionless, at the window of his bedroom overlooking the harbor, with his head held low, his elbows on the stone sill, his hands over his ears, turning his back on the world, his eyes fixed on the old iron ring in the wall of the house, a few feet below the window, where the Durande used to be moored—watching the rust gathering on the ring.

Mess Lethierry was now reduced to the mere mechanical habit of living.

The most valiant of men come to this when they are deprived of their ruling idea: it is the effect of an existence emptied of its substance. Life is a journey and an idea is the itinerary. Without an itinerary the journey comes to an end. The objective is lost, and the strength to pursue it has gone. Fate has a mysterious discretionary power. It can touch with its rod even our moral being. Despair is almost the destitution of the soul. Only the greatest spirits hold out against it; and perhaps not even they.

Mess Lethierry meditated continually, if absorption can be called meditation, in the depths of a kind of turbid abyss. Sometimes a few heartbroken words would escape him, like: "The only thing now is to ask *up there* for a ticket of leave."

There was a contradiction in Lethierry's nature, a nature as complex as the sea, of which, as it were, he was the product. Mess Lethierry did not pray.

To be powerless is a strength. In the presence of those two blind forces, destiny and nature, man in his very powerlessness has found a support in prayer.

Man seeks help from his dread; he asks his fears for aid; anxiety bids him kneel.

Prayer is a tremendous force peculiar to the soul and of the same kind as mystery. Prayer appeals to the magnanimity of the world of shadows; it looks on the mystery of being with the eyes of darkness itself; and we feel it possible that, faced with the powerful fixity of this suppliant glance, the Unknown may be disarmed. Even the glimpse of this possibility is a consolation.

But Lethierry did not pray.

In happier days God had existed for him—almost, as it were, in flesh and blood. He spoke to Him, pledged his word to Him, from time to time almost shook His hand. But in his hours of trouble, which occurred fairly often, God was eclipsed. This is what happens when we have made ourselves a good God, a friendly personal God.

In Lethierry's present state of mind there was only one clear vision—Déruchette's smile. Beyond that everything was black.

For some time now, no doubt because of the loss of the Durande, Déruchette's charming smile had been seen more rarely. She seemed preoccupied. Her birdlike and childlike little ways had gone. She was no longer to be seen curtseying to welcome the rising sun when the cannon fired at daybreak: "Good morning, day! Do come in!" At times she had a very serious air—a sad change in this sweet creature. She tried, however, to laugh with Mess Lethierry and to divert him; but day by day her gaiety was increasingly tarnished and covered with dust, like the wings of a butterfly with a pin through its body. Moreover, whether from chagrin at her uncle's chagrin—for there are griefs that are the reflection of other griefs—or for some other reason, she seemed now to be much inclined toward religion. In the time of the old rector, Mr. Jaquemin Hérode, she had been accustomed to go to church no more than four times a year, but now she was assiduous in her attendance. She never missed a service either on Sunday or Thursday. The pious souls of the parish were pleased to see this improvement; for it is a great happiness when a young girl, who is exposed to so many dangers in the world of men, turns to God. This at least sets the minds of her parents at rest in the matter of love affairs.

In the evening, whenever the weather allowed, she would walk for an hour or two in the garden of Les Bravées. At these times she was almost as thoughtful as Mess Lethierry, and was always alone. She was always the last to go to bed. This did not prevent Douce and Grace from always to some extent keeping an eye on her, with the instinctive watchfulness that goes with domestic service, as some relief from the dullness of service.

In his present abstracted state of mind Mess Lethierry failed to observe these little changes in Déruchette's habits. In any case he was not a born duenna. He did not even notice her punctuality in attending church. Tenacious as he was in his prejudice against the clergy and all their doings, he would not have looked with pleasure on her churchgoing.

Nevertheless, his own moral situation was in the process of changing. Chagrin is a cloud that changes its form.

As we have said, robust souls are sometimes almost, but not entirely, overthrown by strokes of misfortune. Virile characters like Lethierry recover after a time. Despair has steps leading upward. From total depression we rise to despondency, from despondency to affliction, from affliction to melancholy. Melancholy is a twilight state in which suffering transmutes into a somber joy.

Melancholy is the enjoyment of being sad.

Such elegiac consolations were not for Lethierry; neither the nature of his temperament nor the circumstances of his misfortune left any room for such subtle nuances. But at the present time the dreamy contemplation of his first despair had been tending for the last week or so to dissipate. Though still sad, he was less inert; he was still somber, but he was no longer totally overwhelmed; he was beginning to take some notice of facts and events; and he was beginning to feel something of the phenomenon that might be called a return to reality.

Thus during the day, in the ground-floor room of his house, he did not listen to what people were saying, but he heard them. One morning Grace came, quite triumphant, to tell Déruchette that Mess Lethierry had opened a newspaper.

This half-acceptance of reality is in itself a favorable symptom, a sign of convalescence. Great misfortunes have a deadening effect. It is by such little acts that a man recovers from his stupor. But this improvement seems at first to aggravate his condition. His earlier dreamlike condition of mind dulled the pain; his sight was blurred and he was insensitive to feeling; but now that he can see clearly, nothing escapes him and everything draws blood. The wound reopens. The pain is increased by all the details that he now apprehends. He sees it all again in memory, and memory brings regret. This return to reality is accompanied by all kinds of bitter aftertastes. You are better, and yet worse. This was what Lethierry was now experiencing: his suffering had become more distinct.

What had brought him back to reality was a shock he had received. One afternoon about the fifteenth or twentieth of April, the postman's double knock had been heard on the door of the ground-floor room in Les Bravées. Douce had opened the door and a letter was delivered. It was a sea letter addressed to Mess Lethierry, bearing the postmark *Lisboa*. Douce had taken the letter to Mess Lethierry, who was shut up in his room. He had taken the letter, laid it down mechanically on the table, and left it unopened. It had then remained on the table for a full week, still unopened.

One morning, however, Douce asked Mess Lethierry: "Shall I brush off the dust from the letter lying on your table, sir?" Lethierry seemed to rouse himself. "Yes, do," he said, and opened the letter. It was in the following terms:

At sea, 10th March.
Mess Lethierry, St. Sampson.

You will no doubt be glad to hear from me.

I am on board the *Tamaulipas,* heading for Never-Come-Back. One of the crew is a sailor from Guernsey named Ahier-Tostevin who is on his way home and will be able to give you some news. We have fallen in with the *Hernán Cortés,* making for Lisbon, and I am taking advantage of the chance to send you this letter.

You will be surprised to learn that I am an honest man. As honest as Sieur Clubin.

I think you may already know about certain recent occurrences, but perhaps I should still tell you about them.

This is the position:

I have returned your money to you.

I had borrowed from you, somewhat improperly, fifty thousand francs. Before leaving Saint-Malo I handed over to Sieur Clubin, your trustworthy agent, three banknotes, each for a thousand pounds, amounting to seventy-five thousand francs. No doubt you will regard this reimbursement as sufficient.

Sieur Clubin looked after your interests and accepted your money with some energy. He seemed, indeed, remarkably zealous. That is why I tell you this.

YOUR OTHER TRUSTWORTHY AGENT,
RANTAINE.

P.S. Sieur Clubin had a revolver, which is why I have no receipt.

Touch a torpedo fish, touch a fully charged Leyden jar, and you will have some idea of what Mess Lethierry felt on reading this letter. In the envelope, on the sheet of paper folded in four to which he had at first paid so little attention, there was an electric shock. He recognized the writing and he recognized the signature; but at first sight he could make nothing of the letter's contents. The shock was such that it set his mind going again. The story of the seventy-five thousand francs given by Rantaine to Clubin was an enigma, but the positive side of the shock was that it forced Lethierry's brain to work. To make a conjecture is a healthy occupation for a man's mind. It stimulates the power of reasoning and calls logic into play.

For some time now, public opinion on Guernsey had been reviewing its judgment of Clubin, that honest citizen who for so many years had been unanimously regarded with esteem. People were wondering about him, were beginning to have doubts; there were speculations both in his favor and against him. Unexpected bits of information had emerged. Clubin was beginning to appear more clearly: that is, to appear blacker.

A judicial enquiry had been carried out in Saint-Malo into the disappearance of coastguardsman No. 619; but the legal minds involved in the enquiry had got on to the wrong track, as not infrequently happens. They had adopted the theory that the coastguardsman had been impressed by Zuela and had sailed for Chile in the *Tamaulipas*. This ingenious hypothesis had led them into a series of aberrations. In their shortsightedness the investigators had taken no notice of Rantaine. But in the course of their work the magistrates in charge of the investigation had turned up other lines of enquiry. The affair, already obscure, had become still more complicated. Clubin had now entered into the enigma. A coincidence—a possible relationship—had been established between the departure of the *Tamaulipas* and the loss of the Durande. In the tavern at the Porte Dinan where Clubin thought he was not known he had been recognized; the landlord had talked, and revealed that Clubin had bought a bottle of brandy. Who was it for? The gunsmith of Rue Saint-Vincent had talked: Clubin had bought a revolver. For whom was it meant? The landlord of the Auberge Jean had talked: Clubin had been away from the inn on unknown business. Captain Gertrais-Gaboureau had talked: Clubin had been determined to set sail, though he had been warned and was well aware that he was likely to run into fog. The crew of the Durande had talked: the cargo had not been fully loaded and was badly stowed—carelessness that was understandable if the captain intended to wreck the ship. The passenger from Guernsey had talked: Clubin thought he had run aground on the Hanois. People in Torteval had talked: Clubin had been there a few days before the loss of the Durande and had gone off toward Pleinmont, near the Hanois. He had been carrying a traveling bag; he had left with it and returned without it. The bird's-nesters had talked: it seemed that their story might be connected with Clubin's disappearance, if the spirits they had seen were in fact smugglers. Finally, the haunted house at Pleinmont had talked: some inquisitive locals had climbed into it and discovered Clubin's traveling bag. The authorities at Torteval had taken possession of the bag and opened it: it contained food, a telescope, a chronometer, and a man's clothing and underwear marked with Clubin's initials. All this, in the gossip of Saint-Malo and Guernsey, seemed to build up into what looked like fraud. Obscure features were brought together: an unusual disregard of advice, an acceptance of the hazards of fog, a suspicious carelessness in the stowage of cargo, a bottle of brandy, a drunk helmsman, the replacement of the helmsman by the captain, a touch on the rudder that, to say the least, was unskillful. Clubin's heroism in staying on the wreck was now seen as villainy. It seemed that he had made for the wrong reef. Granted an intention to wreck the Durande, it was easy to understand the choice of the Hanois, within swimming distance of the coast, with the haunted house as a place to stay while waiting for the chance to flee. The traveling bag, held ready for that eventuality, completed the demonstration. The link between this adventure and that other adventure, the case of the missing coastguardsman, was not clear. There seemed to be some correlation between the two, but no more than that.

The disappearance of coastguardsman No. 619 suggested some tragic drama. Clubin might have had no part in it, but he was at any rate to be seen in the wings.

Nevertheless, fraud on Clubin's part did not explain everything. There was the matter of the revolver that did not appear to have been used. Probably it belonged to the other affair. Popular feeling is shrewd and accurate. People's instinct excels in reconstructing the truth from bits and pieces of information. But in these various facts, which seemed to point to an act of fraud, there were grave uncertainties. Everything fit together, and the facts were in agreement; but an explanation for them was still lacking.

You do not wreck a ship merely for the pleasure of wrecking it. You do not run all the hazards of fog, going aground on a reef, swimming, seeking refuge and then flight without some good reason. What had been Clubin's reason?

It was possible to understand what he had done, but not why he had done it. This gave rise to doubts in many minds. Where there is no motive for an action there seems to be no action to account for.

This had been a grave lacuna; but the missing link was now supplied by Rantaine's letter. It provided Clubin's motive: the theft of seventy-five thousand francs.

Rantaine was the deus ex machina, descending from the clouds with a candle in his hand. His letter threw the final ray of light on the affair. It explained everything, and in addition it provided another witness in the person of Ahier-Tostevin. The decisive fact was that it explained the use of the revolver. Raintaine evidently knew about the whole business, and his letter made everything clear.

Clubin's villainy was now beyond doubt. He had premeditated the wreck of the Durande, as was proved by the supplies he had deposited in the haunted house. And even supposing him to be innocent of this and accepting that the loss of the Durande was an accident, should he not, having decided at the last moment to remain with the wreck, have handed over the seventy-five thousand francs for Mess Lethierry to the men seeking safety in the ship's boat? The case was proved. But what had become of Clubin? He had probably fallen victim to his mistake: no doubt he had perished on the Douvres reef.

This structure of surmises—all, as we have seen, in agreement with reality—had for several days occupied Mess Lethierry's mind. Rantaine's letter did him a service in forcing him to think. He was at first shaken by his surprise, but soon made the effort of reflecting on the matter. He made the still more difficult effort of seeking further information. He was induced to listen to conversations and even to seek them. By the end of a week he had to some extent returned to practical life; his mind had recovered some of its consistency. He had emerged from his confused state.

If Mess Lethierry had retained any hope of recovering his money from Rantaine, that hope was now totally destroyed by Rantaine's letter. It added to the catastrophe of the Durande this further shipwreck of seventy-five thousand francs. It brought the money only sufficiently within his reach for him to feel its loss. The letter revealed to him the full extent of his ruin.

This was a source of fresh and very painful suffering, as we have just noted. He began to take an interest in his household, in what was to become of it, in what changes needed to be made: matters of which he had taken no heed over the past two months. These trifling cares wounded him with a thousand tiny points, almost harder to bear than his previous despair. It is terrible to suffer your misfortune bit by bit, to dispute possession, foot by foot, of the ground that it is trying to gain. Misfortune in its totality can be borne, but not the dust it scatters. Taken as a whole it overwhelmed you; in detail it tortures you. A little while ago it knocked you out: now it nags at you. Humiliation now aggravates the blow. It is a second annihilation added to the first, and a bitter one. You drop down a further stage into nothingness. Instead of a shroud you now wear rags.

There is no sadder thought than that of coming down in the world. Being ruined seems relatively simple. You suffer a violent blow, and recognize the brutality of fate; it is complete and total catastrophe. So be it: you accept it. Everything is over. You are ruined. Very well, then: you are dead. But no, you are not. You are alive. And at once you become aware of this. How? By a series of pinpricks. You meet someone, and he cuts you; tradesmen's bills rain down on you; you see one of your enemies laughing. He may be laughing at Arnal's[208] latest pun, but no matter: he enjoys the pun so much only because you are ruined. You read your degradation even in looks of indifference; people who used to dine in your house think it is extravagant of you to serve three courses; your deficiencies are evident to all the world; ingratitude, having nothing further to expect, proclaims itself openly; every fool of your acquaintance had foreseen what has happened to you. The malignant pull you to pieces; others, still worse, pity you. And then come a hundred petty details. Nausea gives place to tears. You used to drink wine: now you will only have cider. Two servants, too! Why, one will be too many. You will have to get rid of one and overwork the other. There are too many flowers in the garden: in the future you will have to plant vegetables. You used to give presents of fruit to your friends: in the future you will send it to be sold in the market. And there can now be no question of helping the poor: are you not poor yourself? There is, too, the painful question of dress. What a torment to deprive a woman of a ribbon! She gives you beauty: how can you refuse her some trinket? You will seem such a skinflint! She will perhaps say: "What! Rob my garden of its flowers, and now you want to take them off my bonnet as well!" Alas, too, to condemn her to wearing shabby old dresses! There is no conversation around the family table; you imagine that they resent your behavior. Beloved faces show their anxiety. This is what it means to come down in the world. Every day you die a fresh death. To be struck down is the blast of a furnace: to come down in the world is torture over a slow fire.

Total ruin is like Waterloo; slow decline is St. Helena. Fate in the person of Wellington still retains some dignity; but how wretched when it takes the form of Hudson Lowe![209] Destiny becomes a dastard. We see the man who negotiated the treaty of Campo Formio[210] reduced to haggling over a pair of silk stockings. This diminution of Napoleon had diminished Britain.

A ruined man goes through both of these phases, Waterloo and St. Helena, reduced to the scale of everyday life.

On the day we have mentioned, an evening in early May, Lethierry had gone to bed in a gloomier mood than usual, leaving Déruchette walking in the garden in the moonlight. He was turning over in his mind all these petty and disagreeable details associated with the loss of fortune, all these petty cares, which at first are merely trifling and end up by being lugubrious: a melancholy burden of miseries. Mess Lethierry felt that his fall was irremediable. What was he going to do? What was to become of him? What sacrifices was he going to have to impose on Déruchette? Which of the two maids would he have to dismiss, Douce or Grace? Should he sell Les Bravées? Would he not be reduced to leaving the island? To be nothing where he had been everything was an unendurable decline.

And so it was all over! To think of those crossings between France and the archipelago, the departure on Tuesday, the return on Friday, the crowd on the quay, those heavy cargoes, that industry, that prosperity, those proud direct sailings, that machinery embodying the human will, that all-powerful boiler, that smoke, that reality! The steamship is the necessary counterpart of the compass: the compass shows the right course, the steamship follows it. One proposes, the other does what is required. Where was she, his Durande, that magnificent and sovereign Durande, that mistress of the sea, that queen who made him a king? To have been in his own country the man of an idea, the man who had achieved success, the man who had carried out a revolution—and then to give it all up, to abdicate! To cease to exist! To become a laughingstock! To be an empty sack, a sack that had once been full! To be the past where you have been the future! To suffer the condescending pity of fools! To see the triumph of routine, obstinacy, the humdrum, egotism, and ignorance! To see again the old sailing cutters, relics of the dark ages, tossing on the waves as they sailed to and fro! To see such outdated ways taking on a new lease of life! To have wasted the whole of his own life! To have been a light, and now to suffer eclipse! Ah! What a fine sight it was, that proud funnel, that prodigious cylinder, that pillar with its capital of smoke, that column that was greater than the Vendôme Column,[211] for on one there is only a man, while on the other there is progress. It had vanquished the ocean: it represented certainty in the open sea. It had been seen on this little island, in this little harbor, in this little town of St. Sampson: it had been seen, but now it was to be seen no more!

Lethierry was tortured by this obsession with regrets. We can sob even in thought. Never, perhaps, had he more bitterly felt his loss. Acute suffering of this kind is followed by a certain numbness; and under the weight of his sorrow he dozed off.

He remained with his eyes closed for some two hours, sleeping a little, meditating for much of the time. Such a state of torpor overlies a continuing activity of the brain that is very fatiguing. About the middle of the night, around midnight—a little before or a little after—he shook off his lethargy. He awoke, opened his eyes, and, looking out of the window, which was immediately opposite his hammock, saw an extraordinary sight.

Outside the window was a shape. An unbelievable shape. The funnel of a steamship.

Mess Lethierry sat bolt upright. His hammock oscillated like a swing shaken by a storm. He looked out. In the window was a vision. The harbor, gleaming in the moonlight, was framed in the window-panes, and against this light background there stood out, quite close to the window, a proud silhouette, straight, black, and round. It was the exhaust pipe of a steam engine.

Lethierry sprang down from his hammock, ran to the window, raised the sash, leaned out, and saw what it was: the funnel of the Durande. It was back in its old place. Its four chains held it fast to the planking of a boat, within which, lower down, was a dark mass of complicated shape.

Lethierry turned away, with his back to the window, and sat down in his hammock. Then he turned around, and saw the vision again.

A moment later, with the speed of lightning, he was out on the quay with a lantern in his hand.

Made fast to the Durande's old mooring ring was a boat in which, toward the stern, was a bulky object from which there emerged the erect funnel he had seen in front of the window. The forward part of the boat continued beyond the corner of the house, just above the level of the quay. There was no one in the boat. The boat had very distinctive lines that anyone on Guernsey would have recognized. It was the paunch.

Lethierry jumped on board and ran forward to the mass that he could see beyond the mast. It was the Durande's engines.

They were all there, complete, intact, squarely seated on their cast-iron flooring; the partitions of the boiler were still intact; the axle of the paddle wheels was raised erect and made fast near the boiler; the brine pump was in its place; nothing was missing.

Lethierry examined the engines, with the lantern and the moon helping each other in supplying light. He inspected the whole mechanism. He noticed the two crates beside the engines. He looked at the paddle-wheel axle.

He went into the cabin. It was empty.

He returned to the engines and touched them. He looked into the boiler, kneeling down to see the interior.

He set down his lantern inside the firebox. It illuminated the whole mechanism, almost producing the illusion of an engine with its fire lit.

Then he burst into a laugh, stood up, and, with his eyes fixed on the engines and his arms held out toward the funnel, shouted: "Help!"

The harbor bell was only a few feet away on the quay. He ran up to it, seized the chain, and, impetuously, began to ring the bell.

I I

THE HARBOR BELL AGAIN[212]

Gilliatt's return to St. Sampson was trouble-free but slow because of the weight of the paunch's cargo. He arrived after dark, nearer ten o'clock than nine. He had calculated the time of his return: it was half-tide. There was enough water and there was a moon: it was possible to enter the harbor.

The little harbor of St. Sampson was asleep. A few vessels were moored there, with their sails brailed on the yards, their topsails furled, and without lights. At the far end, high and dry, were a number of boats undergoing repair: large hulls, dismasted, and with gaps in their planking, the curved ends of their timbers nakedly sticking up, looking like beetles lying on their backs with their legs in the air.

After clearing the harbor entrance Gilliatt had examined the port and the quay. There were no lights anywhere, either at Les Bravées or elsewhere. There were no passersby, except perhaps someone, a man, who had just entered or left the parsonage. It was not even possible to be sure that there was someone there, for darkness blurs all outlines and in moonlight everything is indistinct; and distance made things more difficult to distinguish. In those days the parsonage was situated on the far side of the harbor, on a site now occupied by a covered graving dock.

Gilliatt had silently put in under Les Bravées, tied up the paunch to the Durande's mooring ring under Mess Lethierry's window, and leapt ashore. Leaving the paunch behind him at the quay, he turned around the corner of the house, went along a narrow lane and then another, ignored the turning that led to the Bû de la Rue, and in a few minutes stopped at the corner of the wall where there was a wild mallow with pink flowers in June, holly, ivy, and nettles. This was the spot where, sitting on a stone, concealed behind the brambles, he had often, in summer, spent hours for whole months at a time looking over the wall—so low that he was tempted to step over it—into the garden of Les Bravées and watching through the branches of the trees the two windows of one particular room in the house. He found his stone, the brambles, the wall, still as low as ever, and the same hidden corner; and, like a wild animal returning to its lair, slipped into it and crouched down. Then he remained motionless, watching—his eyes again on the garden, the pathways, the shrubs, the flowerbeds, the house, the room with two windows. All this dream was revealed to him by the moon. It is a terrible thing to be compelled to breathe: he did what he could to stop breathing.

He felt that he was seeing a phantom paradise. He was afraid that it might all fly away. It was almost impossible to believe that these things were really under his eyes; and if they were they must necessarily, like all divine things, be on the point of disappearing. A single breath, and it would all vanish. Gilliatt trembled at the thought.

Quite close to him, on one of the garden paths, was a green-painted wooden bench. The reader will remember that bench.

Gilliatt looked at the two windows. He thought of someone who might be sleeping in the room. Beyond that wall she was lying asleep. He wished he was anywhere but where he was; but he would rather have died than go away. He thought of a breath swelling a woman's breast. She was there—that mirage, that vision of whiteness in a cloud, that obsession floating in his mind! He thought of the inaccessible being who was lying there asleep, so close, as if within reach of his ecstasy; he thought of the impossible woman slumbering there, likewise haunted by chimeras—of the creature so much desired, so distant, unattainable, her eyes closed, her hand on her forehead—of the mystery of the sleep of the ideal being—of the dreams that can be dreamed by a dream. He did not dare to carry this thought any further, and yet he continued to think. He was venturing into the impertinences of a daydream, troubled by the thought of how much of a woman's form an angel may possess: the darkness of night emboldens timid eyes to cast furtive glances. He felt guilty for pursuing such thoughts, was afraid of committing a profanation; but in spite of himself—under compulsion, trembling—he continued to look into the invisible. He felt the thrill—almost the distress—of picturing a petticoat hung over a chair, a cloak thrown on the floor, a belt unbuckled, a fichu from a woman's bosom. He imagined a corset with its lacing trailing on the ground, stockings, garters. His soul was up among the stars.

The stars are there for the benefit of any human heart, whether the heart of a poor man like Gilliatt or the heart of a millionaire. At a certain degree of passion every man is subject to a blaze of enchantment: all the more so in rough and primitive natures. An uncultivated mind is readier to dream.

Delight is a fullness that overflows like any other. To look at these windows was almost too much for Gilliatt.

Suddenly he saw her.

From a clump of bushes, their foliage already thickened by spring, there emerged with ineffable slowness, like some specter or celestial being, a figure, a dress, a divine face, almost a shining light under the moon.

Gilliatt felt faint. It was Déruchette.

Déruchette came closer, then stopped. She turned back, stopped again, and then returned and sat down on the wooden bench. The moon shone through the trees, a few clouds were drifting about among the pale stars, the sea was murmuring to the world of darkness, the town was asleep, a haze was rising on the horizon, there was an atmosphere of profound melancholy. Déruchette's head was bent forward, with the pensive glance that stares at nothing. She was sitting sideways to Gilliatt, and was almost bareheaded, wearing only a loose bonnet that left the nape of her delicate neck and the first strands of hair exposed. She was mechanically twining a ribbon of her bonnet around one of her fingers. Shadows in the half-light of evening modeled her hands like those of a statue; her dress was of a shade that appeared white in the darkness. The trees stirred, as if moved by the enchantment that she diffused. The tip of one foot could be seen. Her lowered eyelids had the slight contraction that betokens a tear checked in its course or a thought repressed. Her arms had a charming indecision, as if finding no support to lean on; there was something fluid about her posture; she was a gleam rather than a light, one of the Graces rather than a goddess. The folds in her skirt were exquisite. Her adorable face was sunk in virginal meditation. She was so close that it was almost unendurable; he could hear her very breathing.

Somewhere in the darkness a nightingale was singing. The passing of the wind through the branches brought the ineffable silence of night into movement. Déruchette—beautiful, divine—seemed in this twilight a creation of these rays and these perfumes; this immense diffused charm was mysteriously centered and concentrated in her, and she was its embodiment. She seemed the flower at the heart of all this world of shadow.

All this shadow, floating in the person of Déruchette, weighed on Gilliatt. He was in a daze. His feelings could not be expressed in words. Emotion is always new, and words are well worn: hence the impossibility of expressing emotion. Delight can overwhelm a man. To see Déruchette, to see her in person, to see her dress, to see her bonnet, to see the ribbon she was twisting around her finger: could one imagine such a thing? To be close to her: was that really possible? To hear her breathing, to think that she actually breathed: then the stars must also breathe! Gilliatt trembled. He was the most miserable and the most enraptured of men. He did not know what to do. The delirious joy of seeing her prostrated him. Was it really she who was there and he who was here? His thoughts, dazzled and unwavering, were centered on this being as on a precious stone. He looked at her neck and her hair, saying to himself that all this was now his and that soon—perhaps tomorrow—he would have the right to undo that bonnet and untie that ribbon. He would not for a moment have had the audacity to think of doing so. Touching in thought was almost the same as touching with the hand. For Gilliatt love was like honey to a bear, an exquisite, delicate dream. His thoughts were in confusion. He did not know what possessed him. The nightingale was singing. He felt as if he were expiring.

The idea of getting up, stepping over the wall, approaching Déruchette, saying "Here I am!" and speaking to her did not even occur to him. If she had come up to him he would have turned and fled. If anything resembling a thought had shaped itself in his mind, it was this: that Déruchette was there, that he wanted nothing more, and that eternity was beginning. Suddenly a noise roused Déruchette from her reverie and Gilliatt from his ecstasy. Someone was walking in the garden. Because of the trees it was not possible to see who it was. It was a man's footstep.

Déruchette raised her eyes.

The footsteps drew nearer and then ceased. The walker had paused. He must be quite near.

The path on which the bench stood ran between two clumps of trees. Somewhere in there was the stranger, only a few steps from the bench.

Chance had so arranged the branches of the trees that Déruchette could see him but Gilliatt could not.

The moon projected a shadow on the ground between the trees and the bench. Gilliatt saw the shadow. He looked at Déruchette.

She was very pale, and her lips were half open, as if in a cry of surprise. She had half risen from the bench and then sunk back again; her attitude suggested both flight and fascination. Her astonishment reflected delight mingled with fear. On her lips there was almost the dawning of a smile, in her eyes the gleaming of tears. She was as if transfigured by a presence, as if the being whom she saw was not of this earth. Her glance seemed to be reflecting the vision of an angel.

The stranger, who was for Gilliatt no more than a shadow, now spoke. A voice emerged from the trees; it was gentler than a woman's voice and yet it was a man's. Gilliatt heard what he said:

"Mademoiselle, I see you every Thursday and every Sunday. I have been told that you did not use to come so often. It is what people say: I beg your pardon for mentioning it. I have never spoken to you: it was my duty not to. I speak to you today: it is now my duty to speak. It is right that I should speak to you first. The *Cashmere* sails tomorrow, and so I have come here today. You walk in your garden every evening. It would be wrong of me to know your habits but for the thought that is in my mind. Mademoiselle, you are poor: from this morning I have been rich. Will you take me as your husband?"

Déruchette clasped her hands together as if in entreaty and looked at the speaker—silent, her eyes fixed, trembling from head to foot.

The voice went on:

"I love you. God did not make the heart of a man to be silent. Since God promises us eternity, it means that He wants man and woman to be joined. For me there is only one woman on the earth: it is you. I think of you as of a prayer. My faith is in God and my hope is in you. What wings I have, it is you who bear them. You are my life; already you are my heaven."

"Oh, sir!" said Déruchette: "there is no one in the house to answer."

The stranger spoke again:

"I have had this sweet dream. God has not forbidden us to dream. You are like a glory in my eyes. I love you passionately, mademoiselle. To me you are blessed innocence itself. I know that this is a time when people in your house are asleep, but I had not the choice of any other time. Do you remember the passage in the Bible that was read to us in church? Genesis, chapter twenty-five. I have kept thinking about it ever since, and have read it often. The Reverend Mr. Hérode used to say to me: 'You need a rich wife.' I replied: 'No: I need a poor wife.' Mademoiselle, I am speaking to you without venturing to come close to you, and I will draw even farther away if you do not want my shadow to touch your feet. You are sovereign; you will come to me if such is your will. I love and wait. You are the living form of a benediction."

"I did not know, sir," stammered Déruchette, "that I had been seen on Sundays and Thursdays."

The voice continued:

"Man is powerless against things celestial. The whole of the law is love. Marriage is the land of Canaan. You are the promised beauty. Hail to thee, full of grace as thou art!"

Déruchette replied:

"I did not think that I did wrong more than others who went regularly to church."

The voice went on:

"God has manifested His intentions in flowers, in the dawn, in spring, and He desires that we should love. In this sacred obscurity of night you are beautiful. This garden has been tended by you, and in its perfumes there is something of your breath. Mademoiselle, meetings between souls do not depend on themselves. It is not our fault. You were present, that is all; I was there, that is all. I did nothing but feel that I loved you. Sometimes my eyes looked upon you. I was wrong, but how could I help it? It all happened because I looked at you. We cannot help ourselves. There are mysterious wills operating above us. The chief of all temples is the heart. To have your soul in my house: that is the terrestrial paradise I aspire to. Will you have me? When I was poor I did not speak. I know how old you are. You are twenty-one; I am twenty-six. I leave tomorrow; if you refuse me I shall not come back. Will you become my betrothed? More than once, in spite of myself, my eyes have put that question to yours. I love you: you must give me an answer. I shall speak to your uncle as soon as he is ready to see me; but I turn first to you. One must plead for Rebecca to Rebecca. Unless you do not love me."

Déruchette, looking down, murmured: "Ah! I do love him," in such a low voice that only Gilliatt heard the words.

She was still looking down, as if the face that was shrouded in shadow was committing its thoughts to the shadows.

There was a pause. Not a leaf in the trees stirred. It was the quiet and solemn time when things as well as living creatures are asleep and the night seems to be listening to the beating heart of nature. This mood of quiet contemplation was broken only, like a harmony complementing a silence, by the mighty roar of the sea.

The voice was heard again:

"Mademoiselle!"

Déruchette started.

The voice went on:

"Ah! I am waiting."

"What are you waiting for?"

"Your answer."

"God has heard it," said Déruchette.

Then the voice became almost sonorous, and at the same time still softer than before. From the clump of trees, as from a burning bush, there emerged these words:

"You are my betrothed. Arise and come to me. Let this blue ceiling above us with all the stars be present at this acceptance by your soul of my soul, and may our first kiss mingle with the firmament!"

Déruchette rose and stayed for an instant motionless, looking straight ahead of her, no doubt meeting another glance. Then, slowly, her head held high, her arms hanging loose, and her fingers outspread as when we are walking on unfamiliar ground, she moved toward the clump of trees and disappeared into it.

A moment later, in place of one shadow on the sand there were two mingling into one, and Gilliatt saw at his feet the embrace of these two shadows.

Time flows from us as from an hourglass, and we are not conscious of its flight, particularly in certain supreme moments. On one side there was this couple, who were unaware of this witness and could not see him, and on the other the witness, who could not see the couple but knew that they were there: how many minutes did they remain thus, in this mysterious state of suspension? Impossible to say. Suddenly there was a burst of noise in the distance, a voice was heard crying "Help!" and the harbor bell began to ring. The tumult was probably not heard by the happy pair, drunk with celestial bliss.

The bell continued to ring. Anyone looking for Gilliatt in his corner by the wall would have found him no longer there.

BOOK II

GRATITUDE IN A DESPOTISM

I

JOY SURROUNDED BY ANGUISH

Mess Lethierry tugged vigorously at the bell; then suddenly stopped. A man had turned the corner of the quay. It was Gilliatt.

Mess Lethierry ran up to him, or rather flung himself upon him, took Gilliatt's hand in both of his, and looked into his eyes for a moment in silence—one of those silences that reflect an explosion unable to find a way out.

Then, shaking him and embracing him, he pulled Gilliatt into the ground-floor room of Les Bravées, kicking the door with his foot and leaving it half open, and sat down, or rather sank into a chair beside a large table illuminated by the moon, the reflection of which gave a vague pallor to Gilliatt's face, and cried, in a voice mingling laughter and tears:

"Oh, my son! the man with the bagpipes! Gilliatt! I knew it was you! That paunch of yours—tell me all about it! So you went there? A hundred years ago you would have been burned at the stake! It is pure magic! There's not a screw missing. I've examined it all, recognized it all, handled it all. I guessed that the paddle wheels were in the two crates. And so here you are at last! I have been looking for you in your cabin. I rang the bell. I was looking for you. I was saying to myself, 'Where is he? I want to eat him!' Well, I must say, the most extraordinary things do happen. Here's this fellow back from the Douvres. He brings me back my life. Heavens above! You are an angel. Yes, yes, yes: it's my engines. Nobody will believe it. They'll look at it, they'll say, 'It's not true.' It's all there, too! It's all there! There's not a tap, not a pin missing! The feed pipe has not moved an inch. You just can't believe that there's no damage! All it needs is a little oil. But how did you manage it? And to think that the Durande is going to sail again! The paddle-wheel axle has been dismantled by a proper craftsman! Tell me, on your word of honor, that I'm not crazy!"

He stood up, drew breath, and went on:

"Swear it! What a revolution! I have to pinch myself to make sure I'm not dreaming. You are my child, you are my boy, you are my God! Oh, my son! To go out to get that brute of a machine! In the open sea, too! To that devilish reef! I've seen some pretty queer things in my life, but never anything to equal this. I've seen Parisians who were real Satans, but I'll warrant they could never do this. It beats the Bastille. I've seen gauchos plowing in the pampas: all they have for a plow is a crooked branch of a tree, and for a harrow a bunch of thornbushes drawn by a leather rope, and yet they manage to harvest grains of corn the size of a hazelnut. But that's nothing compared with what you have done. It was a miracle—a real miracle. What a rascal you are! I must hug you. You've made the fortune of the whole district. And aren't they going to gripe in St. Sampson! I'm going to set about rebuilding the boat at once. It's astonishing: the crank is none the worse. Just think of it! He has been to the Douvres. To the Douvres, I say! There isn't a worse rock in the sea. Have you heard, Gilliatt? It's proved, Clubin wrecked the Durande on purpose to swindle me out of the money he was supposed to bring me. He made Tangrouille drunk. It's a long story: I'll tell you another day about his pirate's trick. What a fool I was to have confidence in Clubin! But he was caught, the villain, for he can't have got away with it. There is a God after all, you blackguard! So we're going to rebuild the Durande, Gilliatt—at once, double-quick, right away! We'll make her twenty feet longer. They build them longer these days. I'll buy wood at Danzig and Bremen. Now that I have the engines, I'll be able to get credit. They'll have confidence in me again."

Mess Lethierry stopped, raised his eyes in the kind of glance that sees the heavens through the ceiling, and said between his teeth: "Yes, there is one."

Then he laid the middle finger of his right hand between his eyebrows, with the nail resting on the root of the nose—an action that indicates a project passing through the mind—and went on:

"All the same, to let me begin again on a large scale, a little ready money would have been a great help. Ah, if I only had my three banknotes, the seventy-five thousand francs which that brigand Rantaine returned to me and that other brigand Clubin stole from me!"

Gilliatt, in silence, felt in his pocket for something and put it down in front of him. It was the leather belt he had brought back with him. He opened it up and spread it out on the table. In the moonlight the name *Clubin* could be picked out on the inside of the belt. Then he drew a box out of the pocket in the belt and extracted from it three folded slips of paper, which he unfolded and passed to Mess Lethierry.

Mess Lethierry examined the three slips of paper. There was enough light to make out the figure 1,000 and the word *thousand*. Mess Lethierry took the three banknotes, put them down on the table one beside the other, looked at them, looked at Gilliatt, and for a moment seemed dumbfounded. Then he burst out, in an eruption following his earlier explosion:

"You've got them, too! What a fellow you are! All three of my banknotes! My seventy-five thousand francs! So you must have gone down to hell to get them. It is Clubin's belt. Of course! I can read his accursed name. Gilliatt brings back both the engines and the money! Here's a fine story for the newspapers! I'll buy top-quality wood. I suppose you found his carcass—Clubin rotting in some corner. We'll get the fir wood in Danzig and the oak in Bremen; we'll have first-rate planking, oak inside and fir outside. In the past they didn't build ships so well, but they lasted longer: the timber was better seasoned, because they didn't build so many. Perhaps we should make the hull of elm. Elm is good for the parts under water. When timber is sometimes dry and sometimes wet it tends to rot; but elm likes being always wet, it feeds on water. What a fine Durande we're going to have! They're not going to lay down the law to me! I shan't need to get credit: I have the money. Was there ever such a man as this Gilliatt! I was struck to the ground, laid low, a dead man; and he has set me up again on my two feet. And I wasn't even thinking about him! He'd passed completely out of my mind. It all comes back to me now. Poor fellow! And now, of course, you'll marry Déruchette."

Gilliatt sank back against the wall, like a man who is unsteady on his feet, and in a low voice, but very distinctly, said:

"No."

Mess Lethierry started up.

"What do you mean, No?"

Gilliatt replied:

"I do not love her."

Mess Lethierry went to the window, opened it and closed it again, returned to the table, took the three banknotes, folded them, put the iron box on top of them, scratched his head, seized Clubin's belt, threw it violently against the wall, and said:

"There's something funny here."

Thrusting his hands in his pockets, he went on:

"You don't love Déruchette! So when you played your bagpipes you were playing for me?"

Gilliatt, still leaning against the wall, paled like a man about to expire. As he grew pale, Mess Lethierry grew red.

"Here's a fine fool! He doesn't love Déruchette! Well, just make up your mind to love her, for she's not going to marry anyone but you. What sort of a cock-and-bull story is this of yours? You're not going to get me to believe it! Are you ill? Then send for the doctor, but don't talk such nonsense! You haven't had time to quarrel and fall out with her. Lovers, of course, are so silly! Come now: have you any reasons? If you have, tell me what they are. There must be some reason for behaving so foolishly. After the shock I have had there is cotton wool in my ears: perhaps I didn't hear properly. Tell me again what you said just now."

Gilliatt replied:

"I said No."

"You said No! He sticks to it, the brute! There's something wrong with you, that's for sure! This is stupidity beyond belief! People get ducked for a lot less than this! So you don't love Déruchette! Then it must have been for love of the old man that you've done what you've done? It was for his sake that you went to the Douvres, that you put up with cold and heat, that you were tormented by hunger and thirst, that you ate the vermin of the rocks, that you slept at night in fog, rain, and wind, that you managed to bring me back my engines, as you might bring back to a pretty woman a canary that had escaped from its cage! And just think of the storm we had the other day! Don't imagine that I don't realize what it was like. You must have had a rough time all right! It was for the sake of my old noddle that you cut and hacked away and shaped and twisted and dragged about and glued and sawed and nailed together and worked out what to do and scratched around and worked more miracles, all on your own, than all the saints in paradise? Oh, what a fool you must be! And you were such a torment to me with your bagpipes, too! They call them *biniou* in Brittany. Always the same tune, God help me! And so you don't love Déruchette! I don't know what's wrong with you! I remember it all perfectly well now: I was in the corner over there, and Déruchette said, 'I'll marry him.' And she *will* marry you! You don't love her, you say. I still don't understand. Either you are mad or I am. And he still doesn't say a word! You can't do all that you have done and then come back and say: 'I don't love Déruchette.' People don't do services to others in order to put them in a rage. Very well: if you don't marry her, then she'll remain a spinster. Besides, *I* need you. You will be the Durande's pilot. You don't imagine I'm going to let you go off like that? No, no, my fine fellow, I've got you and I'm not going to let you go. I won't hear of it. Where is a seaman like you to be found? You're the man for me. But for God's sake say something!"

Meanwhile the harbor bell had awakened the household and the whole neighborhood.

Douce and Grace had got up and had just come into the room, struck dumb with astonishment. Grace had a candle in her hand. A group of neighbors, townspeople, seamen, and countryfolk had rushed out of their houses and were standing on the quay, gazing in wonderment at the funnel of the Durande in the paunch. Some of them, hearing Mess Lethierry's voice in the ground-floor room, were slipping silently into the room through the half-open door. Between the faces of two gossips could be seen the head of Sieur Landoys, who had the good fortune always to be there when something was happening that he would have been sorry to miss.

In moments of great joy people are glad to have an audience. They like a crowd for the platform it offers; it gives them a fresh boost. Mess Lethierry suddenly realized that he had people around him, and at once welcomed his audience.

"Ah, there you are, my friends. That's good. You have heard the news. This fellow here has been there, and has brought the thing back. How d'you do, Sieur Landoys? When I awoke just now I saw the funnel. It was under my window. There's not a screw missing in the whole thing. They produce prints of Napoleon's feats; but *I* prefer this to the Battle of Austerlitz. You are just out of your beds, good people. The Durande arrived while you were still asleep. While you are putting on your nightcaps and blowing out your candles there are others who are heroes. We are a lot of faint-hearts and do-nothings, coddling our rheumatism; but thankfully there are other daredevil characters who go out to where they are needed and do what has to be done. The man who lives at the Bû de la Rue is just back from the Douvres reef. He has rescued the Durande from the bottom of the sea and fished out my money from Clubin's pockets, still deeper down.—But how did you manage it? All the devil's works were against you, the wind and the tide, the tide and the wind. It's true that you're a warlock. Those who say so are not far wrong. The Durande is back! The storms can rage, but they've been put in their place smartly! I tell you, my friends, there has been no shipwreck. I've examined the engines: they are as good as new, complete and undamaged. The pistons work easily, as if they were made yesterday. You know that waste water from the engines is discharged in a tube that is inside the tube feeding water in, so as to use the heat: well, both tubes are still there. She's all there, including the paddle wheels. Ah, you shall marry her!"

"Marry whom—the engines?" asked Sieur Landoys.

"No, the girl. Yes, the engines. Both. He'll be my son-in-law twice over. He'll be captain. Welcome on board, Captain Gilliatt! There's going to be a new Durande! We're going to do good business, with passengers and goods and cargoes of cattle and sheep! I wouldn't exchange St. Sampson for London itself! And here's the man who did it. I tell you, what a deed it was! You'll read about it on Saturday in old Mauger's *Gazette*. Gilliatt the Cunning One is cunning, all right!—But what are these louis d'or I see?"

Mess Lethierry had just noticed, under the half-open lid of the box holding down the banknotes, that the box contained a number of gold coins. He took up the box, opened it fully, emptied it into his hand, and put the handful of guineas on the table.

"These are for the poor. Sieur Landoys, give this money from me to the constable of St. Sampson. You know about Rantaine's letter: I showed it to you, Well, now I've got the banknotes. They'll allow us to buy oak and fir and set to work. Just look! You remember the weather we had three days ago? What a battering of wind and rain! The heavens were firing all they had at us! Gilliatt was faced with all that on the Douvres reef, but he still managed to pick up the Durande as easily as I would pick up my watch. Thanks to him I am on my legs again. Old Lethierry's galliot is going to sail again. A walnut shell with two wheels and a funnel—I've always had my heart set on that. I've always said to myself, I'll make one of these! The idea first came to me in Paris, in the café at the corner of Rue Christine and Rue Dauphine, when I read about it in a newspaper. I tell you, Gilliatt could have put the Marly waterworks[213] in his pocket and gone for a walk with them! He's made of wrought iron, that man—of tempered steel, of diamond; he's a seaman that hasn't his like anywhere, a blacksmith, a tremendous fellow, a more astonishing character than the prince of Hohenlohe.[214] That's what I call a man of spirit! None of the rest of us are up to much: old sea dogs we—you or I—may call ourselves, but the lion of the sea is this man here. Hurrah for Gilliatt! I don't know how he did it, but certainly he's a devil of a fellow all right; and what can I do but give him Déruchette!"

A few moments ago Déruchette had come into the room. She had said nothing and made no noise, but had glided in like a shadow. She had sat down, almost unnoticed, on a chair behind Mess Lethierry, who was still standing, in a most joyful mood, pouring out a storm of words in a loud voice and gesturing vigorously. Soon after her arrival there was another silent apparition. A man dressed in black, with a white cravat, holding his hat in his hand, had stopped in the doorway. The number of people in the room had slowly increased, and several of them were holding candles. They illuminated the profile of the man in black, which was of a charming, youthful whiteness and stood out against the dark background with the sharpness of a figure on a medal. He was leaning his elbow against one corner of a panel on the door and holding his forehead in his right hand, in an attitude of unconscious grace, the smallness of his hand bringing out the height of his brow. His lips were pursed in an expression of anguish. He watched and listened with profound attention. The people in the room, recognizing the Reverend Mr. Caudray, rector of the parish, had drawn aside to let him through, but he had remained standing on the threshold. There was an air of hesitation in his posture and of decision in his glance. Now and then his eyes met Déruchette's.

Gilliatt, meanwhile, whether by chance or design, was in shadow and could not be seen clearly.

Mess Lethierry did not at first notice the rector, but he saw Déruchette. He went up to her and kissed her with all the passion that a kiss on the forehead can contain, at the same time extending his arm toward the dark corner of the room where Gilliatt was standing.

"Déruchette," he said, "now you are rich again, and there is your husband."

Déruchette looked up in bewilderment and gazed into the obscurity.

Mess Lethierry went on:

"We'll have the marriage right away, tomorrow if possible. We'll have the necessary dispensations; in any case, the formalities here are not troublesome; the dean can do what he pleases, people are married before they can turn around—it's not like France, where you have to have banns and publications and delays and all the rest of it. Then you will be able to boast of having a good husband, and there's no question about it, he's a first-class seaman: I've thought that ever since the day when he brought back the little cannon from Herm. Now he's back from the Douvres, with his fortune, and mine, and the fortune of the whole district. He's a man the world will hear a deal more of one of these days. You said once, 'I will marry him'; and so you shall. And you will have children, and I shall be a grandfather, and you'll have the good fortune to be the wife of an honest fellow, a hard worker, a handy man, a character full of surprises who's worth a hundred others, a man who saves the inventions of other people, who is a real providence. At least you won't be like almost all the shrews in the neighborhood who have married soldiers or priests, the men who kill and the men who lie. But what are you doing in that corner, Gilliatt? We can't see you. Douce! Grace! Everybody! Let us have some light, so that we can see my son-in-law by the light of day. I betroth you to each other, my children. Here is your husband, and here is my son-in-law: it is Gilliatt of the Bû de la Rue, that good fellow, that great seaman. I shall have no other son-in-law, and you will have no other husband, I pledge my word before God again. Ah, there you are, rector: you will marry these two young people for me." His eye had just fallen on the Reverend Ebenezer Caudray.

Douce and Grace had carried out their master's order. The two candles they had set on the table lit up Gilliatt from head to foot.

"How handsome he is!" cried Lethierry.

Gilliatt was a hideous sight. He was still in the condition he had been in when he left the Douvres reef that morning—in rags, out at elbow, his beard long, his hair shaggy, his eyes bloodshot, the skin on his face peeling, his hands bleeding, his feet bare. Some of the pustules from the devilfish could still be seen on his hairy arms.

Lethierry looked at him.

"He's the right son-in-law for me. How he fought with the sea! He's all in rags! What shoulders! What hands! What a handsome fellow you are!"

Grace ran up to Déruchette and supported her head. She had fainted.

II

THE LEATHER TRUNK

St. Sampson was up at dawn, and people from St. Peter Port were beginning to make their way there. The resurrection of the Durande caused as much excitement on the island as did the apparition at La Salette[215] in the south of France. There was a crowd on the quay looking at the funnel emerging from the paunch. They would have liked to see and touch the engines; but Lethierry, after another triumphant examination of them in daylight, had posted two men in the paunch to keep people off. They were quite content, however, to be able to contemplate the funnel. It was a great cause of wonder. All the talk was of Gilliatt. They made great play with the name he was known by, Gilliatt the Cunning, and their admiration was often followed up by the reflection that it wasn't always agreeable to have people on the island who could achieve feats like this.

From outside the house Mess Lethierry could be seen sitting at his table by the window and writing, with one eye on the paper and the other on the engines. He was so deeply absorbed in his work that he interrupted it only once to call Douce and ask about Déruchette. Douce had replied that she was up and had gone out. Lethierry had said: "It's good for her to get some fresh air. She was a little unwell last night because of the heat. There were a lot of people in the room; and then the surprise, the joy! Besides, the windows had been closed. She's going to have a husband to be proud of!" And he had returned to his writing. He had already signed and sealed two letters to the leading shipbuilders of Bremen and had just wafered the third.

He looked up at the sound of a wheel on the quay, leaned out of the window, and saw a boy pushing a wheelbarrow coming out of the lane leading to the Bû de la Rue and making for the road to St. Peter Port. In the barrow was a trunk of yellow leather studded with copper and pewter nails. He called to the boy:

"Where are you off to, lad?"

The boy stopped and replied: "To the *Cashmere*."

"What for?"

"To put this trunk on board."

"Well then, you can take these three letters as well."

Mess Lethierry opened the drawer in the table, took out a piece of string, tied his three letters together, and threw the packet to the boy, who caught it in both hands.

"Tell the captain of the *Cashmere* that they are from me, and to take care of them. They are for Germany. Bremen via London."

"I can't tell the captain that, Mess Lethierry."

"Why not?"

"Because the *Cashmere* is not at the quay."

"Oh?"

"She is at anchor in the roads."

"I see: because of the sea."

"I can only speak to the boatman who takes things out to the ship."

"Well, tell him to look to my letters."

"Yes, Mess Lethierry."

"When does the *Cashmere* sail?"

"At noon."

"By then the tide will be coming in. She'll have the tide against her."

"But she'll have the wind with her."

"Boy," said Mess Lethierry, pointing to the Durande's funnel, "do you see that? It doesn't have to worry about winds and tides."

The boy put the letters in his pocket, took up the shafts of the barrow, and continued on his way to the town. Mess Lethierry called out: "Douce! Grace!"

Grace appeared in the half-open door.

"What is it, sir?"

"Come in, and wait a moment."

Mess Lethierry took a sheet of paper and began to write. If Grace, standing behind him, had had the curiosity to look she would have read this note over his shoulder:

> I have written to Bremen for timber. I shall be engaged all day with carpenters about the estimate. You must go to see the dean about a license. I want the marriage to take place as soon as possible: immediately would be best. I am looking after the Durande. It is for you to look after Déruchette.

He dated the letter and signed "Lethierry."

He did not take the trouble to seal the note but merely folded it in four and handed it to Grace.

"Take that to Gilliatt."

"At the Bû de la Rue?"

"Yes, at the Bû de la Rue."

BOOK III

THE SAILING OF THE *CASHMERE*

I

THE CHURCH NEAR HAVELET BAY

When there is a crowd in St. Sampson, St. Peter Port is sure to be deserted. Any event of interest in one place acts as a pump, sucking people in from elsewhere. News travels fast in small places, and since the first light of dawn the great concern of the people of Guernsey had been going to see the Durande's funnel under Mess Lethierry's windows. Any other event paled into insignificance compared with that. The death of the dean of St. Asaph's had been quite forgotten; there was no further talk about the Reverend Ebenezer Caudray, nor his sudden wealth, nor his departure on the *Cashmere*. The recovery of the Durande's engines from the Douvres was the great subject of the day. People did not believe it. The wreck of the ship had seemed extraordinary enough, but its salvage seemed impossible. Everyone was anxious to confirm with their own eyes that the story was true. All other preoccupations were suspended. Streams of townsfolk with their families, from the rank of "Neighbor" to that of "Mess"—men, women, gentlemen, mothers with their children, and children with their dolls—were coming by every road and track to see the great attraction of the day at Les Bravées and were turning their backs on St. Peter Port. Many shops in St. Peter Port were closed. In the Commercial Arcade all business was at a standstill, and attention was centered on the Durande. Not a single shopkeeper had sold anything except a jeweler who, to his great surprise, had sold a gold wedding ring to "a man who had seemed to be in a great hurry and had asked where the dean's house was." Any shops that had remained open were centers of gossip where there were lively discussions of the miraculous rescue. Not a passerby was to be seen on L'Hyvreuse, nowadays known for some reason as Cambridge Park; there was no one on High Street, then called the Grand-Rue, nor on Smith Street, then called the Rue des Forges; no one in Hauteville; and the Esplanade itself was deserted. It was like a Sunday. A visiting royal highness reviewing the militia at L'Ancresse would not have emptied the town more effectively. All this fuss about a nobody like Gilliatt caused much shrugging of the shoulders among sober citizens and persons of propriety.

The church of St. Peter Port, with its three gable-ends, its transept, and its spire, stands at the water's edge on the inner side of the harbor, almost on the landing stage, offering a welcome to those arriving and a farewell to those departing. It is the capital letter of the long line formed by the town's front on the ocean. It is both the parish church of St. Peter Port and the church of the dean of Guernsey. Its officiating priest is the suffragan dean, a clergyman in full orders. St. Peter Port's harbor, now a large and handsome port, was in those days, and as recently as ten years ago, smaller than the harbor of St. Sampson. It was formed by two great curved cyclopean walls reaching out from the shoreline to starboard and port and coming together almost at their ends, where there was a small white lighthouse. Below the lighthouse was the narrow entrance, still preserving two links of the chain that had closed the harbor in medieval times. Imagine a lobster's pincer, slightly open, and you have the harbor of St. Peter Port. This outstretched claw took from the abyss a portion of sea that it compelled to remain calm. But when an east wind was blowing there was a considerable swell at the mouth of the harbor, the water inside it was disturbed, and it was wiser not to enter. On this particular day the *Cashmere* had decided not to attempt an entry and had anchored in the roads.

This was the course followed by most ships when there was an east wind, and it had the additional advantage of saving them harbor dues. On these occasions boatmen licensed by the town—a fine breed of seamen whom the new harbor has deprived of their livelihood— picked up passengers at the landing stage or at other points on the coast and conveyed them and their luggage, often through heavy seas and always without mishap, to the vessels about to sail. The east wind is an offshore wind that is good for the passage to England; vessels roll but they do not pitch.

When a vessel about to depart was moored in the harbor, passengers embarked there. When it was anchored in the roads they had the choice of leaving from any point on the coast conveniently near the place of anchorage. In all the creeks around the coast there were boatmen ready to offer their services.

Havelet Bay was one of these creeks. This little haven (*havelet*) was quite close to the town but so isolated that it seemed a long way away. Its isolation was the result of its situation at an opening in the tall cliffs of Fort George, which loom over this discreet little inlet. There were several paths leading to Havelet Bay. The most direct ran along the water's edge; it had the advantage of leading to the town and the church in five minutes, and the disadvantage of being under water twice a day. Other paths, in varying degrees of steepness, led down to the bay through gaps and irregularities in the cliffs. Havelet Bay lay in shadow even in broad daylight. Overhanging cliffs on all sides and a dense growth of bushes and brambles cast a kind of gentle twilight on the confusion of rocks and waves below. Nothing could be more peaceful than this spot in calm weather, nothing more tumultuous in heavy seas. The tips of branches were perpetually bathed in foam. In spring the bay was alive with flowers, nests, fragrances, birds, butterflies, and bees. As a result of recent improvements this wild nook no longer exists, replaced by fine straight lines. There are now stone walls, quays, and gardens; there has been much earth-moving, and modern taste has got rid of the eccentricities of the cliffs and the irregularities of the rocks.

II

DESPAIR CONFRONTING DESPAIR

It was just short of ten o'clock in the morning—a quarter to, as they say on Guernsey. The crowds in St. Sampson, to all appearance, were still increasing. The mass of the population, consumed with curiosity, had flocked to the north of the island, and Havelet Bay, lying to the south, was even more deserted than usual.

But there was one boat in the bay, and one boatman. In the boat was a traveling bag. The boatman seemed to be waiting for someone.

The *Cashmere* could be seen at anchor in the roads. Since it was not due to sail until noon, it was making no preparations for departure.

Anyone passing by on one of the stepped footpaths in the cliffs would have heard the murmur of voices, and if he had looked down over the overhanging cliffs he would have seen, at some distance from the boat, in a nook amid the rocks and branches, out of the boatman's sight, two people: a man and a woman. It was Ebenezer Caudray and Déruchette.

These quiet little corners on the coast, which tempt women bathers, are not always as lonely as they seem. Anyone frequenting them can sometimes be observed and overheard. Thanks to the multiplicity and complication of the cliff paths, those who seek refuge and shelter there can easily be followed. The granite and the trees that conceal a private encounter may also conceal a witness.

Déruchette and Ebenezer were standing face-to-face, looking into each other's eyes, and holding each other by the hand. Déruchette was speaking. Ebenezer was silent. A tear that had gathered on his lashes hung there but did not fall.

The priest's forehead bore the imprint of grief and passion. There, too, was a poignant air of resignation—hostile to faith, though springing from it. On his face, until then of an angelic purity, were the beginnings of an expression of submission to fate. A man who had hitherto meditated only on dogma was now having to meditate on fate: an unhealthy meditation for a priest. Faith breaks down in such meditations. Nothing is more disturbing than surrendering to the unknown. Man is at the mercy of events. Life is a perpetual succession of events, and we must submit to it. We never know from what quarter the sudden blow of chance will come. Catastrophe and good fortune come upon us and then depart, like unexpected visitors. They have their own laws, their own orbits, their own gravitational force, all independent of man. Virtue does not bring happiness, crime does not bring unhappiness; our consciousness has one logic, fate another, and the two never coincide. Nothing can be foreseen. We live in uncertainty and from moment to moment. Consciousness is a straight line, but life is a whirlwind, which casts down on man's head, unpredictably, black chaos or blue skies. Fate is not skilled at transitions. Sometimes the wheel turns so rapidly that man can barely distinguish the interval between one event and another or the link between yesterday and today. Ebenezer Caudray was a believer with an admixture of reasoning and a priest whose life had been complicated by passion. Religions that impose celibacy know what they are about. Nothing so unmans a priest as loving a woman. Ebenezer's mind was darkened by all sorts of clouds.

He was looking at Déruchette—looking too long. These two beings worshiped each other. In Ebenezer's eye there was the mute adoration of despair.

Déruchette was saying:

"You mustn't go. I can't bear it. I thought I would be able to say good-bye to you, but I just can't. It's too much to ask. Why did you come yesterday? You shouldn't have come if you wanted to go away. I had never spoken to you. I loved you, but I didn't know I did. Only, that first day when Mr. Hérode read the story of Rebecca and your eyes met mine I felt my cheeks on fire and I thought, 'Oh! how Rebecca must have turned red!' But even so, the day before yesterday, if anyone had said to me, 'You are in love with the rector,' I would have laughed. That is the terrible thing about love: it comes on you unawares. I paid no heed. I went to church, I saw you there, and I thought that everyone was like me. I don't blame you: you did nothing to make me love you; you didn't do anything but look at me; it's not your fault if you look at people; but you did look at me, and so I fell in love with you. I didn't know I had. When you took up the book it was a flood of light; when others did it was just a book. You sometimes raised your eyes to look at me. You spoke of archangels; but you were my archangel. Whatever you said I believed in at once. Before I saw you I didn't know whether I believed in God or not. Since I have known you I have learned to pray. I used to say to Douce: 'Dress me quickly so that I shan't be late for the service.' And I hurried to the church. So that is what being in love with a man means. I did not realize it. I used to think, How devout I am becoming! It was you who taught me that I wasn't going to church to worship God: I was going for you, I know. You are handsome, you speak well; and when you raised your arms to heaven I felt that you were holding my heart in your two white hands. I was foolish; I didn't know it. You were wrong to come into the garden yesterday and speak to me. If you had said nothing I should have known nothing. You might have gone away, and I might have been sad; but now if you go I shall die. Now that I know I love you, you can't possibly go away. What are you thinking of? I don't believe you are listening to me!"

Ebenezer answered:

"You heard what was said yesterday."

"Alas!"

"How can I help it?!"

They were silent for a moment. Then Ebenezer went on:

"There is only one thing for me to do. I must leave."

"And for me there is nothing left but to die. Oh, how I wish that there was no sea—that there was nothing but the sky! That would make everything right, and we should both leave at the same time. You shouldn't have spoken to me. Why did you speak to me? Well, then, since you did you mustn't go away. What will become of me? I tell you, I shall die. What will you feel like when I'm in my grave? Oh, my heart is broken! I am so wretched! Yet my uncle isn't unkind."

It was the first time that Déruchette had spoken of Mess Lethierry as her uncle. Hitherto she had always said "my father."

Ebenezer stepped back and made a sign to the boatman. There was the sound of the boat hook on the shingle and the man's footstep on the gunwale of his boat.

"No, no!" cried Déruchette.

Ebenezer drew closer to her.

"I must go, Déruchette."

"No, never! Because of a bit of machinery! How can it be? Did you see that horrible man yesterday? You cannot abandon me. You are clever, you will find some way. You cannot have asked me to meet you this morning with the idea of leaving me. I have done nothing to deserve this. You cannot complain about me. You want to leave on that ship? I don't want you to go. You mustn't leave me. You cannot open up heaven and then close it so soon. I tell you, you must stay. Anyway it's not time to go yet. Oh! I love you!"

And, pressing against him, she clasped her hands together around his neck, as if to hold on to him with her arms and to join her hands in a prayer to God. He freed himself from this gentle embrace, which resisted as strongly as it could. Déruchette sank down on an ivy-clad projection of the rock, mechanically pulling up the sleeve of her dress to the elbow to show her charming bare arm, with a pale diffused light in her fixed eyes. The boat was drawing near.

Ebenezer took her head in his two hands; this virgin had the air of a widow, this young man the air of a grandfather. He touched her hair with a kind of religious caution, looked fixedly at her for some moments, and planted on her forehead one of those kisses that it seems would cause a star to shine forth and, in a voice trembling with supreme anguish that reflected the devastation of his soul, said the word that is instinct with the deepest emotion: "Good-bye!"

Déruchette burst into sobs.

At this moment they heard a slow, grave voice saying:

"Why don't you get married?"

Ebenezer turned his head. Déruchette raised her eyes. It was Gilliatt, who had approached on a path from the side.

Gilliatt was no longer the same man as on the previous night. He had combed his hair and shaved, and was wearing a white sailor's shirt with a turned-down collar and his newest seaman's clothes. On his little finger was a gold ring. He seemed profoundly calm. His sunburned face was pale, with the hue of sickly bronze.

They looked at him, bewildered. Although he was almost unrecognizable, Déruchette recognized him. But the words he had just spoken were so remote from what was passing in their minds that they had left no impression.

Gilliatt went on:

"Why do you need to say good-bye? Get married, and you can leave together."

Déruchette trembled from head to foot.

Gilliatt continued:

"Miss Déruchette is twenty-one. She is her own mistress. Her uncle is only her uncle. You love each other—"

Déruchette interrupted in a gentle voice:

"How did you come here?"

"Get married," repeated Gilliatt.

Déruchette was beginning to realize what this man was saying to her. She stammered out:

"My poor uncle—"

"He would object if you went to him and said you wanted to get married," said Gilliatt, "but if you were actually married he would give his consent. Besides, you are going away: when you come back he will forgive you."

He added, with a touch of bitterness: "Anyway, now he's thinking only of rebuilding his boat. That will occupy him while you are away. He has the Durande to console him."

"I don't want to leave unhappiness behind me," murmured Déruchette, still in a state of stupor but with a gleam of joy.

"It won't last long," said Gilliatt.

Ebenezer and Déruchette had been bewildered, but were now recovering. As their agitation diminished they began to grasp the meaning of Gilliatt's words. There was still something of a cloud hanging over them, but it was not for them to resist. We yield easily to those who offer to save us. Objections to a return to Eden are not strongly pressed. There was something in the attitude of Déruchette, as she leaned imperceptibly on Ebenezer, that made common cause with what Gilliatt was saying. As for the enigma of this man's presence and his words, which in Déruchette's mind in particular gave rise to various kinds of astonishment, these were secondary questions. He was telling them to get married: that at least was clear. He was taking all responsibility. Déruchette had a confused feeling that, for various reasons, he had the right to do so. What he said about Mess Lethierry was true.

Ebenezer, plunged in thought, murmured: "An uncle is not a father." He was suffering the corruption of an unexpected stroke of good fortune. The scruples that a priest might be expected to feel were melting and dissolving in this poor love-struck heart.

Gilliatt's voice became short and hard, with something like the throbbing of a fever:

"You must be quick. The *Cashmere* sails in two hours. You still have time, but only just. Come with me."

Ebenezer, who had been observing him attentively, suddenly exclaimed:

"I know who you are. It was you who saved my life."

Gilliatt replied:

"I don't think so."

"Over there, at the tip of the Banks."

"I don't know that place."

"It was on the day I arrived here."

"We have no time to lose," said Gilliatt.

"And I'm sure you were the man we saw last night."

"That's as may be."

"What's your name?"

Gilliatt raised his voice:

"Boatman, wait for us here. We shall come back. Miss Déruchette, you asked me how I came here. The answer is very simple: I was walking behind you. You are twenty-one. In this country, when people are of age and dependent only on themselves, they can get married in a quarter of an hour. Let us take the path along the shore. It is quite safe: the sea will not cover it until midday. We must go at once. Follow me!"

Déruchette and Ebenezer were exchanging glances as if in consultation. They were standing close together, motionless; it was as if they were drunk. There are strange hesitations on the edge of that abyss that is happiness. They understood without understanding.

"His name is Gilliatt," Déruchette whispered to Ebenezer.

Gilliatt spoke with a kind of authority:

"What are you waiting for? You must follow me."

"Where to?" asked Ebenezer.

"There." And Gilliatt pointed to the spire of the church.

They followed him. Gilliatt went in front, walking with a firm step. The others were unsteady on their feet.

As they drew nearer the church spire an expression dawned on these two pure and beautiful faces that would shortly turn into a smile. As they approached the church their faces lit up. In Gilliatt's hollow eyes was the darkness of night. It was like a specter leading two souls to paradise.

Ebenezer and Déruchette were barely conscious of what was happening. This man's intervention was the straw at which a drowning man clutches. They followed Gilliatt with the docility of despair, as they would have followed anyone. A man who feels himself dying is ready to accept whatever may befall him. Déruchette, more ignorant of life, was more confident. Ebenezer was thoughtful. Déruchette was of age. The formalities of marriage in England are very simple, particularly in self-governing areas where the rector of a parish has an almost discretionary power; but still, would the dean agree to celebrate the marriage without even enquiring whether her uncle agreed? They could not be sure. But at any rate they could try. They would have to wait and see.

But who was this man? If he was the man whom Mess Lethierry had declared last night to be his son-in-law, how was his present behavior to be explained? He who had seemed to be an obstacle was turning into a providence. Ebenezer was prepared to accept his help, but it was the hasty and unspoken acceptance of a man who feels that he has been rescued.

The path was uneven, and sometimes wet and difficult. Ebenezer, absorbed in his thoughts, was not watching for the pools of water and the rocks on the path. From time to time Gilliatt looked around to him, saying: "Look out for the stones. Give her your hand."

III

THE FORETHOUGHT OF ABNEGATION

The clock was striking half-past ten as they entered St. Sampson's church. Because of the time, and also because of the abandonment of the town by its inhabitants on this particular day, the church was empty.

At the far end, however, near the table which in Protestant churches replaces the altar, were three people—the dean, his curate, and the registrar. The dean, the Reverend Jaquemin Hérode, was seated; the curate and the registrar stood beside him.

A Bible lay open on the table. On a side table was another book, the parish register, which was also open; an observant eye might have noticed that one page was freshly written, the ink not yet dry. A pen and a writing case lay beside the register.

Seeing the Reverend Ebenezer Caudray entering the church, the Reverend Jaquemin Hérode rose.

"I have been expecting you," he said. "Everything is ready." He was already wearing his vestments.

Ebenezer looked at Gilliatt.

The dean said, "I am at your service, sir." He bowed. His bow strayed neither to right nor to left. It was evident from the direction of his eyes that for him Ebenezer alone existed. Ebenezer was a clergyman and a gentleman. The dean did not include in his bow either Déruchette, who was standing on one side, or Gilliatt, who stood behind. In his glance there was a parenthesis that included only Ebenezer. The maintenance of such distinctions is an essential part of good order in human relations, and it consolidates a society.

The dean went on, gracefully and with dignity:

"I have to congratulate you on two things, sir. Your uncle has died and you are taking a wife; you are blessed with wealth on the one hand and happiness on the other. Moreover, thanks to this steamship that is to be rebuilt, Miss Lethierry is also rich, which is as it should be. Miss Lethierry was born in this parish, and I have checked her date of birth from the register. She is of age and her own mistress. In any case her uncle, who is the only family she has, has given his consent. You want to get married at once because of your departure. I understand this, though since this is the marriage of the rector of a parish I should have liked a little ceremony. I will not detain you any longer than necessary. The essentials are soon complied with. The form of marriage has already been drawn up in the register, and only the names remain to be filled in. In terms of law and custom the marriage may be celebrated immediately after it has been entered in the register. The necessary declaration for a license has been made in due form. I take upon myself a slight irregularity, for the application for a license should have been registered seven days in advance; but I yield to necessity and the urgency of your departure. Be it so, then: I shall now proceed with the ceremony. My curate will be witness for the bridegroom; as for the bride's witness—" He turned to Gilliatt.

Gilliatt nodded.

"Good," said the dean.

Ebenezer still stood motionless. Déruchette was petrified in ecstasy. The dean continued:

"There is still, however, an obstacle."

Déruchette started.

He went on:

"Mess Lethierry's representative, here present, who asked for the license and signed the declaration in the register"—he indicated Gilliatt with the thumb of his left hand, thus avoiding the necessity of mentioning his outlandish name—"told me this morning that Mess Lethierry, being too busy to come in person, desired that the marriage should be performed at once. But a mere verbal expression of this desire is not sufficient. In consequence of the dispensations required and the irregularity I am taking on myself I cannot overlook this difficulty without asking Mess Lethierry himself, or at least having his signature. However accommodating I am prepared to be, I cannot be content with a statement at second hand. I must have something in writing."

"There is no difficulty about that," said Gilliatt, handing the dean a sheet of paper.

The dean took the paper, glanced quickly through it, appeared to pass over the first few lines, which seemed to be of less consequence, and then read aloud:

"You must go to see the dean about a license. I want the marriage to take place as soon as possible: immediately would be best."

He put the paper down on the table, and went on:

"Signed Lethierry. It would have been more respectful to address the letter to me; but since it is the marriage of a colleague I am satisfied with this."

Ebenezer looked at Gilliatt again. There are moments of understanding between two souls. Ebenezer sensed that there was some deceit; but he had not the strength, and perhaps not the desire, to expose it. Perhaps from respect for a latent heroism of which he had gained some inkling or because his conscience was deadened by the lightning stroke of happiness, he said nothing.

The dean took up the pen and, with the help of the registrar, filled in the blanks on the page written in the register. Then he stood up and, with a gesture of his hand, invited Ebenezer and Déruchette to come up to the table.

The ceremony began.

It was a strange moment. Ebenezer and Déruchette were standing side by side in front of the minister. Anyone who has had a dream of being married will have experienced what they were experiencing.

Gilliatt was standing back in the obscurity of the pillars.

On rising that morning Déruchette, in despair, with her mind on graves and grave clothes, had dressed in white. White, the color of mourning, was also right for a marriage. A white dress at once turns a girl into a bride. The grave is also a betrothal.

Déruchette emitted a kind of radiance. She had never before been as she was at this moment. Her fault was perhaps to be too pretty and not sufficiently beautiful. The defect of her beauty, if it is a defect, was an excess of grace. In a state of repose—that is, disturbed neither by passion nor by grief—her charm lay mainly in her sweetness. A charming girl, transfigured, becomes the ideal virgin. Déruchette, matured by love and suffering, had—if the phrase be permitted—undergone this promotion. She still had the same candor, with more dignity, and the same freshness, with more fragrance. It was like a daisy turning into a lily.

The moisture of the tears that were no longer flowing had dried on her cheeks, though there was perhaps still a tear in the corner of her smile. Dried tears, barely visible, are a sweet, somber adornment of happiness.

The dean, standing by the table, laid a finger on the open Bible and asked in a loud voice:

"Does any man know of any impediment to this marriage?"

There was no reply.

"Amen," said the dean.

Ebenezer and Déruchette advanced toward the table.

The dean said:

"Joseph Ebenezer Caudray, wilt thou have this woman to thy wedded wife?"

Ebenezer responded:

"I will."

The dean continued:

"Durande Déruchette Lethierry, wilt thou have this man to thy wedded husband?"

Déruchette, in the agony of her soul from excess of joy, like a lamp with too much oil in it, murmured rather than spoke:

"I will."

Then, following the beautiful Anglican marriage service, the dean looked around him and asked solemnly, in the darkness of the church:

"Who giveth this woman to be married unto this man?"

"I do," said Gilliatt.

There was a silence. Ebenezer, in the midst of their delight, felt a vague sense of oppression.

The dean put Déruchette's right hand in Ebenezer's right hand, and Ebenezer said to Déruchette:

"I take thee, Déruchette, to my wedded wife, for better, for worse, for richer, for poorer, in sickness and in health, to love and to cherish until death us do part, and thereto I plight thee my troth."

The dean put Ebenezer's right hand in Déruchette's right hand, and Déruchette said to Ebenezer:

"I take thee, Ebenezer, to my wedded husband, for better, for worse, for richer, for poorer, in sickness and in health, to love and to obey until death us do part, and thereto I plight thee my troth."

The dean asked:

"Where is the ring?"

This was a request they had not been prepared for. Ebenezer had no ring.

Gilliatt took off the gold ring that he had on his little finger and presented it to the dean.

It was probably the wedding ring that had been bought that morning from the jeweler in the Commercial Arcade.

The dean laid the ring on the Bible, and then handed it to Ebenezer.

Ebenezer took Déruchette's little left hand, now trembling, and put the ring on her fourth finger, saying:

"With this ring I thee wed."

"In the name of the Father, and of the Son, and of the Holy Ghost," said the dean.

"Amen," said the curate.

The dean raised his voice:

"You are now man and wife."

"Amen," said the curate.

The dean said:

"Let us pray."

Ebenezer and Déruchette turned toward the table and knelt.

Gilliatt remained standing, with bent head.

They were kneeling before God. He was bending under destiny.

IV

"For Your Wife, When You Marry"

When they left the church they saw that the *Cashmere* was making preparations for departure.

"You are in time," said Gilliatt.

They took the same path back to Havelet Bay. Ebenezer and Déruchette walked in front, with Gilliatt following behind. They were two sleepwalkers. It was as if they had moved from one daze to another. They did not know where they were or what they were doing; they hurried mechanically on their way, forgetting the existence of everything else, feeling only that they belonged to each other, and incapable of stringing two ideas together. One no more thinks when in ecstasy than one would try to swim in a torrent. From the midst of shadows they had suddenly fallen into a Niagara of joy. It could be said that they were in process of being emparadised. They did not speak to each other, having too much to communicate with their souls. Déruchette hung on Ebenezer's arm.

Gilliatt's footsteps behind them reminded them from time to time that he was there. They were deeply moved, but said no word to each other: an excess of emotion brings on a kind of stupor. Their stupor was delightful, but overwhelming. They were married: everything else could wait. They would see Gilliatt again; meanwhile all that he was doing was for the best. From the bottom of their hearts they thanked him, ardently but vaguely. Déruchette thought to herself that there was something that needed to be cleared up, later. In the meantime they accepted the situation. They felt themselves under the control of this man, so decisive and so sudden, who was conferring happiness on them with such an air of authority. To ask him questions, to talk to him, was impossible. Too many impressions were crowding in on their minds at the same time. Their absorption could be excused.

Facts are sometimes like a hailstorm. They bombard you; they deafen you. Events falling unexpectedly into existences that are normally calm soon make the events unintelligible to those who suffer by them or benefit from them. You cannot keep up with the adventure of your life. You are crushed without suspecting why; you are crowned without understanding why. In the last few hours Déruchette in particular had undergone every kind of shock: first delight, Ebenezer in the garden; then the nightmare, that monster declared her husband; then despair, the angel spreading his wings and preparing to depart; and now it was joy, a joy such as she had never known before, originating from something inexplicable; the monster giving her the angel; anguish giving place to marriage; this Gilliatt, yesterday a catastrophe, today her salvation. She could make nothing of all this. It was clear that since this morning Gilliatt had had no other concern than to see them married; he had done everything; he had answered for Mess Lethierry, seen the dean, applied for the license, signed the necessary declaration; and this was how the marriage had come about. But Déruchette did not understand it; and even if she had understood how it had happened she would not have understood why.

All that was left to her was to close her eyes, give thanks mentally, allow herself to be carried off to heaven by this good demon. An explanation would have taken too long; an expression of thanks was too little. She remained silent in a gentle daze of happiness.

What little power of thought the couple retained was sufficient only to carry them on their way. Under water there are parts of a sponge that remain white. They had just the degree of lucidity necessary to allow them to distinguish the sea from the land and the *Cashmere* from any other vessel.

In a short time they were in Havelet Bay.

Ebenezer got into the boat first. Then, just as Déruchette was following him, she felt a gentle pull on her sleeve. It was Gilliatt laying a finger on a fold in her dress.

"Madame," he said, "you did not expect to be going away. I thought that you might perhaps need something to wear. On the *Cashmere* you will find a trunk containing some woman's things. It came to me from my mother. It was meant for the woman I married. Will you accept it from me?"

Déruchette, half roused from her dream, turned toward him. In a low, barely audible voice, Gilliatt went on:

"I don't want to hold you back, but I think I must explain something to you. On the day the misfortune happened you were sitting in the ground-floor room, and you said something. You don't remember: it is easy to forget. You can't be expected to remember every word you say. Mess Lethierry was in great distress. It was a fine boat, that's certain, and one that had served him well. A catastrophe had occurred, and everyone was upset. These are things, of course, that are afterward forgotten. It wasn't the only vessel to be lost on the rocks. You cannot keep thinking about accidents that happen. Only I wanted to tell you that, when people were saying that no one would go there, I went. They said that it was impossible; but it wasn't. Thank you for listening to me for a moment. You must understand that in going there I had no idea of displeasing you. Besides, it was long ago. I know that you are in a hurry. If we had time, if we could talk about it, you might remember; but what's the use? The thing goes back to a time when there was snow on the ground. And one day when I passed you I thought that you smiled. That's how it all came about. As for last night, I hadn't had time to go home; I had come straight from my labors and was all torn and ragged; I frightened you, and you fainted. It was my fault: you shouldn't turn up like that in someone's house—please forgive me. That's about all I wanted to say. You are about to leave. You will have good weather: the wind is in the east. Good-bye! You don't mind my saying a few words to you, do you? This is the last moment."

"I am thinking about the trunk," said Déruchette. "Why don't you keep it for your wife when you get married?"

"I shall probably never marry," said Gilliatt.

"That would be a pity, for you are so good and kind. Thank you!"

Déruchette smiled. Gilliatt returned her smile, then helped her into the boat.

In less than a quarter of an hour the boat carrying Ebenezer and Déruchette was alongside the *Cashmere.*

V

THE GREAT TOMB

Gilliatt took the path along the shore, passed quickly through St. Peter Port and then turned toward St. Sampson along the coast, and, anxious to avoid meeting anyone, kept off the roads, which were crowded with people on his account.

He had long had his own way of moving about the countryside in all directions without being seen. He knew all the footpaths and had worked out solitary, winding routes for himself. He had the retiring habits of a man who felt himself to be unloved, and remained a being apart. While still a child, seeing few welcoming looks in people's faces, he had developed this habit of isolating himself that had now become instinctive.

He passed the Esplanade, and then the Salerie. From time to time he turned around and looked back to see the *Cashmere* in the roads, now beginning to set sail. There was very little wind, and Gilliatt made faster progress than the *Cashmere,* walking with bent head on the rocks at the water's edge. The tide was beginning to come in.

At one point he stopped and, turning his back on the sea, looked for some minutes at a clump of oak trees beyond some rocks that concealed the road to the Vale. These were the oaks at the Basses Maisons. There, under these trees, Déruchette had once written Gilliatt's name in the snow—snow that had long since melted.

He continued on his way.

It was a beautiful day—the finest that year so far. The morning had something of a nuptial air. It was one of those spring days when May pours forth all its profusion, when the creation seems to have no other thought than to rejoice and be happy. Under all the sounds of forest and village, of sea and air, could be heard a murmur like the cooing of doves. The first butterflies were settling on the first roses. Everything in nature was new—the grass, the moss, the leaves, the perfumes, the rays of light. The sun shone as if it had never shone before. The very pebbles were freshly washed. The deep song in the trees was sung by birds born only yesterday. Probably their shells, broken by their little beaks, were still lying in the nest. Amid the quivering of the branches was the fluttering of their newfound wings. They were singing their first songs and launching on their first flights. It was a sweet jargoning, all together, of hoopoes, tits, woodpeckers, goldfinches, bullfinches, sparrows, and thrushes. Lilacs, lily-of-the-valley, daphnes, and wisterias made a varied show of color in the thickets. A very pretty kind of duckweed that grows in Guernsey covered ponds and pools with emerald green. Wagtails and tree-creepers, which make such graceful little nests, came down to bathe in them. Through all the interstices in the vegetation could be seen the blue of the sky. A few wanton clouds pursued one another in the azure depths with the undulating movements of nymphs. There was a feeling of kisses from invisible mouths passing through the air. No old wall but had, like a bridegroom, its bouquet of wallflowers. The plum trees and the laburnums were in blossom, their white and yellow masses gleaming through the interlacing branches. Spring showered all its silver and gold into the immense openwork basket of the woods. The new shoots were green and fresh. Cries of welcome could be heard in the air. Summer was hospitably opening its doors to birds from afar. It was the swallows' time of arrival. The banks edging sunk lanes were lined by the inflorescences of the furze, to be followed soon by those of the hawthorn. The beautiful and the merely pretty rubbed shoulders; grandeur and grace complemented each other; small things were not put out of countenance by large ones. Not a note in the great concert was lost; microscopic splendors had their place in the vast universal beauty; and everything could be clearly distinguished as in a pool of limpid water. Everywhere a divine fullness and a mysterious swelling betokened the panic[216] and sacred working of the sap. What shone, shone more brightly; who loved, loved more tenderly. There was something of the quality of a hymn in a flower, something of brilliance in a noise. The great diffuse harmony of nature was manifest everywhere. What was beginning to shoot provoked what was ready to burst forth. Hearts, vulnerable to the scattered subterranean influences of germinating seeds, were troubled by a vague feeling of unsettlement, coming from below but also from above. Flowers gave promise of the coming fruit; maidens dreamed; the reproduction of life, premeditated by the immense soul of the shadow world, was being accomplished in the irradiation of things. There were betrothals everywhere, marriages without end. Life, which is the female, was coupling with the infinite, which is the male. It was fine, it was bright, it was warm. In the fields, through the hedges, could be seen laughing children. Some of them were playing at hopscotch. The apple trees, peach trees, cherry trees, and pear trees were covering the orchards with their tufts of white and pink blossom. In the grass were primroses, periwinkles, yarrow, daisies, amaryllis, bluebells, violets, and speedwells. There was a profusion of blue borage, yellow irises, and the beautiful little pink stars that always flower in great masses and are accordingly known as companions. Little creatures, all golden, scurried between the stones. Thatched roofs were gay with flowering houseleeks. The women working with the hives were out and about, and the bees were foraging. Everywhere there was the murmur of the sea and the buzzing of flies. All nature, lying open to permeation by spring, was moist with desire.

When Gilliatt arrived at St. Sampson the incoming tide had not yet reached the far end of the harbor, and he was able to walk across it dryshod, unperceived behind the hulls of boats under repair. He was helped by a series of flat stones set at intervals across the harbor bottom.

He was unnoticed. The crowd was at the other end of the harbor, near the entrance, at Les Bravées. There his name was in every mouth. People were talking so much about him that they paid no attention to the man himself. Gilliatt passed on his way—hidden, as it were, by the excitement he was causing.

He caught a distant sight of the paunch, still at the place where he had moored it, the funnel still held by its chains, a group of carpenters at work, the outlines of people coming and going, and he heard the loud and joyous voice of Mess Lethierry, giving orders.

He turned into the lanes behind Les Bravées. There was no one on this side of the house, the general curiosity being concentrated on the front. He took the path running along the low wall of the garden. He stopped at the corner where the wild mallow grew; he saw the stone on which he had once sat; he saw the wooden bench on which Déruchette had been sitting. He looked at the earth of the path on which he had seen two shadows embracing—shadows that had then disappeared.

He continued on his way. He climbed the hill on which stands Vale Castle, went down the other side, and headed for the Bû de la Rue.

Houmet Paradis was in solitude.

His house was just as he had left it that morning after dressing to go to St. Peter Port. One window was open, and through it he could see his bagpipes hanging from a nail on the wall. On the table could be seen the small Bible given to him in token of gratitude by an unknown man who had turned out to be Ebenezer Caudray.

The key was in the door. He went up to it, double-locked the door, put the key in his pocket, and left.

This time he walked not in the direction of the town but toward the sea. He cut across the garden by the shortest route, with little regard for the plants, though he was careful not to trample on the sea kale that he had planted because Déruchette liked it. Then, stepping over the garden wall, he made his way down to the rocks along the shore. Keeping straight ahead, he followed the long, narrow line of reefs that linked the Bû de la Rue with the great granite obelisk, standing erect in the middle of the sea, known as the Beast's Horn. This was where the Seat of Gild-Holm-'Ur was. He leapt from one rock to another like a giant walking from peak to peak. Stepping from one to another of these jagged rocks was like walking along the ridge of a roof.

A woman fishing with a hand net who was paddling barefoot in the sea pools some distance away and returning toward the shore shouted to him: "Watch out! The tide is coming in."

He went on, paying no heed.

Reaching the great rock on the point, the Beast's Horn, which rose like a pinnacle above the sea, he paused. The land came to an end here. It was the tip of the little promontory.

He looked around him. Off shore a few boats lay at anchor, fishing. From time to time there was a glitter of silver as the boats hauled in their nets and rivulets of falling water shone in the sun. The *Cashmere* was not yet off St. Sampson; she had now set her main topsail. She was between Herm and Jethou.

Gilliatt turned around the rock and came under the Seat of Gild-Holm-'Ur, at the foot of the kind of steep staircase down which he had helped Ebenezer Caudray less than three months before. He now climbed up.

Most of the steps were already under water. Only two or three were still dry. He managed to scale them.

These steps led up to the Seat of Gild-Holm-'Ur. He reached the seat, looked at it for a moment, and passed his hand over his eyes, letting it slip slowly from one eyebrow to the other, in the gesture that seems intended to wipe out the past; then he sat down in the hollow on the rock, with the steep cliff face at his back and the ocean at his feet.

The *Cashmere* was now passing the large, half-submerged round tower, guarded by a sergeant and one cannon, which marks the halfway point in the roads between Herm and St. Peter Port.

Above Gilliatt's head, in crevices in the rock, a few rock plants quivered. The water was blue as far as the eye could reach. The wind being in the east, there was very little surf around Sark, only the west coast of which is visible from Guernsey. In the distance could be seen the coast of France, marked by a line of mist and the long yellow strip of sand around Carteret. Now and then a white butterfly fluttered past. Butterflies like flying over the sea.

There was a very light breeze. All the expanse of blue, both above and below, was motionless. Not a tremor disturbed those snakelike markings of a lighter or darker blue that reflect on the surface of the sea the latent torsions in the depths.

The *Cashmere,* receiving little impulsion from the wind, had set her studding sails to catch the breeze. All her canvas was now spread, but, with a contrary wind, the effect of the studding sails forced her to hug the coast of Guernsey. She had passed the St. Sampson beacon and was just coming to the hill on which Vale Castle stands. She would shortly be rounding the point at the Bû de la Rue.

Gilliatt watched her approach.

The wind and the waves seemed to have been lulled to sleep. The tide was coming in, not in breakers but in a gentle swell. The water level was rising, but without any palpitation. The muffled sound of the open sea was like a child's breath.

From the direction of St. Sampson harbor could be heard dull knocking sounds—the strokes of hammers. It was probably the carpenters erecting the tackle and gear for hoisting the Durande's engines out of the paunch. The sounds barely reached Gilliatt because of the mass of granite at his back.

The *Cashmere* was approaching with the slowness of a phantom.

Gilliatt waited.

Suddenly a plashing sound and a sensation of cold made him look down. The sea was touching his feet. He looked up again.

The *Cashmere* was quite close.

The rock face from which rain had carved the Seat of Gild-Holm-'Ur was so sheer and there was such a depth of water that in calm weather ships could safely pass within a few cable lengths.

The *Cashmere* now came abreast of the rock. She reared up; she seemed to grow in the water. It was like a shadow increasing in size. The rigging stood out in black against the sky in the magnificent swaying motion of the sea. The long sails, passing for a moment in front of the sun, seemed almost pink, with an ineffable transparency. There was an indistinct murmuring from the sea. Not a sound disturbed the majestic passage of this silhouette. The deck could be seen as clearly as if you were on it.

The *Cashmere* almost grazed the rock.

The helmsman was at the tiller, a boy was aloft on the shrouds, a few passengers were leaning on the bulwarks enjoying the fine weather, the captain was smoking. But Gilliatt saw none of all this.

There was one spot on the deck that was bathed in sunshine, and it was this he was looking at. In this patch of sunlight were Ebenezer and Déruchette. They were sitting side by side, nestling close together, like two birds warming themselves in the noonday sun, on one of those benches sheltered under a tarpaulin awning that well-equipped vessels provide for their passengers, labeled, in the case of an English vessel, FOR LADIES ONLY. Déruchette's head was on Ebenezer's shoulder and his arm was around her waist; they held each other's hands, the fingers intertwined. The difference between one angel and the other was reflected in these two exquisite faces informed by innocence. One was more virginal, the other more astral. Their chaste embrace was expressive: it held all the closeness of marriage, and all its modesty. The bench they were sitting on was a private nook, almost a nest. It was, too, a glory: the gentle glory of love fleeing in a cloud.

The silence was celestial.

Ebenezer's eye was giving thanks and contemplating, Déruchette's lips were moving; and in this charming silence, since the wind was blowing onshore, Gilliatt heard, in the fleeting moment when the sloop was slipping past the Seat of Gild-Holm-'Ur only a few fathoms away, Déruchette's tender, delicate voice saying:

"Look: isn't there a man on the rock?"

The apparition passed.

The *Cashmere* left the point at the Bû de la Rue behind her and plunged into the deep, rolling waves. In less than a quarter of an hour her masts and sails were no more than a kind of white obelisk on the sea, gradually diminishing on the horizon. The water was now up to Gilliatt's knees.

He watched the sloop sailing into the distance.

Out at sea the wind freshened. He could see the *Cashmere* running out her lower studding sails and staysails to take advantage of the rising wind. The *Cashmere* was already out of Guernsey waters. Gilliatt kept his eyes fixed on her.

The sea was now up to his waist.

The tide was rising. Time was passing.

The seagulls and cormorants flew about him, anxious, as if warning him. Perhaps among all these birds there was one from the Douvres that recognized him.

An hour passed.

The wind from the sea was barely felt in the roads, but the *Cashmere* was now diminishing rapidly in size. To all appearance she was making good speed. She was now almost opposite the Casquets.

There was no foam around the Gild-Holm-'Ur, no waves beating against the granite. The sea was swelling gently. It was now almost up to Gilliatt's shoulders.

Another hour passed.

The *Cashmere* was now beyond the waters around Alderney. She was hidden for a moment by the Ortach rock. After passing behind it she reemerged, as if from eclipse. She was now making rapidly northward, and had reached the open sea. She was no more than a speck on the horizon, scintillating in the sun like a light.

The birds hovered around Gilliatt, uttering sharp cries.

Only his head was now visible.

The sea continued to rise with sinister gentleness.

Gilliatt, motionless, watched the *Cashmere* disappearing.

The tide was now almost at the full. Evening was coming on. Behind Gilliatt, in the roads, a few fishing boats were returning to harbor.

His eye was still fixed on the distant sloop. This fixed eye was like nothing to be seen on earth. In its calm and tragic depths there was something inexpressible. It contained such consolation as can be found for a dream not realized; it was the mournful acceptance of something that was now over. The passing of a shooting star must surely be followed by glances like this. From moment to moment the darkness of the skies was increasing in these eyes, still fixed on a point in space. At the same time as the infinite sea was rising around the Gild-Holm-'Ur rock, the immense tranquillity of the land of shadows was mounting in the depths of Gilliatt's eye.

The *Cashmere*, now imperceptible, was no more than a speck hidden in the mist, distinguishable only by an eye that knew where it was.

Gradually the speck, now no more than a vague shape, grew pale.

Then it diminished.

Then it disappeared.

At the same moment the head disappeared under the water. There was now nothing but the sea.

NOTES

1. ananke: Greek term for necessity.
2. *Cuges or Gémenos:* villages on the Mediterranean coast of France.
3. *overfall:* a turbulent stretch of open water caused by a strong current or tide over a submarine ridge or by a meeting of currents.
4. *Tewdrig:* king of Gwent in the sixth and seventh centuries. *Emyr Lhydau:* father of Umbrafel and Amon Dhû, who was the father of the sixth-century saint Sampson of Brittany.
5. *Ribeyrolles:* a journalist and politician who shared Hugo's exile in the Channel Islands.
6. *Madame de Staël:* Germaine de Staël (1766–1817), French novelist and woman of letters. *Chateaubriand:* François-René de Chateaubriand (1768–1848), French writer of the Romantic period and later a leading politician.
7. *Ernani and Astigarraga:* in the Basque country of northeastern Spain.
8. *marabout:* a shrine marking the burial place of a Muslim hermit or holy man.
9. *hobgoblins and auxcriniers:* witches and warlocks. The name *auxcriniers* was invented by Hugo.
10. *prince:* Albert, Queen Victoria's Prince Consort.
11. *Premières:* a village near Dijon. The director of the manufactory was Dr. Lavalle, not Lasalle.
12. *Chaussée d'Antin … Faubourg Saint-Germain:* the Chaussée d'Antin was the fashionable district of Paris; the Faubourg Saint-Germain was its aristocratic quarter.
13. *Zaatcha:* in Algeria.
14. soudards: an old word for a rough or ruffianly soldier—perhaps recalling Wellington's own comments on the quality of his troops.
15. *doubles:* A double was a small copper coin worth one-eighth of a penny or one-sixth of a sou.
16. *Pollet:* the fishermen's quarter of Dieppe.
17. *tower:* the Victoria Tower, commemorating the queen's visit in 1846.

18. *Chouan:* participant in a royalist uprising in western France during the French Revolution, the Chouannerie.

19. unda *and* unde…ou *and* où: Latin *unda* = "wave," *unde* = "whence"; French *ou* = "or," *où* = "where."

20. *Rollo:* the Norse chieftain who became first duke of Normandy.

21. Haro: originally a call to a dog to attack someone or something; *crier haro,* to launch a hue and cry.

22. *Du Guesclin:* Bertrand du Guesclin, constable of France in the fourteenth century.

23. *Pantagruel:* a variant version of Rabelais's genealogy of Pantagruel.

24. *Puseyism:* the nineteenth-century Catholic revival in England known as the Oxford movement.

25. *Dr. Colenso's book:* John Colenso (1814–83), the liberal bishop of Natal whose book *The Pentateuch and Book of Joshua Critically Examined* led to a charge of heresy.

26. *Calas, Sirven…count for nothing:* Voltaire campaigned vigorously against the persecution of the Protestants Sirven and Calas. The dragonnades involved the quartering of dragoons in Protestant households.

27. *his speech:* evidently a reference to a speech by Hugo himself seeking support for Garibaldi.

28. *de Maistre:* Joseph de Maistre (1753–1821), theoretician of the Christian counterrevolution of the early nineteenth century. *d'Eckstein:* Ferdinand d'Eckstein (1790–1861), Catholic thinker and mystical writer.

29. *Moulin-Quignon:* near Abbeville in northern France.

30. *Furetière:* Antoine Furetière (1619–88), French satirist and lexicographer.

31. *Valognes:* a little town near Cherbourg.

32. eremos: Greek, "solitude, wilderness." An inventive but unlikely etymology by Hugo.

33. *double:* See note 15.

34. *Pasquier…Royer-Collard:* French politicians of the Restoration period.

35. *Bagpipe!…Guernsey remained calm:* The reference is to Gilliatt's bagpipes (p. 67).

36. *I am not entitled to be called Mess:* For the Guernsey social hierarchy, see p. 107.

37. *Ribeyrolles:* See note 5.

38. *chapters of this book:* "The Bû de la Rue," pp. 60–64.

39. *Tancred…Mazeppa:* Tancred features in Tasso's poem "Jerusalem Delivered." Mazeppa was a seventeenth-century Cossack chief who was the subject of poems by Byron and Hugo.

40. *Île Saint-Louis…Quai des Ormes:* an isle and embankment in central Paris.

41. *"unknown Normandy":* a reference to a book published by Hugo's son François-Victor.

42. *John Brown:* the militant American abolitionist whose raid on the federal arsenal at Harpers Ferry in 1859 made him a martyr to the antislavery cause.

43. *Vadius and Trissotin:* in Molière's *Femmes Savantes* the pedant and the poet.

44. *"J'ai pien... conjugal scenes here."):* The joke turns on the Alsatian's Teutonic pronunciation, which confuses *patois* with *badois* (the language of Baden).

45. *Montmorency:* the Montmorencys were one of France's greatest noble families.

46. *Cahaigne:* a writer and politician who, like Hugo, was exiled to Jersey.

47. *... whom it immortalizes:* In fact, there was no mystery about it: it represented George II, but Hugo deliberately ignores this.

48. *Beccaria:* the great eighteenth-century economist and criminologist. *Monsieur Dupin:* a minor French politician of the early nineteenth century.

49. *Tapner:* Tapner was hanged in 1854; Hugo had made an appeal for his reprieve.

50. Jambage... poulage: compulsory deliveries of hams and poultry.

51. *"Elle a-z-une..."*: The intrusive *z* is a mispronunciation.

52. *Frobisher:* Sir Martin Frobisher, the sixteenth-century English navigator and explorer of Canada's northeast coast.

53. *Du Cange:* a seventeenth-century scholar who published a glossary of medieval Latin. *Barleycourt's:* Barleycourt was the pseudonym of a certain Abbé Hugo whom Hugo liked to claim as an ancestor. *Teutatès:* the Celtic god of war.

54. centeniers, vingteniers, *and* douzeniers: local officials at different levels. vingtaine *and* cueillette: subdivisions of the parish.

55. *the viscount:* a judge; also called the sheriff.

56. *Bishop Colenso: See note 25. Elliott:* John Elliott was a seventeenth-century doctor who made the remark about the sun in a private letter but was in fact brought before the court for attempted murder.

57. *Chateaubriand: See note 6.*

58. reminiscitur Argos: "Remembers Argos" is a quotation from Virgil's *Aeneid,* referring to a Greek nostalgic for his homeland.

59. *the Edict of Nantes:* edict that granted religious freedom to Protestants, which was revoked by Louis XIV in 1695, leading to a large-scale exodus of Huguenots from France.

60. *duc de Berry... Louvel:* The duc de Berry, heir to the French throne, was assassinated by a fanatic named Louvel in 1820.

61. *...the country he had lost:* Hugo arrived in Guernsey in 1855; *Les Travailleurs de la Mer* was published in 1866.
62. La clef...amourettes!: "The key of the fields, the key of the woods, the key of love affairs!" *Prendre la clef des champs* (to take the key of the fields) means escape to the country, to freedom.
63. Homo Edax: "Man the devourer"; an adaptation by Hugo of a phrase in a poem by Ovid.
64. *Brèche de Roland:* a narrow gorge in the Pyrenees, said by legend to have been cut by Charlemagne's paladin Roland with his sword.
65. *Xerxes:* During his war against the Greeks, the Persian king Xerxes cut a channel across the isthmus on which Mount Athos stands.
66. *Trinacria:* the "three-cornered" island; the original name of Sicily.
67. *Robert Wace:* a twelfth-century Anglo-Norman poet, author of two verse chronicles, the *Roman de Brut* and the *Roman de Rou. Pierson:* Major Pierson was killed while fighting off a French attack on Jersey in 1781.
68. *dromond...* monstrum!: The dromond was a large boat used in medieval times for either war or commerce. *Homo homini monstrum* (Man is a monster to man): an adaptation by Hugo of a tag from Plautus, *Homo homini lupus* (Man is a wolf to man).
69. *Bû de la Rue:* The name ("Bout de la Rue," "End of the Street") is symbolic of the remoteness of the place. Beyond it there is nothing but the sea: cf. the last words of the novel.
70. *Houmet Paradis:* a small offshore island.
71. Amant alterna catenae: "Chains like changes": an adaptation by Hugo of a phrase in Virgil's *Bucolics.*
72. *rods: vergées.* There are two and a half *vergées* to the acre.
73. *dénerel:* a sixth of a bushel.
74. *Rosier's* Dictionary...Advice to the People on Heath: The names of the books point to "left wing" interests that would shock the Reverend Jaquemin Hérode and the émigré noble.
75. sarregousets...sins: apparently some kind of hobgoblins; the term *sin* is not otherwise known.
76. *the Sommeilleuses:* cliffs on the south coast of Guernsey.
77. *Catioroc:* off the northeast coast of Guernsey.
78. *one St. Michael and the other:* St. Michael's Mount in Cornwall and Mont Saint-Michel in Normandy.
79. douzaine: the bench of twelve magistrates (*douzeniers*) that was the local governmental authority in each parish.
80. vingtaine: a subdivision of a parish.
81. *Gilliatt the Cunning One:* Gilliatt le Malin. *Malin* is ambiguous: it means "cunning," but "le Malin" is an old name for the Devil.

82. *Mess:* short for Messire; see the description of Guernsey's social hierarchy on p. 107.

83. *Martin:* Thomas Martin, a plowman who became famous for his visions in the early nineteenth century.

84. *Busios:* the first month of the year in the calendar of Delphi.

85. *bisquine:* a three-masted fishing boat used in Normandy for catching oysters.

86. *Bailli de Suffren:* the celebrated eighteenth-century French admiral who fought against the British in America and India.

87. *Portbail:* a little port on the Cotentin peninsula, south of Cherbourg.

88. *Jean Bart:* the celebrated seventeenth-century French admiral who fought against the British in America and India.

89. *Admiral Tourville:* seventeenth-century French admiral who fought British and Dutch naval forces in European waters.

90. *Ango:* a leading sixteenth-century shipowner.

91. *duc de Vivonne:* seventeenth-century French marshal and naval commander.

92. *Duquesne:* seventeenth-century French naval officer. *Duguay-Trouin:* eighteenth-century French naval officer and privateer.

93. *Duperré:* the French admiral who took Algiers in 1830.

94. *La Bourdonnais:* eighteenth-century French sailor and government official.

95. *"... with powder":* The reference is to a firearm loaded with powder but not with ball. The old émigré was implying that Déruchette was unwittingly provocative.

96. *Bible... help of chloroform:* Genesis 3:16: "In sorrow thou shalt bring forth children."

97. *"Is it... work together?":* Cf. Genesis 1:6.

98. La Croix-de-Jésus: a work of popular piety.

99. cabeza de moro: a Moor's head, acting as a punchball or arcade game target.

100. *Oomrawuttee:* Amravati, on the east coast of India.

101. *... an immense white plume:* The whole description of Rantaine reveals him as a royalist. He could recite Voltaire's *Henriade,* a glorification of Henry IV. He knew by heart "Les Tombeaux de Saint-Denis," a lachrymose poem on the royal skeletons in the abbey of Saint-Denis. Souloque was a black slave who rose to become emperor of Haiti. The Verdets ("Greens") were bands of royalists who ran a campaign of terror in the south of France in 1815.

102. neboissed: the term is unexplained. No connection with Turkish can be detected. A derivation from Russian has been suggested but seems unlikely. *thaleb:* student of Islamic doctrine.

103. Montebello: an American warship launched in 1812.

104. *two leagues an hour:* six knots.

105. *galgal:* a combination of lime, oil, and tar.

106. *afloat: À flot,* "afloat," can also mean "doing well, prospering."

107. *"In the future... Lons-le-Saulnier?":* a play on words: Nancy and Lons-le-Saulnier are both towns in eastern France.

108. *"a husband and a donkey":* another play on words: A husband is *mari,* a donkey is *âne.*

109. *Et vidit quod esset bonum:* "And He saw that it was good" (Genesis 1:31).

110. *Edward the Confessor:* Hugo deliberately hyphenates the name Édou-ard.

111. *Savoyard vicar:* a character in Rousseau's *Émile* who preached tolerance.

112. *philosopher:* The reference is to the eighteenth-century French *philosophes* like Voltaire.

113. *Montlosier:* the Comte de Montlosier, an opponent of the clericalism of the extreme right during the Restoration.

114. *"Bourmont... on purpose":* Bourmont was one of Napoleon's generals who went over to Louis XVIII four days before Waterloo. There is an untranslatable pun in Lethierry's remark. It replaces the term *trait d'union* (hyphen, link) with *traître d'union* (traitor of union).

115. *Raca:* See Matthew 5:22.

116. *Chaussée d'Antin:* See note 12.

117. *Mariotte:* Edme Mariotte, a famous seventeenth-century French physicist who formulated what is known in English as Boyle's Law (in France, Mariotte's Law).

118. *Saint-Servan:* a little town just outside Saint-Malo.

119. *Villèle:* French prime minister, was forced to resign in 1828. *two towns on the River Plate:* Montevideo in Uruguay and Buenos Aires in Argentina, which are on opposite sides of the Rio de la Plata.

120. *Diebitsch:* a Russian general who passed through the Balkans on his way to defeating the Turkish army in 1828. *Leo XII:* Pope Leo XII died in 1829.

121. *Berton:* a French general who organized an insurrection in Saumur and was tried and executed in 1822. *the Bidassoa:* a Spanish river on the frontier with France, where a group of rebels tried to prevent French intervention in Spain.

122. *Restoration:* of the Bourbon monarchy in France, 1815–30.

123. *... the social order of the day:* The names in this paragraph are of various rebels and conspirators against the established order; the places that people avoided were the scenes of acts of repression by the Restoration government.

124. *The men... Champ d'Asile:* The men of the Loire were a group of French soldiers, demobilized on the Loire after Waterloo, who set out to establish a settlement on the Gulf of Mexico, the Champ d'Asile or Field of Refuge.

125. *the Convention:* the Revolutionary assembly that governed France between 1792 and 1795.
126. *Bourgain … Séguin:* financiers of the Revolutionary period.
127. *Mandrin:* a famous eighteenth-century bandit and smuggler. *Comte de Charolais:* a nobleman notorious for his violence and debauchery.
128. *Sagane:* a sorceress mentioned in a poem by Horace. *Mademoiselle Lenormand:* a clairvoyant and soothsayer.
129. *Brocken:* the mountain in the Harz that is the scene of the witches' sabbath in Goethe's *Faust. Armuyr:* identified by Hugo in *Les Misérables* (Part IV, Book XI, Chapter II) as the heath on which Macbeth encountered the witches in Shakespeare's play.
130. *This was what the ghosts were saying:* Hugo gives the conversation in Spanish (not reproduced here), followed by a French translation.
131. "Egurraldia gaïztoa?": "In bad weather?" (Basque).
132. *Pundonor:* "Point of honor" (Spanish).
133. *Noguette:* a bell brought from Brazil by the celebrated eighteenth-century privateer Duguay-Trouin.
134. *Lacenaire:* a notorious murderer of the early nineteenth century.
135. *setier:* an old measure of capacity that varied from region to region and according to the substance measured. *liard:* a quarter of a sou, which was five centimes.
136. *Talleyrand:* French statesman noted for his capacity for political survival, serving successive regimes from the Revolution to the July Monarchy (Louis Philippe). Dictionary of Weathervanes: The *Dictionnaire des Girouettes,* published in 1815, listed the many changes of allegiance among politicians since the French Revolution.
137. *"How d'you do?":* Hugo, who made a point of not knowing English, actually puts the greeting "Good-bye" in the old sea-captain's mouth.
138. *Douvres:* There is a group of rocks off Guernsey known as the Douvres, but not at the position assigned to them by Hugo.
139. *the Moines:* the Monks.
140. *the Canard:* the Duck.
141. *Malouins:* "Malouin, malin"; a play on words (*malin* means shrewd, cunning).
142. *the Maisons:* the Houses.
143. *Surcouf:* Robert Surcouf (1773–1827), a French seaman; originally a privateer who preyed on British shipping in the Indian Ocean, later a wealthy shipowner.
144. *Duguay-Trouin: See note 92.*
145. *Odéon:* the Théâtre de l'Odéon in Paris, which was twice destroyed by fire.
146. *a square toise:* about forty square feet.

147. *Marie Alacoque:* a seventeenth-century nun who had visions of the Sacred Heart. *Cadière and the nun of Louviers:* Catherine Cadière and Madeleine Bavent, the nun of Louviers, were seduced by their confessors and subsequently accused of witchcraft.

148. *Escobar:* A famous eighteenth-century casuist, Escobar was a Spanish Jesuit. *Léotade:* a French friar, found guilty in 1848 of the murder and attempted rape of a girl of fourteen.

149. *Boue Corneille:* A *boue* is an underwater rock.

150. *gestatorial chair:* a chair in which the pope was carried on certain occasions. in abito paonazzo: the purple robes of a monsignore (the honorific title of a prelate or officer of the papal court).

151. *the Sorbonne:* Paris's university, originally a theological college and ecclesiastical tribunal.

152. Solus eris: "You will be alone." From a poem by Ovid, written during his exile from Rome.

153. *It was ... his father Zibeon:* the reference is to Genesis 36:24. The Authorized Version differs from the text cited by Dr. Hérode, which follows the Vulgate.

154. *deputy viscount:* a traditional title on Jersey, equivalent to deputy sheriff.

155. *Barjesus:* Acts 13:6–11. *Elkesai:* a first-century heretic. *Aholibamah ... Judith:* Genesis 26:34 and 36:14. *Reuben:* the reference to Isaac's firstborn son is not explained in the Old Testament. *Peniel:* apparently an invented name.

156. Genesis 24:62–67.

157. *and then they bleat:* There seems to be an inventive pun here. The word *moutonner* (from *mouton,* sheep) that Hugo uses means, when applied to the sea, "to be flecked with foam"; but in the present context there is surely a reference to sheep bleating.

158. *Gulf of Stora:* in Algeria.

159. *strangury:* a medical term for retention of urine.

160. *the Eel Bank:* a submarine bank off the southern tip of Africa. *Dumont-d'Urville:* a celebrated early-nineteenth-century French navigator and explorer.

161. *Toluca:* in Mexico.

162. *de Ruyter:* the great seventeenth-century Dutch admiral.

163. *Lisbon earthquake:* the famous earthquake of 1755, which destroyed much of the city.

164. *Firth of Forth ... Scotland:* What Hugo actually wrote is a prime example of his determination not to know the English language as well as his shaky knowledge of British geography. He gives the name of the cliff, in English, as the "First of the Fourth."

165. *Annweiler valley:* in the German Rhineland.

166. *confervae:* a species of alga.

167. Importunaeque Volucres: "And the birds of ill omen…" A quotation from Virgil's *Georgics.*

168. cagniardelle: an early-nineteenth-century invention, which used the principle of the Archimedean screw to produce a draft. trompe: a mechanism that produced a draft by the flow of water through a funnel.

169. *gladiator:* Hugo uses the term *belluaire,* a gladiator who fought against wild animals. Hence the reference in the next sentence to Gilliatt as a "tamer."

170. *Danaids:* In Greek mythology, the Danaids were condemned eternally to pour water into bottomless pots as punishment for murdering their husbands.

171. *syrinxes:* passages in ancient Egyptian rock-cut royal tombs.

172. *Enceladus:* in classical mythology, a Titan imprisoned under Mount Etna whose breath caused eruptions of the volcano.

173. *Amontons:* a seventeenth-century physicist. *Lahire:* a seventeenth-century astronomer and mathematician. *Coulomb:* an eighteenth-century physicist.

174. *… the man who performed this miracle:* There is some doubt about the authenticity of this story.

175. *Balmat:* Jacques Balmat, a Chamonix guide, climbed Mont Blanc in 1786, and in the following year climbed it again with the Swiss naturalist and physicist Horace-Bénédict de Saussure.

176. *Marly waterworks:* Marly was a small palace near Paris built for Louis XIV. The "waterworks" raised water from the Seine to supply the palace of Versailles.

177. Sub Re: Hugo seems to take this phrase (literally, "under the thing") to refer to the task with which Gilliatt was now faced.

178. Sub Umbra: "In the shadows."

179. *Thomas:* Alexandre Thomas was imprisoned on Mont Saint-Michel in 1840. *Boisrosé:* Captain Boisrosé and his men scaled a cliff near Fécamp in 1592 to take an enemy fort. *Trenck:* Baron von Trenck escaped from a Prussian fortress in 1746. *Latude:* Jean-Henri Latude was an eighteenth-century French adventurer who escaped once from the Bastille and twice from the prison of Vincennes.

180. *Jean Bart: See note 88.*

181. *groyne … dike:* The French term is *épi;* "groyne" seems the nearest English equivalent. "Dike" is presumably what Hugo intends with his word *dick.*

182. *syzygies:* conjunctions of the sun, moon, and earth.

183. Solem quis dicere falsum audeat?: "Who would dare to call the sun false?" (Virgil's *Georgics*).

184. *"an eel under a rock":* the French equivalent of a snake in the grass.

185. *Surcouf: See note 143.*

186. *Napier:* Admiral Sir Charles Napier (1786–1860).
187. *Weepers' Tower:* It was from the Weepers' Tower (Schreierstoren) in Amsterdam that sailors' wives watched their menfolk going off to sea.
188. *Ango: See note 90.*
189. *Messier:* Charles Messier (1730–1817).
190. *Ceto:* in classical mythology a Nereid, daughter of Earth and Sea.
191. Turba, Turma: "The crowd, the troop."
192. *Lémery:* Nicolas Lémery (1645–1715), French physician and chemist.
193. Malo viento toma contra el sol: "An ill wind turns against the sun."
194. *Cap de Fer:* on the coast of Algeria.
195. *Stevenson:* Robert Stevenson (1772–1850), the Scottish engineer famed for his lighthouses.
196. *Enceladus: See note 172.*
197. *Thomas Fuller:* English theologian and historian (1608–61).
198. *Piddington:* Henry Piddington (1797–1858), English meteorologist.
199. *devilfish:* an old name for the octopus. The word used by Hugo is *pieuvre,* the term for an octopus in the dialect of the Channel Islands. Thanks to the popularity of Hugo's novel, *pieuvre* has largely displaced the older French term *poulpe.*
200. *jararaca:* a venomous snake of Brazil.
201. *buthus:* a particularly venomous yellow scorpion found in the south of France.
202. *ell:* English unit of measure; equals 45 inches.
203. *Buffon:* the celebrated eighteenth-century naturalist, author of a monumental *Natural History. Denys Montfort, Bory de Saint-Vincent, Péron, Lamarck:* eighteenth- and nineteenth-century French naturalists.
204. *The entrance is also the exit:* Not so: the octopus has in fact two orifices.
205. *radiates:* animals with radial structure, like polyps and sea anemones: one of the great divisions of the animal world under Cuvier's now discarded system.
206. De Profundis ad Altum: "From the depths to the height": a reference to Psalm 129:1 in the Vulgate (Psalm 130 in the Authorized Version).
207. *There Is an Ear in the Unknown:* The title of the previous chapter referred to Psalm 129:1 in the Vulgate (Psalm 130 in the Authorized Version). The title of this chapter refers to verse 2, the answer to the appeal in verse 1.
208. *Arnal's:* Étienne Arnal was a famous comic actor of the early nineteenth century.
209. *Hudson Lowe:* governor of St. Helena during Napoleon's confinement on the island.

210. *the treaty of Campo Formio:* treaty between France and Austria in 1797 that preserved most of Napoleon's conquests and marked the completion of his victory over the First Coalition.

211. *Vendôme Column:* in the Place Vendôme in Paris. Topped by a statue of Napoleon, it was pulled down in 1871 during the Commune and re-erected under the Third Republic.

212. *The Harbor Bell Again:* The title is designed to suggest a parallel between Lethierry's vision of the Durande in the previous chapter and Gilliatt's vision of Déruchette in this chapter.

213. *Marly waterworks: See note 176.*

214. *prince of Hohenlohe:* a German prince who fought in the émigré army against the French revolutionary forces, took French nationality, and was later appointed marshal and a peer.

215. *La Salette:* the apparition of the Virgin to two shepherds at La Salette (Isère) in 1846.

216. *of panic:* associated with the god Pan.

A NOTE ON THE DRAWINGS OF VICTOR HUGO

Throughout his life and illustrious career, Victor Hugo, somewhat surreptitiously, produced thousands of extraordinary drawings. From the unconscious meanderings of a brown ink pen that prefigure the abstract experiments of modernism, to skillfully executed landscapes and seascapes of uncommon beauty, Victor Hugo's drawings, little known to his contemporaries, have increasingly captured the public's attention over the past century. In keeping with the ongoing discovery of these masterly creations, the Modern Library has reproduced five of Hugo's brown ink renderings, executed with brush and pen on cream paper, in this new edition of *The Toilers of the Sea*. Though not specifically created to illustrate the text, the drawings were nonetheless in such perfect harmony with Hugo's novel of sea, storm, and shipwreck that he pasted them into the manuscript to illuminate particular passages and scenes. The five works available to us of the thirty-six Hugo had originally selected have been positioned in keeping with the author's original design.

ABOUT THE TRANSLATOR

JAMES HOGARTH was educated at Edinburgh University and the Sorbonne. While serving in the army during World War II he became a codebreaker at Bletchley Park, and was later undersecretary in the Scottish Office. His recent translations include works from German and French.

A NOTE ON THE TYPE

The principal text of this Modern Library edition
was set in a digitized version of Janson,
a typeface that dates from about 1690 and was cut by Nicholas Kis,
a Hungarian working in Amsterdam. The original matrices have
survived and are held by the Stempel foundry in Germany.
Hermann Zapf redesigned some of the weights and sizes for Stempel,
basing his revisions on the original design.

Printed in the United States
by Baker & Taylor Publisher Services